tempting
isabel

He tempts her. She tempts fate.

RISSA
BRAHM

WANT MORE OF RISSA BRAHM'S PARADISE SOUTH—FOR FREE?

Hello Rockin' Romance Readers!

Sign up for my newsletter and get a deleted scene from *Tempting Isabel*—plus juicy extras from the entire Paradise South series—and lots more exclusive content...all for **free!**

Details can be found in the ***Author's Note*** at the end of *Tempting Isabel*. Until then, enjoy your journey through Book 1 and I'll see ya after the HEA!

Copyright Information

ISBN 978-1-944557-00-3 (print)

ISBN 978-1-944557-01-0 (epub)

ISBN 978-1-944557-02-7 (mobi)

Published by: *108 degrees*™

Brahm, Rissa (2016-04-01)

Illustrated Romance Cover design by: Damonza

Tempting Isabel (Paradise South, Book 1)

TKA Distribution. Kindle Edition.

To Sara, Shiv, and VK, my ever-guides.

And to my two suns and moons, AC and KC, who have supported
the writing of this series, day and night, night and day.

CHAPTER 1

HEAD DOWN, ZACHARY James held up his index finger and tapped his empty glass. "Another scotch please, José."

"José's gone for the night, Mr. James. I'm Angel."

Zack lifted his gaze. The sensual rasp in the sweet rolling Castilian accent had come to his ears through dark lush lips. A spectacular Spanish beauty. But even she couldn't hold his focus. Tonight his attentions were strictly geared to the highball glass in his hands.

"Nice to meet you, Angel. The top-shelf Dalton, please. On the rocks."

"Of course, Mr. James. José told me—and he'd also said to take very special care of you." Probably due to the hefty tips he'd thrown down since he'd gotten to the resort's outdoor patio bar overlooking the beach and the bay. He inhaled the sea air coming in off the water thinking how the warm Vallarta breeze was no doubt better than his suite's artificially chilled and recycled air stream. And the fact that his penthouse mini-bar didn't come with someone to pour.

No. He rubbed his temples. No interest, not tonight.

He nodded his thanks as Angel poured the liquid amber. A soothing sound, scotch over crackling cubes of ice. It almost soothed his despondent mind, but not quite.

Then from the other direction, an obnoxious slurping sound met his ear. A new bar mate. *Perfect.* Zack clenched his jaw tight and consciously made no eye contact whatsoever with the other man who grabbed a bar stool to join Zack.

Without a "please," the guy ordered a new drink from the buxom bartender who went down the way to grab a bottle of the low-end choice.

Meanwhile, the man stared at Zack. "Jet lag?" A thick Jersey accent, or was it Brooklyn?

"Jet lag's an understatement," Zack said, calling up a polite smile while hoping like hell that would be the first and last response he'd have to give the guy, or anyone for that matter, for the rest of the night.

He had landed in Puerto Vallarta from Bangkok via Abu Dhabi just before sunset, and now, as twilight swallowed the Bay of Banderas on the Pacific coast of Mexico, he intended to dwell on or drown out the resounding monotony that had hit him two days before on the far side of the world. And so far neither option, the dwelling nor the drowning, was working worth a damn.

"I'm Johnnie. Just got here for some much needed leisure in paradise, myself. And I'll tell yaaa…" The guy paused with raised brows.

"Oh, uh…Zack." *Shit.*

"Cool, cool…well, I'll tell ya Zack, those two prime specimens over there, the gorgeous redhead and her sumptuous blond friend, they're jonesin' hard for you, and if you don't give 'em something, a smile with a wink or a round of shots, then I'm gonna have to. Those fine hot things are just too perfect a pair of pussy to let go to waste."

Zack winced at the guy's choice of words, then reluctantly expended the energy to look his interrupter in the face. The guy had to be in his early twenties, if that. Near the same age as his kid brother, Darren, who, Zack was proud to say, he'd all but raised himself. Shown him how to be a strong and respectful man, by the way. A damn good man.

This dipshit, though, was smug and cocky without merit. And that was fine, especially if it meant he'd take his arrogant ass out of Zack's face and do what he was just threatening he'd do—go hit up the *ladies* at the end of the bar. Anyway, Zack hadn't even noticed the supposed eyes on him, nor did he have any interest. He didn't want to entertain, talk to, listen to, or deal with anyone, even if they were a "perfect pair of pussy."

"Hadn't noticed, man," Zack said, then continued to glare at the kid to best communicate his desire for him to go the fuck away—with the girls or without them.

"I'll take that as an official go-head," the kid said, then nodded a thanks and goodbye as he slid off his barstool. Angel returned just then to pour the kid's drink, and with no tip, no thanks, the kid took it and left.

Schmuck.

But maybe used to cheap assholes, Angel seemed unfazed by the kid's rudeness, more confirmation as to why Zack was getting such attentive service.

"Good luck there," she called to the kid, who threw a look over his shoulder as if to say, 'No need, I got this,' then continued down the length of the bar. The kid approached the two ladies-in-waiting with his chest puffed out, chin held high.

*

Hmm. This should be somewhat interesting, if not comical. A slightly welcome break in that sudden and now lingering numbness that had hit him those two days ago.

Yeah, Zack had woken up that one morning alone, completely confused, and almost panicked—unlike the usually calm and confident Zachary James. In his haze he'd managed to dial the concierge to ask where the hell in the world he was, because he had no goddamn clue. Had the whirlwind of his fast and luxurious lifestyle finally caught up to him, spoiled him numb?

Who the fuck knew? But whatever the cause, it was affecting him physically. Even before the drinking marathon he'd begun on his jet from Abu Dhabi en route to Vallarta, his knotted gut and pounding head had caught him off guard. But his ailments rocked on and all Zack could think to do was drink more, numb the pain away. So he took another pull from his glass as he watched the kid make his move. Meanwhile, from his peripheral, he caught both gorgeous ladies beckoning Zack with searing eyes still.

Poor kid.

"I'm glad someone's making an effort," Angel said as she propped her elbows up on the bar and leaned into Zack's personal space with a bright smile and generous cleavage.

"Yeah, right. At least someone is…" He smiled graciously while keeping the far-off scene in view.

"Hey, this stuff's my entertainment…and you, Mr. James, were frankly starting to bore me," she said with a wink and a stroke across the top of his hand with her slender middle finger.

Zack only shook his head and gave her his most respectful, thin-lined smile. A gentle rejection. He didn't want to be rude; she was nice. But again, he was just not in any mood for anyone.

"*Entiendo*," she said with a single nod of her head. Then she topped off his scotch as if to say she really was cool with the brush-off, seemingly confident enough to take it, and then the two continued to watch the show down the way.

Too far to hear anything, he did make out a pen in the redhead's hand. She put it to a napkin on the bar's surface then handed it to the kid, motioning her pretty doll head back towards Zack. She was sending the kid back to where he'd come from. *Ouch.* And all the while her gaze maintained sniper-like focus on him, her original target.

Zack hid his smirk behind another pull from his scotch as the kid made the long, emasculating walk back down the bar.

"How'd it go?" Angel asked, absolutely *not* hiding her grin.

The young guy slapped the napkin on the bar top in front of Zack.

"It happens to the best of us," Angel soothed. "Even to me," she said, winking at Zack.

Zack let his lip curl as he met her gaze, fairly certain she'd never been turned down before. Likely not, she was factually hot. *But rejection builds character.* And who knew, maybe his usual spark would reignite a few drinks down the line and by the end of her shift, he'd be game. Fuck he hoped so, because he was getting worried.

The kid rolled his eyes at Zack. "Guess it's your lucky night, dude. Your lucky fucking night…"

Luck? Zack cleared his throat and faced the kid. "I don't believe in luck, man."

"Whatever, dude, call it what you want." The kid slid the napkin—with its hand-written message—toward Zack. "Whatever the fuck you wanna call it, man, but this is for you."

Zack grimaced, sighed and grabbed the napkin. *Bring your drink and your fine ass to the hot tub. Ten minutes. J&T.* He shook his head and fisted the napkin in his hand while not missing the kid's glare from his peripheral.

"Dude, what the fuck's your deal? Why aren't you all over this? Are you fuckin' gay?"

"No man, I'm straight...but tired. Business meetings in three countries in two days...jet lag, like you said." The kid was entertaining, to say the least.

"Whatever, I just really resent lucky fucks like you."

Right. That word again. A burn rocketed up him as he took his next sip of scotch to keep his cool.

Luck. *Fuck luck.* He didn't take that accusation lightly. Never had. Zack James worked his goddamn ass off to get where he was. He and he alone had earned his fortune, his success. And he'd be damned if he had to hear this little prick insinuate otherwise. Like this kid knew him at all. Like he knew anything about anything. "Johnnie, right?"

"Yeah, it's Johnnie. My father's—"

"Look, Johnnie, I don't really care who your father is. Like I said before, I don't believe in luck. Luck has not a goddamn thing to do with anything, not a goddamn thing to do with me."

"Okay dude, okay...fine. But even still, it's fucked up to take this"—he held up the napkin—"for granted, while us regular guys have to sweat and suck to get one semi-decent piece of pussy."

Angel flinched then glared at the kid, a scowl forming on her magazine-cover face.

Zack shook his head. "Have some respect, man." *Jesus.* Not in front of a lady.

Now it wasn't like Zack hadn't used such derogatory terms before to refer to a woman. In context, it's just a part of how guys talk. But shit, not in front of a woman, classy or otherwise. There's a line.

Johnnie was red in the face, shifting his eyes like a kid in trouble. "Sorry lady," he muttered to Angel, then returned to Zack. "But whatever, dude. Those bitches gave me no respect, sending me back like a fucking messenger boy." *So, not apologizing then.* "No, they don't deserve my respect or my attention. Stupid cunts." He mumbled the last bit under his breath, then tapped his empty glass and lifted his eyebrows at Angel.

Whoa. Piece of pussy. Bitches. Cunts? Then the little prick with the big-man talk demands another drink from Angel? The incensed woman stood in front of them, generous chest heaving—she seemed just about ready to crack a bottle over the kid's head.

A disgust, raw and real, swelled in Zack's stomach, up into his chest, then to his already pounding head. Because beyond being in awe of his favorite woman on Earth, his mother, Zack loved and respected women. In general. He appreciated them; their strength, their spirit, their fight, their ability to juggle everything and then some, and…

…hell yes, their beauty. He loved the female form in all its splendor, including and especially their velvet folds and the sleek juncture in the divine center.

Not a cunt. Silken petals of pure perfection.

And, in all honesty in the past, he'd maybe enjoyed and taken for granted a few too many women. But he'd always treated the women he'd been with well, pleased them no doubt, and had given them his respect; from female associates in his business dealings to exotic dancers and every type of woman in between.

But this little prick! The kid was an embarrassment to men everywhere. Zack hoped he'd never sounded remotely like him, drunk or sober. This asshole had no appreciation or respect, no finesse, no class, no goddamn clue. And just in case, for any time Zack hadn't shown enough respect to a lady, and on behalf of Angel and his mother and for other men—real men who knew better, just like Zack knew better—Zack wanted to shove his now-empty scotch glass so far up this guy's ass that it reached his eye sockets. It just might provide him a clearer perspective—Johnnie needed to see through a very different lens that women were far more than the combination of their goddamn parts, or holes, as it were.

But Zack was in Mexico for two reasons, and neither of those reasons would be served from a Mexican jail cell—which he foresaw being thrown into if he did what he wanted to do to this dickhead, no matter the clout he had in Vallarta and in that resort from his years of loyal patronage. The international vacation haven of Puerto Vallarta, Mexico was still Mexico, after all.

No. Instead, he'd play to the kid's sore spot.

"Hey, you know…you may be right, man. I mean, why the hell not?" Maybe if he could skip the small talk with the two hungry and determined ladies and sink himself into their delectable and welcoming bodies—give them the pleasure they so clearly sought— maybe that would be his jumpstart back to his usual, electrically charged existence?

Zack slid off his stool, pulled a big bill from his wallet for Angel, then kissed her hand in thanks for her service and company, albeit short-lived. "Maybe some other time? I'm here for several weeks yet," he said and smiled, turning his prior rejection into a possibility. Then Zack, feeling bad for leaving poor Angel cold, and for leaving her alone with the little dickhead to his left, swept his arm wide across the bar and 'accidentally' knocked his unfinished scotch onto the kid's lap.

"Sorry man. Probably gonna wanna go and change your pants now." And without looking back, he took himself and his newfound motivation to the far end of the bar. He wouldn't meet the two ladies at the hot tub per their written request, but rather, like a gentleman, he'd escort the two sexually assertive women to his penthouse suite for a nightcap. And would go from there.

But as he strode over to the eager ladies while Little Johnnie's glare pierced the back of his head, he couldn't ignore what his gut already knew. True satisfaction wouldn't be had this way. No, it would end the same way it started. With him on empty.

The hard question—what *would* fulfill him?

What the hell would?

CHAPTER 2

S HE ROLLED HER eyes as she declined the phone call, the third one that morning—and the sun was hardly up yet.

As her hard rock playlist resumed, she inhaled the ocean air to clear her lungs and her head and got back to it. Working her guilt-riddled excitement and confusion and nagging sorrow out through the tightening muscles in her back and arms, she pushed those jumbled emotions down and out through the long red mop handle. Each back and forth along the already clean tile floor made her feel like she was doing something. Making a difference. In control.

Hah. What a ridiculous cosmic joke.

Just like the farce of a legal battle that had ended at three minutes after six in the evening last night. After ten infinite months, her mother's siblings and the chauvinistic Mexican legal estate process had lost, and the official transfer went through. Isabel Angelica Ruiz was now the sole owner of her *abuelo's* seaside condo situated far south of town.

And God, it was surreal. A dream, really. *My far off sanctuary.* Just too crazy to think the words, let alone say them, or else, poof! Like everything else good in her life, it'd be gone. Just like that. Just like Sebastian, her soul mate, her one true love.

She dipped the mop head into the sudsy bucket and continued to pummel the hell out of the tile floor. Because if she just thrusted hard enough, she'd annihilate all the guilt and the hurt with just that mop and soapy water and her always-earnest elbow grease.

If only.

*

He woke up panicked, short of breath, pulse sprinting. The bad dream that had startled him awake leaked into his consciousness, some version of the Bangkok hotel scene again. Same confusion, same void.

Yeah, the lingering void, *as goddamn expected.*

The one difference this time, he wasn't alone.

The two bar beauties weren't stirring. Even with how cold the room was while their bare bodies lay completely uncovered, they remained deep in sleep.

He sat up to get a look at the bedside clock. *Shit!* The condo closing—one of the two reasons that had brought him to Vallarta. No way he'd be late for this. He'd waited too long as it was.

He crawled to the foot of the bed and touched the toe of the redhead, her slender arm dangling over the edge of the mattress in deep, lazy sleep.

"Hey…time to wake up." He paused three beats. "Hey, hello…I've got to go, ladies."

Zack stood up and stretched then shook his head at the tangle of beauties. Gazing at them he wondered why he didn't feel sated on any level, because he definitely should have. He knew any man on the planet would have.

But instead, he felt slightly sick to his stomach, to add to the same throbbing headache he'd had the night before. He went and grabbed an antacid, an aspirin, and a Super B from his toiletry kit, and came back to the bedside.

"Girls…it's time! Up and at 'em!"

He imagined the would-be words of his buddies, his attorney and his brother. Any of them would have died to be in his shoes right then, staring down at those magnificent female forms he had fucked the hell out of all night long. "Lifelong lucky streak," they'd say. Just like that prick at the bar last night.

Lucky streak, my ass. They had no idea. What about his father ditching him, leaving him to care for his brother and mother, only a damn kid himself for fuck's sake. Yeah, they had no idea what Zack James had been through. And what he'd overcome to reach his current heights.

He continued to stare at the naked beauties still rolled in the sheets of the grand king-size bed, their limbs entwined like a delicious abstract painting.

Damn it. It would've helped if he could remember either of their names. *J&T*—shit! He did remember that although last night's motivation had been to prove that shady dickhead at the bar wrong, the girls had definitely made out. And he got off once, a decent release from his very real jet lag.

But none of it mattered. His efforts hadn't done anything to stop the droning lull inside. Why the hell was his gut still filled with this cavernous void?

He shook his head. Just pathetic. A goddamn walking, talking, fucking cliché. What was this? A bout of conscience…or guilt maybe? Fucking depression, like his mother? Or some psychosomatic bullshit? Was he looking too deep? Maybe it was nothing more than sheer world-weary boredom.

The other reason he was in Vallarta was to play Best Man at his kid brother's wedding. But the wrench in his psyche couldn't have had anything to do with that. He was happy for Darren. The thought made the corners of Zack's mouth lift—a first in literally days.

Marriage wasn't in the cards for Zack, but for his brother, he couldn't have been more relieved that their parents hadn't annihilated the institution of holy matrimony for both the James boys. Thankfully, Darren was too young to remember much of the devastating split. And so his kid brother, untainted, found a girl—*the* girl—and if anyone could settle down with one woman for life, it'd be Darren.

But for Zack, his unattached lifestyle was the way. At least it had been, damn it. He'd relished the pure, unadulterated freedom of being a filthy fucking rich bachelor. And just as he reminded himself that he'd been made for the fast life, the blonde moaned and stretched. Yeah, he was meant for *this*, he thought, watching her bright blue eyes highlighted by her smudged black eyeliner glare savagely at him at the foot of the bed.

Mopped into a corner, she was trapped against a catch-all box of her *abuelo's* keepsakes, there just collecting dust.

She took a swig of water then hoisted the heavy box up onto the kitchen counter. There, teetering on top of the pile of random things, she noticed a framed black and white photo of her grandparents. She'd never met her grandmother, but God, the woman was beautiful. It was obvious that her *abuelo* thought so too. She took the frame off the top of the precarious pile to study it more closely—and to save herself the very likely mess on the floor. And, God, broken glass to boot!—never a good sign. The last thing she needed was a bad omen on her first morning in her new home. *Please, Jesus.*

She wiped the dust layer off the glass and smiled at the looks of depth and serenity her grandparents had for each other. Sweet, familiar. That was the kind of love, selfless and unending, that she and Sebastian had shared.

A surge of burning pain traveled up her spine. Knowing that type of adoration had ever even existed was heart ripping. It was so rare after all to see two truly connected souls, even with how many couples she works with in her day-to-day. God, ignorance would have been such bliss, if she'd just never known it in the first place. But she had— and she'd never know it again, at least, not for herself.

She flipped the photo frame over, wedged it deep and safe inside the box, and then shoved the entire heaping thing into the center of the counter.

Get back to it, Isa. She gripped the mop again and hit the volume control on her phone three times, tricking her lingering tears to halt in their tracks. *Now scrub, damn it.*

Her new and far-off home had to be her focus.

And her career—despite its admitted and torturous irony.

Yes, despite her propensity for breakages, mishaps and the like, she was an expert at strategizing and planning successful destination weddings in her coastal hometown of Puerto Vallarta. And she loved the work, again, even with the in-her-face pain of it.

And she'd had no reason to consider herself a masochist when she'd accepted the opportunity at nineteen. She'd been naive then, engaged to

Sebastian in a whirlwind of magical bliss. But now, after losing her true love and two arranged fiancés after that, her remaining family continually asked Isabel why she kept doing such excruciating work.

It was torture, yes, but it was what made her feel anything anymore. It combatted the chilling numbness in her heart. It was her self-punishment. And now it was decidedly her realized purpose: helping tie the bonds of love for other hopeful souls while fate kept her from tying her own. Fate's cruel joke was her test-turned-mission.

So now her new home and her work were her life, and she was reconciled to that fact.

As the sun rose higher in the sky, it got hot, almost sweltering. With the lack of air conditioning, the summer heat knocking at May's door, and her deep angry effort at that clean start, she knotted her hair in a bun and tied up her sweat-soaked top to just below her bust line. Cooler, better. She looked down and grinned—her in a crop tank and panties? Yes. In *her* place, not a soul around for the first time in her life—hell yes!

Half-naked freedom!

And why the hell not? Her condo complex was even empty of vacationers until October, and her direct neighbors had up and left—when her *abuelo* died, rumor of her moving in had circulated like wildfire.

So, she'd conquer her new home *this* way, *her* way!—with her hard rock music blasting, arms and legs and back busting ass, and loose strands of her dark locks sticking to her sweat-kissed and smiling face.

*

She had to remember her client meetings in town, so she paused to check her progress and the clock. Only the filth-covered windows and sliding glass door to go, with more than an hour to do it in. Yeah, she'd be fine. "But so much for the cleaning service, though," she murmured to herself and the wind.

They'd obviously rushed through the place, but with just a little more effort, she'd be able to see out to the beach and the bay where some of her fondest childhood memories had been made. The children of vacationing foreigners staying at her *abuelo's* condo complex had been her only playmates growing up, because those kids hadn't known of the little gray cloud that followed her wherever she went.

Other than time spent at her *abuelo's*, she grew up more or less friendless. Well, except for Roberto, a fellow outcast since second grade and loyal to the end. Oh, and her brother, Ray, only sixteen months older than her, who'd shared common interests in fashion and beauty products, so even her lack of long-term girlfriends hadn't been too hard on her. *Not really.*

Anyway, Isabel didn't blame the kids at school, the neighbors, or the folks at church—and now the majority of her own family—for their fearful distance. As far back as she could remember she'd had to struggle to keep things from breaking, falling, crashing, and crumbling around her. She wouldn't want to be in her wake either if she were in any of their shoes.

Especially as she matured, because so did the hovering darkness. Larger incidents happened that no one could explain, except that Isabel seemed to always be at the center of them. And by adulthood, the dark nimbus cloud that was her curse burst open, breaking her heart and crumbling her soul.

She grabbed a rag and spray bottle and began cleaning the glass door from top to bottom, sunlight streaming through each new swipe—"Jesus Rays" are what she and her siblings had called them. After that first full pass, the initial layer of dirt vanished, and the room already became a different place. She even felt lighter. But how sad that her grandfather's home had gotten so dank and filthy since he'd gone. Well, she was there now and would be sure to keep the place pristine and fresh, worthy of her sweet *abuelo's* memory.

She sighed then stepped way back to see her progress. A crack in the lower right corner caught her eye and made her jaw clench. *Of course.* Why was every glimpse of hope met with an ill omen?

The bay breeze flooded her face from the open door, and she took it in and swallowed it back. *You know what? Screw it.* Because again, what control did she have anyway? If things were gonna go to hell, there was not a damn thing she could do about it, right?

So she keyed into the hard rock ballad filling the place, grabbed the spray bottle microphone-style with white knuckles, and made like a rock star in a music video. With the windows and slider open to the moving ocean air, her mostly bare, sweat-soaked skin prickled as the breeze met her. This was a literal and figurative cleansing—of her new home, of her pride and conscience, and of her past, damn it! She felt powerful. Optimistic, even. The rough, head-banging freedom of belting out the words to the heavens, to Fate herself, was a liberating release.

And just as she got to the raging chorus of the song, her streaming hard rock got rudely interrupted, replaced by a joyful mariachi ring tone. Her oldest sister Celeste. Calling again. Attempt number four.

She huffed then glared at her phone. She placed the spray bottle down, moved the mop blocking her path carefully against the wall, wiped her brow with the back of her hand, and stepped toward her phone. But as she reached for the device, she tripped over the bucket at her feet, bringing her back to reality, the reality where she had no hope and no control. *There it is, Isabel.* Fate had the control and wouldn't dare let her forget it.

*

She got to it on the fourth ring, "Celi, hey...are you there?" Her voice as sweet as crème caramel.

"Little sister, how are you? I've tried you, like, a billion times!"

Ah, the exaggeration. "Sorry, Celi...is everything okay? The girls alright?" Her three nieces, whom she never saw anymore, had been like her surrogate children. But by her own insistence, she refused to put them at risk. She did miss them terribly, and the few photos Celeste texted her did little to fill the void.

"The girls are fine, Isa. Yeah, they're great. Will send you the clip of their dance recital...so adorable."

"Oh, good, I'd love that," she said, shoving the pangs of envy deep down, below the scars.

"But Isa, I was calling because I wanted to be the second to congratulate you! Antonio said it's done—you're a homeowner now!"

"I am. I am a homeowner." She shook her head at hearing the words. *Crazy.* Then she knocked on the wood door frame.

"I'm so happy for you, Isa! How was your first night's sleep?"

"Not bad. A bit choppy…from the excitement of it all. I'm still, well…a little floored. Literally." She laughed, the puddles of splattered mop water she'd spilled mocking her from below. "I'm just knee deep in suds and pine scent right now."

"I thought the maid service cleaned yesterday?"

"Yeah, the place was cleaned, but you know, not to my standards." She laughed again.

"Your OCD standards, yes," Celeste teased. "I know them well."

"Yes, but that's why Lucinda throws me as many events as she does. Because of my 'perfectionist tendencies.'" And Isabel's incessant need to compensate, fix, or undo the constant crap that happened around her. Lucinda was pretty damn awesome to overlook half of it.

"True. Just don't go overboard like you do and hurt your back or something. Then how will that woman run you ragged?"

"I love my work, Celi, and now I'll need it all the more. For gas money alone, with how far out of town I am. But anyway"—*shift to the positive, Isabel*—"I do love it out here."

"God, Isa, I couldn't be happier for you. A place of your own. Now we just need to find you a man to share it with."

"Don't you dare start," she warned, trying to check her tone. She knew Celeste loved her and always meant well—hell, the woman had practically raised her—but challenging Isabel's decision to steer clear of relationships was not needed. Nor welcome. "I know you want me to be happy, Celi, but I just can't go there. Not after all that's happened. I just need to keep to myself."

Celeste owned the opinion that Isabel's curse and the danger she posed shouldn't prevent her from finding a man and "from really living." But how could Celeste understand? Her sister carried no burden on *her* shoulders. And hey, she didn't hear Celi fight Isabel's decision to keep away from the girls. But putting others in danger was fine, right? It baffled Isabel, truly.

"Look, Isa, I don't want to dampen your new-house high. You just enjoy your new place and when you get settled, I'll come by for a quick visit. We'll talk then."

But Isabel wasn't game for that talk, not again.

Just because Celeste's ex, Juan, had left her and her three little girls cold, and Celi was now on the hunt, it didn't mean Isabel wanted a man. She didn't. She was done hoping. What was the point anyway? She'd already found, and then lost, Sebastian. And you only get one soulmate per lifetime, right?

Right. And so, since the most recent tragedy, she'd formulated rules for herself. Isabel would continue to keep loved ones at a distance and not allow new ties. No relationships, period—especially not romantic ones. She'd take the occasional quick fling with one of Vallarta's vacationing foreigners who knew nothing of her curse, and usually, in her experience, didn't believe in such "superstitious crap" anyways. It was a perfect situation, unattached and safe release. A win-win.

After all, she was only twenty-five years old, and *she* wasn't dead yet—for whatever reason. And for safety's sake, she kept her sexcapades anonymous. No full names, no numbers. Guilt and danger free.

But her sister didn't understand her—her curse or her vacuous extra-curriculars that led to nowhere on purpose—so, as always, Isabel just appeased Celi on the surface and ended their *talks* as quickly as possible. "Okay, Celi, sounds good."

"Oh, hey! I'll see you tonight? Antonio had said seven o'clock, I think. At our usual spot."

"Yes, right! I almost forgot. See you at dinner." Balanced with her two remaining brothers, dinner with Celeste wouldn't be so bad. That is, as long as there was no repeat of last time, when Celeste brought a "friend" for Isabel. *God, that was awful.* But Ray and his boyfriend Eddie had monopolized the conversation as usual, so she'd managed.

"Okay *m'ija. Hasta luego. A las siete en las tarde.*"

"Right. Seven. *Ciao.*" Isabel sighed as she hit "end" on her screen, and her playlist automatically resumed.

She set her phone on the coffee table with a long sigh, then got right back into her hard rock distraction.

She shut her eyes tight, and whipping her hair around wildly, she unwound again. With every head-banging nod, back to freedom. No pressure, no curse, no loneliness.

And when the song ended and switched to the next, she opened her eyes…

…and screamed bloody murder.

*

A face. At the still-slightly-hazy rear slider.

"Cover yourself, Isabel…you're killing me!" Roberto said as he moved to the open doorway.

"*Por Dios!* You scared the hell out of me, Roberto! Jesus!" In a veiled huff, she ducked into her bedroom as he made his entrance. In Mexico, the unannounced and uninvited were never turned away, an unspoken code that basically applied to any time of day at all. But it didn't mean she couldn't be pissed-as-hell by it. She'd loved the sweeping freedom of being half-naked in her far off piece of solitude. And, damn it, now she'd have to hunt for something to put on.

But also, this was the fourth time this week Roberto had stopped by. First at her cramped room-share in town and now at her new home, a thirty-minute drive south of Vallarta. She could safely assume this visit would be like the others, rehashing an already extremely tired conversation. She was feeling too elated and, at the same time, too exhausted to hear his rant about how they were meant to be together. And he wouldn't let it go.

"Give me a second!" she called from her bedroom. "Hey, can you pause my playlist?" she asked him, unable to hear herself think as she searched around her room for a not-so-small box of her more comfortable clothes.

But except for her professional outfits she'd already hung in her closet, the box of her hang-around clothes was out in the main room. "Hey, just sit and make yourself at home. Or better yet, grab a drink from the sink. It's so hot out already!" she called, hoping to redirect him to the kitchen while she made a run for the box.

"It is hot, outside and in!" he called back to her, a wink in his voice.

She poked her head out. His back was to her, at the sink filling two glasses. She made a tiptoeing run for the box, only ten feet away from her door toward the slider.

"Shit!" she screamed, only a foot from her goal.

"What, Isa? What is it?" he said, spinning around.

Her foot. The right one. It throbbed and dripped red. *Damn it!* She hopped the short distance to the box to grab whatever was on top—her yellow satin robe—then threw it on. She scoffed at the dark red droplets all over her newly cleaned tile floor. From the corner of her eye she saw Roberto moving in her direction to help. "I'm fine. Just sit on the couch. Please…"

Her foot pulsated in pain while hot embarrassment flared in her cheeks. But more than that, the loss of the serenity she'd had just minutes before Roberto's appearance, and hell, Celeste's phone call, was filling her with pure anxiety.

"Isa, please let me—"

"I got it, Roberto. Thanks, though." She closed the robe at her front as she hopped to her room, sank to the floor, and pulled out a tiny tortilla chip-shaped piece of glass. It matched the lower right corner of the slider. *Of course.*

She pulled herself up and limped her way to the bathroom, leaving more red spots in her wake.

*

Bandages. She hadn't unpacked those either, but her grandfather had always kept first aid stuff in the powder room. Albeit two or three decades old now, she was sure something was there to do the job. Annoyed by the entire turn of events, even though she should be quite used to happenings like these, she adjusted the long sleeves of her robe down toward her hands and hopped back out to the main room, this time with a towel at the bottom of her foot as not to extend the bloody trail. She moved past Roberto, who stood to help again. Her palm went up. "Really, just sit there…and relax."

She threw on the light to the powder room and just narrowly avoided seeing herself in the mirror with the large spider-web crack resonating from its center. "For God's sake!"

"What now?"

She shook her head and blew a sigh of relief. "Just a broken mirror's all!" she said with intended sarcasm.

Owning a broken mirror was even worse than having plain cracked glass. But seeing your own splintered reflection! It was almost laughable—seven years' bad luck on top of her infinite curse? *Mother in heaven...*

Yes, in her country, deep-seated superstition and ancient beliefs in the unseen dictated many people's lives. All of her family's endless and usually inconvenient Mexican-Mayan rituals were both nostalgically heartwarming and depressing, being that most of their fears were centered around her very existence. *Isabel the walking jinx.*

Sighing out her frustration, she rinsed and then bandaged her foot, hung a towel over the mirror from the cockeyed light fixture above, and went back out to Roberto, who kept himself seated on the sofa this time.

"You really okay? Need stitches?"

"No, no, I am fine, thanks. And hey, sorry I snapped at you," she said, limping over to the mop while pretending not to have seen him shudder as he eyed her robe draping down over her breasts. She blushed, then felt her nipples tighten from a new hard breeze coming in off the bay. And the slippery satin fabric wasn't helping. She quickly moved away from his obvious gaze as if she'd resumed cleaning, and took the opportunity to readjust her robe's neckline. God, she hated how awkward things were with Roberto now.

It'd been this way since that blackout drunken night more than a week ago, and his damn infatuation was just too much to take. Waking up naked in his arms had been mortifying enough, but he still wouldn't let it go. More importantly, despite Roberto's skeptical take on her situation, she believed the incident to be a potentially fatal mistake. But all the proof and dissuasion in the world had no effect on his stubborn insistence that they were each other's soulmates.

"Salt water will do a deep cut good. Come to the beach with me, Isa."

"I can't. I have three back-to-back meetings—shoot, starting in an hour! And it's at the Five Breezes on the north side of town," she said, noticing the time on her microwave.

"Just come to the bedroom with me real quick then, for a foot rub, a body rub, whatever…" He winked. "Or I can take you right here and now. Let me relax you, soothe you." Then he held out his hand to her, a little wilted wildflower in his fingertips. "I'm still under your spell, Isabel. A flower…for my flower."

She rolled her eyes at him and at the dying little weed, although she knew he was just trying to be sweet. Still, it was too much already! Just too damn much. "Enough of that, Roberto!" Then, half-playing to hide her true aversion, she threw a rag at him, which knocked over the spray bottle on the end table. In an attempt to catch the bottle, she bumped into the mop bucket. Again.

Another round of dirty water spilled all over her newly cleaned floor, except that it didn't help dilute any of the nearly dried blood droplets. She could only stare while Roberto jumped up to grab paper towels from the kitchen.

"Damn it," she grumbled, frustrated with his sexual innuendo, her lack of time, and her unending clumsiness. "Roberto, I love you. You are my oldest and dearest friend. But you're driving me nuts! For the last time and for your own good, best friends are all we can be. Ever. You *know* my rule—"

"And you know what I think of your rule and of your supposed curse." He made emphatic air quotes and rolled his eyes. His family, French Canadian, didn't share the deep-rooted beliefs hers did.

"Here we go again. Okay, so you don't remember any of the four funerals over the last four years?" A rhetorical question posed in her angriest tone. "Or growing up together and the crazy things that happened to me and to everyone around me? Daily?" She pointed to a scar on his chin from when she'd collided with him head-on in the third grade. "And the things that still happen?" She nodded toward the bucket and then held up her bandaged foot.

"All chance happenings, Isabel," he said, moving to inspect her foot as she was now within arms' reach, but she pulled away.

"Chance? Right. *Chance.* Coincidence. Look, we can agree to disagree once and for all, but the annual *loss of life,* Roberto…there's not a day that goes by that I don't…see their faces. And no one has to shoulder that pain and guilt but me," she said with a hint of quivering emotion in her voice. To buy time for composure, she adjusted the satin sleeves of her robe to be sure they covered her arms fully and crossed them over her now heaving chest.

"Isa, you don't have to shoulder it alone. I'm here for you, and I always will be."

"If you don't even believe me, Roberto, how can you really be here for me?" She shook her head. "That's not even the point, though. Believe it or not, I have a fatal track record, and your life is not something I'm willing to screw with. You shouldn't even be hanging around as often as you do! Roberto, you're my only friend, and I don't want to lose you, too."

"Isabel Angelica Ruiz, you won't lose me. We've been friends since we were seven, for Christ's sake. And I'm still here! I'll tell you again, it's all a self-fulfilling prophecy, your bad luck. If you could just change the way you think, not let the damn neighbors and your family get to you—"

"It's not what people think or say, it's what *I know*… Oh for God's sake, Roberto, this is like a dog chasing its tail. I don't want to talk about this anymore. I can't."

"No. You've got to end this craziness once and for all, Isa. No more running away! Listen to me. Just hear my logic. Take Filipe, for example," he said as she moved into the kitchen to put the spray bottle and rags away, slamming the cabinet doors as she went. But he continued just the same. "I mean, he was close to the coffin before your father even arranged that whole fiasco."

"Filipe died a week before the wedding, Roberto…clutching *my* damn photo to his chest!"

"He was a chain-smoking alcoholic, Isa! And pushing sixty." Roberto held out his hands as if they held proof of the ridiculousness of her theory. "Why do you have to put so much emphasis on your losses by trying to find meaning behind them? Why can't they just be horrible tragedies that happened and move the hell on? You're just closing doors, opportunities with this insanity! Stop dwelling and look ahead…look at me, Isa! Look. At. Me." He paused then, but she wouldn't look at him. Her glare remained fixed on the blood on her floor, but she sensed his stare. It burned a hole in her forehead.

*

Roberto leaned forward, grabbed her cellphone from the coffee table, and a few swipes later, he slammed it down again. Face up.

Her favorite picture of Sebastian—his deep jade eyes illuminated the screen. Her Sebastian, who wouldn't heed anyone's warnings. The man who had to have her, and in the end, died to have her. And he still had her. He'd always have her.

"Sebastian is gone, Isabel! It just wasn't meant to be. But I'm alive, right here, with you. And we *are* meant…to be!"

Had he really gone there? Her heart filled her throat, choking her out because, yes, he definitely had.

And she saw red. Literally. Her thumbnail had dug a hole in her wrist. She stared at the trickle of blood. She swallowed hard, as if that would put her pounding heart back in her chest where it belonged. But it didn't. She tried to slow her breath and remain calm as she kept her threatening eyes there on her new wound, just below her other scars that lay covered by the pale yellow robe.

But if she hadn't kept her eyes focused there on her self-inflicted gash, her angered look alone might have murdered Roberto right there and then, piercing a torturous tunnel right through him. He had crossed an invisible line, one she thought she'd never have to draw for him, not for her most faithful friend.

For Roberto to even speak that name. *Sebastian.* Sebastian belonged to Isabel. Her first love, her deepest love. He was goddamn off-limits!

*

"Mmmm, wow. That was, like, the best sleep ever!" The blonde's morning stretch dragged her hard rose-hued nipples up the slender back of Red-Hot who was still sleeping on top of the tussled mess of sheets.

Zack felt a sudden throbbing below. His erection felt a slight draft from the room through the slit in his boxers. Blondie eyed him hungrily, his apparent bulge making her giggle and purr. Wide awake now, she pushed herself up by leveraging the inner thigh of Red-Hot and crawled her way down the bed while zeroing in on Zack's stiff cock.

"Oh no, sweetheart. No, no, no…it's time to get up and out now," he told her.

"I know. It's time to get up and out." She grabbed at his shorts before he could step back.

One side of his lip curled, but he quickly caught her hands in his. "I can't be late for my morning meeting. Some other time maybe…" He blew out a stream of air from the shock of her ice-cold touch brushing his scorching hard-on. Then he smacked her smooth pale ass and moved away from the bed's edge to go to get his clothes on.

"But, baby," she called after him, "how do we contact you for that 'some other time,' huh? You never even told us your name, Mr. Long-and-Strong!" She baited him, begging, still on her knees at the bed's edge. Zack looked back at her with a polite smile and then continued to his closet. He chose a pair of light ultra-casual linen pants to throw on, as was the fashion in Vallarta. He jumped into them and then hurried back across the room for his shirt. He ignored the bombshell who still hadn't given up, trying to tempt him with her right index finger as it slinked down her body and past her blond curly mound to play with herself.

"Well"—deciding to keep his name to himself—"I guess if it's meant to be," he teased. *Hah, meant to be.* What pseudo-deep superstitious bullshit.

Now at the windows, he threw open the floor-to-ceiling drapes, hoping to move things along for his other guest, the still-sleeping beauty.

The bright Vallarta sun flooded the room, causing Red-Hot to shove her head under her pillow while Blondie stopped her whirling-finger to cover her squinting eyes with both hands. He grabbed his watch, his keys and wallet, and then slipped on his brown leather sandals.

"Housekeeping will be here in a minute, ladies!" he announced in a final attempt. There was no way he could wait for them to leave before having to run out himself. "There's a continental breakfast downstairs you can grab on your way out," he coaxed as he adjusted himself and zipped his forgotten fly. He patted his pockets and looked around the room to be sure he didn't forget anything. "Shit, my phone…"

The redhead sat up slowly, holding his cell in her slender hand. She teased him with it as he came toward her, trying for a kiss. He snatched it from her with a coy smile but no other contact and walked toward the door while texting his attorney that he was on his way to meet him at the Five Breezes.

After hitting "send," he felt a wave of relief in his chest, blood flowing, a slight spark, and for a split-second he forgot about the hollow cavern inside. He was finally purchasing the condo, the beachside vacation spot where he'd spent his childhood summers and holidays. It was also the culminating purchase of his career, a personal goal of more than a decade and a half. He would finally own every piece of property in his bastard father's real estate portfolio.

"You know what, girls? Just stay… I need to celebrate when I get back. Call room service for food, anything you want, and then rest up! I plan to tire you out again when I get back in a few hours."

And he left his penthouse suite to high-pitched squeals of joy.

*

Roberto's voice finally drilled through Isabel's zone of fury, snapping her back to her pained reality. "*Tranquila*, Isa. You need to relax. Just sit out on the deck with me for a minute." He widened his spellbinding baby blues to help his case.

No jodas! "I said I can't, Roberto." She shook her head at his persistence, but couldn't find it in her to be harsh. Because she could be way too harsh and shatter him, and then lose her only solid friend, not to her curse, but to her temper. "Crap…the time…my meetings!" She picked up her pace, injured foot aside, and put away her cleaning supplies and then scurried into her bedroom to shower. She hoped to God Roberto would get the hint and go before she came out again.

She hurried out of her room in an ivory skirt suit with her subtly low-cut white satin camisole to go under the professional little blazer jacket she carried over her shoulder. Though lightweight, she hated to put the darn thing on just yet. With the sweltering heat inside the house—and her seething anger at Roberto who still hadn't moved an inch toward the front door!—it stifled her just imagining her arms inside the long, suffocating sleeves. Then add the definite swelter outside with the midday Vallarta sun at its height—yeah, she'd force herself to put the blazer on at her first meeting, but not a moment earlier.

"Hey, you wanna meet for drinks after work?" Roberto asked, sinking further into the sofa. *God, can he take a hint or five?*

"No, sorry. I'll hardly be on time for dinner with my sister and brothers as it is." She'd usually invite Roberto along to a family dinner, but she just couldn't stomach it. She needed space from him, or more like *he* needed space from her.

She collected her silver cuff bracelet and watch from the side table by the front door. She slid the bracelet on her left wrist and the watch on the other; her tablet and charger at arm's distance both went into her shoulder bag. Then she scooped up her keys and her feet found and slipped into the strappy heels lying underneath the table. She clipped to the front door, ignoring her throbbing foot—she'd pop a pain reliever in the car.

"Okay, I'm ready."

"Your phone?" Roberto held up the device with Sebastian's gleaming green eyes still on the screen.

She grabbed it, swallowed back a surge of renewed rage as she powered it off, then shoved it into her bag. "Okay then…" She looked at Roberto with lifted brows, a final, unnecessary push, but he only sat there, a look of disappointment in his narrowed eyes.

"So do you mind if I stay and chill on the back deck for a couple of hours? Alone I guess, since you're abandoning me! It's my day off…and I drove all the way out here," he pleaded.

She so wasn't in the mood for this. *I mean, I didn't ask you to drive out here!*

He went on though. "Don't worry, I'll lock up for you when I leave."

Roberto had always had a house key to her old place, so the precedent had been set long ago. But now, with his strange obsessive behavior, she hesitated. She missed her best friend so much. God, how she regretted that one smashed-out-of-her-head night. And she couldn't even remember it. Not a single damn detail!

His wide smile and round puppy-dog eyes stared at her, waiting.

Damn it. Saying no to him would be too insulting. She tossed him her spare house key and a fake smile to go with it. "I broke the slider door lock this morning. Until my brother comes to fix it, just use that wood rod for a security pole."

"No problem. And...I'll see you over the weekend?"

"Uh, no...I have two weddings to run. But I'll call you."

*

She rushed out, closing the front door behind her. She was definitely relieved to be in a different air space than Roberto, but stepping into the radiant heat of the day was just a different kind of stifling.

She tossed her jacket onto the front seat of her ancient sedan and immediately wished for the freedom, the peace, the nearly naked liberation she'd owned earlier that morning.

She sighed and started the ignition; she didn't want to be late. She was off to the paradisiac patio restaurant at the Five Breezes Resort to meet with hopeful and love-struck brides, all anxious and starry-eyed, ready to plan their perfect, dream-worthy destination weddings with Isabel Ruiz of Golden Rings Wedding and Event Planning. She pulled a breath then backed out of her parking spot with extreme care—*as always.* Her rosary dangled from her rearview, a mocking reminder of her past...and now of her current purpose—to forge the lasting bonds of love for other souls. *And never my own.*

She spiked the volume of her 90s hardcore playlist again, drowning out the deluge of thoughts and the repressive loneliness that came with them. *Isabel, just focus on the road and the day ahead.*

She ran down her day's agenda and took a quick peek in her rearview to see if her hasty makeup job sufficed—which reminded her, she had to call someone to replace that broken mirror in her powder room. She'd do that between meetings. Then after her five o'clock, she'd meet her family for dinner—and pray that Celeste would come alone.

With a deep sigh, she tried to will the tension from her shoulders and neck.

She needed to relax…and she knew just how to do it. After dinner with her family tonight, she'd grab "some dessert of the male variety," as her boss, Lucinda, would put it. In celebration of the condo and her new start, she'd snag a fine nameless distraction for the night. She deserved a good, hard, mind-freeing release.

Because, screw fate! *I'll get you by getting mine.* She pressed her right foot to the gas and flew down the cliffside byway to her meetings, tempting fate the entire way, just on goddamn principle.

CHAPTER 3

AT THE FIVE Breezes Resort, Zack James had just finished celebratory drinks with his attorney, Armando Sanchez. They had closed on the condo, the fifty-fifth and final property of Bennet James' real estate portfolio, which Zack had set his sights on after his father had left Zack, Darren, and their mother, Elaine, for the other man's much younger and knocked-up French mistress.

But even that sense of accomplishment, that bit of justice served, hadn't gotten rid of that damn sinkhole inside, or the accompanying headache still pounding away in his skull. Beyond the sheer annoyance of it, he began to get concerned. Ailments like these were rare for him, and it now dampened his celebratory mood—*totally unacceptable.*

Armando stood up to leave. "I'll have Tania call you with my doctor's contact info. Oh, and the carpenter's, for that entertainment unit idea. He's really excellent," he said to Zack, who stood as well, ready to shake his loyal and skilled attorney's hand. The man had treated Zack like a second son from the start. Zack kept a team of attorneys the world over, but Armando was more like family than legal counsel. He thanked Armando with a final wave as the man exited the restaurant, and then moved to take his seat again as the waiter set an espresso down at Zack's place.

"*Gracias, amigo.*"

"*De nada, Señor.*" The young waiter spun to leave and slammed right into a woman—or rather, an angel—in soft creamy white against bronze shimmering skin.

Zack, strangely frozen in his seat, watched as she fell to the ground in what felt like slow motion. His breath halted, too, as if the Earth had paused on its axis a beat.

Stand up, man, and help her! He jumped from his chair to join the waiter in helping her up from the patio pavers.

"I'm so clumsy, God," the woman said from the ground with a light laugh to follow. She took the waiter's hand for leverage, and as calm as the tropicbirds strolling around the patio, she pulled herself up to stand. She brushed her backside off, ridding it of patio dust, then straightened her professional fitted skirt that he couldn't *not* notice.

God, top to bottom, she was a Latin beauty—much like Angel the bartender from last night. Similar lustrous black hair and mocha skin tone, but less magazine-seductive and more...what? Professional? Yes, but that hardly covered it. Something more. She didn't blush or flush with embarrassment from the fall, but she wasn't frustrated or defensive either. She was humble, as if surrendered to the occurrence of this kind of accident. As if it happened all the time. No big deal.

Graceful! That was it. She was graceful. A graceful—and yes, gorgeous—klutz. Yes. Even though her fall hadn't been her fault and she immediately took the blame anyway, her grace and serene calm was what caught him. Especially since he couldn't remember a single time a woman hadn't fawned or melted or flustered in his presence, whatever the context.

This woman was different. Refreshing. Confident and carefree.

Well, speak to her then!

Right. "Are you alright?" Zack's voice cracked. Jesus, what the hell was wrong with him?

She nodded and smiled with her eyes, just as her body began leaning to the right. His hand flew to her back, his other held her elbow. "Are you light-headed?" he asked, trying like hell to ignore the spiking sensation shooting through him from the mere feel of her skin. Smooth, soft, and warm. Like silky sand at dusk.

"Oh, no, not lightheaded, just a little off balance."

"*Dios mío*, I'm so sorry, *Señorita*," the waiter said without looking either of them in the face, as if embarrassed and maybe even worried about his job.

"Really, I'm okay, thank you," she said, looking down at her feet. And then she let out a little chuckle. "Ah, there's the issue. I broke the heel off my shoe, is all." Her left leg bent to accommodate her shortened right one, while the displaced four-inch spike lay at their feet. "And, hey, it could have been a broken ankle, right?"

"*Sí, sí. Tenemos mucha suerte*," the waiter said half under his breath.

"Oh, no. I don't believe in luck," she said to the waiter, picking up the separated stem of her stiletto.

A fellow unbeliever?

"Or should I say, luck doesn't believe in me. But hey, I'm thankful nonetheless." She smiled, a kind, genuine smile.

The waiter nodded, then left them while Zack could only stare. And stare some more.

*

She let a smile lift her face. God, a smile so sweet it was sensual. He got a chest pain, a good pain, from that smile. Zack smiled back at her. Just staring and smiling, until her smile took on a more questioning look. Her gorgeous head tilted. Maybe unsure of what else to say? Because he sure as hell was.

Another silent beat went by until she noticed her purse on the ground. Zack felt panic shoot up his spine. *Shit.* She was about to leave his vicinity, his world. *Damn it, say something, asshole.*

But then she bent over for the purse. Her firm yet gloriously voluptuous figure, hugged by that professional little skirt, just right in his face—God, he hated himself. He felt like a fiend, a dirty rotten monster for wanting her the way he did, imagining that ass pounding against his bare thighs. He was disgusted with himself for having such a primal desire for such an unknowingly exquisite being.

He composed himself as she stood up, and before she turned around, a small coffee-colored blotch on her back caught his eye. A tiny birthmark peeked out from her low-backed top in the shape of a puzzle piece, situated on a slight angle. It just floated there, lost-like. He kept his eyes on it until she pivoted around on her uneven heels to face him. He swallowed and cleared his throat. She smirked then nodded one last thanks to him and his awkward ass, and then left him standing there—his pride in the fetal position at his feet.

And Jesus, no hesitation, no glance back over her shoulder, just…nothing. Was she playing hard to get? No. She seemed too self-assured to play that game, and she didn't have the attitude, either. She had a kindness in her eyes, a stoic sweetness. Games just didn't seem her style.

Maybe married? But he hadn't seen a ring. He would have noticed a ring.

No, it was all so much worse. He didn't exist for her, just not on her radar, or in her very recent past, or even on her planet. She hadn't been rude or snotty in the slightest, just wholly uninterested.

An earthquake just shook his world to a standstill. A woman, an angel, rather, just limped away from Zachary James in her one high heel without a qualm, without a care, without giving him a first, let alone a second, thought.

*

Although his headache and that mysterious void in his gut were gone—replaced by mush and goddamn butterflies!—he couldn't catch a full breath. And when he opened his mouth to say something, to stop her, to keep her for even a moment longer, no words came out. Zack James, smooth as silk with all life matters, had become completely and hopelessly inept around a woman. Now all he could do was watch the puzzle piece on her back get smaller and smaller as she moved farther away from him.

His gaze kept on it, though, as if it was his missing piece to reclaim.

In awe of himself, he watched her get to a far off table where another woman—a much taller, older lady—stood waiting. It looked like they were about to leave. *Shit.* He needed an excuse, a quick reason to go over there. To grab a second chance, probably his last chance in gaining this angel's attention, her electric presence. Because, now, in sharp contrast to the last few dismal days, Zack wanted something. Like a pirate wants his sunken treasure.

No, not wants—needs. And it was drifting away from him on an ocean wave without a goddamn care.

Think! He scanned his mind, then surveyed the restaurant and the other patrons, but nothing came to him. He looked down, sprinting through ideas of what the hell to do to stop the cure to his deep void before she left.

Then the glaring sunlight caught a sparkling something on the ground. An earring. A small gold hoop lying right where she'd fallen.

He couldn't remember if she'd had earrings on. He could only remember the sweet coconut scent of her long wavy hair, the color of moonless midnight, and her heavenly doe eyes of deep desert brown outlined by a river of rich dark chocolate as she'd thanked him. And, God, the heat of her skin.

But even if the earring wasn't hers, it would get him over there before she left the restaurant, before she vanished from his meaningless and fleeting movie-of-a-life for good. And he couldn't let that happen, this woman captivated him like none he could remember. She was like a magnetic force, framed by the sun and sea. She could have very well been a mirage, if he hadn't already touched her, smelled her, heard her voice minutes before and known she was real.

His angelic target and her friend had thankfully paused their departure. Why, he didn't know, but their eyes referenced him a time or two. He might just catch her, at least he had reason to hope.

*

He began the long walk across the patio toward her table, nervous though, as if walking the plank. He gripped the earring in his sweaty hand like his life depended on it, his mind strangely blank, unsure of what he'd say when he got there, which made him question the location of his balls. "Man up, goddammit!" he mumbled to himself—another scary first. *Jesus.*

As he closed in, he watched the other woman give his goddess in creamy white a kiss on the cheek, and then left her standing at the white-clothed table topped with half-empty wine glasses and a bouquet of white lilies in the center.

The other lady, with her regal-bordering-on-haughty stride, passed right by Zack to leave the restaurant, and on her way by him she whispered, "Treat her like a queen," in his ear.

Zack smiled politely at the tall stranger and nodded his understanding. He wouldn't ever want to get on the bad side of the Amazonian. Then he resumed his focus on the angel with a new confidence, close to his usual level of suave solidity. The tall woman's message had been a sure sign that his angel was waiting for him, whether by choice—God, he hoped—or by pressure from departing "mother hen." Either way, he'd treat her like a queen, all right. Fuck yes, he would.

*

He watched her like a laser as he closed in. She teetered, uneven on her feet, then finally pulled her chair out to sit. Her curvy hips folded into the seat. Zack had to stop from biting down on his fist as he pictured her sitting right down on his lap, on his hard, throbbing cock, ready to give her the ride of her life, rising and falling with his emphatic, ecstatic thrusts. But he kept his fist by his side with sheer will, white-knuckling it to the point of pain for having such thoughts, such dirty, impure, sinful, thoughts.

Only twenty feet from her, he watched her scoot her chair in and bump the table in the process. The glass closest to her tipped over—red wine crept in a blotchy expanse over the white cloth surface.

The soft ocean breeze became a gust in an instant which helped the glass roll and then teeter at the table's edge in the opposite direction of his magnificent target. Quick-paced, he got to the table with hand extended, ready for the glass to roll smoothly into it. But he stumbled, and the glass bobbled at the tips of his fingers and then shattered to the ground in sharp array of wide-spread humiliation.

She looked up at him with a sweet, apologetic expression, her lush lips in a half smirk, but apparent mortification filled her almond-shaped eyes. Maybe her embarrassment was for him? Either way, Zack felt like a complete ass as he stood in a pile of a billion tiny glass shards. "I'm so sorry. I, uh, almost had it," he said with heated cheeks, unable to remove his gaze from hers to assess the damage.

She shook her head. "It's not your fault—it's for sure mine. This kind of thing always happens to me...or around me."

He snickered, then nothing. An awkward silence ensued that he just didn't know how to fill. He was still too distracted by her enigmatic presence to find coherent words.

The earring, dumbass, remember the damn earring!

Yes! He held open his left hand to show her the gold hoop, which he saw now was a match to the one in her right ear. And behind that ear, an exotic white lily.

Wide eyed with that nectar-sweet yet undeniably erotic smile, she fingered her goddamn-kissable lobes. Finding no hoop in her left ear, her lips parted for a light gasp of surprise. "Oh, my goodness, thank you! I didn't even know I'd lost it!"

Her fingers tickled his palm as she plucked the gold hoop up, sending a reverberating shock through his entire body. He visibly shivered. And he couldn't even hope to hide his physical reaction to her, it being a thick and humid ninety degrees outside.

His palms were sweating still and his pulse was on uppers. It was her eroticism mixed with her sweetness and calm. And that fragrance—ocean breeze and that sweet coconut—all of it made him struggle for composure, which again was usually so easy for him to come by.

Has he fallen into a damn vortex or something?—because he had no control over anything anymore, and it freaked him out but thrilled him at the same time.

Get it together for fuck's sake. He saw her smile widen as his voice, finally found, cracked to a start—*again*. "Lilies are very exotic...intoxicating," he said with a pseudo-confidence he pulled from somewhere. Then he leaned into her personal space and smelled the white, satin-like petals above her ear. "It's really lovely, but you..." He stepped back to take her all in, ignoring the crunching sound under his feet. "*You* are just...stunning," he said, his delivery smooth as fake silk.

Her smile grew, widened, and then her hand flew to her lips. Despite her apparent effort, it was no use. A small giggle escaped first, then came all-out laughter. "I am so, so sorry. The glass, it just crunched at the *perfect* moment, like it was scripted…with the pick-up line from a B-grade romantic comedy," she said, gasping through her laughter as she slapped then grasped his elbow for leverage through her fit.

Having her hand hot on his skin, he didn't even mind her amusement at his expense. He couldn't imagine being anywhere else. He finally looked down at the pile of glass he stood in, sighed, and started nodding his head in surrender. Yeah, the entire scene was ridiculous. He was ridiculous. And she was ridiculously goddamn amazing.

"I'm Isabel," she said, once she found air. She held out her delicate hand to him and moved her other hand from his elbow toward the chair next to her, inviting him to sit down at the warzone of a table.

Isabel. Angelic Isabel.

Before his next breath, he'd taken a seat. He pulled his chair in closer to hers but it wasn't enough. He already missed her searing touch—his arm still tingled, like the moment after entering a perfectly scalding shower. And God, that touch—and now the lack of it—had done something to him. It had erased the earlier guilt he'd felt for wanting to take and possess this sweet angel of a woman, to own her. She was still an angel, deserving the sweetest, most delicate care. But his type of care would bring her to her knees, inciting pleasure throughout every part of her being, which in turn would rock him to his core.

He hadn't felt so alive in as long as he could remember. Maybe not ever.

CHAPTER 4

WHEN LUCINDA HAD left her there on purpose—such a matchmaker, just like her sister—Isabel had felt her cheeks flare up immediately with red hot embarrassment. First off, she liked to pick up her one-nighters on her own. Not with her boss! Or rather, by her boss.

Second, she preferred hitting up the bars and nightclubs, despite their seediness. She shared a common goal with bar and club-goers: pleasure, anonymity, and *just one night*. And the low-light atmosphere of those spots covered her clumsiness better. Having just fallen on her ass in front of this guy in broad daylight proved her point to a tee.

And third, her picks were of a very specific type. Clean and well dressed, yes. Nice and respectful, too. Well-off enough to buy her a drink and take her to a safe, clean, comfortable hotel room at a reputable resort, but not too wealthy to draw attention to them, or to drive her insane with his "look how big my wallet and cock are" stories. He had to be just attractive enough, but not a man she'd melt over—most hotties were either too hot headed, too big headed, or both. But she didn't want the shining personality either, not too funny or smart or witty or, God help her, sweet-and-swooning. She couldn't take swooning. But really *any* combination of those traits might make it hard to say goodbye at the end of the night, and that goodbye…it was non-negotiable.

Now, as she cursed Lucinda to the depths, she found herself sitting next to a man who was, simply put, gorgeous beyond belief. Too gorgeous for either of their own good. He was also very well off, if his logoed attire and his designer watch were anything to go by. But his slight nervousness and comic, almost endearing clown act contrasted with the cockiness she'd been used to with these types of men. He made her smile, then laugh, then smile some more. Again, he was the multitude of types she kept far, far away from. This rare, all-encompassing combination more than worried her—beyond the probability that he was some married axe murderer, for Christ's sake. Just too good to be true.

Oh, then add the shattered glass at his feet. No, not a good start at all.

Yeah, you should go, Isabel. Definitely leave now.

*

She placed her uneven feet on the patio pavers to push the chair back. To go. But couldn't.

The metal legs of the chair were wedged in the paver crevices, and he was so close to her, and the leverage to push or shift or free the chair legs with her one good heel, and, well…damn it! She didn't really want to go!

Between his unbelievable man scent, his searing gaze, and the convenience of him being there and obviously interested—as opposed to the idea of suffering through a dinner with her harping sister, then to have to find a new one-night friend?—no, she could do this. Combat the potential consequences for her breach in criteria. She was strong enough.

And God, so was he. With his well-defined arms with an admittedly sexy tribal tattoo around the right bicep. And then there were his robust facial features which she dared to look at only for a few seconds at a time. Because that look in his eyes, which she swore could melt the polar ice caps, had a definite hunger in them, a carnal focus that made her numbness fade if only for the time being.

Yeah, she could do this for a night. Yes she could. And she would, so help her.

*

So it was settled. She let her shoulders ease and her lips curl into a smooth and somewhat suggestive smile, then she looked up at him. Into his eyes.

Then froze.

They were a translucent jade in color with flecks of contrasting emerald. Her heartbeat echoed in her ears. Haunting eyes, those eyes. She pushed aside her sudden images of Sebastian, shaking his ghost out of her head.

Don't act insane, Isabel…

Her cheeks got hot again as she tried to redirect her focus and to end the awkward silence she'd created, thick as the Vallarta heat. "God, I'm sorry, you know, for laughing…before. That pick-up line was solid. Classic, really." Intended yet gentle sarcasm laced her tone. "But, I should say, the bar is set pretty low these days. Pick-up lines are hardly even needed. If you're walking, breathing, preferably male and in Vallarta on vacation, then I'm pretty much game," she teased, motioning with a nod toward a man with a very healthy beer gut, a fanny pack, and a camera around his sweaty neck being seated at the next table. Her companion, the finely built American now only half a foot from her face, cracked up without taking his insanely mesmerizing eyes off her. But on impulse, she looked down at her hands.

Explain, Isabel, or end it here. "Really, I'm, uh, just out to have a fun time for a night, nothing serious, and so I don't need to be picky, you know?" She flashed a quick smile and ventured a peek at him again. At that face, that gorgeous, dangerous face that made her tense and hot below her belly and tightened her chest. But in a blink, her eyes were on her hands again.

"On the rebound, are we?"

She snorted. Or in other words, "What's the deal?—a moderately attractive woman like you…sans boyfriend?" And, God, that could never be explained, not to an unbelieving gringo at any rate.

She looked from the red-stained tablecloth to his face. "Something like that." She half-smiled, but then got caught by those green crystal eyes again, those eyes that dug into her way too deep. But this time, strangely, they didn't bring up that haunted image with the longing, the guilt, the strife.

She swallowed and took a deep, clearing breath in. Instead, somehow, a wave of…comfort? Yes, comfort had overtaken her. The living man in front of her made her feet feel firmly planted on the ground, despite her uneven heels, the glass-covered brick floor, and the general on-edge feeling she always carried with her.

Don't get comfortable here, Isabel.

Right. She had to keep it light, keep it fun, and keep it short.

So…smile, flirt, something!

She flashed a smile, reached for what was left of Lucinda's wine glass, and finished it in one pull. "Hot out here." *Oh Lord, Isabel, keep it together.*

*

"Can I"—he waved at the waiter—"get you another drink?" The waiter held up an index finger and headed back to the bar, probably for a broom and dustpan. "I was wondering when he was going to sweep this up."

"Welcome to my Mexico," she said with a laugh strung through her words. "We could be here all night and I bet this pile of glass, along with this red and white splotched tablecloth, would remain untouched."

"We? All night? That sounds good to me," he said with lifted brows framing a hopeful look.

She smiled at him with a deliberately seductive glimmer. How forward and smooth, yet still…totally cheesy, cute.

And as she'd planned that morning, and now after a long day of back-to-back meetings, she definitely agreed that 'all night' sounded nice. *Hold it!* Much of the night. Or just some. No, only a few hours. Damn this sinfully attractive man sitting next to her with the charm and the fumbling and the eyes.

The waiter was suddenly tableside, glass crunching under his feet—but no broom, no dustpan. Holding back her laughter, Isabel looked at her new friend, the gorgeous man obviously trying to contain his outburst too. But they both successfully swallowed their shared joke and let the waiter speak. "What can I get you both?"

"An *horchata* water, please." In English, for her company. "Oh, and this time, do bring it in a regular glass, not the stemware, please." She offered a thin-lipped grin, having asked the inattentive waiter for a regular glass originally, but now thought it best to run preventative maintenance for her and her new friend.

Her beautifully scintillating companion asked for a Mexican microbrew that only her richest local event clients knew about.

"Sorry, sir, we don't carry that type of specialty beer," said the waiter in a lackadaisical tone.

"The darkest stout you have, then." The waiter rolled his eyes not too subtly and left them while Isabel's company refocused his gaze on her.

"I'd much prefer your waiter, the one who knocked me on my ass." She giggled. "He was at least nice."

"True. But this guy leaves us be, even if it is to a fault. I like the privacy," he said, an intimate gleam in his eyes.

Oh Jesus. No holds barred, he wanted her. The tingling sensation up her spine shocked her. Thrilled her. Scared her.

Not good, Isabel. But so good at the same time.

*

She cleared her throat and squirmed a bit under his steady stare, her right hand nervously adjusting her cuff bracelet at her wrist. He seemed almost glad for any small display of her possible anxiety, because he only grinned wider. Maybe he liked that it evened the playing field of heightened nerves, sexual tension, and awkwardness.

"So paradisiacal, that flower in your hair, the ocean backdrop with the setting sun highlighting your entrancing shape..." *Oh God.* Even he was blushing as his words fell out of his delicious mouth.

"Entrancing, huh?" she teased, tilting her head just so, feeling ever more confident with every bumbling comment he made.

He gave her an almost bashful smile, looked down at his hands flat on the tabletop, and shook his head to himself. "Jesus, I, uh, I usually, you know, don't need...or use pick-up lines. Like ever. But for some reason, I'm just...I'm all nerves with you. I can't keep it together."

She loved his vulnerability, defending his pathetic lines for the record. And his sweet nervousness around her?

Por Dios, who is this man?

And, *shit!* Who the hell is this man?

Unsure of what to say back, her own cheeks suddenly flushed, she fingered the lily in her hair. "You know…the woman I just met brought these lilies to show us for an event she's holding. So, crazy as it sounds, her future mother-in-law is allergic to lilies, right? And you know what she's doing?"

"What's that?" he asked, obviously relieved she'd taken the baton.

"She's ordering two hundred of them!" She shook her head laughing. "Sick, right?"

"A bit, yes, bordering on evil," he said with a hazy smile, only half listening to her as told by his relentless stare hard-set on her with, God, those crystalline eyes of his!

"Lilies are a love-hate proposition, you know? I happen to love them— white lilies are my absolute favorite," she said then smiled through a new round of slightly awkward but somehow thrilling silence.

He kept his attention on her, laser sharp and ravenous.

"So you know, I didn't get your name…"

"Oh shit, I'm such a jackass. My name's Zack. Zack J—"

"Zack." No last names, per her rulebook. "What brings you to town, Zack?"

"Business mostly, pleasure always." He shook his head again, probably at his continued bout of corniness. Isabel lifted her eyebrows, forgiving him as if he had the hiccups. "Seriously, though," he recovered, "I have real estate matters that have me down here a couple of times a year. But I've been coming down to Vallarta with my family for as long as I can remember. This place hooks you, you know?"

"Don't I. Puerto Vallarta, born and bred, and I've never left." Despite the alienation and the hardships she'd endured, she wouldn't leave her seaside town or her country for anyone or anything in the world.

He smiled. "I'm actually also here for my—" An incoming call interrupted his train of thought as he checked his phone screen. "Shoot. Gotta take this. Please excuse me for a minute?" He left the table and answered in a deep but tender voice.

She waited. Probably his wife or a girlfriend. *I knew it was too good...*

Damn it, why was she even still sitting here? God, she almost did hope he had a girlfriend or a wife. Yes, then she'd be out a minute ago—another rule, never ever knowingly mess with someone's family life.

He returned after two minutes.

Screw it... "Girlfriend, or wife?" She'd never been accused of being indirect or understated.

"Neither. I come to Vallarta a free man." He winked at her.

She cocked her head at him, with slight surprise that her gut instinct was off.

He held up his phone. "When my mother calls, I always answer," he told her. "Always." A small icon of an older woman with sweet and sullen eyes was set in the corner of the screen.

Isabel didn't know what to make of him, but she was definitely taken aback.

"Anyway," he continued, "speaking of being free...are you free tonight? *Now*, I mean? I can show you where all the *gringos* go to party."

She wasn't free, but a quick text to her brothers and she'd be good to go. So, she flirted back. "Why not? Please, show me your hot spots."

CHAPTER 5

ISABEL'S INTRIGUE GREW.

Beyond his looks and the sweet-and-stumbling thing he had going on, there was something else. In his demeanor and in the softness of his smile, the gentle upward curve of his full and fallen lips as he spoke. She felt comfortable and anchored, an anomaly for her. And it was almost as if he saw beyond her shield, the one she used to hide her never-ending loneliness. It was as if he understood it himself, a deep-seated and genuine empathy.

And it scared her to death.

Yet still, she stayed.

She stayed and flirted over starter drinks and appetizers until dark by somehow managing to shut her contesting brain off. Because she was enjoying herself, his company. And, damn it, he was funny. The foreign or forgotten sound of her own laugh surprised her, thrilled her, soothed her.

"You have not!" she challenged.

"*Oh* yeah…on US Skies and FlyGlobal. Oh, and Jetta Air. Man, that was a close call, but a cooler than cool flight attendant looked the other way."

"That's insane!"

He gave her a coy smile. "Flying commercial is worth it just for the restrooms!"

She watched him in awe and wondered how two people could even fit in the tiny airplane bathrooms. She hadn't been on an airplane to know, but had an image from television, and it just didn't seem very easy, or comfortable. Awkward was more like it.

"You didn't bang into the door by mistake, and fall out—the both of you? A show for all?" she asked, cracking up at the image.

"Nah, not a chance. I told you, I'm usually super-smooth." He laughed as he shook his head, turning a light shade of red for the millionth time. "I'm not ever this far off my game."

Contrarily, Isabel had never been so accident-free, smooth, and confident. In her. Entire. Life.

"But," he said with a revived confidence in his voice, waggling his brows for effect, "I wouldn't mind if the door did fly open. Exhibitionism is a definite turn-on for me!" He stood up, threatening to strip his shirt off, which she honestly wouldn't have minded at all. God he was so hot, and she was so buzzed. So buzzed that she'd even forgotten about the cut on her foot that had been throbbing since morning and the tiny degree of nagging guilt for skipping out on dinner with her family.

She sighed and stared at Zack. Buzzed or not, she was shocked by her level of lust for this stranger, despite or because of his high school boy demeanor in a magazine model's body. He made her damp and hot and anxious to get more closely connected. And contrasting his awkwardness with her newfound calm and cool, she felt like a queen, a confident seductress. She was ready, excited even, to seduce her new friend Zack. Last name, still perfectly unknown.

*

He couldn't take his eyes off her, awkward or not. But as the night wore on and shots flowed down, the awkward factor dropped too. He relaxed into their groove, though still randomly tongue-tied. Isabel had her buzz on, as told by the glazed look in her eyes and the ease of her laugh. *Mmmm, that laugh.* He could listen to it all night and not do anything else.

Well, he could, but, no. He definitely wanted more. As the drinks loosened him and his nerves, they also increased his ravenous hunger for her, as if that were even possible. It got harder to control himself. Much, much harder.

The sun had long since set over the bay, cooling the night off a bit, and seeing her goose bumps up and down her arms, he had an uncontrollable urge to take her in his arms and warm her. But instead, he took it upon himself to help her into her little suit jacket, his fingers brushing her neck as the collar landed square. So he got to play gentleman and cash in the excuse to touch her, to connect. A teaser. A teaser for more—hopefully sooner than later.

*

God, she liked this. Liked who she was now, here, with him. And how steady he made her feel. The more drunk she got, the more grounded she felt. How was that even possible?

Who cares how? She deserved to feel this way, even for just a night. A uniquely solid and strangely riveting night out with a man like Zack. Why not, right?

But then what?

More torture.

Not if she stuck to the plan. *Only one night, period.*

She watched him down another shot, then slid him another.

"Here's to a damn great night," she said as she raised then slammed her drink, signaled for the check, and collected her purse. "Ready to go."

"Okay, then." He laughed then helped her out of her chair and over the pile of glass shards. "Hey, you called it," he said with a wink.

"Yup." She definitely knew her Mexico. "So where to now?" *Please say your hotel.* Because, God she wanted him. And she really didn't trust herself at this point, for so many reasons, on so many levels. More schmoozing and dragging this out, *no bueno.*

"The dance club I wanna take you to is right across from here. We can walk, but your broken heel! How can you walk, or dance for that matter?"

There was her excuse. Her perfect out. Skip the dancing and move to the intimate peak of the night. *Then done.* "Dancing sounds great and no worries," she said, motioning to her feet. "I have a pair of sandals in my car as backup."

Wait, what just happened? What happened to skipping the club, on to the hotel?

She damn well knew better, but…she wanted to go dancing, damn it! With him! And that was exactly what she was going to do, so help her. *To a damn great night, remember?*

*

She switched shoes and followed his lead across the street to *La Sexta Noche*, a newer club Zack said he'd been to several times on his last trip down.

She'd been there too, but didn't mention it. He seemed so excited to show her his find. And maybe she didn't need him knowing that she, a local, had frequented a touristy night spot.

Either way, it was an upscale club with a higher cover charge than most in the area, so it brought in a slightly more mature crowd. In high season there were usually lines around the building on the fifth or sixth night of the week, but because it was a weekday night, not even a bouncer stood at the door.

Once inside, Isabel didn't dance around her goal. She felt electrically charged being near Zack and wasn't afraid to show it. His eyes, hands, and body responded in kind, touching her arms, her back, her backside every chance he got. And once another round of tequila shots were slammed, the two of them went straight to the dance floor and couldn't have gotten their clothed bodies any closer.

*

"You're driving me insane," he breathed into her ear, grinding her from behind.

Insane? God, the sensation was mutual. Although the idea of hitting a club with Zack, spending more time talking and laughing—and yes, up-close dancing with him—had thrilled her, now Isabel wasn't sure how long she could control herself. He just hit all her buttons, and as she pushed her backside into him with rhythmic angst, feeling him, solid and hard, with every pounding beat the club's DJ put out, it was almost too much. They continued their grind for only one more song until she rolled to face him, her hand clutching his ass, unable to wait anymore.

"Where are you staying?"

"The Airington. You know it?"

"Yeah, I know it," she said. "I remember the awesome view of the bay, but it's been a while. You wanna show me your view?" she teased, her buzz allowing her to speak as loosely as she damn well pleased.

"Sure, I'm up for it." And he was, his erection now bulging through his khakis against her tensed midriff. She felt it and needed it. She clenched in response, already wet and well beyond primed to get more familiar with his body. Over the bass, he shouted, "I'm up in the penthouse. The view is spectacular."

"What are we waiting for?" She rolled her body keeping hard against his stiff, beckoning manhood, then grabbed his hand and led him out of the club. All done with the formalities. All done.

*

She was on a high.

When they left the club, the thick Vallarta humidity immediately smothered them. It had just rained, torrentially so, it seemed. Isabel dodged and sidestepped around puddles in her tall, narrow-heeled sandals.

Why she wore anything but flats when she knew she was one big accident waiting to happen, she'd never say out loud. But at five-foot-two, she justified that style and stature were just too important. Especially in her line of work. And since fate had left her alive to breathe and walk, then she'd damn well look decent doing it.

And Zack offered her his hand like a gentleman, making sure she didn't fall. Vallarta's cobblestoned streets and potholed roads were a challenge. And although she was becoming somewhat of a master at navigating life's uneven ground, she'd had plenty of collisions with the earth because of the inconsistent stone streets of her Vallarta.

Yeah it's the cobblestone, or the waiter, or the mop bucket, Isabel, that's the issue. Right.

Whatever, she was just glad to have her hand in his, for balance and for the seemingly perfect fit of their fingers.

Don't get used to this, Isabel! Just don't.

They reached his parking spot on the street back at the Five Breezes Resort, and she smiled at the hot red sports car. Such a bachelor, but one with damn fine taste. And rarely did one of her evening companions open the car door for her. It was sweet. He was sweet.

And God, too damn sexy.

But he made her feel just as sumptuous. She felt his eyes indulge from behind and sensed him examining her every curve as she smoothly and deliberately folded herself into his passenger seat.

"Thank you," she said, getting wetter between her thighs with the idea of him above her. Soon. But, God, not soon enough.

With a wink and that delicious smile of his, he shut her car door. And at that exact moment, a bus passed, followed by a tidal wave from a Vallarta street puddle. It rose up and over him. And his car. And clear over to the sidewalk.

Isabel shook her head, scared to look. When she did open her eyes, she saw Zack dripping wet outside her window, like a sad, wet dog, a look of awe on his face, his hard chest heaving.

And there it is.

Case in point for her one-date rule. Thankfully, a minor one. Past examples on her sexual escapades—a fender bender with John a month back, and three weeks ago, Drew from Germany had incurred a huge bruise to the head, and to his ego, from a tree limb they'd walked under—all served as important reminders for why she'd made her rule in the first place. If broken, the puddle or the concussion no doubt led to something far worse, far more permanent.

Never again.

She pulled a scarf from her purse and put it on the leather-upholstered driver's seat as he moped around the front of the car, not even attempting to wipe the muddy street water from his face. She couldn't see his expression, but it didn't matter when the clouds opened for another round of rain. She almost laughed, but caught herself so that when he opened the car door, he was greeted by her infinitely warm and empathetic smile.

With one soggy foot inside, he picked up her scarf. "No, please, take it. I don't want to ruin this. The car's a rental anyway. And I am hopelessly waterlogged, it wouldn't even help." He tossed the scarf onto her lap as he squished into the bucket seat.

"It was my fault, anyway," she muttered, even though he couldn't possibly understand why.

"Yeah it was. If you weren't so goddamn gorgeous, attracting the attention of every man, woman, *and* roadside puddle...or rather, lake..." He snickered, one sultry eyebrow raised.

She reached over the gearshift and with the tip of the scarf, she tenderly wiped away the rolling droplets cascading down his nose. "Strange, because I didn't notice any one else's attention but yours." She smirked, blinked then stared—God, she could drown in those sea green eyes.

"Mmmm." The deep rumble in his chest hit her ears. Her answer pleased him.

And his obvious hunger pleased her. But it was when his lip curled with sinister delight, and his forever-gaze deepened, and the rain turned from pattering to pounding all around them, that the all-out crescendo of the combination made her core's ache billow to overwhelming lust for this man. This stranger.

Only one beat passed before their hands reached for each other in unison, and mouths crashed. An inhaling, all-powering kiss. Fast and furious and rain soaked. Breath caught and found, then lost again. Too much, and not enough.

*

"Let's get back to your room," she panted through entwined lips, "and get you out of these wet clothes."

And his reply? More depth, more fire, more insane heat infused into the connection their lips had already made.

God, that kiss. It stole her breath, her sight, her hearing. And her soul screamed for more still.

But Zack pulled away, wide-eyed, surprised, shocked even. Had he felt the same indescribable intensity that she had? Overpowering. Surreal.

She hunted for the answer in his face as he caught his breath. She broke a smile, because his narrowed eyes searched her face with what seemed like the very same question.

He took one last lungful of air, then nodded his head. "Yes, wet clothes," he stammered, started the vehicle and pulled out of the spot, his front tire bumping the curb before screeching into traffic. They were obviously heading farther uptown toward his hotel, and with more speed than was safe on a rainy Vallarta night.

CHAPTER 6

THAT KISS. HOLY fuck, *that kiss*. Where the hell had this woman come from?

He'd never known such an attraction, an in-sync connection, one that was powered beyond sexual energy. What he felt with Isabel was beyond imagination.

And that robotic monotony he'd felt only hours ago was replaced by an energy, a fulfillment. And then that fucking kiss!

Her hand on his thigh, his pulse pounding in every part of his body, he was enthralled and entranced by this woman. Enlivened.

His ass began buzzing with an incoming text.

"That's something…new." Isabel smirked.

"Shit—my phone! It must be soaked." He struggled to get it from his rear pocket.

"Please, let me." She slid her slender hand under his right ass cheek, into his pocket and pulled out his cell. He caught a glimmer in her eye, and he couldn't contain his need to touch her, to feel some part of her electric flesh against his ice-cold hand.

"I'll read it at the light," he said, reaching under her skirt instead. He squeezed her warm and welcoming thigh, then slowly slid his way up, creeping farther still until he met her sweet spot, already wet. Yes, just for him. He plucked the thin strand of her thong, which had been wedged between her silken velvet lips. Then he massaged his way back down to her knee, a small disappointed groan coming from her with his hand's withdrawal. Goddamn, he wanted to tease her all night long. And he would, and couldn't wait.

At the red light—the damn time-wasting red light—he glanced at the missed text. "Shit. That's tomorrow," he thought out loud. Then he turned to Isabel hopefully, trying not to stammer over his words, which was still a goddamn challenge since they'd met earlier that afternoon.

"So, uh, not to jump the metaphorical gun, but tomorrow morning I have a brunch to hit for my attorney's charity group. Everyone is supposed to bring someone new…so, if you eat…food…" He paused, trying to resurrect the self-assured Zack James from wherever he'd gone. At least his cock was still standing strong—it was just his damn words that kept falling short.

He took a good breath and continued. "I assure you, after tonight, you'll be absolutely famished. You should be my breakfast date." That at least came out in one piece.

"Thanks, but no, really, I can't."

"You don't eat? It's gratis!" he teased.

She glared back. "It's not that, fuck you very much." She glared with puckered lips.

"It's cool. I just thought, we've had so much fun up to now, and we'll have even more fun in my suite. A good meal among…friends? A nice topper, that's all I'm saying." He glanced at her to see if his nonchalant argument was making an impact, swaying her whatsoever.

Just then, a woman with a baby in her arms stepped into the road. Zack screeched to a stop just in time. Fuck those randomly placed, albeit beautifully landscaped Vallarta street dividers, all with unmarked crosswalk paths. *Jesus Christ.*

The woman just stared at them through the windshield, then continued on, as if it wasn't 1:00 AM and pitch black on an 80 km-zoned roadway she had just happened across. With an infant in arms!

"Holy shit, that was just way too close!" Zack's hands were gripping the steering wheel with all he had. "Puerto Vallarta, damn it! I love her…but, really? I'd rather *not* be put away in a Mexican prison for vehicular manslaughter because they damn near encourage jaywalking! All those manicured grass dividers with a billion paths to death. They're all along the highway lanes! And then add the insane cabs, ancient buses, random horses, and pizza scooters. Fuck!" he ranted.

"That poor child," Isabel said quietly and obviously ignoring his frustration, her eyes following the woman and baby, almost as if she was willing them to safety on the far side of the road.

Zack smiled at her sweet side amidst their palpable heat. "Yeah, but who takes a baby out this late at night? Shit, never mind," he said, pissed that his heightened blood flow was now diverted from his cock up to his racing heart because of his near heart attack from the close call.

She stopped clutching the passenger seat for dear life, moved her hand back to his thigh, bringing him back to the present, and said, "So, I have a rule."

"Only one? Is it about jaywalking?"

"No, actually. It's a one-screw rule. It ups my game. I always put in my all," she said jokingly. "And the rule has an obvious subsection: no relationships."

She was so serious all of a sudden. A different side to her, still sexy, but it threw him a little.

"I like a woman with a strong work ethic," he answered to part one of her comment. "But as for a relationship, I would hardly say a brunch counts. An innocent late morning meal between…friends, physically close friends, is nothing to fear, right?" he asked her as he turned into the portico of the Airington.

The conversation paused there as Zack handed the valet his keys, and then went around the car to usher Isabel out, taking her hand, and keeping it in his grasp.

The silence and lust between them was thick as he led her through the lobby and into the elevator.

*

The elevator doors slid shut.

He pressed the penthouse floor.

Then he pushed her sumptuous ass into the elevator handrail and ground into the center of her smooth mocha thighs. "But one thing you *should* fear," he continued their car talk, "is an addictive sexual encounter with me." He breathed into her right ear with an intentional tone of arrogance. He might have been a Jittery Jason when it came to casual conversation with this woman, but his usual stride was all there when it came to the topic of pleasuring the living daylights out of this woman.

She played coy, not letting his desperately seeking mouth reach hers, and his lust magnified with every teasing twist of her head.

The elevator stopped at the penthouse, and he let her feet down to the floor. They exited the elevator, and as they walked, his hand slid into place low on her hip. Then he gently pushed her in front of him, wanting to watch her walk, her buttocks swaying, calling to him. His gaze moved up her back stopping at *his* puzzle piece. He wanted so bad to outline it with the tip of his tongue, then down her spine, all the way down to her smooth, round ass, and then around to the front to what his fingers gleaned from the car ride was a freshly shaven mound. *Heaven.*

He stuck his hotel key into the slit, and the door opened gracefully. Before entering, Isabel hesitated. "Hey."

"Hey, yourself."

She smiled, no eye contact. "Zack, just wanting to be clear. I like to keep it casual. I draw my line at one night. That's really all we've got."

His eyes focused on her like lasers, not worried about her lines. Not worried at all. Because for all the self-assurance he lacked around this woman, he had an overwhelming amount of confidence in the undeniable fire ignited between them. That fire would turn any and all lines either of them dared to draw to fine, wind-strewn ash.

"Got it." And he escorted her into his suite and shut the door behind them.

CHAPTER 7

I SABEL STEPPED THROUGH the door, slick heat running through her and pooling at her core. She let her jacket fall at her feet while Zack hiked her skirt up to her hips, exposing her thin string thong against her smooth-as-silk mound, which she always kept groomed for this exact occasion.

In a flash, he had his hands on the back of her thighs, hoisting her up and pressing her back against the wall at the penthouse entrance before she could even check out that bay view he had bragged about.

But she couldn't have cared less about the view fifty stories up, because—*oh, God*—he was more amazing to look at than Heaven and Earth combined!

His mouth ravaged hers as she tore her hands through his hair, just-long-enough waves of auburn for her to grab and pull. "Let's definitely get you out of these wet clothes," she whispered, and then felt his whole body shiver, pinned there by her tight but trembling legs.

His hand pulled her shirt down at the neckline to devour her right breast, heavy and exposed above her black lace demi-bra. He popped her nipple out from under its blanket of frill and twirled the hard button with the tip of his tongue. Then, going crazy from the overstimulation, she pulled his face back up to her mouth and she devoured him right back.

He cupped her ass and carried her further inside the suite while she pulled her mouth away to gasp for air. Lungs replenished, she went in for another delectable taste of him…but noticed his once-hungry eyes had flicked to the minibar.

"What is it?" she breathed, brushing her lips against his neck, her body's angle against his rock hard cock making her need spike a million degrees.

"Nothing's wrong. Nothing in the entire universe is wrong right now! Isabel…Jesus, you are so fucking right, it hurts," he managed through panted breath.

He carried her across the room, her nose nuzzled in the crook of his neck. Between her heart pumping triple time, her increasing lack of oxygen, his incredible scent penetrating her nostrils, remnants of her tequila buzz, and the peripheral view out of the floor-to-ceiling windows, she felt completely dizzy.

But when they landed on the sofa, him grinding into her arousal, she became anchored again, safe under his protective cage of bulk manhood. His mouth delivering a torrent of sensual, focused attention to hers.

It felt divine. Indescribable.

Right up until he stopped, backed off and stepped back, hands up in the air as if surrendering to something or someone.

*

"What? What is it?" she asked, slightly out of breath, a little frustrated and definitely confused. She couldn't imagine what was going through his mind right then, but judging from his intense erection begging to be rescued from his pants, he wasn't backing away from her because of…*her*. Right?

"I can't go so fast," he stammered then raked his hands through his hair. "You are too fucking…amazing, Isabel."

She watched his Adam's apple bob up then down in his thick, ropey neck, while her heart did the same in her chest. Was he for real? Or was this the end of their heated play? Because it felt like something had cut the power at the electrical box.

"I need a drink, you?" He spun around then walked over to the minibar.

Yes, it seems like we're done. She leaned forward on the sofa, her chest still heaving while he pulled out a glass from below the bar counter, then glanced up at her. "Isabel...I need to drag this out... I need to...savor you."

She blinked then squinted at him from across the room. *Okay.* Somewhat cheesy, but she could like being savored. She relaxed a bit into the sofa's mold and let her lip curl a fraction, relief and a new round of heat resuming below her middle. "Sounds okay to me."

A quick exhale of relief, then a nod. "So a drink?"

"Yeah, I'll take one, thanks," she said then smiled, but couldn't shake the weird feeling in her gut that had only crept in since moving into the expansive hotel suite.

He winked and grinned back while, with attempted subtlety, he snatched some logoed paper from the bar-top and then craned his neck around the corner, toward another internal doorway. She assumed...the master bedroom? He looked at the paper with wide eyes and then seemed to sigh with relief.

"Everything okay?"

"Yeah, yes. I just...had a massage last night—long flight—and housekeeping left the bill. Anyway, let me pour you—what? I've got vodka? Then I can come over there and give *you* a massage...one you damn-well won't forget!" He winked again then poured their drinks, ignoring the splashes leaping over the sides of each glass.

She watched him and heard him, but somehow something in his demeanor had changed. Maybe still off his game like he had said—possibly nervous about performing? She didn't think he had anything to worry about, but she knew that between psych classes, years' worth of talking down nervous grooms, and her own sexcapades, sexual performance was such a mental thing for guys. And for women, for that matter.

Or, what if she had freaked him out with the one-night thing? What if he was really into her, and she'd led him on—maybe told him her rule too late? Most foreigners were thrilled at the prospect of no-strings-sex, but maybe Zack was different. She did feel different with him, an *amazing* different. And that was bad. While detachment was good and necessary, 'amazing'—definitely not good. It was dangerous. And if he felt the same way—even worse.

Maybe she should go? Yeah, she should definitely go.

But watching him smile at her from across the room, she didn't want to go. Her throbbing clit was screaming, "Stay!"—and the hot need deep in her belly would be less than satiated with her vibrator at home.

She was strong enough, objective enough to stay. For a stellar night of off-the-charts sex, for a night, for the record books, heck yes she'd stay. And then she'd leave. Who wouldn't want that and only that?

"Before the drink, may I use the restroom?" she said, asking permission with her eyes to enter the bedroom.

"Uh, sure, of course, back and to the right," Zack said, gesturing with a nod to go ahead in—then followed her. To be sure she found the right door, she guessed? She thought it was funny, cute, and only slightly awkward. She waved with a smirk then closed the bathroom door behind her.

She flipped on the light. She wasn't shocked to see her hair a complete disaster—a beautiful, make-out session mess.

What shocked her was the lipstick-written message on the grand vanity mirror and the two pairs of lace panties, each one intelligently hung from a light bulb above it, already creating a burning plastic odor. The message read: *We waited, baby, but had to scoot. As a THX for the HOT SEX last night, we left you gifts. We'll be back for them and for you! J & T.*

A bubble heart for the "&."

Really?

*

Her head tilted to the side, just staring at the mirror, at the message, then at herself. She took in a huge breath, filling her lungs to capacity, then exhaled, releasing the air until her shoulders hung.

Straightening her head, chest out, she made her decision.

Of the casual sex partners she'd distracted herself with over the past months, all of them had met only moderate standards, again, per her design. But that day, with Zack, everything had been so vastly different, unusual—to her core, unique. Even, dare she say, *special?*

But she'd been taken—taken by a brilliant player, a masterful artist who had made her feel and breathe and laugh, and none of it mattered. Isabel Ruiz had standards. She had God-given pride. Third in line for a screw? Nope. Not a chance.

*

She flipped off the bathroom light, shut the bathroom door quietly, walked out of the bedroom, and up to the bar.

Zack's back was to her, putting the vodka bottle away. She gently picked up that bill he had been distracted by earlier. A lipstick kiss and a handwritten note stared up at her. She read the note to herself—*Bye, Baby! And thanks! Jeannie and Tina*—then slid it back to its unobtrusive spot on the counter.

Zack turned around, lifted his eyebrows at her, one corner of his lip curling up, his hunger apparent.

She smiled oh-so-sweetly back at him, picked up the drink he had poured her, and leaned closer to him. Seducing him still closer, she pressed a kiss to his cheek. After she pulled away, she smiled, lifted a brow, then emptied her drink over his head.

She caught his look of utter awe, nodded at him, then calmly walked out of Zack's luxurious penthouse suite with the oh-so-grand view.

CHAPTER 8

THE DOOR SHUT behind her.

His mouth still hung open.

And Zack's stomach immediately twisted and burned, motivating his sprint to the bathroom. His guts retched while his skull pounded. He couldn't understand it, such a physical response, so violent and sudden. The instant Isabel marched out of his hotel suite—damn it, out of his life?—this gut pain hit, and that fucking void returned with it, tenfold.

From the toilet to the sink to clean himself up, he tried to figure out what the hell had happened to make her leave like that.

Then he glanced up at himself in the mirror.

"Fuck me!" he yelled at the message written in hot red lipstick slightly to the left of his distraught and flushed face in the reflection.

Yes, he had forgotten the girls he'd left for safekeeping in his penthouse suite. And yes, he only remembered them when he saw the room service bill on the minibar. But the girls' note on the bill confirmed they were no longer in the room, so all was fine, or it should have been!

After all, Isabel had taken him by storm, a complete mind, heart, and soul tsunami. And that wild, treacherous cleansing had left him vibrating and calm all at once. Needless to say, she distracted him to the ultimate extent.

And wouldn't it be a compliment to Isabel that he'd completely forgotten about the girls in his room? Really, what man forgets about round two of a threesome with supermodels, if not for something, or someone, exponentially more enthralling? Like Isabel.

He surmised that after seeing the message in the mirror, Isabel must have revised her initial impression of him. But, goddammit, her initial impression of him was the right one! The real one! Or at least was the *new* real one. Only days before had he become indifferent to the pleasures he was used to, including connecting with those girls, which was just a reaction to that asshole at the bar, and then morphed into a mindless distraction, an activity to pass the time, and an attempted cure for his despairing soul.

Because, damn it, a transformation had occurred in him. His eyes now saw the truth of his false fucking existence. And Isabel was the light at the end of the bleak tunnel that was his life! But she would probably never give him the time of day to even let him explain! Now he was just another sleazy scumbag in her eyes. Just like the kid in the bar.

His stomach churned again, and he slammed his fist down on the sink counter. No, goddammit, this wasn't how it would go down. He had to find her. He had to find Isabel and get that feeling back, that fulfillment, that pure ecstatic bliss.

Around Isabel, there was an immense freedom he'd found. And crazy shit, like his frequent inability to speak and function around her like he normally did, both shocked and exhilarated him. He literally felt like a teenager again, fumbling words, clammy hands, cracking voice. When near her, that sudden wave of whatever it was, call it insecurity, led to broken glass, rain and puddle soakings, close-calls. All things that never fucking happened to Zachary James.

But, weirdly, they were all welcome mishaps. Each one made him feel newly alive. He could breathe while before he was choking on his own phony way of life, that deluxe yet mundane treadmill that ran down his soul, one long nowhere-stride at a time.

But not when he was with her. And now knowing that she existed—the something, or someone, that filled his void—he couldn't go on without her.

He'd find her, even with no phone number and, damn it, not even a last name! They'd talked and flirted for hours, and he didn't even know where she lived or what exactly she did for a living. Their connection had overshadowed all of that. They had been so in the present, so in the moment together, he had no information on her at all.

He hunched over as another wave of nausea hit him along with a sharp, dagger-like heat stabbing him from the inside out.

He *would* find Isabel, or he'd die trying.

*

Unlocking her own front door felt good. It was a relief to be home after such a long mind-game of a day. She'd spent her car ride dwelling on how wrong she'd been about Zack, but was at least glad she hadn't wasted even one orgasm on him.

She'd just have to settle on her friend with benefits, aka her vibrator, for comfort just as soon as she'd showered off any remnants of that man.

She got inside and freely tossed her purse on the sofa.

"What the...!" came a man's voice—in shock and apparently in a small amount of pain.

She grabbed an umbrella from the holder at the entrance, point extended toward the voice.

"Who's there?" No air, pulse crashing her eardrums.

"Isa, it's me." Roberto's face came into view once her eyes adjusted to the dark.

Exhale, hot rage. *Calm yourself.*

"I swear, Roberto. What. In the hell?"

"I guess I fell asleep waiting for you," he said in an overly sweet tone, his eyes wide and anxious.

"Roberto...Jesus Christ! I don't want that! I don't need that!"

"But I need you, Isabel. And you do need me!"

Damn it! What she needed was for him to hear her, understand her. She loved Roberto with a deep, platonic and loyal love. And even without the curse chained to her ankle, she would only love him in that way.

And time and patience were not helping. Before now, she hadn't thought she had it in her to slap him out of his obsession like she'd like to think she would have with any other man. Roberto was the one person on Earth besides her two brothers, Antonio and Ray, and her sister, Celeste, who had stayed by her side over the years. But this thing with Roberto was unhealthy. She had to get through to him somehow.

And it looked like harsh was how it had to be.

"Roberto, I do *not* love you!" she exploded. Then she recoiled, his look filled with pain, heartache. She knew it well, for herself. "Except as my best friend in the entire universe—"

He shook his head, as if erasing the last quarter minute of their lives. "That's fine. Your love will grow—"

"No," she said in an even, firm tone, "it won't." Chest heaving, fists clenched, she had to stop this.

"Roberto, I don't even remember being with you that night. And...I don't want to remember it, because that is not how I think of you. You're like a brother. Not a lover. You're my best friend, and whether you believe in my hex or not, it's not safe to be around me." She sighed as a regretful truth hit her square in the face. "This is my fault. I should have been more direct, but I didn't want to hurt you, your feelings. Listen, I think you shouldn't be around me for a little while. I mean, at all. We need...a break. I'm sorry."

He stared and stewed in silence, but he didn't move a muscle.

Come on, not again. "It's 3:30 in the morning and I need to be up for work in only four hours," she nudged, impatience more than apparent in her voice.

He got up off her sofa and headed to her front door. As he passed her, he stuck his nose deep into her hair, inhaled, and continued his way to the door. "You smell like sex, Isa. I hope your quick fuck was worth standing us all up for—for *your* celebration dinner!"

She knew she smelled like Zack from messing around with him earlier, and she wanted nothing more than to shower the man off of her. But the close-to-sexual encounter with Zack, let alone that with any man, was none of Roberto's damn business.

And as for the family dinner, the one Roberto wasn't even invited to, yes, now she regretted skipping it, but her siblings were always understanding. As for Roberto, she could tell he was just wounded, confused, lonely, like she was lonely.

"Roberto—"

"Enjoy your new home," he said in an indignant whisper before heading out the door.

"Wait! Roberto…my key?"

He paused, glared at her, then easily pulled her house key from his pocket and tossed it with a flippant flick of his wrist.

The key made a perfect arch through the air toward her, but slipped through her shaky hands when the door slammed behind him, the jolting blast clobbering her ears, which somehow harmonized with the sound of the metal key's reverberating clang as it hit the floor at her feet. She stood frozen, stunned, ears ringing. Scary—the sounds from the prior moment weren't nearly as jarring, as deafening even, as the new level of loneliness echoing in her already-scarred heart.

CHAPTER 9

TWO WEEKS HAD passed since she had met and left Zack in his extravagant penthouse suite.

And those same two weeks had gone by with no sign or word from Roberto, like she had asked for, but regretted at the same time. She missed calling him, sharing her day with him, and being distracted by the details of his day. She definitely missed her devoted friend, just not the obsessed version.

She hadn't been out of her house since that night, except for a mandatory client meeting and one weekend event. She'd worked from home otherwise.

And it being the height of wedding season, she was slammed anyway. She puppet-mastered from her desk in her bedroom, windows open, floor fan on. To her dismay, she didn't even have time to enjoy her back deck at all, but hey, she could at least hear the rolling tide coming in. And she'd taken to traipsing around her sanctuary near-naked, enjoying ocean-breeze kisses and unadulterated freedom.

And she wasn't a total hermit. Her brother, Ray, stopped by once, and so did Celeste—thankfully a quickie, on the way to grab the girls from dance class. Every few days she'd spoken to Lucinda and also to her brother Antonio, whose limo company she hired for all of her events.

Basically, though, she stuck to her plan, keeping to herself. Safe and sound for all.

But the quiet hours of her day allowed her mind to wander. And where her thoughts went, and who they rested on, were far from healthy. Dangerous waters, those piercing, bottle-green eyes. Zack. *Asshole.*

His stories had made her laugh until she cried, and his touch had sent such sensations through her, she could still feel the remnant vibrations. All of it swarmed her brain. His scent of man and that intoxicating cologne, and oh, his body, all-encompassing and surrounding her. The steadiness and security she felt when around him—intangible, but it lingered just the same. Zack and that entire night hadn't faded from her senses, but neither had the memory, the wakeup call written on the bathroom mirror.

The doorbell rang and snapped her out of her trance.

"It's me, love. Let me in to your paradise by the sea!"

Louder than a timeshare hawker, *Lucinda.*

An hour early, Lucinda! Isabel threw on clothes and ran to the door.

Lucinda stood a towering six-foot-one. A French-Canadian cougar with a deep and husky voice. One could peg her a chain-smoking drag queen, but she was neither.

She was, however, the founder of the most successful wedding and event planning company in Vallarta, with too many A-listers under her belt to count. Extremely dedicated, she lived and breathed work, and would do practically anything for a client in the name of revenue, which was what made Golden Rings the biggest and best, the woman's pride and joy. Lucinda's baby.

And how had "Isabel the Walking Curse" landed a job with the great Lucinda Carlyle? It just so happened that Lucinda had been the dearest friend of Isabel's late mother, Yesinia Ruiz. And as a favor to Yesinia, and despite Isabel's accident-prone existence, Lucinda had given the youngest Ruiz a chance and the training to become a wedding and event coordinator with Lucinda's foreigner-focused company. Yes, another singular blessing, one that Isabel knew better than to think too hard on or take for granted, lest she jinx it. *And poof!*

Isabel quickly earned the title "protégé" for being, as her mentor stated in all introductions to new wedding clients, "deeply loyal, a relentlessly hard worker, bilingual and brilliant, hyper-focused and the deepest believer in true, unadulterated love." It was the script Lucinda went by, and, Isabel felt, an authentic sentiment. Yes, Lucinda was a true blessing, and Isabel wouldn't disappoint the woman, not for anything in the world.

"Ready to talk nitty-gritty, love?" Lucinda was an hour early for their meeting to discuss the Rine/James wedding, the biggest-ticket affair her boss had ever entrusted Isabel with. And Lucinda was never early. Isabel nodded, eager to calm the woman's nerves, having prepared all the details her boss would want.

The woman came in and threw herself on Isabel's sofa, lying on it Cleopatra style. "Oh, before we start, love, pour me a vodka, would you? On the rocks."

"Of course." *And alcohol…just before noon…an additional way to unwind.*

In the kitchen, Isabel smirked while she got the glass for her boss's midday drink. Then she reached into the freezer. When the entire tray of ice cubes fell onto the kitchen floor, she shook her head and cursed under her breath. She grabbed a few pieces still stuck in the tray, threw them in the glass, then carefully poured the alcohol.

Before serving it, she bent down to pick up the mess of slippery ice from the floor. While freezing her fingertips, a realization hit her and she grunted. During her time with Zack, except for her fall at his feet and her wine spill, she'd been completely accident-free. The entire rest of their time together, eight solid hours, had been without mishap. There had been a complete reprieve, never known to her before or since.

And Zack, on the other hand, had sworn that he was never that clumsy, never so 'off his game.' Only around her, he'd said. He'd been nervous like a schoolboy with her. A puff of a laugh—could he have soaked up her bad juju? His clumsy, blathering, stumbling words and his cheesy-ass pick-up lines, the ones he'd explained were so out of character for him.

Why *wasn't* it possible?

Because, what of Zack's stellar confidence in other areas? His lips, his expert tongue, his hands, his hard steel and grinding hips, they were all anything but clumsy during their foreplay, even though it had all damn well led to nothing.

But maybe the sweet-and-stuttering, blushing thing was just an act to get her usually blundering ass into bed? And hell, it had almost worked!

If that was his strategy, then thank Jesus for the two pairs of melting panties on the vanity light fixture! Yeah, for a guy to snag two women in a night and have them waiting their turn for a second round the very next, he had to be slick, strategic, *sad*. Sleazy.

But, on the other hand, maybe the women he got with were all empty-headed bimbos who didn't speak in the first place. Such a sizzling-hot catch like Zack wouldn't even have to talk about the weather before panties were flying.

So, maybe that was it? She was the first woman he'd hit on who had any-thing between her ears? And maybe the brilliant comic-clown act was *not* an act! He *was* dumbstruck and nervous around her. Like he'd said.

Hah!

And, *oh shit*.

Now so glad she'd left when she had, she really hoped she wouldn't ever see him again.

At least she wanted to hope that.

She dried her hands, wiping the entire thought stream from her mind at the same time. *Back to business, Isabel. Head in the game.*

*

Isabel handed her boss the drink, then took out her tablet. Lucinda immedi-ately got working on her buzz while Isabel pulled up her notes for the Rine/James affair.

"The event block is Friday-Sunday, May 30th -June 1st, but the bridal group arrives Wednesday the 28th for their bachelor and bachelorette par-ties, which, of course, they're handling themselves." Golden Rings didn't do tacky or crude. Lucinda didn't need the hassle, the liability, or the chance at staining the company's reputation.

To Lucinda, reputation was everything. Isabel had learned from Lucinda how their business was hugely dependent on word of mouth. And since the real money for the Puerto Vallarta wedding industry was found in the wealthier, albeit more finicky, foreign markets, that word of mouth needed to be far-reaching and exemplary.

And, it so happened, that the foreign focus was perfect, no, necessary for Isabel. If Lucinda's clientele was based on the local area instead, the woman couldn't have kept Isabel on, no matter how close Lucinda had been to Isabel's mother. Isabel's locally infamous hex would have created havoc for Lucinda's business. But their wealthy foreign clients didn't know about Isabel's curse, nor did they believe in such "mumbo-jumbo" as Lucinda lovingly called the area's superstitions. So Lucinda only saw Isabel as an asset, always on her game. Or *striving* to be, at least.

But there was that one major reputation killer that Lucinda never hesitated to warn Isabel and the other attractive junior planners about, especially with the liquor-driven nature of the weddings they managed. In the name of professionalism, planners and staff could never, absolutely ever, fraternize with their guests. Isabel had watched her assistant get fired just last month, and Lucinda made sure Janine was blacklisted from all the event planning outfits up and down the Pacific coast. Beyond watching out for their own agencies, owners had to also zoom out and take care of the entire region's reputation, or else all Pacific Coast planning companies would be out of the running for American and European wedding business.

So, for Isabel, the nightclubs and bars were safest for those intermittent distractions. *Es todo—that's it.*

Isabel continued running through the logistics of her biggest-ticket wedding ever, but glanced up from her notes when she heard the sound of clinking ice cubes. Lucinda was swirling her empty glass as she stared out at the bay, maybe listening to the sound of the high tide rushing in...or to the unimaginable and eccentric dialogue in the woman's own extravagant mind.

Isabel could have refilled the glass, but doing so would be committing to an entire day with her boss, because the woman shouldn't be driving sober let alone buzzed, and Isabel really didn't want to drive the woman all the way into town. Also, she wanted to get through this monologue of a meeting and be done, as she had tons of other work to do.

"So the amenities are all opulent elegance—I am of course bending over backwards." Lucinda knew Isabel went all out for clients. She gave her a satisfied wink. "I even have a courier making ten round trips over the border with the bride's must-have Californian wedding wine, you know, since Customs doesn't allow more than the nine liters over per run. But Amy Rine said that 'the sky is the limit' since her father, Daniel Rine, is footing the bill." Her eyebrows lifted for emphasis.

Lucinda's attention sparked to the here and now. "Ah, yes, the shipbuilding tycoon. Very nice." She smiled while she fingered her empty glass, perhaps predicting the total invoice in her money-happy head. "Isabel, love… you keep clinching bigger and bigger clients and giving them what they want, and soon enough you'll be running the show…and I'll retire into the lap of a fine young Mexican *tamale*." She laughed, obviously pleased with her wit and her future.

"Sounds…spectacular Lucinda. I mean, running the show, that is." Isabel flashed a slight smile, cheeks warm.

She did relish the thought of heading up the company. After so many tragedies in her life, it was something to strive for, to look forward to. And if there's any glimpse of a silver lining to those heart-wrenching incidents, it's that no one could compete with her through-the-roof threshold for pain and high pressure, two inevitable components of any high-end destination wedding. And, also, the job's rapid pace made her blood flow, it made her feel alive. And the fact that she was damn good at her job didn't hurt.

"By the way, Isabel, what happened with that gorgeous American steed of a man from the Five Breezes a few weeks back? Did ya screw him? Oh God, please just tell me. Let me live vicariously through you, dear. I have needs…"

Isabel gave her boss a cockeyed smile. Lucinda was shameless.

"What? It's for work, love. Research. Unions are our business," Lucinda justified, guffawing and slapping her lap.

Isabel's employer—her mentor, her sometime matchmaker, her delving, digging friend and sort of motherly stand-in—just never ceased to amaze her. The woman was majorly self-centered and money-focused, but Isabel got to know and near-enjoy Lucinda's softer, more human side—however awkward and embarrassing, frustrating and circular the resulting conversations became.

"No. Almost…but no." Isabel paused, regretting her use of the word "almost," hoping it wouldn't open a huge can of worms, with Lucinda asking for all the gory details. "He turned out to be a bit of a scumbag…but better that than some Prince Charming!" she said while avoiding eye contact—Isabel already knew what expression was held on her skeptical boss's sun-wrinkled face.

"Isabel." Lucinda shook her head, kind disappointment in her face. "I swear, Isa, you Mexicans and your superstitions…twenty-five years old, gorgeous, smart, and for God's sakes, giving up on romance entirely! And what a bride you'd make…if you'd just let me find you the right man!"

"He'd need to be invincible…immortal. Maybe a vampire?" Isabel half joked. At least she kept her sense of humor. It helped her endure the same optimistic spiel by her boss almost weekly. Between Celeste, Roberto, and Lucinda, she swore she'd lose her damn mind.

And it was especially laughable hearing it from her boss all these times, because Lucinda Carlyle was very much the expert on 'the right man.' With three ex-husbands and the fourth one in process, she could write a book or four.

As always, Lucinda went on whether Isabel wanted her to or not. "I'm a thirty-year veteran of the wedding industry. Love is my damn business! I can call the success rate of any couple I marry, almost to the day, and you've seen me do it!" she bragged, forehead wrinkles pronounced to drive her point home.

Oh, her point… God, did the woman miss it each and every time.

"I'm really *fine*, Lucinda, being on my own." Isabel really believed it—and never allowed herself to wonder if there was something beyond just *fine*, because going there was just a waste of time leading to more pain. Inevitable pain. Why not let Lucinda shove Isabel's already-scarred heart into pellets of dry ice? At least the mist would look lovely to their wedding clients. But Lucinda wouldn't understand, couldn't relate, and Isabel couldn't fault her for it. "Look at it this way. I had a true love once. That's one more than many can say they've had in their entire lives!"

"Nice try, sweetheart, with the ultra-positive outlook. I'm telling you that you're not fine, Isabel. You are brilliant, gorgeous and alone. A complete waste of perfectly good pussy!"

"Lucinda!" she cried as heat rushed to her cheeks. She swatted at her boss, knocking over Lucinda's empty glass on the coffee table in the process. Isabel was anything but a prude, but to hear her sixty-something-year-old boss reference her cunt was just way beyond *not-okay*.

Besides, her pussy got use—a nice, occasional variety of use. And she didn't need three—almost four—divorces behind her to boast that.

She had to think of a proper response, though, one that would hopefully end that day's session of *Poor Isabel's Pussy*. But in the nick of time, her cell phone buzzed.

She read the new text and shot to her feet. "It's Madeline's. They have a question about the cake flavor for the Nilson/Edmond gig tomorrow. The clinical sanity of the bride is also up for debate, which makes sense having met her. They want me down there…like, yesterday."

So much for not driving into town. Isabel got her keys from the coffee table where she had knocked over Lucinda's glass. She gave the keys a quick shake to dry them and moved toward the front door, very glad to be going. This was becoming a common theme, Isabel wanting to escape her own home along with the visitor inside it.

"I'll drive you, love. We can discuss more in the car, and I'll bring you home after. We'll have girl time!" Lucinda exclaimed. Isabel recognized the loneliness in her boss's voice and eyes. "And your place is so peaceful, I wouldn't mind having a drink out on the back deck at sunset."

Although she'd always folded to her mentor's whims in past, a flash of random fear halted her default response. It was the drive into town and back—with Lucinda at the wheel. The thought shot an icy chill up her spine. The winding cliffside road into Vallarta—more than a hundred feet above the bay—took hold of her mind. But why the hell was she so scared? She hadn't thought of her own safety in forever. In fact, death had been a very welcome thought after Sebastian, her mother, and the others. But this new worry for her own life? The end isn't so scary when a person has nothing and no one to live for. So why now was she so terrified? What had changed? What had entered her life that made her so fearful of leaving it?

"You know what, Lucinda? You stay, I'll go. Relax on the back deck with another drink and I'll come back to join you within the hour."

"Okay, love...okay. You know, you are the absolute best, Isabel, dear. A true treasure."

*

"I really would love to, man, but a lot has come up, issues with this...price-less... deal I've been working on." Dwelling in self-pity and wallowing in a depressive tailspin over Isabel had been truly time-consuming. "I mean, don't get me wrong! Hand interviewing strippers is a welcome task by me, any day, but I really don't have the extra time right now," Zack said trying to act nor-mal, well, according to his brother, and whatever that meant anymore.

"Yeah, I get it—but, dude! The bachelor party is the best man's job. Since the dawn of time, bro!"

Zack had always given in to Darren's whim, probably because Zack felt he had to compensate his kid brother for their bastard father's early exit. "Little brother, listen...I'm absolutely pumped for your wedding...and my role in it!—not that I needed the title since I know that *you* know I'm the absolute fucking best," he cracked. "But I bet Wret or John would do such a better job with the bachelor party than I would right now. I'm just going through some shit with this one damn...deal," he said, catching himself again. Zack wouldn't burden Darren with Zack's reality, what with the wed-ding being so close. He wouldn't show this unprecedented vulnerability to his kid brother, either.

No, he would hold back on what was actually eating him alive—that a woman, the all-consuming Isabel, had just evaporated from his world. What did it matter? Wherever she now existed, she despised him. Then to add insult to injury, he had set out on a mission to find her, and having failed up to that point, he was feeling close to insane. Failure was not something Zack James was at all used to.

"You're full of shit and you know it! Wret and John? Zack, you're the ultimate pimp of the entire fucking universe! And you know Vallarta like the back of your hand. Plus, you know me better than I know myself. You fucking raised me, dude! So don't tell me anyone else but you can plan this thing!"

He sighed into the phone. "I'll fucking do it. Yes, I'll plan your bachelor party, damn it. But I'll expect Wret and John to handle the logistics the night of!"

"Yes, absolutely. Definitely! You're the best, Zack. Seriously! And with your pull, I bet you can get some supermodels or even a celebrity or two!" Darren said, sounding like an excited puppy before his food bowl got set down.

"Don't push it, Darren James!" Zack said like a father, one who'd just been designated to get his surrogate son sloshed off his ass then spanked and molested by strippers before his wedding day arrived.

"Look, brother, you know you can just snap your fingers and get centerfolds from Norway and a flippin' princess from Spain if you wanted to!"

"Whoa there, you pushy little shit!" Zack warned. "Yes, you are getting married, the whole *man* and wife thing, but you're still my kid brother, the one I beat on as a child." He laughed into the phone. "Listen, it'll be a great time, trust me. But you'll be so knocked-off-your-ass drunk you won't know your own name, my name, the strippers' names…or where the hell they come from!"

Zack could hardly think of putting his attention to a bachelor party in his state, let alone going all-out—making calls, trading favors, or string-pulling with his high-end connections. And, *goddamn it*, his little brother had always thought things came so easy to him. 'With a snap of his fingers!' Zack's ass, it was that easy. In general, Darren had been too young to know how hard Zack had worked for everything. In fact, Zack made sure Darren had no clue. Protecting Darren had become his top priority since their father left— Darren had just turned eight and Zack had a year to go before he could even vote! And their mother? She'd slipped into an indefinite depression.

No, nothing was ever as easy as it seemed.

"I know, Zack. It'll be all-good. That's why I asked you. I think I'm just…you know…"

"What, you nervous?"

"Yeah, dude! But not, like, about Amy. I mean, I *know* with her—she is my…*one*. It's more like…I won't let us be like Mom and Dad. This will be it, so, well, I want it to be perfect. Shit, I sound like a fucking bride, don't I?"

"Yeah, man"—Zack snickered then cleared his throat—"and you're fine. Big man's makin' the big move. It's natural…and all good."

Darren kept silent for a beat then snorted. "It is good, right? Really good.… Hey, you know something?"

"What's that?"

"When Dad left Mom and us for Sabrina, I remember thinking marriage must be like…like the circus. You know, they go all-out with the big top, the animals, the trapeze setup and all, but then it just picks up and leaves…onto another fucking town. Like, 'Okay, Dad's going to live in France now with his new family,' while we were just the town he'd left behind…you know what I mean?"

Zack hated talking about their father, especially with Darren. He never wanted Darren affected by the bullshit that came with Bennet James. But he definitely understood Darren and his metaphor completely. And it was right-on, too, except that a circus leaves a dustbowl of a parking lot in its wake, while Bennet James had actually left his sons with a get-out-guilt-free card—a tremendous, multimillion dollar trust fund. Oh, and a note—*Sorry, sons…Be good boys, be good men…etc.*

Then the "ring master" of the allegorical circus bailed. Not a word ever after.

"Isn't that crazy about Amy's dad? Zack? Zack! Hey, you still there, bro?"

"Yeah, sorry. I'm here."

"Hey man, you okay? You're not all here, like, at all. That property deal is really running you for your money, huh?"

"Yeah, I guess so… It's fine though. I'm just working late hours." Drinking away his sorrow late into the night for two weeks straight was hitting him hard. But drowning in a liquor-induced coma felt better than doing nothing—and female distractions weren't even an option. Thinking or looking at a woman who wasn't Isabel made his stomach rage, so the idea of sleeping with one near killed him. In fact, the only sex he'd had over the past weeks was with himself while fantasizing about Isabel, and that was torture enough.

"Well, just get focused and be ready to have a blast when we get down there. Like I said, it's my one wedding, bro, and you are, like, one of the most important parts of it."

Zack cleared his throat again. "Just get your whipped ass down here so I can get it whipped for real." Zack dug up the ability to laugh, trying hard to get into the spirit of things for his brother. "I hear The Inferno has got some great S&M girls. You should be more careful about what you wish for, little brother."

"I'll be fine, man! No need to worry about me," Darren defended. "Oh, hey, listen. Even though Amy has the wedding planner handling the airport pickup with limos and all, I want you at the airport too. This shindig has got to start with seeing you first thing, dude! First thing!"

Zack smiled at his end of the phone. "Yeah, sure, brother. I'll be at the airport." A warmth that only Darren could strike in his heart rose up and got caught in the throat. "And by the way, Darren, I'm really happy for you. Really damn happy."

"I know it brother…and thanks, for everything." Two beats of silence followed. "So, see you then?"

"With fucking garters, titty tassels, and bells on!"

"Abso-fucking-lutely! Later, Zack."

Zack hung up, tossed his phone on the bed, and stared up at the ceiling. His kid brother was getting hitched. A crazy thought. An insane fucking thought.

And then an even crazier feeling surfaced—unfamiliar, unidentifiable, uncomfortable. It made his shoulders tight and his jaw clench. This nagging emotion had visited him a time or two before, most recently…when? At the condo closing! *Yes, that was it.* When he'd seen his attorney, Armando, with his son, Juan. Juan was joining the Sanchez firm, and the pride in Armando's eyes had been undeniable, glowing. Their camaraderie, the mutual respect, it had been obvious and solid. Zack had everything in the world, but he didn't have that. Not from his own father. And he never would.

Envy. It was goddamn envy, and it burned.

And now he envied his little brother, who had found and grabbed the love of his life. Never, ever before had Zack wanted that for himself. But now that he knew of Isabel, his potential match, his missing, floating puzzle piece…that she even existed on Earth was a goddamn miracle.

He hadn't felt whole before or since meeting Isabel.

But Zack couldn't find her anywhere, and even if he did find her, she wouldn't want him. She thought he was a total asshole. And he was, or at least he had been! But he'd changed. She had changed him. And he had to find her and show her. His only focus was Isabel.

But, *shit!*—Darren's bachelor party. He was so not looking forward to the task his brother had just put to him. A cramp sparked up on his right side just thinking about it. Then he heard the minibar calling.

No! He had to get this shit done. The expectations of his kid brother were just that much louder.

He reached for his cell and dialed Armando. His lawyer never stopped bragging about his one client who owned the major strip club in town, a quicker ticket to a party-in-a-box, way less hassle.

Zack needed to speak to the man anyway. He'd lost the doctor's number Armando had given him and his stomach had been killing him slowly since the night Isabel had left.

And Armando knew a PI. If anyone could take the search for Isabel to the next level, it was Armando's guy, because, at that point, Zack had exhausted all other obvious avenues. He had already spoken to the local staff at the Five Breezes and at the Airington, three times each, but they'd been no help.

He waited for the call to pick up as it rang for the fifth time. He knew Armando's secretary juggled a billion things at once, so he just hung on while his mind wandered. By the eighth ring, he literally laughed out loud—never in his life would he have imagined himself desperately seeking a woman, least of all one particular woman, and going to such lengths to do so. Only a couple of weeks ago, one gorgeous female had been the same as another.

And he sure as hell wouldn't have procrastinated when it came to arranging a bachelor party! Close and personal interviews with exotic dancers and he'd have been all in!

Damn it, Isabel. Where the hell are you?

CHAPTER 10

S ITTING AT THE café table under a ceiling fan, Zack took out his cell to text Armando.

I'm here. Just swing by. At Marcello's Café.

He'd ordered then downed a quick espresso shot by the time his attorney pulled up.

"Excited, are we? You're *always* late for our meetings!" he cracked at his lawyer as he got into the car.

"This is different. Hold on." Armando drove Zack in the new black treat he'd bought himself after Zack's condo had closed. The tires screeched onto the main road as they headed to The Inferno for the bachelor party planning session. Armando insisted on taking him personally, "to make introductions."

They entered the club, and Zack felt an immediate flood of stale sex and spilled beer in the air, and it was only 4:00 PM with no action to speak of yet.

He couldn't help but want to be done there as quickly as possible. Armando, on the other hand, searched for any tits and any ass anywhere and came up to the empty bar, disappointment in his old-man eyes, like a tired, sad hound dog who'd lost the scent.

Jake Demonte, the owner of the spot, came up behind them and slammed Armando on the back in greeting. Apparently, most of their meetings took place at Armando's office or by phone. Jake seemed proud of his place, glad to show it off.

After Zack was introduced, planning began.

Armando lit up when the strobes turned on, a pounding bass vibrated the space, and a parade of dancers made their way out onto the stage. Zack turned on his bar stool while Armando had already gone stage-side.

"Nice selection, huh? No one beats my parade of pussy, I will tell you that," Jake said in a thick New York accent, nudging Zack with his elbow. Zack cringed and cleared his throat of the welling disgust, but he knew full well that it came with the territory.

He took a sip of water to reset, then tried to hurry the process along. "It's hard to choose man, but hey, let's make it easier." *And quicker.* "First off, let's steer clear of brunettes, or raven for that matter. My brother's fiancée is a pretty brunette, and my mom's dark haired, too. Darren won't do well with any kind of resemblances."

"Redheads and blondes only!" Jake called out to the stage.

Redheads and blondes. "J&T" and hanging panties and lipstick on a mirror all slammed to mind. *Isabel.* God how badly he wanted to get out of this place.

"Any other specs, man? Our hot pussy comes in every shape and size, color and age," the guy said, grinning from ear to ear. That grin, it reminded Zack of the little prick from his first night in town. It was weird, they even looked a little alike. Probably just their goddamn sleaze factor in common, was all.

Fuck, I so wanna get outta here.

He put his focus back on the stage. "Just, whichever girls are the most assertive, man." He knew his little brother needed an onslaught of attentive dancers so he could take a more passive role. A more guiltless role. Tits smashed in his face, and not the other way around. Zack had been the playboy, not Darren. Not even close.

Minutes later, the job was done. The bachelor party was arranged and paid for, with all the flair Darren and his friends could want; private room in the back, lap dances galore, the works. And then, to Armando's disappointment, the meeting was over. The blinding strobes and pounding bass stopped, as did the girls' parade. Zack thanked Jake and got the hell outside, beating Armando by several long minutes.

When his attorney did finally get out to the parking lot, the man held out a strip of paper to Zack, smiling wide while trying to catch his breath. "You forgot your receipt, and, you lucky bastard, the redhead with freckles, the one with the tiny heart tattoo on her baby-smooth mound, she wants you to call her after she gets off tonight! And, God Almighty, at first I thought she was giving me her number! I swear I almost had a heart attack!"

Ignoring the "luck" reference, Zack glanced at the receipt then flipped it over to a handwritten name and number. *Destiny*. He scoffed at the name, then stuffed it in his pocket and got into the car. Sinking into Armando's passenger seat, he could only think of Isabel. He only craved Isabel. "Any news from your guy with that woman I'm looking for?"

"Not yet. 'Isabel' is a popular name down here."

"But she's uncommonly beautiful. Did you tell him that? And the birthmark?"

"Zack, I told him. Still a tough one, but give it time. Until then, call that damn number on the receipt! Distract yourself, for Christ's sake! You look like hell."

Zack shook his head. Armando was a good man, but he wouldn't understand. He called both of his divorces blessings and proudly announced his commitment to his job, which Zack selfishly appreciated. But at the same time, the man couldn't know what Zack had found in Isabel. His potentially perfect fit, lost. For now.

CHAPTER 11

ZACK CRANED HIS neck to spot his brother and entourage wading through the timeshare hawkers at the airport exit. He saw Amy and her sister Stephanie first, both with enough luggage to clothe a small Mexican village.

He waved.

Amy and Stephanie were followed by their mother, Annette, and three other ladies, all with matching personalized wedding-themed beach bags. As they all came through the gateway, a mariachi band began with a boom, and still louder than the blasting accordion, horn, and joyful wailing of the traditional *Jalisco*-style ensemble, the women chattered to each other.

"He is so beautiful…mesmerizing…delicious!" Stephanie told Amy, again, not quietly.

Zack politely ignored the comment and its maker and went directly to Amy, his future sister-in-law, and hugged her tight, swinging her around and around in welcome.

"Great to see you too, Zack!" Amy said. She was glowing, obviously ecstatic about her big extravaganza.

"And hello, ladies." Zack, ever the gentleman, greeted Amy's mother, then each of the bridal party, all of whom he didn't know, nor care to, and lastly the maid of honor, Stephanie.

Zack had met Stephanie at a few combined-family gatherings for Darren and Amy. The woman was a bit eccentric, to say the least. Her outspoken take on people's auras, karmic connections and astrological charts were just too much for him to stomach, as was her obvious infatuation with him.

"You look very well, Zachary James. Very healthy, centered," Stephanie said to him as he backed away after the obligatory kiss on the cheek. She glanced at the other women, as if to be sure they noticed her confidence— her assertive air—as she offered Zack her analysis.

"You look centered yourself, Stephanie. Like the stars are aligned for you right now," Zack returned, feigning seriousness and civility with not-so-subtle undertones of sarcasm that only Amy seemed to catch.

Amy glared at him and whispered, "Behave yourself, sir."

He winked at her and redirected, "Ready to be a James?"

She smirked at him, then cocked her head. "Just be nice to her."

"I'm always nice." But Amy's wedding week or not, he was not about to be pushed together with Stephanie under any circumstance. Even if it was to give the happy couple a break from the high-maintenance maid of honor. "Now answer the question. Ready for the James name or what?"

"Absolutely. Despite…well…*that.*" She shook her head as her groom sauntered in their direction with a sombrero on his head and a margarita in his hand.

Darren's eyes widened and lit up when he spotted Zack from under the hat's rim, dropped his luggage where he stood, and then picked up his pace to a clumsy jog. The hat flew off before he got to Zack, but Darren didn't stop until he was locked in a bear hug with him, a bit of the margarita pouring down Zack's back. "So damn great to see you, man! My best man! My brother!" said Darren, his speech only slightly slurred.

"Always." Zack cleared an emotional knot in his throat, and then pushed his brother off him to check him out. "The groom. Looking good. Definitely marriage material."

John and Wret had picked up one bag each for Darren and joined the reunion. The three other groomsmen, guys Zack had never met, approached too, one with Darren's huge sombrero in hand.

"Dude, your brother doesn't fly well," Wret said, shaking Zack's hand and pounding him hard on the back.

Zack had forgotten that fact and laughed while greeting and meeting the other guys. "So the drinks started pouring early, huh? Nice. Very nice. Well let's get everyone settled back at the resort. I see the limo driver over there," he said, pointing to a tall clean-cut guy holding a sign. "The Rine/James Wedding."

Zack got the ragtag group moving toward the limos. "Let the wedding week begin, everyone!"

Darren, beaming, buzzed, and proudly gawking at his bride-to-be as she climbed into the limo in front of him called out, "What my brother said, people! Whatever my brother says."

CHAPTER 12

I SABEL WAS EARLY to their usual spot. She felt bad about missing the last family dinner for what turned out to be such a worthless cause, so she made sure to get there early to save their table in the "quiet corner," and pre-order starter apps and a round of drinks.

They'd been gathering at the touristy Las Tequilas for years now, just every month or so. Infrequent equaled safe. And while the vacationers were often obnoxious and rowdy, Isabel and her remaining family could at least relax invisibly with one another, without the fearful looks from her own people in the local hangouts.

As for the rest of Isabel's eight siblings, they'd all left for other cities in Mexico, the United States, or Canada after the tragedies connected to her began to turn fatal. Her mother's demise was the last straw for most of them, as Yesinia Ruiz had been the very glue that had held the entire family together. And Isabel needed no ghostly image of her ravishing mother to flash before her eyes for the writhing guilt to surface. She had the scars on her wrist to remind her constantly. Healed now, the raised knife-lines matched her mother's—same place on the left wrist, four slash lines all of equal length. But different than her mother's tragic scenario, Isabel was found in her bathtub just before she bled out. Celeste's intrusiveness, that time, had definitely saved her life—to Isabel's dismay at the time. Now, though, for the sake of her remaining family at least, Isabel had decided to stay on Earth and suffer and cause no further heartache to them. She sighed and looked down at her drink. *Don't think on it, Isa. Just don't.*

And when she looked up, Antonio was there. He hugged her warmly, and went to sit just as Ray and Eddie appeared. Real love, she thought to herself. *This* is real love.

The four immediately began eating, drinking and chatting while waiting for Celeste who was always fashionably late—exactly how Isabel preferred it, so her sister couldn't corner her alone and start in on the usual 'find a man' pitch. Anyway, when Celeste finally did show, Antonio pushed a drink her way so she'd catch up and unwind from moment one.

Loud cheers and toasts erupted at the other end of the bar, which they all ignored as commonplace, while they continued to crack up over Ray and Eddie's antics, Isabel's bride-and-groom sagas, Celeste's own manhunt tales, and Antonio's limousine adventures, most of which got pretty raunchy. After they'd finished the first round of tapas and beer, Isabel headed to the bartender whom she knew from her events and could get a few free drinks out of without a problem.

She got André's attention right away, and they chatted as he poured her order, which, as she hoped, was on him. She thanked him sweetly and turned to leave with the drinks, always extra careful not to spill or drop or fumble one or all. But she involuntarily paused, as if on autopilot. A tribal tattoo caught her eye, and up from it was a somewhat familiar set of shoulders, wide and strong. The tattoo owner was sitting only five stools down. Her gaze dropped back down to the torqued biceps wrapped in a tight black polo. She refocused her eyes on the tat, now making out its distinct red detail within the intricate black ink. And while the familiar scent of cologne and masculine musk hitting her nostrils could have been from any of the men sitting between her and Black Muscle Shirt, she didn't need to see the chiseled face and the emerald eyes to know.

She turned in the opposite direction like a shot and without dropping a bottle or sloshing an ounce—amazingly—she fled.

Dear God, thank you for not letting him see me.

Undiscovered and relieved for it, she set the first few drinks down on the table.

"Thanks, Isa," Ray said reaching for his glass.

"Not a problem," she sang as she placed the next two down, proud of her surprising grace and ease. She snapped her arm back as if she'd performed magic…

…and knocked her own drink over in doing so. Her glass rolled off the table and onto the floor in front of her stoic, sullen eyes. Lips pursed, nostrils flared, she huffed in frustration.

"That's what you get, baby sister," Ray said, snickering. Isabel rolled her eyes at him.

"I'll go get you a new one, Isa. You just sit and relax," Antonio said on his way to standing. But she shook her head and stopped him with one hand on his shoulder.

"No, it's okay. I got it. I get it free, and well, you're just not as pretty as I am." She winked at her brother, and then spun in the direction of the bar with a sigh. Zack would for sure be gone by then. Already at a far off table with his drink and whatever woman or women he'd brought with him. *Definitely.*

But on her walk back to André to get her replacement beverage, she asked God to please make it so, just in case.

*

Zack somehow heard his phone ring over the volume of the pre-party and the surrounding bar-goers. He backed away from the bar and returned to his table to take the call. "This is Zack," he shouted into his cell.

"It's Amy! I know I'm not supposed to be calling, but how is he?"

"More like, how are you?" Zack asked, hearing the thumping bass behind Amy's muffled voice.

"Oh, Zack, there's just not enough alcohol in the world. This place Stephanie picked…wait a minute, let me find a quieter spot…okay, well she thought it had male dancers—" A thud rocked Zack's eardrum, Amy must've dropped the phone.

"Sorry, a girl, or guy, not sure which, lost his…her…balance and bumped me. Anyway, the Rainbow Club is for gay men, albeit, hot gay men. Bottom line, we're not the most attended-to people in the place!"

Zack, who had pieced the choppy details together, hadn't had that good a laugh in a while.

Actually, not since that night he'd met Isabel, whom he was fully preoccupied with not having found. Still.

He had practically camped out at the Five Breezes in hopes Isabel would have other meetings there. He also began asking around about the tall older woman who had been with Isabel the day they'd met, but he'd still come up with nothing. And the PI was supposed to have something back to him before the weekend.

"Zack? You there?"

"Shit, sorry Amy."

"So all's good with my groom?"

"Yes, absolutely—Darren's fine, being watched over like a hawk. No problems. Just go and get your freak on. We'll see you tomorrow afternoon."

*

When the call ended, his lip lifted at the sweet concern behind Amy's call. She was good for Darren. She was really good for him.

The line for drinks at the bar had gotten long, so he decided to wait a while, and just resumed his watch over his brother and mates. An unclaimed tequila shot conveniently left by one of the guys was right within reach. A nice gift. He grabbed it and slammed it back. Getting wasted was probably not the best move, even Armando's doctor who had come to Zack's suite a few nights back had told him that. For his stomach's sake, he'd be best to take a break from alcohol, all spicy food, and coffee. But he'd straight-out ignored the advice. His stomach wasn't fucked up from any of those things. He knew damn well what was twisting his insides.

And drinking made the night he'd planned for Darren move along faster. While he kept a plastered smile on his face for show, he watched the scene around him unfold through dour eyes—everything seemed to be moving in super-slow motion. But at least, everyone seemed to be having a blast, which was of course the goal. Darren deserved this.

"Upfront pussy and backroom lap dances, dude!" Wret said from out of nowhere, slapping Zack on the shoulder. "Can't fuckin' wait!"

Zack mustered an appeasing smile and a nod at his brother's best friend. "Yeah, man. It'll be great, no doubt," he lied. Because as the guys anticipated The Inferno, Zack found himself dreading it more and more. He couldn't think of a worse place to go, knowing that the only woman he wanted to devour and fantasize about and hold in his arms the entire night after wouldn't be there. *In fact, she was absolutely fucking nowhere, goddammit.* Nowhere at all!

Stir-crazy and tired of sulking, he needed to move, to get up, change views. He walked back toward the bar, passing Darren on the way. "I'm getting another tequila shot, brother. You want one, or five?" He slapped his extremely inebriated baby brother square on the back.

"Yeah, a few for you and me!" Darren slurred, then raised his voice for the whole bar to hear. "And a round for everyone! I'm getting MARRIED!"

The entire bar cheered.

Zack laughed, loving to see his brother so happy, then headed to the bartender to pay for his brother's gracious bar-wide drink order.

He weaved through the hefty crowd to a barstool. While waiting his turn, he looked down the length of the bar at the array of drunken people for distraction's sake alone.

The next instant, *hypnotization.* His pulse moved to his ears while his air caught in his chest. A woman. *That woman.* At the end of the bar. He swallowed hard, heat and hope flooding his body. Her smooth bare skin showed through an open-backed halter top, a long dark braid hanging down the middle. Down went his gaze to the fully magnificent bottom of an hourglass figure, the ass of his dreams, snug black skirt hugging that fully sensual shape.

She shifted her stance, leaning her right elbow on the bar. Her braid swished to the right, leaving for Zack's eyes a small splash of a birthmark in the shape of a lost-soul puzzle piece.

Isabel? Oh God, Isabel.

His heart leapt up into his throat so fast he actually coughed. He turned away to clear his throat, but he couldn't stop the coughing fit. He felt volcanic heat in his ears and cheeks. The bartender passed a glass of water to him quickly and shouted, "You're welcome," before he could even try to voice a thank you. He checked to see if Isabel had caught sight of him during his choking stint, which would have made his face burn up more, but she hadn't.

No, she was busy talking nonstop to the other bartender. Far too busy. He felt a growl in his chest. He watched her luscious lips as inaudible words fell out, talking and talking to the admittedly attractive man behind the bar. And the whole scene burned him. Yeah, it fucking burned. The guy now handed her a double shot. She paused her words, parted her mouth just so, and poured the drink down her throat.

Fuck! Zack wanted to punch the guy in the face for watching her lips so closely. And for some reason, that burning possessiveness he felt wasn't unreasonable to Zack. For as much as he had thought about her, hunted for her, wished for her, dreamed of her, he did feel like she was his.

After smiling her thanks and tipping the barman, she turned her sultry body around to leave. Zack strained to keep sight of her and of her smooth, defined back, until some fifty-something silver fox approached her, blocking her exit and Zack's streamlined view.

Definitely unsolicited from the looks of it, the guy slid his hand down her exquisite back, then farther still until his palm circled her right ass cheek, no qualms, no hesitation.

And that was all it took. Zack's instincts ramped into gear, and he darted in her direction. At the same time, he saw another man coming from the opposite direction in a rush of *Save the Damsel*, too. Piercing crystal-blue eyes, intent on Isabel.

Isabel turned her head first to Zack and then to Blue Eyes. "Roberto?" she said to Blue Eyes. "Um, Zack?" A look of pure perplexity mixed with frustration splashed her in the face. "Wait! Just hold it!"

She unloaded her hands of the two beer bottles. "I can handle this gentleman all by myself, thank you *both* very much." Then she reached her hand behind her, grabbed the man's hand, and twisted. Not to break his arm, because from the sharp look in her eye, she really could have, but maybe just to scare the guy into thinking so?

"I actually kill men who get too close to me," she said to the lecherous bastard, "but it looks like you're on your last legs anyway, so just please, back the hell up and off. Now." Punctuated with a thin-lined grin and narrowed eyes.

Zack fucking loved it. She was unbelievable! He absolutely wanted her right there, right then…more than he'd thought possible over the last excruciating weeks. But his attention was forced away from her as the embarrassed asshole she'd just *handled* fumed, the guy's hot breath filling Zack's left ear.

How would this asshole regain his pride after such a forward and public turndown? Maybe not wanting to stoop as low as to hit a woman, he turned his frustration on Zack. The guy pulled back to throw a punch, but Blue Eyes, who was still on the other side of the sleazebag, quickly grabbed the bar bowl of chips and poured them over the older guy's head.

And Isabel yanked Zack back and away, narrowly rescuing him from the swinging blast to his face.

A blink later, he found himself outside, behind the bar with his lost-but-found angel on the sandy white beach with the sun in its final descent over the shimmering bay.

CHAPTER 13

ALONE, TOGETHER, SHE stared at him, unsure of what the hell had possessed her to help this…this player! And more, what had motivated her to escape with him outside? Again—*alone, together!*

As if on autopilot, adrenaline had juiced her body's reactions, all without her mind's permission. The result, a complete lapse of judgment. *Damn it, Isabel!*

But it got worse. Zack's eyes were hard on her, quivering with energy, burning her like the blinding orange glare of the setting sun. She felt an unwarranted flood of heat start low and deep. It rose up through her and reached her face. Anger and denied-arousal clouded her vision.

Struggling with her body's reaction to this mind-screwing, womanizing player, she took a deep breath, readying herself to get the hell away from him. *Go already.*

But first, words fell out of her mouth, words completely unapproved by her brain. "I, uh, didn't want you taking a punch to that handsome face of yours for *me*," she instigated, a flirty sarcasm betraying her pride. She stepped back toward the bar to counter the traitorous act of speaking to him, all the while trying to ignore her body's screams of protest for the incremental distance. But words poured out again, this time her heart played the betraying culprit. "After all, those lace-panty owners wouldn't be able to recognize you if your face was all bruised up, and we couldn't have that, now, could we?" *Really?*

For God's sakes, Isabel—leave. Now!

"So, okay then...take care." And her foot pressed deeper into the sand to begin her retreat.

But in a flash his hand held her left wrist, just above her cuff bracelet. His grasp was gentle, but firm enough to keep her there and to transfer his damned electricity through her entire body. But when he caught her look of warning, he released his grip.

"Listen to me, Isabel—you need to know something."

She was surprised by the command in Zack's voice. Although brushed with a slight and genuine sweetness, he sounded firm, assertive. Far less wavering than last time. Now his voice matched the unbelievable control and power he'd exhibited when last they touched, kissed, and devoured each other whole. "I've been looking for you. Trying to find you. God, it's been—"

"Wait a minute...hold on. Looking for me? Why look for me? Seemed to me like you had a line out your penthouse door!"

She felt his glowing green eyes detach from hers, angling up as if to devise a new strategy. And damn it, she wanted his gaze back. She so hated that she wanted his gaze back!

A moment later, she got her wish as he refocused his eyes on hers while biting his bottom pout—a touch of humility, maybe? Whatever it was, he'd somehow toned down his intensity—so he wouldn't scare her away?

Because, truth be told, she was absolutely terrified and wanted nothing more than to run. But her feet were frozen and sinking into what felt like quicksand beneath her feet. "I left those panties at the front desk for immediate pickup and have been entirely too busy looking for you to have time for a new collection of lace undergarments, or any other variety of underwear for that matter." He grinned, a hopeful and apologetic look spun around his lighthearted words. "Please...can we just talk, like we did before we even went up to my penthouse that night?"

An airy laugh escaped her lips and she let her eyes smile at him. Just her eyes. "Talk, huh?" What was there to talk about? And again, why the hell was she still standing there? Even *talking* about talking to this asshole was self-degradation.

And she highly doubted he was interested in just talk. She knew *she* wasn't. Her betraying body vibrated and there was nothing she could do to steady herself. Self-hatred began to flood her core, or was that pure, unadulterated goddamn arousal?

And she still couldn't move herself away from him.

But maybe she could get him to walk the hell away from her before she caved? "You should go back inside to your friends, Zack. There was a round of drinks for someone getting hitched in there, yeah? Go get your free drink on…have fun. I'm fine right here. Good bye, Zack. And take care." She took a step back in the sinking white sand. Shocked at that small step, she spun around to face the bay. And that was it—all her body would allow. It was, at least, movement in the right direction.

But from the sound of his breath, way too close for her comfort, she knew he was completely ignoring her parting words. Then his breath magnified, now warming the nape of her neck, fanning her in synch with the lulling rhythm of the incoming tide. Tingling waves of electricity shot down her spine. Damn him. And damn his heat.

"Isabel."

She shuddered. God, his deep, sultry baritone—thick, sensual—a sharp contrast to the silent anticipation of him finally, hopefully leaving her there, leaving her be.

But the hypnotic magnetism of his damn presence overshadowed all. Their bodies were so close. She felt his radiating heat. She could smell him, that particular brand of his, of man and delectable power. And from her memory she could almost taste him.

"Who was the blue-eyed knight in shining armor at the bar?" he whispered in her ear.

An unintentional smile spread across her mouth. Isabel couldn't help but enjoy the possible motivation behind his question. Was he jealous at the thought of a competing stag rushing in to save her?

Then she wanted to kick herself for getting a jolt from that possibility.

"My oldest friend-turned-stalker. He's like a brother. Why? What does it matter?" she asked, instigating without shame.

Zack said nothing. His breathing just got fuller and hotter on her neck.

A few beats passed. She got done waiting, done with him. "Zack, I'd really like to be alone out here, if you don't mind." With her back still to him, she attempted to focus on any of the many far off boats out on the bay—they looked like sparkling stars on a midnight-blue sky. She listened and held in a lungful of ocean air, waiting for proof of his departure, waiting for the removal of his sweet, searing breath on her skin.

But no proof came.

*

Instead, his rough hand grabbed her left arm again and spun her around. "You want me. You do," he said with an arrogant smile on his lips. His eyes narrowed, glistening green.

"You cocky bastard! If I wanted you, you'd—"

His mouth interrupted her argument—muted by a deep, unwelcome kiss.

Unreserved and lustful, as if he'd been waiting years, decades, lifetimes—like he couldn't wait another moment.

Held captive—her mouth, her tongue, her lips, all recollected the deluge of fire he'd ignited inside her just weeks ago. Down to her core, she remembered. And the next thing she knew, her mouth attacked back with equal force, equal passion.

She was taken. And taking back. Dangerously, vitally consumed within each other's grasp.

Deep moments passed until he paused to look at her. She couldn't catch her breath even if she tried, trapped by his gaze. That haunting gaze. Then his hand met her cheek, slid back behind her ear, down to the nape of her neck, then he moved his mouth to hers again, easing into sweet, slow-motion ecstasy. His lips—delicious, moist, and soft as velvet—caressed and tripped over hers.

In perfect synch, she slowed and held his top lip, sucking gently, her tongue savoring his taste, that familiar decadence. Zack's hands moved to cradle her face, then her hands covered his.

And with as much control as she gave him, he moved his overwhelming vastness a step closer to her, their bodies meeting, unable to get any closer. He brought his muscular arms down, wrapping around her in a smooth, deliberate, possessive stance, squeezing her to him, just shy of depleting all oxygen. Or was her continued inability to catch her breath something beyond physics, far deeper than words could explain?

His wide, slightly rough hands slid in all directions across her back, rubbing, pressing, and then grazing her skin as if memorizing its every dip and definition. His fingers glided underneath the satiny fabric of her open-back top, curling around to the sensitive bloom of her breasts just brimming at her sides. His delicate touch sent her reeling, nipples sharpened, and Isabel pushed hard into Zack's broad chest to alleviate the painful delight of not being naked, skin-to-skin, in his entire, heavenly grasp.

She could hardly stand. Her legs were useless weights pulling her down, down into that deadly quicksand. She was melting and didn't have the strength to stop it. But he did. His rock-hard arms came down to her hips, hoisting her up. He placed her arms tight around his neck, her feet dangling, just hovering above the white sand. He held her, floating, as if weightless, locked in their continued, incapacitating kiss.

Her body had definitely defeated her judgment. She couldn't even hear her mind's scolding voice over the loud thud of her heart and the throbbing in all of her most crucially sensitive points.

Zack, her puppet master, pulled her in any direction he wished. She'd become so under his control, so heavy in his hold.

And when she took a brief break for air, her peripheral caught sight of Roberto standing in the back doorway of the bar, she couldn't have cared less. She watched her friend fume his way back inside as she melted deeper into Zack's all-encompassing embrace.

*

Like a dream that Zack refused to wake up from, he held Isabel in his grasp, inhaled her, absorbed her, but did so with as much delicacy and subtlety as he could muster. He couldn't afford to frighten her away. His intensity even overwhelmed him. And beyond fucking things up last time with the girls-in-waiting and all, he knew she was skittish about commitment, about connection beyond one night. Hell, he would have freaked the fuck out if he were in her shoes, and in fact, he'd been that commitment-phobe. All the way up until meeting her, he'd been running from the long-term, the *any*-term.

So, yeah, he had to move slowly, and that would be unthinkably fucking hard to do now that he'd found her, finally—a lifesaving shot-of-adrenaline-to-the-heart find. When Isabel had spun away from him there on that beach, he'd nearly keeled over from the pain in his middle, but she hadn't walked away. No. She stayed just within arms' reach.

He couldn't let-on that she had consumed his mind and soul since their first meeting, but he had to grab her, take her. And it'd worked. She was kissing him back, surrendered in his arms.

Still connected, lips gliding over one another's, teeth nipping, and tongues searching hungrily for more, he lifted her higher into the air and breathed her in before placing her down in the sand again, hating to separate from her mind-bending reciprocal hold. "Go. Get your purse," he ordered in a hazy whisper. "I'll tell my friends something much more important came up." And he directed her to the bar's back door, ready to follow behind her divine silhouette.

But her feet sank into the soft sand before taking a forward step, despite his gentle push at her lustrous lower back.

She pivoted to face him, hesitating—a look of resistance had wiped over her face. She took his hands in hers. "Zack…"

God, hearing his name from her mouth, he pulled her into him, unable to stay even inches apart and wrapped her in his arms again, pressing his lips to hers for one more taste.

But she stopped him, taking a step back. "Zack, wait…"

Her arms reached around her, moving his right hand from the cusp of her lower back to her right ass cheek. "Feel that? My ID, cash and credit card. Inside my secret skirt pocket." She grinned.

God he wanted to rip the skirt with the goddamn secret pocket right off her fine ass. *Now.*

Then her left hand moved to the sweat-glistening dimple at the top of her chest and slid her index finger down to the rim of her halter. Once she'd arrived at her fleshy left bosom, she pulled the lace material out and down. *Dear Jesus.* "And my cell."

"Yes, I see…your cell phone. I'm very jealous of your cell phone."

She blushed. "I can text them. So we're ready to go. Now." She smiled.

"No, Isabel. You need to go in and tell the people you're with that you're leaving, or else they'll think you were abducted." He grabbed a handful of her sweet ass. "Then meet me out front."

*

Reluctantly, she went back to her table, zigzagging her way through the packed bar. Her admittedly voluptuous curves bumped people's chairs along the way, but she was in such a hazy state of hot arousal and robotic hypnosis she couldn't have cared less.

Well, except for the people that she was being forced to say goodbye to. Namely, Roberto, who she knew would be waiting with her siblings, ready to give her an earful. Even though, damn it, what was he even doing here?

She got to the corner where her family and Roberto sat. *Deep breath.*

She slid into her chair, conveniently situated next to Roberto's newly added seat and place setting. "What are you doing here?" she whispered in his ear.

"I'm out at a bar…the bar we all always go to. Nothing wrong with that, right?" Roberto blurted out, obviously unwilling to keep things mellow and undramatic. Everyone paused and stared. Roberto nodded to everyone, eyebrows raised while Isabel took in her second large gulp of oxygen.

Her brothers and sister all knew that Isabel had asked Roberto to give her some space. It was no secret. But knowing Roberto's more recent state, and her current and exploding desire to get the hell out of there—with Zack—she didn't want a scene or an unending discussion to go down there at the table. It would just slow down her exit.

From across the table, Antonio checked in with Isabel with a single look. She gave her older brother a nod and a convincing-enough smile, hopefully staving off his protective instincts for a short goodbye, then out. "Roberto"—said through gritted teeth and plastered grin—"I just meant...I didn't expect you here, is all. It doesn't matter. Thanks for helping out with that sleaze at the bar."

"No problem, sweetheart. But it looks like you have more help than you can handle tonight." He lifted a brow at her—the vibrations of his bruised ego and his clear reference to Zack were no doubt received.

Not willing to feed the fire, Isabel turned away from Roberto and focused on Antonio and the rest of the table. "Hey...so, I just bumped into an old friend, and we're gonna go catch up before he leaves Vallarta." She moved toward her sister, kissed her goodbye, and whispered, "Use this when you guys are done for the night." She put a wad of bills in Celeste's hand. "Drinks and dinner on me."

Celeste took the cash with a small reluctant eye roll, and then hugged her sister. "Have fun. And please, keep an open mind, Isa?" she whispered in Isabel's ear.

"Where are you going?" Roberto asked.

Like it was any of his business! Isabel was trying to be patient and civil, but Jesus! If he'd remembered how to be a best friend and not a relentless, self-absorbed stalker, she'd have confided in Roberto from moment one. But Roberto wasn't there for her. He wasn't listening to her words, her explanation of how she felt toward him, her platonic, and solely platonic, love for him.

If Roberto had been the usual support system he had been for all the years before their drunken-mistake-of-a-night, she'd have told him how Zack had invaded her mind and body these past weeks, and of the war playing out within her at that very moment. Of how weak she felt for even entertaining the idea of going anywhere with Zack—last name still thankfully unknown—the gorgeous American player!

But no. Roberto wasn't there to play that role for her, not anymore.

"Not sure," she said, making no eye contact with him whatsoever. She leaned across the table toward Eddie then to Ray to kiss them each goodbye.

Next Antonio. At the edge of her seat, ready to reach her oldest brother, Roberto leaned into her.

"I just saw you out back on the beach, Isa," Roberto whispered. "With that *gringo*…more than a friend, I'd say. What happened to your one-night rule, anyway?"

Her cheeks burned up red, not from embarrassment since no one at the table had heard his comment, but from anger. Pure, hot anger.

*

Using the reasoning she'd given Roberto against her, and automatically assuming, what? That every guy she kissed was someone she'd already slept with? Roberto was obviously hurt, emotional, irrational, and didn't care who knew it.

But it just so happened that contrary to Roberto's jealousy-based assumptions, she hadn't fully been with Zack at all yet and wasn't technically breaking her rule. She was only in the gray with regard to her own self-worth and her greedy need stemming from deep within her core—an intense and raw desire for a man she had stomped out on only weeks ago. He had insulted her intelligence and made her potential sloppy-thirds. There had been a damn waiting list of women for him to screw for heaven's sake, or so said the hanging panties and their accompanied lipsticked-note!

She had to get the hell out of there before she talked herself out of *Zack* altogether, and her throbbing clit wouldn't have been so forgiving. It'd be only one night, for heaven's sake. And Zack had been desperately searching for her over the past weeks, so said his convincingly sweet eyes when he stopped her from leaving him out there on the beach.

Oh God, on that beach behind the bar only minutes ago. The blissful, floating feeling of being wrapped in Zack's arms flooded her senses, and she couldn't hide her smile. Roberto rolled his eyes at her as if he'd read her thoughts and then slowly shook his head in disappointment.

Screw you, Roberto, and screw this. A resurgence of anger put to immediate death her internal voice of self-judgment, self-doubt, and second-guessing. She'd show Roberto what it looked like when her foot came down. She was going with Zack, and there wasn't a damn thing he could do or say to stop her. She was a grown woman, and she would indulge in Green Eyes that night and damn well enjoy it.

And the minutes she'd spent away from Zack were already too long—her quickened heartbeat was starting to thump in her ears now. Without more theatrics to delay her from being back in that smoldering man's gaze, she said to Roberto in a quiet growl, "I'm sure you're well-meaning…but it's none of your concern." Then, to the rest of the table, "Okay, talk to you all over the week."

"You can't go. You're being goddamn…reckless," Roberto snapped at her in her ear, still just decibels below hearing range so that her family missed the comment.

With that, her frustration level peaked. She filled her lungs then hissed back, "Last I knew, my father checked out of my life, and I definitely didn't apply for a new one. Thanks, though." She spun away from Roberto, gave a strained smile to her siblings, and pushed her chair out from the table. Roberto began to follow suit, but Antonio stood up from his seat before Roberto's chair screeched back any further. Tall, well-built, and always calm, cool, and controlled, Antonio, a martial arts master and second oldest Ruiz brother, walked over to Isabel while keeping Roberto in his chair with a single glance.

Antonio kissed Isabel on the cheek. "Have fun. Take care of yourself." He pushed her gently toward the bar's exit. "Text me when you're home."

"I always do, big brother," she said with a thankful smile then lifted to her toes to give him a quick hug. Admittedly strong and stubborn by nature, she knew Antonio's protectiveness—always given with room to breathe— was the only brand her pride and strong-willed nature could take.

She gave them all a final wave goodbye and headed out. With the exit targeted, she heard Roberto push his chair out in a huff, then from her side view she watched him vanish into the sea of people at the bar. She shook it off, replacing anger with sheer, core-pounding desire, and made a beeline toward the exit to reunite with Zack outside.

Zack came up on Isabel's blindside as she reached the door. Her pulse triple-timed. He took her hand in his.

"That took way longer than I wanted," she said and squeezed his hand with renewed excitement.

"Maybe you should've called?"

She sighed with her eyes then smiled. "I told you."

"Well, we're out now. Come on."

With his hand still clutching hers, he opened the door for her and pulled her across the threshold. She hadn't met the bar's outside steps before she noticed Roberto out of the corner of her eye—at the side door, leaving too, and in a more than obvious rage.

Who cares? Roberto wasn't going to ruin her night.

Nothing would.

She beamed at Zack, tantalizing as all hell. A feeling engulfed her like the ecstasy she'd known on that first morning in her new home—working her ass off, free of clothing and judging eyes, with the windows open to the sweet sea air.

Same sensation now, with Zack—liberation mixed with an overwhelming sense of yearning. Hand-in-hand, they left *Las Tequilas*.

CHAPTER 14

ZACK KEPT FIRM hold of Isabel as they walked one block away to *La Sexta Noche* in the thick Vallarta heat. His need for her was impossible to hide. He had a hot, firm grasp on her hand, their fingers interlocked, his moist palm suctioned to hers. He found himself pumping her hand to the beat of the deep, pounding bass drifting through the air from the club.

But while relishing the electricity spiking up his arm from her hand's tight hold, he could hardly stand the distance between their other body parts. He'd skip the club in a heartbeat and move right to his place in order to gain full access to her delectable body, that is if he didn't think she'd bolt. Even though it seemed she was as anxious as he was to get back to exploring each other in penthouse-privacy, as her hungry and focused gaze suggested. But he wasn't about to risk the modicum of trust he'd somehow won back.

And then later, after attending to each other's primal needs, he'd tell her everything, all of the realizations that'd struck him like lightning since she'd left him two weeks ago, alone and reeling in his void, the void that only Isabel seemed to be able to fill.

They crossed the street at the traffic light, hand-in-hand, with heightening anticipation. An oncoming pickup truck looked as though it wanted to run the red, and Zack tightened his grasp of her hand and picked up their pace, despite Isabel's spiked heels. At the safe side of the road, he made sure she was all right.

She smiled at him sweetly. "Both heels intact."

And twenty syncopated steps later, they were at *La Sexta Noche.*

*

The club was unexpectedly packed with partiers lining up around the building. Despite being a weekday night in the sweltering late May heat, some murmurs of a famous musician having just arrived explained things.

Zack pulled Isabel up to the front of the line, whispered something to the bouncer, and the velvet rope lifted for his immediate entry—but then quickly clipped back into place before Isabel could pass, now taut across her midriff.

"She's with me, man," Zack said with raised eyebrows to his bouncer acquaintance.

"Sorry, man. Not her." And the larger man turned his attention to the next desperate soul in line.

"Seriously, bro, she's my date."

But the bouncer didn't give Zack a second glance.

And Zack James wasn't one to be ignored. *Ever.*

Who the fuck was this oversized chump anyway? Stopping his woman in her tracks? Ignoring and insulting him? And breaking their vibe?

He looked at Isabel. A slightly mortified expression on her gorgeous face.

Fuck. He slipped his hand in and out of his pocket and subtly extended it to the massive man on door duty. "Take this and lift the rope. You need more hot women tonight, anyway."

The bouncer slowly returned his attention to Zack. "You deaf, *gringo?* Not *her.*" The large man referenced Isabel with a nod while obviously avoiding direct eye contact. The bouncer wouldn't even take the wad of bills Zack tried to slip into the man's giant hand.

Zack didn't want to make a scene, and Isabel's shifting stance and downturned eyes told him that she agreed. From across the velvet rope he whispered in her ear, "Go around back. I'll meet you and let you in. Go carefully," he said, looking down at her spiked heels.

Three minutes later, he had made his way through the overflowing dance floor to the rear emergency door. For pride's sake alone he'd sneak her in. Fuck the bouncer.

When he opened the door for Isabel, an ear-shattering alarm went off. It continued until the door slammed shut again, but he and Isabel were already lost in the thick crowd by the time security made it to the fire door.

The entire episode was comical; it made him feel twenty again. He watched her catch her breath after a fit of tearful laughter, a glow coming off her that enticed him all the more.

"Come on," he yelled as he pulled her deeper and deeper into the vibrating crowd. With the pulsating beat and the flashing strobes, the dance floor was alive, rising and falling to the electronica and throbbing bass. Zack found a pocket for them to *be*, pulled her close, and molded his body with hers. Moving in synch with the music, with each other, they became part of the club's rolling wave.

*

Three songs pulsed through them until he needed more accessibility. He couldn't contain his hunger for her. He led her off the dance floor the next instant into a small booth he'd spotted, just barely beating another couple to it.

He ordered them vodka on the rocks, and, since it was so slammed, a next round of shots while they had the waitress's attention.

"What the hell was the bouncer's deal? He acted like he had a personal grudge against you."

"I think…I dated his best friend in high school. Broke a heart or two, I guess." She threw him a coy smile.

"I can only imagine!" Zack smirked as he slid his hand behind her, rubbing small circles with his index finger where he remembered her sexy puzzle-shaped birthmark to be. Then his fingers streamed up and down the bevel of her spine. Fuck, her skin was perfect satin, divine. He wouldn't make it more than a short while this way. He knew that for certain.

The waitress returned with five drinks. He counted from his peripheral since his eyes remained glued to Isabel's almost involuntarily.

"I think there's one too many drinks here…Mandy," he said, glancing for a nanosecond at the waitress's name tag—then back to Isabel.

"This is from the woman at the red booth up there," the waitress said, pointing up to the mezzanine level. Zack shifted his gaze for another blip in time to a brunette supermodel-type who winked on cue.

He raised the glass to the stranger in thanks, and without so much as a hesitation or thought, he put it to Isabel's lips, tipped it back and whispered to her, "Hold it, and give it back to me." He wanted to give his benefactor a show.

Isabel did as she was told. She took the drink in her mouth, then putting her lush lips to his, slowly let the liquor flow into his mouth and down his throat. And with his hand now at the nape of her neck, he kept his lips pressed to hers long after the drink was downed. He tilted his head and teased her with his tongue, dipping into her gaping mouth, tickling and twirling until her tongue joined the dance. The sweet taste of her, combined with the lingering burning-cold vodka, made him harder than steel. He reached a new level of desperation to attack and take her, but quickly pulled away to maintain some element of control at their extremely public booth.

"Mmmm…that was some drink," she said with a trailing contentment in her voice, on her face, and in her slow, deep, panting breath.

"Incredibly ballsy, huh? Women can be such wicked bitches. I mean, sending a man a drink while he is obviously with someone." He wagged his head. "What insecurity…but it's because you are just so much hotter than she is." And he returned his lips to hers as he raked his hand through her hair, holding then pulling just to incite the slightest bit of pain. She moaned. *Fuck!* He needed *this* to end and *them, together, alone,* to start! But he couldn't stop his mouth's assault! The thought of prying himself away, pulling apart, separating for even a moment, it was just too much to bear. His thoughts blurred, his blood rushed. But it got too hot to breathe. Finally, he had to throw his head back to inhale fully and escape her resonating heat.

He grinned just as he started to catch his breath.

"What is it?" Isabel asked, her eyes softening with curiosity and maybe a slight hint of sweet insecurity.

"Look." He stroked her cheek with his hand and nodded to the mezzanine. The brunette who'd sent him the drink, grumbled to her friends and offered up the best damn evil eye he'd ever been "lucky" enough to receive.

*

She was delirious. And guilt spiked up her spine only every other second now. The other fractions of time were infiltrated by Zack's essence in such gloriously close proximity.

She downed her drink leaving only the ice, then slammed down the glass to regain Zack's fullest attention. *Screw that meddling brown-haired bitch.*

"I'm really thirsty too, for some reason." Zack winked at her and then followed suit, slamming his vodka down his throat.

She watched him process the heat of the drink as she filled her mouth with the remaining ice in her glass. He hit his glass to the table when empty and she moved closer to him on the smooth vinyl booth cushion. She put her fingers to her mouth, took out one cube of ice and moved her ice-cold hand with the slowly melting cube under the table, under her skirt, and placed it between her legs, her thighs squeezing it in place. God she needed that, an icy reprieve from the kinetic heat overtaking her at her very core.

Then she took his hand and united it with her now-cooled clit, screaming for warmth once again. God, the contrast. At the same time, her empty yet freezing-cold hand undid the drawstring to his linen pants and slid down to grab his electrified cock.

"Are you sure this is where you want to be right now?" she asked Zack. He beamed his confirmation and groaned to the ceiling. His response got her wetter still.

He laughed, but his expression, icy and serious. "Want? As long as I'm with you, Isabel, I know I'm exactly where I'm *supposed* to be." He moved his fingers masterfully, despite the distraction he faced between his own legs. "I've not been able to get you out of my head, Isabel."

She searched his face then. His tone, so severe, in such sharp, sexually charged contrast to their play beneath the table. And as she fought for focus in order to absorb the meaning behind his words, a man came toward them waving. Isabel recognized the man from somewhere, but she couldn't place his face.

"Isabel, right? How are you? It's me, Chris…the mirror install, a few weeks ago…"

Isabel slowed her stroking hand to a gentle-yet-firm hold so Zack would match her pace with his own hand, which was driving her absolutely insane, wedged in her slick folds, manipulating her throbbing nub with expert-level care. She wouldn't be able to find words for their surprise visitor, let alone gain enough composure to make eye contact, if Zack didn't give her a short-yet-unwanted break.

"Chris, right. Hey, yeah, the mirror… It's still hanging!" she said awkwardly, but thankful anything close to coherent came out.

Isabel's peripheral caught Zack's expression. He stared at the guy interrupting their foreplay, his narrowed gaze only slightly threatening. He seemed confident enough not to be jealous of the tall, tanned, and obviously stoned Canadian. And her giddiness at the potentiality of Zack's possessiveness was overshadowed by her impatient need to get back to Zack's throbbing cock in her fist.

Chris stood there, strangely silent, waiting for something. *Oh God, introductions?* No, that would be bad. The risk of Chris sticking around beyond just polite chitchat would then be way too high. And she didn't know, nor did she want to know, Zack's last name. Meanwhile, Zack had already gotten back to driving her mad, his fingers working her again like a master guitarist, strumming the tight, perfectly tuned strings of a fine mahogany acoustic. She blushed and squirmed while swallowing back her need to squeal.

But Chris finally broke the silence, though he still didn't get the hint to leave them. "I DJ here occasionally," Chris yelled over the reverberating bass, oblivious to her distracted state of bliss. "Ya know, just filling in. But my shift starts now." *Oh thank God!* "So…I guess I'll leave you guys to it, eh?"

Yes, for the love of all that's good and holy! "Good seeing you, Chris."

"Right, you too. Have an awesome night," he said to Isabel, who he winked and smiled at and then gave a somewhat cocky nod to her still-anonymous date before strolling off.

She caught Zack's eyes of glowing green. "That was Chris."

"Yes, I heard. He installed…your mirrors."

"He replaced a broken mirror in my bathroom and I guess he's also a substitute DJ here?"

"Isabel," he said, pausing his fingers' magic down below, making her heart pause a beat. "I don't want to talk about Chris."

A smoldering look melted over his face as he resumed his blissful play at her throbbing juncture. She held back a moan as his thick finger slid between her folds and deep into her begging core, making her cunt clench with need. In turn, she grasped his cock, her thumb relishing the drops of arousal he had for her at the ever-smooth tip of his crown. She used the sticky serum to stroke his pulsating length down to its base and up again.

God she was glad for the club's choice in long tablecloths at that moment, although she wasn't so sure that the lack of them would have stopped their sinful and totally inappropriate play. No, she wasn't so sure at all as he whirled her to the edge.

Then Zack took his finger out from her pooling, wet canal and began plucking her thong string—drawing it back then releasing it, snapping it up again then letting it go, torrentially teasing her hypersensitive clit. Deliberate, cruel, the thin string of her thong just barely stimulated. And the lack of his thick finger's heat and precise manipulation left her tortured and needy.

A fifth time, he lifted her thong from her hungry folds but paused there, giving her full freedom from the string. He held the fabric out for several seconds, still giving her nothing of his touch. He drew his finger back further, up toward her ass. His hand then gave a sharp tug, the thin strip of lace dividing her lips into more oozing pleasure coupled with delicious pain.

"Zack," she hissed then swallowed hard. "We need to go." She needed to be skin to skin with him. Needed it. Now.

CHAPTER 15

S HE COULDN'T STOP creaming in her barely existent panties, despite his socially acceptable distance as they walked through the Airington lobby, only his two fingers at the base of her back ushering her on. His limited touch was torturous, not enough, and just too much to take. She needed him fast and now and nothing less would do.

But she had to wait. He forced her to be patient. The polite space he gave her continued to and inside the elevator, then through the hall to the penthouse door, as if he was conscious of the hotel's cameras this time. Or maybe holding back to counter the association the penthouse held for them, trying to erase last time's incident before tearing her clothes off? Yeah, he was probably just being a gentleman. And if so, that was sweet, and good.

But the lack of his heat, his core-stirring distraction gave her time to think, to question.

That was bad.

The jumbled emotions that had boiled up on the beach behind the bar earlier that night started bubbling again. Doubting again. Underlying warnings in her head followed by Roberto's words crept in. But she fought back, calling up fantastical visions—a wild feast of sensual surges, rippling orgasms—to drown out the memory of last time's degrading episode. The one that'd had her raging off after drenching Zack in a vodka shower.

As he dipped his room key into the slot, his hand swept up her back, the warmth of his palm bringing her back to present, quieting all thoughts.

She felt anchored, secure. It would be okay. He was there. They'd be in each other's arms, in their groove again, in only minutes from now. He'd bring her the awaited release she needed.

And that was all she needed.

*

He escorted her inside. The suite was in a state of tidy chaos. Cleaned by housekeeping, yes, but only around the piles of paperwork, newspapers, maps, and strewn file folders lying on every available surface. *Busy boy.* Even the sofa was taken, his open laptop with its charging cable carelessly strung across the back of it. And under the machine, some 'Spanish for Idiots' guide? *Huh.*

Zack gave her a close-lipped smile and then scurried past her to move the computer and to consolidate the piles.

She watched him hungrily and with some amusement. That slight nervousness in him had returned as soon as they had crossed the suite's threshold, reminding her of his sweet, endearing charm at their first meeting when they'd joked and talked about nothing and everything for hours at The Five Breezes.

He brushed her arm on one walk by, and a shiver shot up her back. That sensual vibe of his trumped all. It had a power over her, a controlling, chilling power.

Zack was almost done shuffling things from one pile to another when she noticed a white linen sleeve hanging from a chair under a teetering pile of newspapers. Her heat turned to nervousness—it was definitely a woman's sleeve, judging from the cuff. Just as she felt a flood of regret replacing the soothing comfort she had felt, Zack caught her eying the pile and moved directly toward it. To cover it up? To make an excuse for another lingering article of some woman's clothing, another insult that her pride just wouldn't be able to take? Another jagged, disappointing end to an otherwise unbelievable, unforgettable night?

He picked up the newspapers and pulled out the white linen article. He brought it to his nose and smelled it as he walked it over to her, a smile in his eyes. "You left it here. It was my ticket to seeing you again. My excuse, so I could apologize, and explain and to"—he grabbed her and pulled her in, her face now inches from his—"be near you again. You're a drug, Isabel. An amazing, healing drug." He followed his words with a slow, tender kiss, gently dipping his tongue into her mouth, then sweetly sucking her top lip. "I really don't have a line of women, at least not since I met you, Isabel. It's not lip service. You've taken me over…entirely."

Warmth spread through her. She became a melting, dripping icicle in his hands, no longer sharp or painfully cold.

She was still mildly embarrassed, though, at her suspiciousness. It may even have been misconstrued by him as jealousy. And she wasn't jealous. He wasn't hers. Nor would she want him to be…or, she wasn't supposed to want him to be.

Whatever. The jacket being hers was a relief. The night could continue— she could allow herself to have him and be had by him, at least for the night. *Only tonight.*

But, Isabel. What he said…when he handed you the jacket.

She tried like hell to ignore the feelings his words had ignited in her, to halt her inner crazy, to switch off the voice of warning inside her.

Just get on with it, Isabel.

Right.

She yanked his shirt up to gain access to his drawstring again and was completely unprepared for the display. His tanned chest made of broad plates of tight muscle halted her breath. His smooth yet rippled stomach begged her fingers to feel, to caress. And yes, her fingertips surrendered, brushing his skin lightly, tracing the definition of his rock-hard middle, each muscular indentation making her sex shudder with anticipation.

But as she took in the sight of him, that damned boding voice of hers spoke up again. His drug reference. Was he *addicted* to her? Infatuated? Like Roberto's obsession, except that Roberto was like a brother while Zack was an ultra-magnetic god, a living pool of ecstasy she couldn't wait to dive into.

Screw the bigger issues. One night was all she asked for. She put her foot down—literally, her right foot stomped the suite's ultra-plush carpeted floor. Her mind had no say in this—as if any part of her being had a say. It was crystal clear that Zack held all the control, like a telepathic, hypnotic, otherworldly hold on her. Under his spell and his heat, her hands continued to fumble like mad with his drawstring, but then his hands came up to hers, gently stopping her anxious efforts.

"Wait." He pulled her hands up and around his neck. "Isabel, I'm so trying not to freak you out right now, but the last two weeks have been a kind of hell for me, not being able to find you. So now that I have you, I just really want, you know, to relish every ounce of you. And I want to explain." He kissed her on the crook of her neck and led her by the hand to the minibar.

Wait? That's all she heard.

Déjà vu. Please, no.

Patience, Isabel. She nodded and blinked at him. "Slow, of course."

She watched him pour the two glasses of vodka then curl his lip as he put hers firmly in her hand. "To drink, not to pour."

She gave him a flirtatious glare and lifted her glass. "To drinking, not pouring…together."

He met her glass with his, then they took their first pulls while holding each other's fiery stares like tigers in heat. She liked this, his attention, their deliberately slow and sensual vibe. *Slow wasn't so bad.* And she'd keep going with the pace he was setting, despite her teetering volition. But if too much more time passed, she knew her mental processes would reign victorious. And if that happened, she'd bolt, no hanging panties needed.

He kept her gaze as he relaxed into his drink, then began to make small talk. She inhaled, seeking more endurance, more energy it took for her not to attack him. The bar between them was already too much hard separation, and idle chatter was not going to help matters. Even his voice—God, so thick and deep—ramped up her arousal.

No, she had to move things along, get closer to her goal, closer to him.

*

She downed the rest of her drink. The glimmer in his eye when she set the empty glass down made her smile and clench hard at her core. The firewater flowed down and through her. Spiking heat and all, she began to forget her worries, her rush, her angst. Suddenly, finally she could just be there with him. God, how at ease she felt. It was more than a comfort level, but an actual physical ease. She even breathed deeper, more fully. She almost felt at home, her shoulders relaxed and lowered, allowing for more air to fill her chest, bringing with it a tingling sensation that rose up to her head, a heightened peace.

And with it came a solid confidence. She tore herself away from his searing gaze and moved to the sofa. She sunk into the plush middle cushion and just watched him, craving him from across the expansive room. His back muscles and shoulder blades flexed and shifted as he returned the liquor bottle to its shelf, the glasses to the sink, and the minibar towel to the counter. She bit her lower lip, her eagerness for him growing, mounting. His burgeoning shoulders framed that chiseled V-shaped torso down to his waist, culminating at his perfectly sculpted ass draped beautifully by his khaki linen pants—those pants that she wanted off him. Badly.

Okay, so the impatience factor had returned full force—though still laced with that *meant-to-be-here* ease. She crossed her right leg over her left to dam the flow of excitement threatening to pour from her sex before he could even make it over to her.

He left the bar just achingly slow while her hunger grew. He finally crossed the room to her, his expression both pensive and determined. His face, tilted slightly, studied her, like he wanted to tell her something. He licked his lips and swallowed hard as if in preparation. Maybe more words to clear the air about last time? But she knew she couldn't handle any further delay, mentally, or, for God's sake, physically. And she didn't want any further explanation from him. She somehow trusted his sincerity, that she wouldn't be disrespected by him again, consciously or otherwise. He had actually gone searching for her with nothing but her first name, hunting for her to apologize.

And, yes, also to have her.

But what did any of that matter, anyway? This would be it. Their one night together, their first and their last. And right then, she needed the night to begin. She just needed him near her, over her, in her, of her.

"May I interrupt your thoughts," he whispered, kneeling in front of her, dragging his thumb along her jawline. "I want to tell you so much, Isabel. So goddamn much. But my willpower is only so strong. I thought the drink would help, but you, on this couch, I...I can tell you what's been on my mind after—"

She pressed her mouth to his to silence him, pulling him by his shirt collar tight against her anguished, throbbing sex right there between her sprawling, wide-open and welcoming legs.

CHAPTER 16

SHE RIPPED AND buttons flew. She untied and unzipped and pulled. And he was all there, his long, hard steel which she'd held, throbbing hot, only a bit ago at the club. But up to that point, she'd only imagined its vital definition and girth in her mind's eye.

Now her eyes, mesmerized, could relish all of him, there in her elated, heart-thumping reality.

She leaned in, starving for a taste. Then she consumed him, a never-ending mouthful of sweet hard candy. Pure bliss. He bore back ecstatically, then leaned forward again, anxious to watch the devouring of his entire cock by her tongue-moistened lips.

She pulled him out quickly, coyly, then smiled at the slight taste of him in her mouth. Her eyes hit his as she left him throbbing and moved to stand. Slowly, methodically, she removed her top overhead and dropped it to the floor. He shifted, his jaw tightening, his hips lifting in the air.

His reaction burned her alive.

Faster now, she undid the clasp of her skirt and wiggled her curves out of it. He inhaled through flared nostrils. And how she loved his frustration, her sex getting wetter and hotter from his intensity alone. She flung her high heels behind her, then looked down at her black lace bra cupping her breasts, her nipples out, begging for his tongue to come and play, to circle, to tease. She tilted her head and moved her eyes to meet his. *Not yet.* She'd make him wait just a little longer. Because he'd kept her waiting.

Her hands slid down to the crotch of her matching and moist lace panties. Her fingers found within her slick folds that tiny bit of material he had used to snap her into reeling lunacy. She pulled that little lace shred to one side, her pulsating clit now free and on clear display for him, just below her utterly silken mound. Her sex beckoned—no, screamed—for his touch.

But teasing him, keeping him deprived and wanting, sparked her senses to a new level. She moved her exposed cunt closer to him, inch-by-aching-inch closer. Then she kicked her leg up on the high back of the sofa, her arousal so near his mouth that he could almost lick her pussy clean. But when he reached for her with his fidgety, anxious hands, she clicked her tongue and shifted her hips back again. "Uh-uh, look from there, buddy." She grinned with an intentional glint of glee in her voice.

Then she slid her index finger into her mouth and got it dripping wet. She slowly slid it down between her heavy breasts, her cleavage glistening with perspiration, then around a nipple twice, making it pebble more, teasing him harder. Her finger continued its downward path, over her stomach, into her navel, dipping in and out, making her squirm for a nanosecond. Then she ran her finger straight down from there, down to her anxious, clenching cunt, which burned, begged for direct and immediate attention.

When her moist trigger finger met her glistening wet clit and began tapping and twirling herself into rolls of ecstasy, she watched his eyes. They were filled with ravenous frustration. She knew he was so close to losing his ability to keep away. She had him where she wanted him, and she loved the control, at least for this one illusory moment.

*

He attacked. His arm wrapped around her perfectly round ass, skin so smooth, radiant, hot. He yanked her onto him. He sank back into the sofa while his two hands lifted her fully, placing her perfect pussy onto his summoning mouth. He needed to taste her. He ripped her thong at the waist to get unbridled access to her glorious, beckoning velvet folds, so anxious, too sweet. She was so swirling wet. He sucked her delicately, drinking her in, lapping her up. Like an elixir from above.

She moaned when he focused his lips at her clit, sucking more, maybe a little too zealously, but ravenous for her, he couldn't hold back.

She grabbed his hair and tightened her thighs around his head. He could tell she was ready, so ready. And then she came, hard and rhythmic, squirting sweet syrup into his mouth, her body above him convulsing with each violent spasm. Oh God, this woman! He stayed at her juncture, his mouth pressed hard and firm to her, unwilling to let her go. He moaned as she finished, moving his hands up her ass, squeezing and massaging, memorizing the feeling of her.

A final hum then whimper, and she slid down and folded into his lap. "My plan has changed," she whispered. Out of breath but not out of energy, she shifted to straddle him. She began grinding into him, her soaking wet pussy gliding over his rock-solid cock.

"Plan?" he asked, locked into her deep golden eyes.

"I think it'll be more like five or six. Not to be selfish, but I can see it won't be any trouble for you," she said, as if he'd read and understood her thoughts.

"Five or six what, angel?" His brain was clouded, the rhythmic motion of her lower lips further hardening his pulsating rod, driving him wild, making it impossible to think.

"Orgasms," she stated in a breathy rasp.

Sweet obliterating orgasms were certainly the plan, but he was a sky's-the-limit kind of guy.

"Oh no, darlin', don't place limits. Not with me." He rolled her from the couch to the floor. Dragged her to the rug in front of the tall frameless windows. Fifty floors above Vallarta, as if on stage, a show for the world, and for her. It was his sense of pride inciting him to deliver to the fullest.

But when he looked down at her, his frame now hovering over her, caging her, owning her, she met his gaze, held it, owning him right the hell back.

Her soul-deep eyes drilled into his, shards of her heat piercing his heart with that look. And all he wanted now was to please her. Screw the outside world, and screw his own needs. Fuck his pride! All he wanted was her pleasure, her release. Jesus, he wanted her happiness, above all else.

With full and utter focus, he tended her.

And teased her. With the dripping tip of his solid-steel cock, he tickled her mound, then her folds and pulled back to line her inner thigh. Shifting his cock forward again, he rounded her velvety lotus. But only for a moment. He pulled away again, wedging his steel this time between her welcoming ass cheeks, slowly dragging a warm line of pre-cum along the way.

"Fuck me!" she cried out. "Fuck me now, damn it!"

"No, no. Not yet, angel."

He shifted far up on her writhing body, his hands holding firm her fleshy breasts. Then he thrust his engorged cock between them, his shimmering crown pressing up against her chin. She bent her head and flicked her tongue at his tip. He gasped. She tickled him again, leaving her sweet saliva on the sensitive spot at the start of his ridge. The massive suite's icy current gave him a chill, forcing him to blow out a hard stream of air, his cock's heightened sensitivity just too much to take.

On his knees, straddling her gossamer body, he paused, in awe, not believing the view beneath him. On stage again, he loved this play, he loved his part in it, and he was enamored by the woman who played opposite him.

*

His thumbs tapped at each of her hard pert nipples, teasing her, making her squirm. His throbbing erection remained cushioned between her weighty tits which glistened with her perspiration. She writhed under his heft, so he reached back with one hand and lodged it between her thighs, cupping her achingly hot mound, keeping her cunt anchored with pressure, just until he was ready to partake.

With her full breasts surrounding his cock, he slid himself forward and back, coming to the edge, too close to exploding over it. Then she brought her fingers to the root of his length, then lower, lightly brushing and kneading his sensitive sac, driving him mad, making him thrust faster and faster.

"Not…yet," he said to himself out loud. He wanted her hot clenching cunt gripping him endlessly when he did finally go.

But he was too goddamn close.

He grabbed her shoulders and flipped her over like a pillow in the middle of the night. His stiff cock hovered, elevated in the air, bobbing until it slapped down on the dip of her lower back. Her birthmark, his missing piece, stared up at him, and he smiled, slowed himself down, remembered how hard it had been to find this angel again. He hadn't even *found* her, he'd just happened upon her again. Thankfully.

He leaned back, taking her smooth mocha body in with his eyes and into his hands. His hands caressed her arms and her back, massaged her sweet round ass, then, reaching behind him, they slid down her silky thighs, calves, ankles, feet, brushing her skin with just his fingertips.

Her breasts pressed against the floor, spilling out from under her. He tilted forward, pressing his needy cock into her as he traced every inch of her with his fingers. She shivered and arched her back from the chill.

Smiling, living for each and every one of her on-cue reactions, he sat up, grabbed his raging hard-on and dribbled his pre-cum down her spine. Then he leaned in and blew a light stream of air over the shimmering trail he'd left. She quivered again, flat on the carpeted floor—a deep, resounding purr trembled out of her.

He leaned down. At her mouth, he kissed her and traced her luscious pout with his anguishing tongue. He was ready, ready to focus on being locked into the angel beneath him, getting as deeply connected as humanly possible.

His mouth still at hers, he drew his hips back then swiftly jammed his thick shaft between her ass cheeks, making her gasp. He inhaled pure pleasure at the sounds she made. He pressed his body into hers, needing her heat, then suddenly pushed up with his arms, planked over her, hovering. A disappointed moan rumbled from her throat, but was replaced with a sated hum the next instant as he dragged his cock down the curve of her ass crack. His magic wand tickled her starburst with its tip on the way to her screaming, velvety core.

She lifted her ass up into the air for him, her hole visibly tightening and opening, calling to him so loudly he could hardly control himself. Then his crown reached just outside of glory and held there, trembling with an overpowering need.

He reached for a condom from the rear pocket of his pants which had been discarded on the floor just feet away. Isabel panted below him while he worked to catch his own breath, his chest heaving from the impossible view she had on display just for him.

Racing against his impending explosion, his teeth tore opened the packet. He rolled on the rubber, parted her luscious folds with the tip of his voracious cock, and slammed into her glorious, oozing sex.

*

Savage fucking sweetness.

Tight and hot—just as he'd dreamed she'd be, an all-encompassing heaven—while, at same time, her canal hugged his length, warm and tender, like he was fucking home.

He pushed himself in just a bit farther and got a guttural moan of delight out of her. Oh God, her noises, they made him lengthen all the more. And the bliss of her clenching cunt, it made him lightheaded. Then he hit her depth. Fucking divine! But his lustful greed for her had no end. No end in sight.

He slid out, slick and wet, then pushed back into her perfection fast and hard. Keeping that rhythm, relishing it, he pushed his throbbing staff to her depths again and again and again.

His surprise ability to hold out was only balanced by the infinite joy of filling her with everything he had. His cock inside her was a perfect fit, and at that moment, he swore he could've gone on inside her forever.

But he had brought her to the point of no return without realizing it, while he almost lost it to her cries. Her body trembled, jerked through her second climax.

"Keep fucking me! I have more…in me. Don't you dare stop!" she demanded, writhing under him, her fists pounding the floor.

"I wouldn't dare, Isabel. Fuck—I wouldn't"—he groaned—"dare"—he grunted—"stop." *Hell, I'd go on for eternity if you'd let me.*

He continued his torrent—glad, proud, elated to put her high peak before his own. He infused her with his *everything*. And delivering full and complete satisfaction gave him renewed energy, control, stamina. He would goddamn earn his release, that he knew. And if he could time it right, he'd come in on one of her waves—her biggest wave, her typhoon.

His onslaught drove on. Judging by her new round of screams, he was bringing her to the ends of the earth. And by proxy, he was right there with her.

She breathed his name over and over while frantically clawing at the carpet. With desperation, she lifted her delectable, full backside to meet him, his steel still inside her warm, wet pussy.

She pushed up, now on her hands and knees. "Now like this," she said panting, showing him how she wanted to get fucked. Zack loved it, her initiative, her ever-sexy goddamn confidence.

Arms straddling hers, he leaned forward and kissed her hard, a second endless and deep connection. Through their mouths' clash she panted, "More. Give me more of you."

Fuck me! He tore his lips away. "What this woman wants"—tongues *re-tangled*, then a gasp for air—"this woman gets." Choppy words, rasped.

Give, he would. He pushed himself up to kneel and braced to pound her harder. With utter focus, his eyes absorbed the view—her curves, her edges and lines, her smooth juts and ledges and cliffs to pure bliss. But his eyes needed more. The pleasure-assault continued while he leaned left to watch her breasts rock and sway with his rhythmic thrusts. They were just begging for attention. He straightened for balance then took one delicious handful, her rock-hard nipple wedged, squeezed between his fingers, while his other hand gripped her hip to jerk her ass back to slap against him. His cock, then just inside her entrance, rocketed into her like a torpedo. She gasped with awe-stricken delight. *Mmmm-hmm.* More fuel, more momentum to keep driving and drilling into her.

And, holy fuck, that echo of slapping skin! It sent a jolting current through him. He needed more of it, more of that cracking sound—like lightning. He slapped her right ass cheek. She squealed. *Fuck, is this a dream?* His desire to fill and fulfill her, rocketed to beyond *never-ending*. He glanced down at his thrusting hips meeting her beautiful bare ass, and, damn, the reverberation of her quaking buttocks and the slight mark of his hand there on her perfectly smooth skin, it was more than enough to send him over the cliff.

But no, not yet, Zack. Don't go yet.

While pumping her still, she twisted her head, mouth gaping for him. He leaned forward and around, his tongue primed to catch hers. Their tongues flicked and twirled and teased—a dance—until he caught her eyes. Hungry eyes with a glint of contrasting sorrow as deep as the sea. His chest filled hot and wide for her. He slowed his plunging hips and kissed then brushed her lips with his. A touch of *tender* to go with their raging lust.

But her left hand flew to his ass, leveraging for balance, grasping for force. Now she owned a fistful of his hardworking ass cheek, slamming him harder into her, each thrust a torrential attack of his hips, his thighs, his booming, ever-hard cock into her almighty center, her celestial goddamn cunt.

Out of his control—and all in hers—frantic tongues tangled once again. His breath got heavy, hurricane force. She somehow turned her gasps and moans into words, her voice weaving through their desperate and savage kiss. "My God, you…go on forever…inside me. So thick and…long. So good… so right."

And that did it. For Zack, nothing else existed in the world. Roaring from the depths of his chest, electrified and in time, he glided in and out of her toward his brink. Knowing that she felt, and loved, every extensive inch of his manhood was too much for him to bear.

And as his eruption threatened, the sound of her rapid breathing froze, caught in a long inhale. He knew her dam was ready to break again too, the impending dive from her ultimate peak. And he felt her shiver in his grasp as she held her breath in until…

Simultaneous eruption.

He dove headfirst with her.

Ecstatic streams of creamy fire shot from him—full, fast, forever. Each and every one of her pussy's tight crushing spasms sent a kinetic shock through him while milking his cock of the forever-flow of thick, hot cum.

He felt her exhale and gasp for oxygen while her glorious body shuddered beneath him.

A final jolt grabbed him as he shot the last of his liquid lust, his hips smashing against her sumptuous behind all the way through.

She looked back at him, her eyes wide and intense, searing into his. A sweet, exhausted smile claimed her face before she surrendered into the floor, shattered.

Sweat-drenched and spent, he gently fell onto her, his chest sticking to her back. He shuddered from the aftershocks. Feeling her intermittent trembling, he mustered up the energy to shift to his side, rolling her bare, limp body with him, keeping her wrapped in his arms while his vibrating-albeit-sheathed cock still reveled in the vast hot pool of her sweet cunt's liquid ecstasy.

"See?" he whispered. "No limits."

She smiled then nodded her agreement. "Now let's move to your bed. I want more."

He shook his head in awe. "You are perfection incarnate, woman. Sheer fucking perfection."

CHAPTER 17

ZACK HAD RAVAGED her, or more, she'd ravaged him—twice more in the comfort of the plush penthouse bed, and although he should have been delirious, he lay propped up on his elbow watching her sleep.

He tittered to himself. However clichéd, she really did look like a shimmering bronze angel. Renaissance-relaxed on her back, one elbow out, hand behind her head—like Venus in Giorgione's masterpiece. And her stunning breasts brimmed over, on display for him. He focused more closely on their rise and fall, as she took slow, deep, quiet breaths, breaths of their shared air. It was a connection he still had with her without being in her.

He had a strange desire to feel her pulse, to feel her physical heartbeat. Her other arm rested along her side, just next to his body. He shifted her snug cuff bracelet up just a bit to access her wrist...

Then he flinched and recoiled. The long thin scars shocked him. Near sickened him.

What the hell had she done to herself? What could have motivated her to attempt—he stopped his thought. His strong, confident, idealized angel had taken to slicing herself, and the image didn't fit. *No.* He wouldn't let it.

It killed him to know she had ever felt that much pain. What agony had led her to this? He took a gulp of mind-clearing air. Swallowing back the knot of this knowledge echoed in his ears.

He watched her more closely. Her soft lids twitched, maybe from a dream. This peaceful angel sleeping next to him was here with him. And that's what mattered, history didn't. Hers or his. *Everyone has skeletons.* And hers wouldn't frighten him away. The opposite, in fact. If Isabel would let him in, he would be there for her—constant and committed, he'd be there. By choice, he'd be there.

With his mother, he'd had no choice. When she fell into her own downward spiral of depression, Zack had been a scared-shitless teenager who had to suck it up and deal. But at least his mother had made no overt suicide attempts—her prescription drug abuse was subtle, hidden behind the door of the well-decorated master bedroom his father had left behind.

He swore to himself then that whatever pain Isabel hid or held or had before would be rooted out, so help him. She goddamn deserved nothing but pure contentment, happiness, pleasure. And he was the one to ensure that. Of that he was positive.

*

Isabel woke up. The clock on the side table read 2:00 AM. *Shit!* She'd fallen asleep in his arms. She should've been gone hours ago. But she didn't want to leave then, and she didn't want to leave now. She wanted to stay and wake up in his grasp, tight against his wide protective chest.

Damn it. Stay or go? Go with her gut, her heart, her desire, or go with her reason?

She looked out to the bay through the bedroom's balcony doors. The view and the promise of the fresh night air coming in off the water were calling her. In the name of procrastination and opportunity to see her beautiful Vallarta from so high up, she got up to head out there. Zack was still asleep after all.

With the bedsheet wrapped around her, she opened the French door to the balcony, but the night chill pushed her back inside. So brisk for Vallarta in late May. She reached for the closest thing to her, a light jacket of Zack's draped over a side chair, and threw it on.

She made her way back outside and blinked at the expansive view. Instantaneous calm. Banderas Bay held her heart, her sweetest memories, and from this high up, it took her breath away. The vastness amazed her.

Then she looked back inside through the French doors at Zack, curled up, sleeping with a pillow in place of her body. His auburn hair was strewn over his sculpted cheek, hiding his sweetly sleeping eyes. He amazed her too. Being in his arms, in his gaze, in his bed—also amazing. And when he was inside her, well, that was implausibly amazing.

Damn it, Isabel.

A cool gust whipped a chill through her. She gripped the collar of the jacket with one hand while she put her other hand into the pocket.

From it she pulled a folded receipt with a handwritten name and number scribbled on it. Her heart froze.

None of your business, Isabel.

But wasn't it? She'd just slept with the man after all, the man who'd supposedly been hunting for her. And now in her hand was *another* goddamn woman's love note! She looked down at it. *Destiny*, it read. She unfolded the paper and flattened it out in her hand, then flipped it over: *The Inferno Club.* Nearly eight thousand dollars? Dated last week. Well-after they'd first met. After she'd left his suite the first time she'd been insulted by this scumbag. Oh, and after his "desperate search" for her had already begun.

Desperately seeking Isabel—*yeah, right.*

*

He jolted awake when his arm fell hard on the empty mattress beside him instead of landing on the heavenly body that had been rising and falling with every deep, sleepy breath she took.

Now she was nowhere. He hadn't even felt her slip out of bed.

A three-minute search of the entire penthouse made him know she'd left. Without a trace.

And goddammit, he hadn't gotten her fucking number! Again! How had he forgotten? Because just like last time, he'd lost his damn mind around her.

But shit, how the hell would he have known she'd damn skip out on him? In the morning he would've remembered to get it, and her fucking last name too.

Why'd she leave this time? Not a word, not a note. Nothing. A commitment-phobe, okay, and with a history of some deep-seated despair, yes. But to damn leave him in the middle of the night after they'd made such a connection? Beyond a connection—a symphonic fucking masterpiece!

And now, goddammit, he sounded like a woman…a woman scorned! What was more, he was suddenly, shamefully aware that he had put countless women in this very position, this same exact spot that had him screaming at the walls of his mind. As bad as that fucker in the bar his first night in town. As bad if not worse even, because Zack James knew better. *Was* better. *Fuck!*

And now, like a perfectly timed clock, he felt the return of that familiar and insatiable sinking hole inside. He'd had a twelve-hour break from it, from the void, just like the last time he'd been with Isabel, that first time they'd met.

Zack closed his eyes. It was bone-chillingly cold in his hotel room. And dead quiet, except for the buzz of the mini fridge in the next room and his sporadic sighs, an emotionally fraught reflex.

He reviewed the evening in his head. He'd been right, Isabel was different. She was real, raw, more grounded than any woman he had ever known. She exuded a humble confidence, like she knew herself and accepted herself while most women he encountered pretended to be anyone *but* who they truly were.

The smell of her coconut scent drifted up to his nose from the pillow she had left empty next to him. He stared up at the ceiling, remembering the confident, cool control she'd exhibited with every stride, every word, and every hot, sensual stroke during their night out in the world.

And how he craved that honest desire she'd exhibited for him when they were in his suite, in private, swimming in each other's bodies. Total interlocked and unadulterated ecstasy. The thought of her body, her eyes, her taste—she'd driven him wild. Drove him wild. Down to his primal center. He started to harden, his erection calling out for her, but of course, she was long fucking gone.

Zack knew that his pining for Isabel was so far beyond the carnal need of his cock. He felt different around her on so many levels—challenged, human, alive. Her strong and objective demeanor toward life and, *for fuck's sake*, toward sex and toward release made his insides vibrate. A new, effervescent rumble in his chest had replaced that inner void a thousand fold when he was in her presence.

He would find her again. He couldn't lose that feeling or last through another torturous period with the void eating at his goddamn soul.

And when he did find her, he would waste no time telling her the things he needed to. Damn his libido. He'd wait and make her wait for their passions' demands. He'd go slow, get to know her, and let her get to know him, the real him she had helped him discover, all without letting her out of his sight again—at least, not without a direct line of communication, damn it!

He could do casual if that's what she wanted. No strings to start. At least he thought he could. He'd try. He was new to giving a fuck, new to caring and wanting, no, rather needing a woman that essentially, that vitally.

And convincing her shouldn't be hard. He was already sure she was on his page with respect to their fit together as lovers. The level of pleasure they had reached together was hard to describe and would be even harder to match with anyone else. He hadn't felt that aroused or climaxed that hard before, ever. And Zack had an enormous and global pool of experience for comparison.

But it was unlike Zack James to jump ahead, emotions at the helm, before organically processing all variables. He had to address the first issue at hand—*Why'd she leave again?* He had done nothing wrong. He knew there were no remnants of other women hanging from light fixtures, no lipsticked messages on mirrors. From the deepest part of himself he knew everything was so absolutely right. And if it was that whole *no-relationships*, one-night-only line, well, again, he understood that stance better than anyone on Earth. But he also knew he had found the exception to his rule, and he was equally positive that he was the exception to hers.

He would just have to prove it to her. But he had to find her first. Again.

Being Zachary James, he would. Without a shadow of a doubt, he would find his angel and make her his.

CHAPTER 18

ISABEL WAS SO relieved to be home. She checked that her sofa was empty before she threw herself onto it, completely drained. Her heart and head were, that is. But as for her body, a high-frequency buzz hummed through her, reverberating echoes of sated pleasure he'd left in her from their endless rounds of raw and rocking sex. And she hated every resounding vibration of it.

She had, of course, intended to leave Zack after she'd gotten her unprecedented climax, or climaxes as it were, and yes, it had been harder to leave than she'd thought.

Hell, finding that receipt had really been a blessing, a reminder of the man's true damn nature.

But what a dumbass she'd been.

Disappointment flooded her, and she felt herself sinking into it neck deep. She tried hard to take a full breath but couldn't. The harder she tried, the shallower and more unfulfilling her breathing became. Damn her faulty intuition, her total absence of judgment. And, yes, her lack of self-control, too. Falling prey to his overpowering, overflowing magnetism, which had led to the most erotic, in-sync sexual experience of her entire ill-fated life, made her wince. The regrettable, pathetic, self-effacing thought of it sucked the air out of her lungs further and churned her stomach too.

She dragged herself from the couch before she fell asleep there, knowing that her back would kill her in the morning if she didn't move to her bed. On her way to the kitchen for water, her microwave clock beamed the time in bright screaming yellow. It already *was* morning. She'd have a total of three hours of sleep before she had to be up and ready for a wedding gig, one she'd have to look and attempt to feel great for. It would no-doubt suck.

She continued to the sink, filled a glass, and walked past her sliding glass door on the way to her room. Motivated by a gut instinct— however well that whole instinct thing had been working for her—she thought to check that the door was secure with a quick lock check. Silly and unnecessary, really, being as far out from town as she was. But with her hand on the handle, she yanked on it.

And she flew with the fast gliding door, her glass of water joining her.

She fell to the floor, just stopping herself from cracking her forehead on the tile by instinctively putting her hands out, palms down. Stunned, pissed and confused, she could only stay there frozen, catching her breath and gathering her wits before getting up, knowing there was a maze of glass shards and water pooling around her. The dark was stark, the moonless night lending not a glint or glow through the somehow unsecured sliding glass door. All she could see was the yellow digital time on the microwave mocking her tired eyes through the reflection on the glass. Her head turned to the side, surrendering onto the back of her hands.

Now, staring at the slider door track, expecting to see a splintered mess of a wooden rod wedged in the track, she noticed instead there was no 'security' pole at all.

A minute later she was calling her brother, Antonio.

"Hey, I'm home…Yeah, no, I'm fine. But, um, did you move that security pole from my slider by chance? From its track? The one I had there because the door lock was broken…remember?"

*

Within twenty minutes, Antonio had come. With his heavy D-cell flashlight in hand for light and as a potential weapon, he checked the condo and its perimeter twice.

He sat down next to her on the sofa. "I definitely didn't move the pole because I hadn't found time to fix the lock yet. Someone else had to have removed it. So, I'm staying here with you until we figure this out, and we'll get all your locks changed tomorrow. I'm sorry I didn't make it a priority in the first place, Isa." He got up then and moved toward the storage closet. "I guess we need another temporary pole"—he stuck his head in the closet—"even if *Abuelo's* place—I mean *your* place—is this far out," he said, slightly muffled as he rummaged through the closet.

"Antonio, my gut is saying something, something I'm really trying to ignore…because I left Roberto here alone to lock up a few weeks ago, but I've had service guys in and out, with the mirror replacement, and the electrician…Lucinda was here, too, but she fell asleep on the couch, didn't even make it outside to have moved the pole."

Antonio brought his head out of the closet. "Well, when *was* the last time you actually noticed the pole there? Try to pinpoint…"

"I, uh…God, I've just been so busy…definitely my first few days here I noticed the rod. And…I guess I haven't been out on the deck since, and hadn't thought to check it except for the first few nights here. Even when I come and go, I just take it for granted because of how far out of town I am, like you said." She paused a beat, then continued to think out loud. "But, shit, forget about the pole…Roberto could've just as easily made a copy of my key in that one day he'd had it. The missing pole wouldn't even have mattered, if he could just come in and out as he pleased through the front door! And maybe he just forgot to put the pole back, or…or he got worried about being seen coming in through the front door in case one of the few people in the complex spotted him and kept the pole so he could get in through the back door. The *silent* sliding back door. Because the front door lock catches, you know. I would've woken up if he'd come in the front! Oh God, Antonio!"

"Whoa, now. Just, let's not jump to conclusions here, *m'ija*," he said, moving back to the couch. He sat down and took her quivering hands in his to steady them. "*Tranquila*, Isa."

She looked out the glass door to the sea of endless black beyond the beach below. The image of Roberto crept into her head, with his peering ice-blue eyes and his hot silenced breath hovering over her as she slept. Potentially any night over the past few weeks Roberto could have entered her home without a sound beyond the smooth and easy glide of her back door. He'd had free rein to watch her, and then he'd be able to leave again without a trace.

Chills ran through her. She felt violated while, at the same time, a sense of guilt filled her chest. The blame *was* hers. His obsession could have been prevented by her in the first place if she had been in control and lucid that one drunken night. Or even after that night, she should have gotten through to him and not brushed off his obvious infatuation.

Mid-thought, she turned to her brother. "But, Antonio…no police. We can't do that to him."

"Again, Isa, if it even *was* Roberto. I mean, what if Ray had taken it to be helpful? Or the service guys who were in and out. And you said Lucinda was here? She could have moved it intending to go out there, right? We know Lucinda, flighty as hell. Or, a real stretch, but *Tío* Raul, being the *cabrón* that he is. He's still pissed that his piece of shit kids didn't get this condo. Either way, right now, no police…only because, what the hell would we tell them? 'I'm calling to report a stolen rod?'" One brow arched. "You know our *policía*. And anyway, a potential break-in with nothing stolen and no one hurt doesn't make for much of a case. Can't see them dusting for prints over it, you know?" He patted her hand. "But I sure as hell am staying here with you until we get this place secured." His tone was quiet but stern.

She nodded, so thankful for him because she really was freaked out. She'd lived in a pretty sketchy rental in town before this, but strangely had never felt as unsafe then as she did now.

He patted her hand, kissed her on the forehead, and went back to the closet to resume his search for a temporary security pole.

"Thank you, Antonio. For coming out, staying with me, being here for me."

"You shouldn't have to thank your family for help, Isabel. You should damn well expect it. I'm sorry you've had such assholes in *your* family to feel like you have to say thank you." Just then he found the mop, unscrewed the head, and stuck the makeshift security pole into the slider track. Then he pulled his keys, wallet, and cell from his pockets and placed them on the coffee table.

"You must be tired. Let me get you bedding for the pullout so you can get some sleep."

She felt horrible about putting him out, despite his reassurances and kind words. Granted, Antonio had no wife or kids of his own to go home to, but his growing limo business, working his ass off day in, day out, managing and being responsible for dozens of employees, and still, without a moment's hesitation he's by her side. And add her hex, potentially risking his safety by being in his mere vicinity for too long—she hated it. But her brother was ever loyal. And when it came to this type of situation—Antonio, the Tae Kwon Do master—there was no one she felt safer with.

Isabel went to the linen closet carrying her nerves and worry with her. Bringing the pile of bedding back to the sofa, she walked past the slider and tried to take a full, clearing breath. She couldn't. Her chest was stuck, her body on high alert along with her mind. She looked at the slider while attempting to swallow back the knot at the start of her throat. Then she noticed something out on the deck.

She took a step toward the glass and squinted her eyes to combat the night's darkness. A tiny wildflower lying just outside the threshold, its color impossible to make out in the staunch blackness, just its silhouette, like the one Roberto had given to her when she'd moved in. Not proof by any means, a sign though for sure. And signs meant everything to her. With this sign, a different kind of chill starting at her feet shot up to her head. It paused her in her tracks. Her whole body shuddered from the sensation and with it, a wave of confident awareness took her. Her jaw clenched. She swallowed again, then turned to Antonio.

"It's Roberto. I know it, in my gut. Antonio, will you go over there? Talk to him? Check. Please?"

Antonio and Ray were the only people on Earth who believed in her curse *and* still stayed by her side despite it. And after her mother's passing, when she announced a gut feeling, Antonio listened.

"You couldn't stop me if you tried, little sister, just let me get the locks changed first and fit an alarm system, too. Then I will. I'll check him out."

She nodded, blinked a thank you, and continued zombie-like to fix the pullout. When done, she kissed his cheek, then shuffled to her bedroom, all in an abysmal daze.

A heavy feeling pushed her into the tile floor, as if it was thick, seizing tar, and with every next step, the more sucked-under she felt. That image of Roberto's eyes intruding on her life, in her home, at her sanctuary, weighed on her, strangling her heart with a mile-long chain.

Roberto, damn it, what the hell are you doing?

CHAPTER 19

ISABEL MET RAQUEL at the Bay View Hotel the next morning, where the Rine/James wedding was being held. She wanted to show her face to the delegates to help bolster her assistant. The banquet manager, the customer service manager and the other jigsaw pieces to the hotel-side of the event puzzle were all at her beck and call. Since Vallarta was heading into hibernation for the hot summer season, weddings were their last hurrah until November. Wedding planners were treated like royalty then.

"The ladies are at the pool already, and I think most of the groomsmen are in the sauna or still sleeping. Late night," Raquel reported. "And by the way…the maid of honor, the bride's older sister, seems pissed that Lucinda isn't heading the event herself. Just be warned, she's a bit of a handful."

"I like a challenge." Isabel winked at her assistant, then moved onto other details—the dresses, the schedule, the vendors—until Charlie, the hotel's customer service manager approached.

"Ah, I found you, Isabel. You just move too fast for me. I'm an old man…have pity." He laughed and kissed her cheek in greeting. "You look lovely, Isabel. As always." Charlie had treated her a bit like a daughter from her very start with Golden Rings.

"Thanks, Charlie." *But I know I look like I feel.* "It's always great to see you."

Between the home security issue and the conflicted sexual nirvana experience with Zack, she knew the shadowy bags under her eyes alone were enough of a giveaway, hardly even concealed by her professional makeup arsenal. Of the two hours she'd slept, she'd been less consumed by hauntings of her suspected home invader, Roberto, but more of visions of Zack, that pleasure-giving asshole.

She put both Zack and Roberto out of her mind and got back to planning. With Charlie, she went over the rooming list for the out of town guests arriving that day and then called Antonio to finalize all of the airport pick-ups. Raquel had reported that the bridesmaids' dresses were brought up to the ladies' rooms the night before while the bridal gown had just arrived, and the tailor was on site if they needed him.

Okay, so she'd have the bride try on the dress for her before taking her to see the church. But before heading up to meet Amy Rine face-to-face for the first time, she detailed the next night's rehearsal dinner with Charlie, which reminded her, she had to stop by the grand ballroom for a last minute measurement. Some things she knew she just had to do herself.

"And Raquel, you'll be here all day as anchor. Get the group whatever they need," she said, finalizing the runaround route in her head. If all went her way, she'd get home early enough to grab a catch-up nap.

Her quick stop in the grand ballroom to grab the table skirt lengths became a small issue because, rifling through her bag, she found that her tailor's measuring tape was missing. It must've fallen out somewhere. She'd have to check the limo if, that is, Antonio was still in the parking lot. She texted him, and as she stood from kneeling, Lucinda's number flashed across her phone screen. She answered while ever so smoothly scurrying out of the hotel.

"Everything okay, Lucinda?"

"Love, remember the backup florist in Sayulita from a month or so ago…need the number."

"Got it, one second." Isabel pulled the phone from her ear to her eyes to be able to read it to Lucinda, speed-walking all the while.

And just as she found the number on her tiny phone screen—an air-stopping, wind-knocking collision.

*

All she could see was a wall of dark blue. A man's torso?

A confirming deep rumble met her ears as her victim cleared his throat.

Yes, it was a real live person, a man. *Jesus, Isabel. It never ends.*

Getting her bearings, she took her face out of her phone and out of the man's noticeably expansive chest. With a sigh, she stepped back. Peering up slowly, reluctantly, her eyes reached the face of her victim.

And she became immediately confused. Standing inches from her was a near duplicate of what had haunted her all night and all morning. It wasn't Zack. This man's vibe, his stance, his scent, and the color of his eyes, a deep chocolate brown, were all definitely different, but the uncanny resemblance in the rest of this man's features freaked her out enough that she lost her words and her balance.

She stumbled back just slightly, but he caught her free hand. She steadied, sighed, and, looking down at their feet, she shook her head.

Get yourself together, for Christ's sake. Reset. Act human.

She began to lift her head up, and as she did, she got an awakening view of the spreading dark blotch across the front of the man's shorts, the crotch, and all the way down his legs. Lifting her gaze a bit further, an empty coffee cup in his grasp.

Then she heard some far-off voice, little, high-pitched, and garbled. *Shit, Lucinda!* Her hands fumbled, phone to ear. "So sorry, Lucinda. Yeah, I'm okay, just, well, can I call you back with that number? Three minutes... Thanks." She hit "end" and looked back up to the face of her victim. "I am so, so sorry! What...how can I—?"

"It's fine, really. If this is the worst thing that happens during my wedding weekend, I'm in damn good shape," the man said, smiling sincerely, hands out in stoic surrender to his shorts.

In May and June, several weddings took place at the Bay View all at the same time, having as many ballrooms as they did. With a big dose of fear lacing her question, she of course had to ask, "You're the groom of which wedding? I mean, congrats, and which wedding is yours? Because I'm actually coordinating a wedding here this weekend."

"Oh, I'm Darren James, marrying the unbelievably amazing Amy Rine."
Of course he was.

*

Isabel smiled widely, showing all teeth, absolutely overcompensating for the two-way torrent of anxiety shooting up and down her body. "Wow, huh, so…this is something. I'm Isabel Ruiz, your wedding planner."

"Isabel! *The* Isabel? *Mucho Gusto!* Really great to meet you. God, Amy can't say enough about you. You've already made things easier for her, and that, you know, makes things easier for me." He cracked a brilliant white smile, just too similar to Zack's for her to look at him for more than a moment before forcing her eyes away.

"Well, easier is only the start. *Smooth, fantastic, perfect* are all to come. And I agree, we should take this," she said pointing at his coffee-stained crotch, "as a good sign. The worst is over. Just some ice, and you'll be just fine for your wedding night," she joked, but immediately felt her cheeks blush.

God, Isabel!

But Darren was very gracious, laughing at his own expense, despite the horribly embarrassing comment that flew out of her mouth.

"Well, listen, it's so great to finally meet you. I'm gonna get inside to my groomsmen for some hardcore sauna time. We had a pretty hard night. You know, the bachelor party, too much alcohol, way too many strippers…so coffee"—he looked down—"and relaxation are the order of the day."

Her head tilted, eyes narrowed, connection made.

Darren, Zack's brother, and Darren's groomsmen were at her bar last night with Zack. And they had moved on to the strip clubs without Zack? Zack chose to be with her instead?

Shit, Zack chose to be with her instead. He skipped a bachelor party, his brother's bachelor party, and Destiny?

All to be with me.

And the whopping receipt was for his brother's bachelor party. Again, the one he'd totally skipped.

For me! Her stomach churned.

"Okay, so…I'll probably see you later then?" Darren broke her stunned train of thought.

"Right, yes. Have a relaxing day, and…I'm off to meet your bride-to-be!" Isabel yanked out a smile.

"Tell her I'm thinking about her, will you?" he said with the sweetest, most genuine expression on his handsome, practically glowing face—while her insides moaned with a tinge of unmistakable envy mixed with sadness and a touch of hope. Yes, hope, and happiness…for the couple.

"I absolutely will, and again, God, I'm just so sorry," she said, waving to him as he made his way into the hotel to join his groomsmen and his brother, whom she'd been wrong about—again. And who was potentially falling for her, dangerous territory she knew, and who she'd have to be in close proximity to for the next several days for photos, rehearsals, fittings. *Jesus.*

She looked up to the rich blue, cloudless Vallarta sky. *God, is this a joke? Zack, the brother of the groom, at my fucking event?*

Her first big-ticket event, to boot. And she'd *already* slept with a guest, the best man, the brother of the groom!

*

Coño! Her mind spun.

She'd have to find Zack, get him in private, explain that they had to act like strangers, all past interaction forgotten. The end. For the sake of her career, her livelihood. And, not that she'd tell him this lest he think her insane, for his sake and safety. All done.

Which is what she thought she'd accomplished with her middle-of-the-night escape!

Okay. All would be fine. She could do this. She had no choice but to pull this off. And he wouldn't have a choice either, damn it.

But all predictions in her gut pointed to inevitable chaos. If not played out in real life, then at least within her, more inner anarchy that she just didn't need. How would she put out the emotional wildfire already sparked by Zack?

Oh God, Zachary James. She now remembered seeing his name on the guest list. Zachary James, who nearly burned her alive last night, igniting parts of her she'd never known. Now, when she had the most extravagant wedding of her life to pull off, she'd be in his scorching presence constantly, like Venus' proximity to the damn sun.

Jesus, Isabel. Buck the hell up. It would only be a few days, and once this charade was over, he'd be on his private jet to wherever the hell he'd come from and she'd still have her job. Maybe even Lucinda's entire company someday.

And he'd be long gone. Out of sight, out of mind.

Yes. That was best. Needed. Vital.

She smiled stoically. Fate, again with her sadistic sense of humor, had insisted on putting her and this temptation named Zachary James together again, scene after scene in her funny little play.

Well, fine. She'd pass this bitch's cruel test this time. *No fraternizing with the wedding guests.* So she wouldn't fraternize and erased her memory that she had. Fraternized. With Zack.

Zack. His name, how she'd whispered and screamed and moaned it only twelve hours ago. *Forget it, Isa! Forget him.* Preserving her job was key…and the perfect excuse for setting her boundaries solidly and keeping to them. Because explaining the real reason she couldn't be with him, not possible. Telling a high-powered American businessman that she was *cursed*? A mortifying disaster. She honestly couldn't stomach the look she imagined in his gorgeous sea-green eyes. Beyond disbelief, they'd reek sheer disgust, and just the thought made her shudder.

A car horn startled her back to reality. "Isa! I've got to make a quick run…you left something in the seat?" Antonio asked through his car window.

She squeezed all thoughts out with a long blink. "Yeah, I think so. Thanks for waiting." She slipped into the passenger seat.

"You okay? I saw you slam into that guy. You need to slow it down, *m'ija!*"

"Yeah, just too many things going on at once, I guess."

"That was Darren James, the groom, wasn't it?"

"Yeah." Her mind's instant replay of the coffee spill made her eyes roll.

"Cool guy. Took him and his group to The Inferno last night. Funny guys. But his brother, I think his name is Zack, wasn't with them, and he's the real big tipper. Met him at the airport, seems above the club scene anyway. Stand-up guy I think. Anyway, I like 'em both."

She smiled in agreement as she switched her focus to the floor for her tape measure. She reached under the seat and felt around. "Ah-hah!" She pulled the thing out, threw it in her bag with her cell phone—"Shit, Lucinda! I promised to her call back"—she found the time on her cell screen—"four minutes ago, damn it!" She sighed then flick-flick-flicked and found Lucinda's amongst her favorites.

"Hold it, little sister."

Her pointer finger paused.

"What's the deal here?" Antonio patted his dash. "What's our plan?"

"Right…well, I still have to double check the bridal gown, then get Amy Rine to the church for her sneak peek all before the first airport pickup. Can you drive us to the church, or do you need to send another car for us?"

"I already have two other cars on the airport runs, so I can do the drive to the church, then take you home afterward. I had Ray meet the alarm installer and locksmith already, so we need to meet him at your place early afternoon for the new keys and codes. And, because that will be done, I asked him to go to Roberto's."

"Antonio, you know Ray's nature. He's such a softie…he'll end up chatting over coffee with him!"

"Not with this level of crazy, Isa. He's freakin' pissed. And anyway, I didn't want it to wait another day, and with this wedding, I wouldn't be able to get to him until Monday."

"I guess sooner is better than later," she said, stepping out of the car. She couldn't think about it now, anyway. Too much crap all at once, even for a master juggler like herself. "Okay, just remind Ray to be tough, tell him to take no shit."

"Isa…he's fuming. No worries."

"Fine. Well, I guess I'll meet you back down here in two hours with the bride."

She pressed Lucinda's number on her touch screen as soon as both feet were on the uneven cobblestone drive. And from the corner of her eye she caught Antonio shaking his head at her, probably for her incessant multitasking. She waved and threw him an acknowledging smile while taking renewed care in her footing as she made her way into the hotel—where she'd no doubt find, *had* to find, the best and worst and most tempting thing to happen to Isabel Ruiz.

That thing's full name—Zachary James.

CHAPTER 20

AFTER ZACK CHECKED out of the Airington and moved himself to the Bay View per his brother's request, he met Darren and the groomsmen in the sauna at the hotel spa. After a late and crazy night, they all looked wrecked. Happily, hazily done in.

As for Zack, his body was still buzzing from Isabel. But his frenetic high was encased in the re-enlivened nothingness he felt in his gut, and he had a pounding headache to go with it. Maybe the guys would be an entertaining distraction for him. After all, he couldn't stay holed up in his room like he wanted to. Darren wouldn't have it.

So it seemed that John, Wret, and the others had shown Darren a great time after Zack had split from the group the night before. Darren only remembered a blur of nipples, he said. He thanked Zack and his best friends for the party, and cited that he was ready and looking forward to his soon-to-be wife's nipples, and only her nipples, from that point forward. They all laughed and punched the crap out of him, then whipped each other's asses with the towels that had been wrapped around their waists.

Such was male bonding in a sauna.

Wret asked if anyone had heard how the girls' night went, and Darren announced his decision to not think on it.

But Zack knew. "Actually, Amy called me early on in the night, checking up on Darren."

All the guys began busting on the groom, the whipping sounds of towels resuming, this time in thin air.

"But Amy sounded pretty distraught. It sounds like the maid of honor arranged the bachelorette party at the Rainbow Club… All the man-on-man action, and none for her and the girls!"

"You aren't serious!" Darren shouted. They all broke out laughing, some of them in tears.

"Wait a minute, wait a minute…hold on! What I want to know is, where did Zack slink off to last night?" John presented to the guys.

Once attention turned to Zack, there was no going back.

"I spotted him at the bar hitting on a jaw-dropping piece of ass. No, dude, she literally had the most fucking amazing ass I have ever seen. And rack! But it was that round, fuckable ass that really got me sprung! If that was who he left with…oh, Lord!" Wret spewed, then pounded Zack on the back for congrats and good measure.

And Zack's anger spiked hotter than the sauna, hotter than the goddamn sun.

*

Rage ripped through him. White-knuckled, Zack clenched his fists at his waist, doing everything he could to keep the cool, straight-lined smile plastered on his face. He locked his jaw.

Say nothing, stay silent.

He kept absolutely still there on the wood-slatted bench, or else, he worried, he'd slam his brother's college roommate in the face. Just dead-on in the nose.

Isabel wasn't even his—far fucking from it with her having vanished again, goddammit—but that wasn't the point. Those assholes weren't even worthy enough to fantasize about her, let alone talk about her.

Zack, just let it go.

He felt Darren nudge him, but he ignored any contact. He was still not okay.

Darren, apparently knowing his brother was trying to keep his temper, quickly steered the subject in a different direction, giving Zack time to cool down in the stifling heat and heightened testosterone of the small wooden space.

*

Within minutes, Darren had drawn attention away from Zack's alleged conquest by way of embellishment. His brother spun a story about Zack, some groupies of a visiting celebrity, a party-turned-orgy, and a yacht.

And even though, God, those comments about Isabel had choked out his ability to keep control, keep calm, Zack had come back down, even fake-laughing along with the guys as if nothing had pissed him off only minutes before. Though he was an expert at keeping his cool in even his most heated business dealings, this had been worlds different, a precedent really. His mother and brother were the only people in his life he'd ever gotten so defensive of. Before Isabel.

But what mattered was that she was no longer a topic, out of all their filthy, undeserving minds, so he just let the tall tales and rumors fly. And after all, only a few weeks ago, grandiose orgies weren't out of the realm of possibility for the great Zack James, so he wasn't about to say anything to dispel the guys' excitement. And hell, no harm in letting his kid brother, who was soon to be hitched, live vicariously through Zack before his big day, even if the new chapter in Zack's story was far from the spun fantasy the guys had created, as far as the sun is from the Earth. His new chapter with Isabel was actually, magically, solidly, down to Earth. Except for the fact that he didn't know where on Earth she was again, his life—with her in it—would no doubt be so raw and real, tangible, whole. His heart slammed his chest from the inside. *So whole.*

*

The men were all at the brink of overheating in the sauna, but the common consensus was to stick it out for a few more death-defying minutes. The steam had helped lighten Zack's mood, getting him even further away from his initial fury over the words said about Isabel earlier.

Still amazed and impossibly jealous over Zack's supposed conquests the night before, the guys were getting more and more daring, really trying to bust his balls.

"This asshole even had one of the strippers last night whining for him, pissed that he wasn't there! I think her name was Deedee or Diamond?" John said.

"Destiny," Wret said. "She was so fine! Man, right-up-in-my-face *fine*, you know? But she wouldn't compare to a floating gangbang! On a yacht, no less."

"That's why he's Mama's lucky charm!" Darren added. Zack grimaced and punched his brother in the arm for telling his friends their mother's nickname for him.

But Zack came back to rile the men up for one more round. "Like luck had anything to do with it! Lady Luck can join the fuck-fest too," he spat. "There's plenty of me to go around!" He ripped off his towel, displaying all that he had for Miss Fortune, giving the men the cocky arrogance they craved. When he threw his towel onto Darren's face, the men roared.

The sauna filled to the max with the men's pumping testosterone, fantastical delusions, and more hot steam.

*

While the guys showered, Darren cornered Zack in the locker room. "What the fuck happened in there earlier? It looked like you wanted to murder John."

"Dude, nothing," Zack shot, a knee-jerk response. Then seeing the look on his brother's face while knowing the man had just totally gotten his back, he reset himself. "Just, not now, man."

"That's just fine," Darren said, expertly guilt-tripping Zack with just his tone.

"For fuck's sake...fine. That woman, at the bar...I'm into her. Really into her."

"Holy hell! Zack James is—"

"Shut the fuck up, dude." *God, some things never change*—Darren's volume hiking five decibels from excitement like his kid brother was…a kid again. All the guys turned to look at them, but Darren brushed them off with a nod of his head.

Back to a whisper, "This is a damn…enigma! A miracle! And at my wedding! You've got to bring her, dude! I have got to meet this woman!"

"I can't. She's MIA." A cramp tore through Zack's middle while his heart pounded in his throat.

"So, she's not into you?" Darren whispered as best he could with even more surprise in his hushed tone.

"I thought she was. Or she is, but I think she's just…a commitment-phobe."

"Not an actual term, but, dude, that's perfect. A perfect goddamn match, because so are you!" Darren laughed, then got another pounding in his arm for the comment and for forgetting to whisper.

*

Amy greeted Isabel with an enormous hug, as if they'd known each other forever. And they had been in close contact throughout the yearlong preparation process. It just so happened that Amy Rine was someone she could stand knowing. So many times, that was not the case with Isabel's brides.

Amy welcomed her into the suite. Isabel pinpointed the maid of honor and the mother of the bride, Annette Rine, hitting the mimosa tray without relent—yeah, she didn't need introductions to know. And wow, they obviously noticed Isabel, performing—and completing—top-to-bottom assessments of her in mother-daughter unison. Isabel just smiled, not unused to such looks by any means.

Amy made quick introductions and then, being obviously out-of-her-head excited to try on her gown, she ran to the back bedroom to do just that. Isabel was left alone with the two women and the room's pervading ice-cold vibe.

It didn't matter, Isabel knew to expect their iciness. As Raquel had forewarned, they wanted the owner of Golden Rings at their beck and call, but they were getting her instead.

Isabel smiled politely. "How has your stay been so far here at the Bay View? Comfortable, I hope."

Stephanie rolled her eyes. "Sorry…Jezebel, was it? I understood my sister's wedding was being arranged by Lucinda Carlyle of Golden Rings Weddings."

"Isabel."

"Who is *Isabel*? My name is Stephanie, remember, from a minute ago, and from the stupid questionnaires? Stephanie Rine, the maid of honor, Amy's sister."

"*Older* sister and not getting any younger either," mumbled Annette Rine, obviously buzzed and not ashamed by it. "This may be the only time I get to be mother of the bride," she stated, certainly directing the comment at Stephanie, whose eye roll Annette seemed glad to ignore. "And so this wedding must be better than perfect. We understood that the woman to make that happen is Lucinda Carlyle."

"Not to worry, Mrs. Rine—"

"*Ms.* Rine." Evil glare.

So subconsciously intentional, Isabel held back a smirk. "Ms. Rine, of course. My name, again, is Isabel, and if there's anything Amy needs, I'm at her absolute disposal. And her wedding will be all she imagined and more. That, I guarantee."

"*You* guarantee, huh?" Stephanie Rine piped.

And sometimes fate throws a bone, as a thankful knock sounded at the door. Isabel went to answer it. "That was fast! Thank you, Anna," Isabel said as the young room service attendant rolled in a cart of morning muffins and a replacement tray of mimosas.

The two women paused their pretentious assault on Isabel and attacked the cart instead. Easy as fresh squeezed orange juice and sparkling wine— they wouldn't be any trouble for her. It also helped that Isabel didn't give a damn what those two thought of her. She was obliged to the bride and the signer/guarantor of the event contract, which was neither Annette nor Stephanie. Isabel would, of course, be respectful to all the family members and guests, but she'd been *hired* by Amy and her father.

*

Amy came out the next instant in her wedding dress.

Isabel was floored.

Amy glowed.

Isabel swallowed back a sudden knot of emotion. Seeing her brides in their dresses always had an impact on her. Her Sebastian floated into her mind like a dagger to the heart each and every time.

"What a stunning gown on an even more stunning bride," Isabel said.

"And where is Lucinda Carlyle, anyway?" the mother of the bride mumbled to the mimosa tray, as if reawakened to the here and now, but was completely ignoring the vision that was her youngest daughter. Amy seemed unfazed by her mother's bypass, it probably happened all the time, Isabel guessed.

Isabel followed Amy's lead and pretended not to have heard the woman.

"It does fit like a dream, doesn't it?" Amy said, spinning, enamored by the train of her gown. "All the bridesmaids tried on their dresses yesterday, and they all fit well, except for Preeya, my college roommate. She flies in tomorrow. Oh, and Stephanie hasn't tried hers on yet," Amy said, eyeing her sister for an instant, and, receiving a glare in return, she headed to the back room. "I'll get changed so we can go see the church, Isabel. I cannot wait to see the aisle I'm walking down on Saturday," she called over her shoulder.

Isabel always took her brides to the church for a preview so they could feel the peace and beauty of it before it was filled with people and before the bride was consumed by nerves. It allowed the bride's wedding fantasy to come to life even before the big day, and it often abolished the common wedding-day jitters altogether, which was Isabel's plan.

But for Isabel, just stepping into the iron-domed sanctuary was always bittersweet. Just like her career choice, the torture of seeing the church where she'd been set to marry her first love sent a surge of agony through her. But it was necessary and cleansing. A tribute. A remembrance. And there was no more beautiful place to be married than at the Church of Our Lady Guadalupe.

In the awkward silence of the suite, she looked down at the floor, then her hands, her wrists, her cuff bracelet. Beyond the forthcoming pain at the church, a new competing torture had been thrust into her life. *Zachary James*. And oh God, did she feel regrettably and wonderfully alive with him. Thinking about Zack, internally debating over him, dreaming of him, hating and re-hating him, it made her blood flow hot and thick through her veins. And now she got to dread the inevitable reunion with him, the best man of Amy and Darren's wedding.

"Isabel...Isabel?"

"Sorry, what was that Amy?"

The bride appeared in an adorable summer dress, heels, and a genuinely sweet smile. "I was just saying that you are taking so much on your shoulders. I just appreciate it so much."

"Oh, sweetie, that *is* my job, and my pleasure. And, goodness, I was just thinking about the church. You're going to absolutely love it, Amy. It's one of my favorite places on Earth, and—"

Her phone buzzed. She glanced at the screen. "Sorry, hun, it's the florist." *Who always blows things out of proportion.* "Let me meet you down in the lobby in about ten minutes, okay?" she said as she headed out of the room to take the call.

She made sure to throw a quick wave goodbye to the *brujas* of the bride, Stephanie and Annette, but they were too busy brooding in the corner of the suite to lift their fingers to wiggle a California-wave back.

And God, she had much bigger things to worry about than those two. Again, the highest priority, she had to find the best man. She needed to explain, get a handle on the situation, make sure Zack was clear. *Strangers.* They were perfect strangers.

Raquel or Charlie, they both had the rooming list. She just needed to call his room. Yes. Easy.

But Darren had said he was meeting his group in the sauna. And, oh God, the time. Either way, she'd have to handle this after checking out the church with Amy.

And shit, the florist! Her phone was still buzzing. "Hello? Anita, sorry, so sorry...Yes the color scheme is *still* white and lavender."

CHAPTER 21

ZACK WAS GETTING raked over the coals by Darren in the men's common suite. "You had weeks, dude! And you 'forgot' to get your tux fitted? You're the tallest muscle-bound gorilla that ever walked the damned Earth! You *know* you need custom! *I* know you need custom."

"No, it's fine! Fits just fine!" Zack said, smirking at the rest of the groomsmen, full well knowing it was tight in all the right places.

"That's it. I'm getting Amy. If you won't believe me, you'll at least believe her!" Darren stormed out of the room, leaving the door wide open in his melodramatic frenzy while all the guys launched into hysterical laughter at the frantic groom's expense.

Zack could hear Darren stomping down the hall, then they all heard a grunt and a woman's muted squeal.

"Sorry, sorry. Are you okay?" Zack heard a woman ask. "Oh my goodness…that's number two." The woman's voice went on, now striking a chord with Zack. It had a familiar warmth to it, combined with a sultry smoothness that gave him a chill, lifting the fine hairs on the back of his neck.

Then Darren laughed. "No coffee this time, though! Lucky for the tux," he said. "So, hey! I could really use your help for a second."

"Sure, I have a second before meeting Amy in the lobby. What's up?" The woman entered the room after the groom.

Zack shook his head in disbelief. A rush of energy sprinted up to his head, then chest, then throughout his entire body. He felt dizzy and hot and confused. But more, he felt release. Out-of-prison, death-escaping, awake-from-a-nightmare release.

Because the claustrophobic emptiness that had started in the lowest and deepest center of him had, since her second disappearance, spread up through his rib cage, tightening his chest. But now that emptiness was gone, at the mere sight of her, gone. It was replaced with new life, new hope. He was elated, in absolute awe. His lungs fully inflated as if for the first time, yet breathless at the same time.

And the rush of heat to his face was out of his hands, as was the further and involuntary tightening of his tux pants. Zack shifted his stance and tried like hell to be smooth, act normal, keep it together as he clasped his hands in front of him.

"Guys, this is Isabel Ruiz, our wedding planner," Darren announced.

Finally, her last name. *Ruiz. Isabel Ruiz.*

*

Here it is! The dreaded reunion that he didn't know was coming, the one she would have chosen to avoid like the plague, but had been at least hoping to grab him in private for clarification of mandatory next steps…and nothing else. But again, the choice was never hers. Damn Fate and her fucked-up sense of humor.

Isabel was without a doubt, jittery. Remembering that she had nothing in her stomach except for one grande mocha, she could blame it on that. But she knew the truth of it, Zack could affect her under any circumstance.

"The best man, his tux…" Darren walked her further into the suite. "Look—"

And there was Zack and his bulging…everything.

And his *everything* made her sex squeeze so tight, she felt her cheeks flush while her vision clouded.

But Zack might have been paler than her.

His stunned face was really closer to ghost-white, then cherry red an instant later. His jade-colored eyes were wide with shock, but with a softness to them, maybe a sense of solace, relief, comfort even?

He finally smiled, a glimmer of knowing in his eyes. And she wanted to run away, right out of the room, scared of caving to his charms and just melting at his feet then and there.

But she couldn't. Instead, she quickly held out her hand to shake his, and gave him a neutral, acquaintance-level smile. "Good to meet you, best man."

"Uh, you too," he replied, narrowing his eyes, cocking his head just enough to show her his confusion, but he thankfully followed her lead.

Yeah, she could do this, just as long as he followed her lead.

And as long as she ignored the familiar, electric sensations rising up her body, similar to those jolts she felt the night before, starting out on the beach when she'd caved.

"He's been in Vallarta for how long and didn't even get fitted? And what multimillionaire doesn't have a damn tux at the ready, anyway?" Darren said to Isabel while keeping his targeted gaze on his brother.

"I don't go to black-tie bullshit often enough," Zack defended while keeping his eyes targeted on Isabel.

"Then, I mean, what the fuck were you doing all this time, or more like, who were you doing? Goddamn priorities," Darren mumbled, not so subtly pissed off at his brother, his best man.

As a matter of fact, *she* had *done* the best man not even twelve hours ago. Her cheeks blushed at the mere thought. She cleared her throat. *Okay. Take some actionable steps here.* Five steps to the room phone, she calmly called the front desk. "Is Arnold still down there? …Okay, is the resort's tailor available, then? …Okay, thanks."

Damn it.

With Zack standing in his porn-star pose in his too-tight tux pants, she'd have to get his measurements herself and drop the garment off at Arnold's offsite shop later. She'd done measurements before when in a bind, but this was so different. This was so bad. She looked over at Zack, his brows lifted, waiting.

She swallowed hard and waved him over to her, where the light was better. She pulled her tailor's tape from her bag while her heartbeat choked off her airway and pulsed at her core. She reminded herself to keep cool. *We don't know each other, and I don't want him. At all. In me. Right now...Jesus Christ, Isabel, stop.*

Without making eye contact, ignoring his wide, toothy grin, she kneeled at his feet to check the hem, then she stood. *Simplest measurements first, his waist.*

"Thank you for your help, *Señorita* Ruiz," he whispered in her ear as she reached around his body, her hands, clammy and trembling as they met at his middle, unable to ignore his washboard stomach. She cleared her throat and noted the measurement on her pad. Then she stepped back. *Outseam now.*

Shit. She exhaled as she bent down to place her pad on the floor. God, if only she could hit fast-forward through the rest of the measurements, because, after this one, it was all straight downhill.

She dragged the tape down the length of his outer leg, then jotted down the outseam. She had to shake her pen twice to get it working when she noticed her arm hair had prickled, the break in physical contact was a kind of relief and agony at the same time.

Now, onto the inseam. She glanced up from crouching and, oh God, she felt like shutting her eyes tight so that maybe the nightmare would end when she opened them again. But she all-too-clearly remembered her hands at his hardened manhood just the night before, eyes closed in deep pleasure rather than her current mortified inhibition. Her mouth went dry. She needed water. Or to lick her parched lips at least. But that would've been just too awkward, undoubtedly misconstrued by the onlookers. Dear God, pant-fitting turned amateur-porn hour, just without the cheese ball music in the background. She just had to go faster and get through this.

You're a professional, Isabel. Come on now.

She inhaled, placed the tip of the tape on the seam of his inner thigh—at his bulging crotch, at face level—and quickly brought the tape down to the floor. Pen to paper, thirty-five inches. Done. She blew a hard breath out.

Then inhaled long and deep. The last measurement, his rise.

She stood, moved around his body to his side. Her breasts were helplessly pressed against his muscular arm. He turned his head just slightly but said nothing, his warm breath just resonating in her ear. She swallowed and with her left hand took the end of the tape to the center of his waistline at the crux of his back. She held the tape there and awkwardly reached her right hand around the front of him and through his legs to grab the tape, keeping her eyes behind him, the lesser of two glorious evils.

She swore under her breath when the tape slipped through her fingers—"Damn it," she muttered. Trying again, she reached further back to catch it. For Christ's sake, could this get any harder? She could hear throats clearing, a few whispers from the male peanut gallery, and a small snicker from the best man himself. Once the damn tape was in hand, she slid it all the way up to the front waistband, careful to keep her fingers from brushing his body. Then she pulled the tape nice and taught. Her eyes flicked at the tape and away—measurement noted. She released the tape from her fingers, then felt her lungs fill with air, not having realized how long she had gone without the vital stuff.

Okay then. *Fate, you horrid bitch.* "You're all set. Just bring the pants down to the front desk for me, and I'll take it from there," she said, already grabbing her bag and walking toward the door.

"Thank you so much!" Darren called after her.

Before exiting the room, she turned back around as not to be rude. "You're welcome," she said, catching most of the groomsmen staring at her behind while Zack had his hand to his forehead. "See you all at the rehearsal dinner tomorrow night."

By her third step down the hallway, she heard one of the guys from inside the room. "That woman's ass could make me its slave! It was as nice as the booty from the bar the other night! Damn!" Laughter and a series of hand slaps followed, fading as Isabel moved farther down the hall.

But a booming baritone stopped her stride and her heart the next moment.

"Shut the fuck up and have some respect, you assholes!"

A loud silence filled the corridor from that point on while a totally unwanted surge of warmth filled her heart.

*

"Isabel!" Zack shouted after her. He could hardly *move* in his pants, let alone run, but he wasn't going to let her out of his sight again, not without a fuck-ing phone number at least!

Zack James, the avid unbeliever of all things cosmic or superstitious, couldn't explain this disappearing-reappearing act with Isabel, his angel. Just a series of coincidences, of course. Whatever, though. He was damn thank-ful. His heart was goddamn thankful.

Isabel stopped short and turned on her high heels. "Yes, Mr. James?"

"What's with the 'Mr. James'?"

She motioned for him to follow her into the elevator alcove, and then set to whisper. "I'm the coordinator for your brother's wedding, Zack. If I'm even suspected of being…*with*…a guest, a guest of my own event, the best man nonetheless, I could get fired, end of career, done."

"Okay…I get it, professionalism and all that, even though we got together before we knew that—"

"*That* doesn't matter, Zack. Not at all."

"Okay, so, I'll, uh, hang back. That's fine. But damn it Isabel, why the hell did you vanish on me? I thought we clicked, you know? I mean, I know we clicked." Sweat dripped down his back.

"Just, please…I can't talk here, now. We can maybe…touch base after the wedding. But Zack, until then, we are strangers. I need to focus, and I need you…to keep your distance. Seriously."

"Oh, like back there in Darren's suite with your hands at my crotch?" he asked, not hiding his frustration at her dismissal of his major issue: her disap-pearance at dawn.

She tilted her head, looking at him with lowered eyes, somehow solemn.

"Please just...act. Even if we are constantly thrown into situations together, you need to act. I can't risk anyone knowing...that we, you know, know each other."

"Fine. But after the wedding, we will talk. *Seriously*, I'm not leaving Vallarta until we do," he asserted. "And I want your cell number. I'm not letting you off the hook, Isabel. I don't do *this*, feel *this way*...ever! About a woman. But you..."

She gulped down air, then squinted at him for a beat. "But you have Destiny's number...why do you need mine?" A smug expression spread over her perfect face.

"What? What does that even mean?" he snapped, trying to keep to a whisper for her.

"Destiny. From The Inferno? Was she on your playlist the night before you found me again? The number on the receipt?"

For fuck's sake. The girl from The Inferno? The one who'd passed her number through Armando on the back of the receipt. Annoyance spiked at this new dramatic element between them, but, in the same vein, he felt his blood pump hot through him at the slight hint of jealousy. "Isabel...I planned my brother's bachelor party, and when I went to the club to arrange and pay for it, like, a week ago, a girl threw her number at me. Written on my receipt, I had to keep it. Doesn't mean I called her."

She shifted nervously, red in the cheeks, flustered. "Are you or aren't you a womanizing prick?" she asked, sounding as if she were asking herself the question at the same time.

"I'm—"

An elevator's arrival bell interrupted him. Then Isabel's glare paused him until the three hotel guests got out of the car.

"The tux will definitely be ready for Saturday," she said in an ultra-professional tone while still holding him quiet with her eyes until the hotel guests were farther down the hall.

"They aren't even part of Darren's wedding."

"I don't know who is or who isn't right now, and it doesn't really matter.

Every staff member at this hotel knows me. This is serious, Zack. My career is my life." Her golden eyes widened with intensity.

God how he wanted her.

"Okay, I hear you." He took a step closer to her, not caring if she liked it or not. "I'm not sure why, but I can't stop thinking about you. I mean, not that I'm not sure why…you are unbelievable…smart, funny, sexy as hell! I meant that I have never been so crazy about one woman. No one else, nothing else, has kept my attention, my interest. Until you."

"Hush, *Jesus*." A harsh whisper. "And I'm so glad I'm 'keeping your attention,' like some fun-time dress-up doll, for Christ's sake—"

"Just please let me finish, would you? As for that stupid phone number, the stripper's, I didn't call her, didn't think about her, couldn't even point her out to you if my life depended on it. I had to arrange my brother's party, and the girl snagged my receipt from my attorney. Honestly, you've taken over my brain, Isabel, there's been no one and nothing that's made my radar."

Isabel looked slightly relieved, but then disappointment, defeat glazed over her face. Why, though? Maybe she didn't want all of this from him, like it was too much for her to take? Too overwhelming? Maybe the stuff in her past, the scars on her wrist? Was it all surfacing and freaking her the hell out?

He wouldn't know until she let him in, gave him a chance. That wouldn't happen until after the wedding, if he could wait that long.

Amy and her bridesmaids could be heard squawking down the hall, getting louder, closer. Isabel quickly hit the elevator call button. She was in the car before Zack could utter another syllable or even blink his eyes. Then the serious expression on her striking face disappeared behind the sliding elevator doors.

And for fuck's sake, she had gotten away from him again without giving him her number.

CHAPTER 22

AFTER TAKING AMY to the church, her *Iglesias de Señora Guadalupe*, Isabel brought the elated bride back to the hotel to meet up with the groom. Amy and Darren wanted to greet their out-of-town guests at the airport, which Isabel thought was sweet. Amy was lovely, and from watching her with Darren for a brief time before they got in the limo to the airport, she thought they were a very well-suited couple. Rare to see, good to see. A breath of fresh air. *Really.*

Isabel continued on with Antonio to meet Ray at her house. She welcomed the break from anything to do with Zack, the wedding, the church; any and all of it. An afternoon at home, and that nap, would be good for her before Friday's big rehearsal dinner.

When they pulled into her driveway, Ray was there waving with one hand, holding her missing security pole in the other.

"So what did Roberto have to say? What did *you* say? Did you threaten him?" She bombarded Ray as she got out of the limo.

"Isa, you'll be relieved. He did take the pole, but…"

"I should be relieved…for what? That he admitted it?" Isabel asked impatiently while Antonio unlocked her front door with the new set of keys Ray had handed him.

Once the door was opened, Ray punched in the code to her new alarm system, then continued. "Well, yes, but no. It sounded like there was nothing *to* admit. He said he took the pole to size out a stronger metal one for you.

He was going to surprise you with it by just returning it to the track. He said he didn't think giving each other space meant that you both couldn't be there for each other like you always have been. Like at the bar that night, with that sleaze bag."

She shook her head. How could Ray be so damn blind? "I asked for my house key back from him for a reason. Didn't that tell him something? Wasn't that pretty clear? In my demand for a break, I hadn't made 'surprises' an exception, not even for a new security pole! In fact, his waiting up for me in *my* home until three in the morning was the very last *surprise* that brought me to my breaking point in the first place! And he obviously made a copy of my key! Doesn't that strike you as odd? Because it freaks me the hell out!"

Ray could only stand there, wide-eyed and speechless, his breath hitched and holding, like it had when he'd gotten caught stealing their mother's makeup at age ten.

But what bullshit!

She shifted her glare from Ray to the ceiling of her front entrance, her jaw tightening, her teeth grinding out her frustration and justified concern, an attempt to keep the threatening explosion from going off and burning her brother alive. He had only been trying to help in Antonio's stead.

Ray jutted his hip, crossed his arms over his chest, and began again with a defensive tone. "So he misunderstood, stepped over the line, but the house is secure now, so it can't happen again anyway. And making a copy of your key is just responsible, Isa. We all do that as a backup for family, and he's been like family for almost twenty years!"

Isabel closed her eyes, her breathing deepened, her lips a hard, straight line.

"And, you should know, he said he agrees with your decision to give each other some space. He said he's feeling good, even glad to have the time to focus on himself, to figure out what he really wants," Ray concluded, trying to convince her and, unfolding his arms, softening, trying to put her at ease.

"Glad you believe him," she cut, having reduced her tirade down to those few words.

"Hey"—Ray touched her arm—"he even went on a date last night. It seems like he is really trying, you know, to get over you."

Isabel shook her head, clenching her teeth harder. She turned to Antonio, the oldest of them, the Ruiz rock, and said behind tightly pursed lips, "I don't buy it. I'm just not convinced."

"I get it, Isa. I do. But the point is that your house is alarmed and the locks are changed. The fence will be finished tomorrow. You're good...honestly. If I'm not worried, neither should you be. I don't believe Roberto would ever hurt you, but he couldn't get to you now, even if he tried."

She followed that neither Ray nor Antonio was worried, but with the major incidents over the past few years due to her horrendous luck, how could they not be?

It was then that a tight nauseating knot in her gut surfaced. A familiar knot, one that brought up terrible visions for her; flashes of hospitals, funeral caskets, bloody wrists—not her own, but her mother's. This familiar knot was the very one that had taunted Isabel the entire day leading up to the most horrific discovery of her life, when Isabel found Yesinia Ruiz lifeless on the bathroom floor of her childhood home. The mother of twelve had blamed *herself* for Isabel's ill-fated existence—and Isabel blamed *herself.*

Isabel pushed past Ray and Antonio and made it to the powder room just in time.

*

Her heaves turned quickly to empty gasps. Her throat sore, her head pounding, she stood and stared at herself in the now seamless mirror. She closed her eyes to reset and calm the burning sensation in her chest. A sudden flash of Roberto's obsessing crystal-blue eyes appeared in her mind, and her lids shot open in an instant. She wouldn't dare close them again, not if it meant seeing that chilling and invasive gaze. That stare. It made her skin crawl.

Instead, she focused on her own welling tears as her stomach-retching queasiness grew to a peak again.

"Isa, are you alright in there?" Antonio called through the door.

She couldn't form words to answer him. "Mm-hmm," was all she could muster with her raw and raspy voice.

But she wasn't okay. And her safety and comfort level aside, she was certain Roberto wasn't alright either. Again, her best friend's obsession had gotten him stuck in a downward spiral because of her and her godforsaken hex. The hex, which there was absolutely nothing she could do about, despite all her efforts. Fate, as always, would do whatever the hell she wanted with Isabel's life and with the lives of those Isabel cared about.

She crouched by the toilet's edge, still on the brink of sickness, waiting for the next wave. It felt like forever, but eventually the nausea waned. She heard Antonio's fading voice and then the sound of her front door shutting as her heavy eyes closed to let sleep take over, right there on her bathroom floor.

*

When she came out of the powder room, hours later according to the microwave, her stomach and emotions had calmed.

But now she was better able to focus, and the main room's drastic reduction in sunlight stunned and chilled her. New blackout curtains across her precious sliding glass door gave a protective wave with the passing of the oscillating floor fan.

Her brothers had definitely gone all-out.

Not wanting to dwell on the loss of her glorious bay view, she continued her scan of the main room. Crazy how dark grey everything seemed; the walls, floor, the breakfast nook—yeah, she was going to sulk. Because now just to see anything, she'd have to surrender to artificial light and, God, she hated the harsh, fake glow. *Forget about the electric bill.* She huffed frustration from her nostrils as she switched on the kitchen light...

...to find, on the kitchen island, one wrapped present with a note.

*

Goosebumps dominoed up her arms. Her shoulders shimmied.

She kept her distance from the present as if it were a bomb, trying to shut her paranoia down so she could mentally process. Be rational, reasonable.

Then came the sound of running water, from her master bathroom?

Frozen thought, breath, feet, knees.

The water-rush stopped.

A nanosecond passed.

Duck, at least.

What, behind the couch?

It didn't matter, her knees were locked.

At least grab something sharp or—

"Oh hey, you're out." Ray stood in her bedroom doorway drying his hands on his jeans, smiling. "You need hand towels in your master bath, Isa. Best to get some with silver accents to match the fixtures. Man, we should've gotten you those instead of, well, what we got you."

She grit her teeth while slowing her breath down from bullet-train speed.

You are so oblivious, Jesus, Ray!

Calm. Do not explode.

But it was damn hard not to, her sense of relief was no match for the extreme panic that had just moments before consumed her being. And as Ray practically bounced his way to the gift—apparently from him?—on the kitchen island, just totally giddy, her temperature climbed higher still. Her eyes followed him, now disbelief trumping all.

"Go ahead and open it. Happy belated house-warming from Eddie and me." He slid it to the edge and handed it to her.

She heaved a breath out. *Don't be pissed. Nice brother. Well-meaning brother.* She somehow mustered a sweet smile for a "thank you" as she took the gift. "I just didn't know who was here, who'd left the gift, you know?"

Because, remember, Ray, when I got violently ill from this whole Roberto thing?

"Oh, yeah, well, Antonio thought one of us should stay until you woke up. Man, were you snoring. Best to just let you sleep, like our partying days, right? Bowing to the porcelain god?" He smiled.

Ray, sweet-natured, oblivious, Ray.

She glanced at him, with a stoic smile. After securing the condo, her brothers were just not concerned about the Roberto-threat and she had to accept that. But it wasn't like they *weren't* taking her seriously; Ray had stayed until she woke up.

And hell, beyond that, maybe they were right? Why worry if everything proactive that could be done had been done. Well, except for the completion of the fence.

But maybe, just maybe, she was overreacting about the entire thing? Paranoia was a way of life for her.

She looked up at Ray who still seemed oblivious to any of her inner turmoil here, way more focused on the wrapped present. Eyeing it, nodding at it, brows waggling at the damn thing.

And it was nice, a present. He'd always been thoughtful that way. No one else brought her a housewarming gift.

"Thank you, Ray. And I'm glad you stayed." She put the box down on the floor and hugged her brother.

"You're welcome, and"—he picked the box up from the ground and shoved it in her arms—"open it already. You're killing me, Isa." He glowed, hands clasped at his chest. "Eddie will be so mad he missed seeing your face, but I have to give it now. It will just make you feel tons better. Maybe I should take a pict—"

"Nope," she said, stopping him from reaching for his cell phone. "Eddie can take our word for how excited the gift made *you*, I mean *me*," she teased.

Eddie and Ray were for all intents and purposes, married. She'd known they'd been together since they were fifteen, but they'd only come out publicly a few years ago. A decade in hiding. But even though attitudes in Mexico had opened up, or at least in Vallarta they had, with the large foreign gay population a sign, Ray and Eddie got almost as many harsh stares as Isabel did. Isabel really had to give Ray credit for having fought the biggest and most important fight of his life—living his truth in their predominantly homophobic world. She really couldn't have been prouder of him. She thought her mother would've been proud too if she'd been around to know.

She unwrapped the present. A pot and pan set. *Wow.* She placed the box down on the counter and put on a wide-ass grin. "God, thanks, Ray, really…"

"What? We wanted to get you something useful!" Disappointment pulled his smile down to the floor.

She pulled him in for a hug, the assured remedy. "Yes, because you know how much I cook!"

"Now you will," he pouted in her ear.

"Hah!"

"You should, you are twenty-five for goodness' sakes! Just don't burn the place down!"

She smiled then sighed at the serious potentiality said in a light-hearted tone.

"Thanks, Brother. You're the best." He really was.

"And what do you think of the drapes? Antonio's idea, but Eddie and I picked the fabric!"

"Yes, the privacy curtains. Definitely a...surprise." Another set up, poor Ray. Yeah, after being in the main room for five minutes now, she officially detested the curtains. They were horrendous and stifling, but yes, necessary. And weighing the fear of Roberto's lurking with this new involuntary claustrophobia, like being trapped in a jail cell right by the expansive sea—the worst kind of tease—she wasn't sure which was worse.

What she did know was that the entire situation sucked.

"Thank you, Ray. They're just what I needed." *Damn it, Roberto.*

"Oh, and I got a call from the fence installers while you were, you know, napping. They're gonna take a few more days than they thought to finish the entire perimeter, but the alarm system is remotely monitored, twenty-four seven, so you're A-Okay, no doubt."

She sighed. "Okay, Ray. Well, thank you, you know, for everything." They walked to the front door.

"Anytime and always, little sis."

Ray kissed her cheek and left, shutting the front door behind him.

"Hey, Isa!" A muffled call from outside. "Lock up and press 'away' on the keypad! And the rest of the codes are on that note in the kitchen! And have fun cooking!"

She smirked as she turned the deadbolt, engaged the alarm, and then listened to the sound of her own breath echoing in the surrounding silence of the now dank and dreary main room.

CHAPTER 23

SINCE THE TUXEDO fitting that morning, Zack had been a wreck. A goddamn mess, for sure.

The entire situation was fucking with his ability to maintain, and maintaining was his forte. For him, multimillion-dollar deals were like tying his shoes. But when it came to Isabel, well, he couldn't even find the damn "shoes" to begin with!

She amazed him. Her fucking stellar performance in the hotel suite in front of his brother and all the guys; the calm, cool strut; and, *oh man,* her teasing touch. She was just so damn smooth.

He had been totally floored when she'd walked in that room with Darren. Her reappearance, a heavenly relief. And he had never known how cold and tight his heart had been until it had opened then, like a first breath of air after drowning in the sea for too damn long.

But now they had to play strangers? He grumbled.

Fuck it. Fine. At least he'd found her. That was all that mattered. Well, except for missing her damn cell number again, but he'd snag that as soon as he saw her next, no doubt at the rehearsal dinner the following night at the very latest.

And a few days of this dumbass charade—for her, he'd do it. But when the wedding's done, he would devour her whole. He swore it.

Until then, he'd try to control himself. Even though he felt like screaming her name from the rooftops. A crude, lavish womanizer turned fucking romantic, Zack was unrecognizable to himself. But he was on a high, tasting another level of sweet contentment that all the money and power in the world couldn't buy.

He needed her, or at the very least, he needed to talk to someone about her. He couldn't tell Darren that *the* woman he'd referenced in the locker room was Isabel. But his mother, Elaine, had arrived only a few hours ago. He could at least tell her. Elaine James was safe with a secret. She didn't speak to people anymore anyway, especially not people in the Rines' class of crowd.

When Darren had texted their mother's arrival at the hotel, Zack had gone to her room straight away. The '*Do Not Disturb*' sign hanging on the doorknob was a disappointment, but he wasn't surprised. He knew she didn't fly well, so he'd have to wait to see her at dinner later.

In the meantime, he pictured the look on her face when he gave her the news that he had found someone, maybe *the one*. He remembered the family dinner a little over a year ago, when their mother had sparked to life with the announcement of Darren and Amy's engagement. It was the first time he'd seen life in her vacant eyes in more than a decade.

Zack knew that Elaine held out little hope for him finding, or even caring about finding, one special woman, but tonight he'd pull her aside, tell her about the angel he'd found, then lost, and thankfully found again. Him having met a woman that had grabbed his heart and twisted it in knots, he knew his mother would weep and sigh with relief. Elaine deserved to feel joy after all she'd been through. And when he did point Isabel out to her for the first time, she'd weep some more. She would just adore Isabel. He was certain of that.

*

He slipped on his sandals, moved to the door, spun around for his room key that he'd forgotten on the dresser, and then headed out of the suite. Darren and Amy were meeting him a couple of hours before the big welcome dinner to grab some happy hour drinks. A last little breather together before the craziness of the wedding weekend really began, and his little brother began his married life.

When Zack entered the pool area, the heat bowled him over. His brother stood across the patio waving him over with the waiter already tableside with a tray of several margaritas. Zack counted four of them as he got closer.

Darren had picked a table in a perfectly shady spot under the farthest cabana; a large column blocked the entire table from his view, and from the sun, which he liked, being so damn hot outside.

As he approached, and the column blocked less of his view, he saw Amy. She was practically glowing as she spoke with deep enthusiasm to someone, the back of whose head he didn't recognize. He could just make out a man's hand lifting the fourth margarita and a sparkling emerald ring on one finger, which caught the sunlight just so. A hazy memory surfaced, but it was interrupted when Darren walked into the sun to hug him, chattering on about the rest of their day at the airport.

Then Darren stopped him at the edge of the cabana. "And Amy kind of arranged a huge surprise for me. I'm not sure how she pulled it off, but it all worked out, even down to the airport pickup." Darren let Zack pass him into the shade of the straw *palapa* to the table where one of those refreshing alcoholic beverages awaited him, as did a shocking and completely unforeseen sight.

Bennet-fucking-James.

*

"Holy shit, Darren!" Zack shot at his brother, backing away from his worst nightmare. "What the fuck!"

"What's your deal, Zack?" Darren said, urgently trying to take things down a few notches.

"What the fuck do you mean, 'what's your deal'? The sight of this... man...is the fucking deal! Why'd you bring him here...invite him here? Why?"

Boiling heat pounded through his body like he'd been injected with liters of snake venom.

Amy started to tear up and then all-out bawled. "I was surprising Darren. We wanted to start our lives together having forgiven all of the people in our past…like I got to forgive my father, so I surprised Darren by finding his dad…so he had a chance to do the same," she sobbed.

Zack couldn't even look at Amy. He kept his furious focus on Darren. "*Forgiving* can be handled on the fucking phone, Darren! And what about Mom, goddammit?"

"Look, bro, I'm sorry you're upset—"

"Upset? Why would I be upset in the presence of this bastard who left us and our mother for some whore in France!" His volume brought the maître d' over to the table, while all the patio guests gawked.

"Listen, Son." Suddenly vocal, Bennet stood up, speaking directly to Darren. "Maybe I should go. Just let things cool down some."

"Son! You don't get to call *him* son!" Zack blasted. "This man is more my son than he ever was yours, you vacating piece of shit!"

"Zack!" Darren grabbed his shoulders and shifted his attention, forcing direct and targeted eye contact. "Listen. You are *not* going to make my bride cry days before her wedding, or at any other time, for that matter! And you may have raised me, but right now, you are acting like a goddamn child!"

"A child! No, Darren, you were *a child* when this asshole left us! You know what…fuck this! If *I'm* the child, you should probably get a different best man. Why don't you ask your fucking father here? Yeah, he's the perfect candidate!"

And Zack stormed off, knocking into patio chairs and a young waitress without apology. Once inside the hotel building, he unclenched his fists to see his hands, his bloodless white palms, shaking out of control.

When he looked up, he was face-to-face with his mother, with her tired eyes and soft smile. "Don't, Mom. Don't go out there."

CHAPTER 24

ISABEL KEPT HER evening free to be ready and rested for the next night's rehearsal dinner. All the out-of-town guests had arrived successfully with the help of Antonio's crew, and Raquel had made sure the bride and the rest of the party were doing fine.

So, instead of ordering delivery, she would try out her new frying pans. Yeah.

But staring at the dark kitchen, feeling the static air, except for the oscillating fan hitting her every minute or so, she got taken over by a hot fury.

Fuck this…and screw him!

She hardly lived as it was. She sure as hell wasn't going to live in fear. She'd been hankering for home and her naked freedom and solitude. She was glad for the precautionary alarm system, the nearly finished fence, even the drapes drawn when she was away, but she wasn't going to hide, not in her own damn home!

She went into her bedroom, showered off the day, and came back out in a towel, throwing open the drapes to let the sunlight in. Then she pulled open the slider to welcome the ocean breeze.

The flower. On the deck floor. That little, wilted, wildflower. Still there. She plucked it up and threw it over the rail down to the beach. "Fuck you!" she yelled, then went back inside, feeling better already.

She dropped her towel where she stood. "I'm ready to cook," she announced to no one. Completely nude for principle's sake, in the quiet of her now bright and airy kitchen, she poured oil into her new pan while humming an old melody Celeste had sung to her as a child. *Yes, this is better.*

Whatever veggies she had in the fridge, she pulled out. White onions first, she knew that much. Chopping them felt fabulous. She threw them in the pan; a sputtering sizzle met her ears. Then she refocused her now-tearing eyes at the colorful array of remaining veggies; bell peppers, mushrooms, red onions, which sure looked purple to her, and broccoli. She cut and diced it all, then tossed them all into the sizzling oil. She didn't really despise cooking, it was more that she never had the time. Now, in her house, she kind of…loved it—the sounds and smells, even the sweltering heat of the stove. All of it.

She added her ready-mix spices and tossed the combination with a flick of her wrist, a simple maneuver she'd seen done a billion times in the back kitchens at her events, but had never dared to try herself. A few pieces of onion flew out of the pan and onto the floor. She giggled as she picked them up and threw back in the pan, abiding by another rule of hers: the five-second one.

She tried the sauté toss again—this time a perfect landing. She smiled and did it again and again, still humming her nostalgic childhood tune.

The aroma drifted up to her nose. Her stomach rumbled in response. She remembered again that the grande mocha was the only thing she'd had the entire day, then add the gut attack from nerves in the early afternoon with her brothers and she was running on absolute empty.

The onions were now translucent and the mushrooms a deepened brown, signs that she'd be eating soon. She continued humming and watching the last subtle changes of the sauté.

But a change in light made the fine hairs on the back of her neck stand on end. It was something like a split second shadow or silhouette cast on the backsplash to her left.

And over the final sputters of the heating veggies, her inner voice raised up, pausing her humming altogether. Was her mind playing tricks on her, or was the brief break in sunlight something…or someone? The whisper of a nagging reality forced her to put her wooden spoon down. Was he lurking?

Peering in at her? She couldn't stop picturing the crystal-blue eyes there now, at her doorway, like his surprise appearances of the recent past. And after the security pole and his freak-out at the bar…*damn it, Roberto!*

She surrendered, grabbing an apron from the pantry and covering herself, tying it off in the back with a double yank. But the bay's soft breeze sent goosebumps up her backside, taunting her, as if to say, "That's far from good enough." And she knew it.

Damn it!

She went to untie the apron and struggled with the massive knot she had just created. She growled, nails and fingertips working and manipulating, and finally, she broke free of the fabric, throwing it to the floor. Then she left the veggies on the hot burner and huffed off to her room to get clothes on.

When she returned from her room, the scent of burned oil and blackened veggies met her with a punch to the face, and sent her into a second fit.

"Fuck you!" she yelled out her back door to the potential someone who was lingering out there. Or was it still only in her mind? She stuck her head out and looked both directions. No one. She was going insane. Definitely going crazy.

Back in the kitchen, she grabbed the hot panhandle and jumped back from the burning shock, dropping the pan on the stovetop with a clatter. She pulled out a potholder after the fact and brought the dead dinner to its funeral by stomping on the pedal of her garbage can and crashing the pan filled with burned sauté down into it. She tossed the pan into her sink and tossed herself onto the sofa. The pan softly sizzled with each drip from her leaky kitchen faucet while tears welled then streamed down her face.

Even her little piece of solitude got yanked from her, goddammit. Everything she cared about got taken.

*

Some calming minutes later, she sat up, done with her *poor me* tantrum. She wiped her face.

Her stomach grumbled and brought her back to the present. She reached for her phone to call for Chinese delivery. Maybe she would try the new pans again next week, after the damn fence was up. That she even needed a damn fence re-enlivened her fury.

She angrily swiped through her favorites list for the restaurant's phone number when a text came in.

The bride.

Amy's message was unintelligible, with more typos than not. Isabel could only make out '*best moon*' and '*Darren's further.*'

To get clear on the matter, dinner would have to wait.

"Hey there, what's going on? …Whoa, okay. Just slow down, Amy, and breathe sweetheart."

Amy took a deep breath and then detailed at length a dramatic scene at the hotel's poolside restaurant. It involved a surprise guest Amy had arranged, a gift for her groom. But Amy had neglected to prepare anyone else for this guest. If she had clued Isabel in, at least, Isabel could have prevented a whole lot of unnecessary drama.

So Darren and Zack's father had arrived in Vallarta for the wedding. And then Zack, the *best man*, had relinquished his role to his father.

"I got this. Where is the ex-best man now?"

"Well, he said something about a meeting at *La Vaca* Ice Creamery at eight."

CHAPTER 25

ISABEL ARRIVED AT *La Vaca* and immediately spotted Zack's hot sports car, then Zack, just down the way. Leaning against a column, he towered over some petite beauty with long auburn curls down her back. The lady, confident in her high heels and skintight jeans, seemed comfortable and animated with Zack. *Familiar.*

A twinge of jealousy spiked up Isabel's spine. Her immediate response was to throw her chest out and set her stance for a more relaxed and poised look, but *Jesus*, why? How ridiculous. Again, Zack wasn't *hers*. And she couldn't have him even if she wanted him. She'd been through this too many times to count.

Isabel, you are only here to collect up the best man for the bride. Do your damn job.

Then Zack leaned down to kiss the small woman goodbye, planting one on her cheek. A wave of guilty relief flooded over Isabel. The petite woman handed Zack a manila envelope and got into a silver sedan to leave. Zack immediately turned to walk back to his car without even waiting for the woman to drive off.

The kiss on the cheek, the lack of lingering as she drove away—Isabel didn't have to be an expert in couples' connections to know that Zack and the woman were definitely not a couple.

Again, so what?

This is what. The undeniable fact was that her deepest self wanted him for herself. The first step to beating addiction was admitting the existence of the problem.

She rolled her eyes and took a step toward him. She had no problem, damn it. She had *this* like she had every other damn wedding guest she'd been charged to handle.

Zack looked up after a few strides toward where he'd parked and where Isabel stood smiling coolly, giving the slightest, most nonchalant wave she could muster.

*

She looked so damn hot, he could have pushed her onto the hood of his car there and then, right in front of the ice cream shop, spectators and all. His cock hardened at the thought of her bronzed skin against the reflective hot red metal.

But when she reached her hand out to him and shook his hand in greeting, her touch sent another sensation flooding to his center. Warmth moved up and filled his chest like it had that morning.

"Waving at me in public? Meeting me away from the wedding venue? This is all a definite no-no," he said with wide eyes framed by raised brows. He tried to hide the heat that had overcome him, but his cheeks and ears were already burning, making him aware that he had lost the fight.

"It's allowed when I'm on the clock. Amy called me. Some drama with the best man?"

"Fuck…yes. I blew up," he said with disappointment in his rich baritone as he unlocked his car. He slid the envelope into the glove compartment—he couldn't afford to lose the original closing documents for the condo. Armando's assistant had emphasized that to him three times before handing the damn envelope over.

He locked the car and rejoined Isabel on the sidewalk. "Call me a fucking drama queen, but, shit, this wasn't like running into an ex from twenty years back. This was being face to face with my deserting piece-of-shit father! Against my will! Did *you* know my father was coming?" He definitely had a new kind of heat in him then. Had she? Had she known?

"Had no idea. And I have the guest list, of course. No notes from the bride about anything *sensitive*."

"Well, this is *sensitive*…to me! The fucker left us! And now Darren wants to forgive and forget! Forget that *I* raised him! I didn't go to college. I didn't date. Instead I worked my ass off and raised him from age eight because my mother had all but vacated too! All the while not taking a dime from that asshole. And Darren invites him to his wedding?" he vented. Then he caught himself, slightly embarrassed about his volume and dramatics in front of the ice cream parlor patrons, mostly parents with their stunned children.

Then his hurt pride rose up. So, just who was this woman, escapee rather, to discuss any of this with him in the first place? They were supposed to be strangers, right? Well, beyond some amazing goddamn sex and two mind-fucking vanishing acts, they *were* strangers! Who was she to discuss his personal life with him? His eyes asked her all of that with not a single spoken word, just his narrowed, penetrating glare.

But Isabel only tilted her head slightly to the left. "Listen, I didn't eat dinner. Or lunch. Or breakfast for that matter, except for a grande injection of caffeine. I'm going to get some mint chocolate chip. Health first, you know?" She smiled. "What flavor for you? My treat."

It pissed him off how she could calm things down with such oozing damn sweetness. At that point, he could've kissed her or shaken her, he wasn't sure which.

Neither. Instead, he decided on the spot to mellow out and play for control.

"Wow…*this* Isabel…she is hot *and* sweet." He smirked to get a rise out of her.

Her mouth formed a straight line, and her left brow lifted. "Nope, just doing my job." Then she whispered, "And we're surrounded by kids, Zack. We're not going there. Get me?"

He smirked again at her embarrassment. "Mint chocolate chip. With hot fudge. And chocolate sprinkles," he whispered back, behaving himself for her. "Oh, no nuts! And make it a large…please," he yelled as she had already sauntered her fine ass to the counter. Fuck, he got so turned on by making her squirm.

He watched her order, pay, and collect the ice creams, then followed her with his eyes to a table as far away from other people as possible. He smirked as she proceeded to place napkins at each bowl—just so—then spoons, each at the proper parallel to the napkin's edge, then she waved him over. A bit OCD, but with an extreme sexiness to it.

Beyond getting a rise out of her, watching her attention to detail got him hard, and how she managed shit for her career in general, like with his tux that morning, just really hot. And being managed *by* her when they were intimate the night before, that drove him buck-ass wild.

But he had to admit, being managed by her when it came to his personal life, well, that just felt…too close for comfort. He'd cooled himself down from his earlier ego attack, but he still hadn't given her the entrance ticket into his damn psyche.

So, in response to her *summons*, his walk of procrastination toward his Mexican goddess couldn't have taken longer if he were standing still.

*

Isabel sensed Zack's discomfort. A self-made, self-assured man like him, especially having reached such success at such a young age, was probably not accustomed to taking advice from anyone, let alone a woman, who, by the way, hardly knew him…well, except intimately.

And the topic was personal. Well, that's an understatement. Probably more like one of the landmarks in time for this man.

"You know"—she paused for a large spoonful of ice cream, then swallowed and smiled—"Amy explained from her perspective. Why don't you tell it from your side?"

"Okay, first off, Ms. Psychoanalysis 101, please, for fuck's sake, speak to *me*, not one of your wedding guests to conquer and control." He placed his hand firmly on the table as he finished the demand. Then he swiped his hand back, and the cup of ice cream went with it, to the floor. "Damn it."

Isabel ran for a pile of napkins at the counter, and on her way realized that she couldn't remember a single time she'd ever had to help someone else clean up *their* spill, solely theirs. Even when they'd first met, the wine glass had been a shared calamity.

Anyway, she got to the counter and was met with a brand new bowl of ice cream, already prepared by the goo-goo eyed teenaged guy wearing the uniform bright pink apron. Smiling a thank you, she made sure there were no nuts but only sprinkles—she now remembered the nut allergy listed on the best man's questionnaire—and then headed back to the table where Zack was taking visibly deep, calming breaths.

She wanted so badly to comfort him and ease his frustration, his pain. She wanted to care for him. And it all annoyed the hell out of her. *Objectivity, Isabel. Get some.*

She got to the table, bent down with the napkins to cover the spill on the floor and stood up again. Zack reached for the ice cream to help her, his fingers skimming hers. They shared a look, then both glanced down at the ice cream. Still gripping the stupid bowl, scared to let it go and have it spill again, she rolled her eyes with a smirk, slid her hand back, and sat down.

He cleared his throat and smiled. "Thanks."

She nodded, and they took a few silent tastes from their bowls.

She felt his eyes on her, mid-bite. Then he began, in an almost too-soft tone, as if to counter his earlier demeanor. "Look, I have justifiable anger toward my father. He abandoned us. Darren didn't ask me, or was it Amy who didn't? Whoever the hell invited the bastard, I was completely taken off guard. My mother couldn't even reach him by phone six years ago for Darren's high school graduation. She was given instructions never to phone again. What kind of man...?" Then he took an angry bite of ice cream.

Isabel held back a smile by taking a bite of her mint chocolate chip dinner, swallowed it down, and looked at him. "Doesn't sound like the kind of man you are. And not the kind of man you helped Darren to become," she said naturally, objectively, knowingly. Strategically.

He looked at her and through her at the same time. He was searching for something, maybe her authenticity, the truth behind her observation. "I tried. I try," he said humbly.

"Here's my question. Does Darren know? I mean, did he know that you're still so angry with your father? Because I get the sense that Darren, and that would mean Amy also, had no idea. Sounds like you held back all criticism of the man, not lowering yourself to your father's level by bad-mouthing him, just to protect your baby brother." She paused and looked him straight in his sea-green eyes. "Did and does your brother have a clue how you feel? And why you feel such...anger?"

"No, of course not. I didn't, and don't, want him to think the way I do about the man, feel this same awful disgust and hate...I mean, fuck!"

He slammed back another spoonful of ice cream, then went on with his mouth still full. "And I would never want Darren to think I resented *him*! I'm angry with my father! For leaving us and leaving me to raise *his* youngest son..." He trailed off as a realization seemed to hit him over the head.

She let the silence be for a beat or two.

"Hey, it's okay that you resent your father. And it's just as okay to acknowledge the fact that you *didn't* ask to raise your kid brother."

"But I'm proud of Darren, and I'm damn proud of the job I did with him. I don't really have any regrets. None in fact. I supported my family without that fucking asshole," he said, shaking his head, nostrils flared, "and I'll be damned if he'll come waltzing in now and be fucking forgiven for all."

"Look at it this way: Your father left, and you're justifiably bitter. Darren is not *as* bitter. Why? Because you jumped in, *more* than compensating for your dad's absence, giving your brother guidance, love, and support, a true guardian. So Darren's life really didn't skip a beat. He never felt a void, at least not like the void you felt. Maybe, because of *you*, he's able to forgive your piece-of-shit dad and not harbor the same animosity you do. All because of the job you did. Because of you!" She paused to let it sink in.

He took a bite of his melting mess, and halfway through the spoonful, he said, "Yeah, Amy was right about one thing. You *are* damn good. And I hate it."

"I am," she said with a smile, "and hate it or not, you'll have to suck on up, buttercup."

"It's 'suck *it* up'," he said, letting one side of his mouth curl through his gravity.

"Right, whatever," she said with an emphatic eye roll which morphed into a thin-lined grin. "Anyway, I'm just being honest, which I can be if I'm *not* talking with a guest at one of my weddings."

"I guess...I appreciate that?" Zack said with a hint of levity in his voice, definitely uncomfortable with the current advisee-advisor roles. "And, wait— not a guest? Sooo..."

She gave him a slow eye-sigh, cleared her throat, then took a big, comment-ignoring bite of ice cream.

*

Three more delicious bites later, she said through frozen lips, "I want you to hear an alternative." Isabel looked at him, waiting for a nod of approval before she went on. And after two pensive spoonfuls of ice cream, he bobbed his head.

"Let's say that Darren knew how much you hated your father, which he didn't. And let's also say Darren sought him out *and* invited him, even if it might upset you, neither of which he did. But Zack, even if he *had* done those things, Darren is a grown man. And it isn't up to you who Darren and Amy invite to *their* wedding." She took another slow spoonful, awaiting a reply.

But none came, Zack just stared and stirred his melted green and black slush.

"Be your brother's best man, Zack, and be supportive of him forgiving your dad. And it wouldn't hurt for you to do the same." She stopped there on instinct. She might have gone too far already, so she chose not to say her next thought: *Sometimes, what we hate most in others is the mirror we see reflected back at us by them.*

Especially by our own blood.

She watched Zack intently. The corners of his mouth, downturned now as he continually bit his bottom pout, maybe stopping himself from saying one thing or another. But it was coming, she knew. A response was in process, she could almost see it brewing. His strong hands occupied themselves with stirring his ice cream to death. The apparent conversation he held with himself, within himself, had him shaking his head from side to side with inaudible mutterings escaping every now and then.

She felt inclined to reach her hand out to his, hoping to bring him back. She swallowed hard as she slid her hand across the table toward his. And when her fingers met his warm, slightly rough skin, his hand flinched, he shot his chair away from the table, and rocketed up to standing.

She inhaled fast, watching his wide green eyes target hers with abrupt and icy harshness. "Listen, I appreciate you helping…Darren and Amy… keeping their wedding in one piece. But it's all damn easy for you to say… *anything*! All can be forgiven from *your* seat!"

Isabel stayed calm and cool, as if all she felt from his dagger-storm of deadly sharp icicles was the crisp air they tore through.

She looked into his face and said in a frosty and firm tone right back at him, "Yes, Zack, it's *really easy* for me. Among too many things to mention, my parents…left me, and most of my brothers and sisters have all but disowned me. All because of…my past. Things I had no control over. So, no, there's no one for me to forgive in *my* life. Because they're all gone. It's all just peaches and fucking cream for me."

Zack froze there, in his tall, arrogant stance, making no eye contact. He seemed smart enough to not dare look at her then, while she on the other hand, wouldn't remove her glare for an instant. He sighed, then laid his hands flat on the tabletop, his chest heaving. He seemed caught. In limbo. Go or stay? *What would it be?* she wondered. He wouldn't look up, still avoiding her eyes, only looking down into his mint green soup. She stayed silent, stuck mid-breath. A second came and went, then another, and another still. They all passed them by, gone forever.

He cleared his throat, swallowed hard, then slowly, pensively sat back down across from her.

So, he was apparently staying.

The tension was still thick though. And in the awkward lull, his eyes still hiding from hers, she smirked to herself. If she were speaking to one of her usual wedding guests, they'd both be schmoozing and laughing over the day's or week's antics already, sipping the last of their melted sweets.

But Zack and Isabel just continued to sit in sharp, frigid silence.

Fireworks on the bay cracked in distraction, brightening up the evening sky. Then came a loud pop, which made Isabel jump in her seat and bump the table. Zack's second bowl of ice cream soup spilled onto his lap.

You've got to be kidding me?

Isabel came around the table to help while he had already patted the spill into his pants with too many napkins, most of them catching the wind, flying across the cobblestone street and away.

She smirked at him, really because this sort of thing usually happened to her, except it was becoming more and more apparent that they didn't happen to *her* when she was around *him*. He got the brunt of it all.

She got some clean napkins and a cup of water from the counter boy, and taking a little spray bottle from her purse without hesitating, attended to Zack's crotch. He didn't stop her or seem to mind, and when she was done, the stain was gone, and he thanked her with his eyes. Those eyes. She'd missed them over the last frosty minutes.

She re-situated herself in her seat. And he brought his seat back close to the small round table as well. Then he glanced at her with a soft, surrendered expression. Like he was done fuming. Like he had come back to the table and come back to her.

She nodded, smiled, then lifted her brows, asking without words if she could speak. He nodded hesitantly and returned his gaze downward.

"A comedy of errors," she said.

"A comedy of errors?"

"Yes. Words I live by these days. So, think about the irony of the entire situation. Start with innocent, young Amy, so in love with her fiancé, wanting to give him a second chance with his dad. She doesn't say anything to anyone about any big scheme she's got cooked up, she doesn't consider consequences or repercussions. There's no forethought, and she knows nothing of the need for careful handling of such a matter. She hasn't had enough *matters* in her life *to* handle."

She paused. The fireworks grand finale had begun, and while it was too loud to talk through it, she also wanted to get a sense of where Zack was with her reasoning. His eyes were still down on his fidgeting fingers. Listening and registering or just brooding, she couldn't know, but he was staying with her at the table for two, nonetheless. A good sign.

She looked up to admire the sparkling light show in the meantime.

As she did, she could immediately feel him watching her. His red-hot vibrations radiated from three feet away. Was it anger? Resentment? Frustration, maybe? She just didn't know. But the strange anchored feeling that enveloped her whenever she was with him was still present, and it kept her there, vested, with a purpose. A purpose beyond being Amy's wedding planner. No, she would stay to make her point and to maybe alleviate his pain. If only a little.

*

Minutes later, the crackling spectacle ended. He looked back down just as she glanced at him again, picking up where she'd left off.

"So…I was saying, can we really get upset with Amy? It's just a case of naiveté meets good intentions, you know?"

Zack's head tilted in consideration.

"And then, there's you, Zack."

His eyes shot up, a slight warning flashing on his face.

Tread delicately. "You're just discovering your own *Catch-22*, which is protecting Darren from being hurt by your recently surfaced resentment of…Darren, your own brother. Seems to me to be, well, a comedy of errors, your dad being the smallest part of the damn joke, but the instigator of it all."

Zack narrowed his eyes and repeated as if to himself, "A comedy of errors."

"The universe has quite the sense of humor, doesn't it?"

"Yeah, right."

Then he lifted his gaze to meet hers. The heavy feeling in her chest lifted slowly.

He swallowed, sighed, then licked his lips, set to speak. "Well, with that said, I wonder what joke it has in store for us next. Because, knowing how self-centered my dick of a father is, he wouldn't be here if it weren't for something…self-serving."

"Possibly."

"Definitely."

"But your father's actions, ill or otherwise, are beyond your control or Darren's. But the relief Darren will feel, and that you *would* feel, if you let the bastard off the hook…a feeling of true indifference. That pathetic asshole would hold no more importance to you than a stranger who steals your parking spot at the grocery store. Then whatever the man's evil and ghastly plans turn out to be, it wouldn't affect you or your brother in the least. You wouldn't care enough to let it. Apathetic freedom."

His lip curled up coyly, as if defeated by her logic. "Text Amy," he ordered. "Tell her that everything is fine and that Zack *is* the best man, the *only* best man." He allowed a small smile to form and added, "I'll text my brother."

CHAPTER 26

H E REVIEWED IN his mind all the hits his pride had taken in the presence of this woman. He had become a clumsy, stuttering asshole; he had been fucked and left by her in the middle of the night; and now, he had been advised and enlightened by her.

And he still wanted her more than anyone or anything else in the world.

He pulled out his phone to text his brother quickly. *Let's talk tonight. Be back soon, your rightful best man.*

"Isabel, walk with me." He came around to her side and pulled her chair out, confirming that his statement wasn't a request.

They moved along the boardwalk, crowded with merchants and hawkers, families and young couples moving in and out of their path. The moonlight showed through patches of clouds, hinting rain, but holding out.

And each time the moon glow broke through the threatening sky, Isabel glowed, and he almost tripped twice from the distraction.

"Isabel, as a wedding planner, you're nosy and meddlesome. I might even add arrogant!" He worked hard to hide his smirk. "But I'm really grateful. Words of wisdom that I probably wouldn't have heard from anyone else."

She smiled, a glimmer of pride in her large doe eyes. And he felt that she was glad to be there with him—or maybe he was just being hopeful. Maybe she was just glad to have been able to help. And—or—to have accomplished the goal of her paying client, the bride. At that point, her motivation didn't matter to him; he was just ecstatic to be near her.

They walked on, both watching the mini-scenes surrounding them. Then she paused and stared hard at the back of some man's head. Zack could tell she wasn't concerned about the man being a wedding guest from the James-Rine party, because she actually moved in tighter to him, as if under his wing.

"Do you know that guy?"

"Oh, no. No. Just thought it was someone." She released the tension in her face and put the space back between them, ready to walk on normally.

After a few steps forward and a long sigh, she paused and looked up at him, as if ready to explain herself, like he'd asked for an explanation.

"This is embarrassing," she said, her sweet, wide eyes catching his, as if to ask him to withhold all comments or laughter. "My longtime friend, actually my best friend, Roberto…well, he's become a bit obsessed. With me. I got pretty smashed one night, and our relationship kinda crossed the line of no return. I mean, I was so drunk that I don't remember any of it, but the next morning it was pretty obvious what had happened…and let's just say he sees things, us, differently now."

"You? Smashed? I would pay to see the slobbering, silly Isabel." Zack laughed out loud, teasing her as he pictured chasing her around his hotel suite, both of them buck naked and giggling. Then him *catching* her. And pleasuring her. Oh God, to pleasure her again. And again.

Whoa. Come the fuck back, Zack.

"I wish it were funny, but it's actually gotten a little creepy."

"Is it Blue Eyes from the bar? Or is this a *different* stalker?"

"Yeah, he was the *other* 'knight in shining armor' at the bar," she said in a teasing tone, accompanied by a hint of surprise in her eyes, like Zack had worked magic somehow in knowing. But it took no fucking magic, the look of desperate need had been written all over that guy's face that night.

"Ah, yes, the *other* knight," he cracked with a grin, her dig by no means escaping him. "So, you've been straight with him? About how you feel?"

"Yes. I told him we needed a break. But he still showed up at the bar that night, among other things. But he's a great guy, like a brother to me. And I didn't know he saw me as anything but a sister. And then that one night happened, damn it!"

"Isabel. Seriously? You have got to know that other than an actual blood brother, there isn't a man on the planet who sees you as a sister."

She blushed a little, a modest smile lifting her face.

"For a brilliant woman, you're naïve as hell, you know that? Bordering on oblivious." He nudged her with his elbow and grinned as a pack of young guys gawked at her, slowing their pace to a crawl as they went by. Zack cleared his throat. "See? My point."

She slapped his arm and then hooked hers through his. So naturally. They walked on in silence for a bit. Fuck, he liked this. Their vibe, their comfort level.

"Hey…I've got my *own* stalker, so don't get yourself a big head."

"Is that so?"

"Yes it is so. The lovely maid of honor wants me. Bad." His eyebrows lifted for emphasis. "And although I think the woman is certifiably insane, I might just have to snag myself a little wedding party hookup," he teased, making Isabel purse her lips and cut him with a look. "What, you're not allowed to play until after the wedding's over," he said, giving her more shit. She just blushed and shook her head at him.

He was loving the subliminal confirmation he got back from her, that she wanted him, maybe even close to as much as he wanted her. But unlikely. Because although it would be his greatest wish, he doubted she could ever want him as infinitely as he wanted her.

"You *so* should. I heard that she's very…deep. She could tell you your horoscope while she has you chained to the refrigerator, and then she could make you a candlelit dinner with the bunny she killed!" She laughed. He loved that laugh of hers from the first time he'd heard it, albeit at his expense at the Five Breezes. It was a whole and hearty laugh, damn sexy, and it got his heart pounding every time.

And that moved the conversation into the realm of endless antics about this wedding and past weddings Isabel had planned.

"I'm used to drama, but the mother and sister of this bride are on a whole different level. I can already tell…a level only reserved for celebrity gigs! Not even my boss will have as many issues with the Marco event as—" She shut her mouth and covered it with her French-manicured fingers. A coy smile crept out from behind.

"Something you aren't supposed to say, Isabel? Half a secret is already spilled. Come on now."

"Can I trust you?"

He could only smirk at her.

"Seriously, if you even say anything to Darren…I can tell he's the type who couldn't keep the color of his morning piss from Amy. And sweet Amy… if she knew, her little bridesmaids would spread it far and wide for sure."

"I can keep a secret. It's cool." She gave a slantways look at him, needing more. "Okay, I promise!" he said laughing, hand over his heart.

"Marco. Golden Rings is handling his wedding in Sayulita this weekend, the same day as your brother's."

"Sorry, Isabel," Zack replied, "but who's Marco?"

"Seriously? And you say you're loyal to Vallarta. Hell, are you loyal to planet Earth? The guy is hot the world over! 'Struck by Luck'?"

"Yeah, I know that song!" He hated that damn song, and it played incessantly on the rental car's preprogrammed radio stations. "Just from being down here this trip, though. What can I say? I'm a healthy blend of world traveling ex-womanizer and introverted loner."

"Or just deaf!" She laughed.

He gave her a look along with a nudge from his overpowering right shoulder. It knocked her off balance but he quickly put his arms around her, preventing her fall. Her body's warmth caught him off guard, having been so hands-off all night. He allowed his grasp to linger there. He had to, or his fuses would short circuit, the stark contrast without her warming vibration would do that, he knew.

So he held on to her, his arms around her waist, his hands flat on her side, just until she looked up at him with a blink and a smile. And God, she melted him with that damn smile.

He wished the night would last forever, her arm in his as they walked, their conversation picking up from where it had paused with her near fall.

"So, yeah, I guess the whole global Marco phenomenon isn't my thing. I'm actually all about 90s rock, you know, the dark, head-banging stuff," he said. "What about you?"

For a split second she had a definite and excited spark in her eyes, which she blinked away on the next beat, as if they might have that in common, and weirdly, she wouldn't dare admit it. She only shrugged. "Not much time for music of my own choosing. Just playlists for you know, weddings…"

Hmmm. "Except for dance music. Strong beats, yes? Like at La Sexta?"

She threw him a coy smile. "Not so much to listen to on my back deck, but yes, to dance to. Like at the club."

God she got him so hot. And just thinking about how she moved her body against his those nights at the club. Hell, he would've done anything to get her back to his suite right now—off the clock.

But he maintained. He actually only thought about slipping himself inside her hot velvet sweetness every few minutes, as opposed to every other second. Because she honestly intrigued him, captivated him like no other woman had, way beyond her exasperating sexual magnetism. He really could listen to her stories, her laugh, her voice all night long.

But, he couldn't lie—that creamy, sensual voice calling out his name over and over again while he brought her to the brink the other night would have been more than welcome, too.

*

They got lost in conversation, in each other, for what turned into hours. They talked about their upbringings. He loved hearing about her large family, twelve children in all. *Jesus!* And he wasn't surprised to know she was the youngest, she had fight in her, something to prove. And in a family that large, he could only imagine how much she'd had to fight and prove just to survive.

They shared more lifetime details. He'd foregone college while Isabel told him about taking night courses in secret on her own dime. Zack had flown around the globe in his own private jet by age twenty-two while she had never left 'her' Mexico.

He told her of his lofty adventures, catching the sense of wonder in her eyes. "I just can't imagine it, a life filled with just…anything you could want. It sounds like…heaven," she said.

"But of all that excitement, luxury, and comfort…all the women…none of it amounted to anything real. Nothing lasting." He looked at her to be sure she caught his deeper admission—*all the women*—and his regret for having unconsciously insulted her when they first met, the whole panties-caper. But more than that, he realized now the waste of time, energy, heart, and soul that his splurges had sucked from him.

But not anymore.

"I've had this pit in my gut, Isabel, like I have everything in the world, but nothing at the same time. The richest food doesn't last past the moments on your tongue, you know? It is all so damn…fleeting. Until this trip to Vallarta."

She stared at him as if he was from a different planet. Did she get that it was her who had plugged the dam for him? Or did she just think he was a spoiled asshole complaining about the pains of being wealthy as hell?

"I can't really relate, but I guess on a much less expensive scale…here I am, living in paradise. Foreigners look at me, maybe envious of me, being able to go to these amazing beaches, surf, breathe this fresh ocean air twenty-four-seven. Oh, hell, never mind…it is flippin' amazing here, and it's real to me every day." She laughed. "They should be jealous!"

He laughed, loving her energy and how perfectly fulfilled she was with her home, the simply spectacular paradise of Puerto Vallarta.

She went on, her voice a melody. "I mean, I imagine life is tough, relatively speaking, for everyone, everywhere. Either physically, mentally, or emotionally, right? Or all three combined! But anyway, for me, when I can't find a reason to get out of bed, I hear the ocean right behind my house and it all fades away."

He was lulled by her words and felt calmed with the hope that maybe she did understand. Maybe he wasn't alone in the stoic nothingness he felt, especially when he was without her. Then he remembered her scars, her marks of misery indelibly splayed on her wrist, and the pain they represented. With no further talk of it, he could trust that she understood the void, probably better than he did, he being a newer member to the 'reality club.' He guessed from her scars that her pain ran several long years deep. Forever and a day deep, even.

Isabel's surfing stories brought him back to present. Her vivid details let Zack imagine her as a little girl fighting mammoth waves and killing it. He smiled because he'd always been scared shitless of surfing, since childhood actually. This woman just kicked his ass at every corner. "I feel most alive when I'm in the water, even though, God, I haven't surfed in years." She trailed off, obviously nostalgic, missing it beyond words.

"I've always been kind of afraid of the ocean, the jellyfish and sharks." He laughed. "And the waves, and the undertow. Ever since I was a kid."

A sweet sympathy crossed her face in response to his admission.

"But, hey, you have enough courage for the both of us, and I just might be ready to conquer my fear now. You can give me a surfing lesson or two, that is, of course, after the wedding's over. I need to start small, but I'd trust my life in your hands, Isabel Ruiz." He smiled at her, but after having put it out there, he both loved and despised his own grand idea. The great, unknown sea—shit, it really more than terrified him. But solidifying a time and place to see her again, he was in love with that thought.

But not so much for her. Her response was only a polite, thin-lipped smile. Warm to cold in an instant.

They walked on, her silence strangling him breathless. Why the sudden shift? She'd basically drowned his attempt. What the hell? The vibe they'd shared throughout the night was so palpable, without a doubt. And he wanted more of it. He wanted to see this woman again, and again, but for some reason, she just left him dangling there.

*

Okay, fine. He was catching on, getting to know her nature. So she was a precision planner by trade, but again, personally, she dreaded the thought of long-term anything. Like he dreaded a shark attack. And again, he'd lived with the relationship-fear too. But Isabel had changed that for him, and, so help him, he would change it for her in return.

But for now, he would merely change the subject, but strategically so.

He opened up about his mother, and *her* past, a difficult subject for him. He figured the more he gave Isabel, the more she'd lower her defenses. And she already knew the deep and dirty about his father, albeit forced upon him. But not having spoken to anyone about his family matters—ever, with anyone—it felt strangely liberating talking to her about it all. Therapeutic. Cathartic, even.

"And, wow, was she the greatest cook, especially expert at anything seafood. It was like she was meant for Vallarta." He smiled at the memories flooding his mind. Elaine James' most glorious days had been in the kitchen of the condo they'd had there, the one he'd just purchased.

"Tell me more," Isabel said, a tender smile all the way up to her eyes.

"Darren, my father and I would go out fishing, and when we got back, Mom would be ready for us and our catches."

"Wait, you guys took a relaxing fishing excursion then she did all the hard work?"

"No, no. Let me tell you how it went. The one who caught the biggest fish, almost always me, would get to skip out on cleaning and scaling. And, oh man, did I love watching Darren and my father roll their eyes at me as I announced the score of whatever game I was watching from the oh-so-comfortable couch." He laughed and Isabel raised her eyebrows at him.

"Anyway, once they finished the prep for Mom, she'd prepare such a delicious feast, and no two meals ever tasted the same. Every time, a completely unique flavor. Unbelievable. I can still taste her mahi-mahi…"

"Sounds amazing."

"Yes, incredible. But she hasn't cooked a single dish since he left. All of Elaine James vanished the day my father did." Zack sucked in his bottom lip in thought. "After the initial years, with her pain pill dependency which almost killed her several times over, she started to get better. More stable. Sliding toward stoic. But always a little sad."

She kept quiet, but nodded, like she knew he needed the silence. Shit. He regretted bringing the mood so low. He sighed, then tried like hell to cut off the thoughts whirling in his head—his mother's lack of laughter over the years, her cracked heart.

Just then, a mariachi trio came upon them—a joyous serenade for "*la encantadora pareja!*" sang the leader.

"Oh, no, please. We aren't...a couple!" But Isabel couldn't be heard over the band, and it wouldn't have mattered anyway. Zack pulled her into him, then swung her around and around while imitating the merry music with his deep baritone. She laughed so hard she could hardly catch her breath, and he only let her pull away when she began coughing.

Holding her chest to calm her breathing, her eyes searched his. What she found, he wasn't sure, but she surprised him by pulling him by the hand, away from the spotlight to continue their stroll.

Man, had she forgotten herself, or lost too much oxygen during their exhilarating mockery of a dance? Because the warmth she was showing him was definitely uncharacteristic in the scope of their "act," but it was welcome, definitely more than welcome.

*

They hit the end of the marina's boardwalk, and he turned, assuming she'd want to head back. But Isabel stayed put. Zack returned to her side when a light laugh escaped her lips.

"What is it?"

"Oh, nothing...just how hooked I am on this breeze. It reminds me—oh, God, never mind."

"That's not allowed, now. No, not cool at all. Whatever it is can't be more personal than your surgical-style meddling into my family's history... or our..." He paused and leaned into her, that coconut scent tickling his receptors. "Our hours of love making."

She gave a little huff, then spun around to face him. Lips pursed, gorgeous and unfairly mesmerizing eyes narrowed, she said, "I mean it, Zack James. We're strangers. Remember?"

She was so obviously convincing herself as much as she was reminding him that it was almost comical. And cruelly, he loved the struggle written all over her face. The effect he had on her was as real as the impact she had on him. She couldn't deny it, but he knew she wouldn't admit it either, at least not now, not tonight, and not until after the wedding.

But it made him feel fucking great. Reciprocated. Un-alone in the merciless vulnerability.

When she tore her gaze away and set her sights back out on the bay, he took one last whiff of her hair and pivoted. "Strangers, of course. Right. Better get back now, stranger. You coming?"

She took his arm again, *just like strangers do, of course,* and they made the long walk back to the start of the marina, their conversation flowing like an elaborate fountain.

Again, like strangers in the night.

*

Her stomach grumbled. It was loud enough to interrupt their chatter about nothing and everything. Her cheeks instantly blushed. "I guess the ice cream wasn't enough for me. Are you hungry?"

God, he adored her. "Definitely. What fabulous Mexican fare in this international foodie haven shall we throw down, *Señorita?*" It seemed that all the locals ate dinner late, so all the food spots up and down the boardwalk were still serving.

"Pizza."

"Pizza? Really?"

She shrugged, a childlike smile lifting her face.

He snorted and took her hand. "Take me to pizza."

She nodded at a stall two down from the enticing Mexican restaurant.

Within minutes they had greasy New York style slices in their hands.

Sitting shoulder to shoulder at the counter, he hadn't realized how hungry he was. For food, that is.

"Oh, can you pass me that bottle?" Her mouth was half full, but she was still sexy as hell. Even with a string of melted mozzarella hanging from the corner of her delectable mouth. How he wanted to lick it right off her. So badly.

"What, the ketchup?"

"Yes, please." Her tone, sweet-but-sassy.

"Ketchup…with pizza?" There was no way he couldn't tease her. Not a chance. But, damn it, he couldn't pay attention to anything but the cheese teasing *him* from the corner of her mouth. *Screw it.* He moved his thumb to her bottom pout, wiped the food away, and licked his thumb. "Now I can focus on your…interesting…choice of pizza condiments." He smirked as her eyes went from wide-surprise to narrowed-and-defensive in a split second.

"That's how we eat pizza here. It's a thing, it's good! Now pass it down, *por favor.*"

But he'd snatched the bottle before she could get it. He'd hold it hostage. Why? Because, aside from the sacrilege of dousing pizza in sweet ketchup, he just craved her raw attention in whatever form he could get it.

She rolled her eyes, huffed, then reached over him, her body now pressed against his, trying like hell to grab the bottle. "Give it! I want what I want!"

Want. Need. Her words, her scent, her skin, her entire being overwhelmed him. Invaded his senses. Like she'd taken him by storm just the night before. In his penthouse suite. God, only one night ago! And while she still fought for the ketchup bottle he held just out of reach, her neck, her ear, her cheek were all just within biting distance. Nibbling and nuzzling distance. Necking, kissing, caressing distance.

He stiffened, his entire body, every part tense with *want.*

Control yourself.

He inhaled her essence, then let out a long, hot hush of words into her ear. "I want what *I* want, Isabel."

She paused, frozen, mid-reach for the condiment bottle, her body leaning across his. He could feel her chest rising and falling against his arm and shoulder, her heaving breath in complete synch with his racing pulse.

He knew she wanted what he wanted. *Just turn to me. Look at me. Surrender.*

*

But no. She denied the desire. She pulled away slowly, slid back onto her stool, resumed *professional* and *distant*. Back to strangers. She stared at her pizza slice, sans ketchup, while he stared at her.

The game was over.

He placed the ketchup bottle in front of her.

"Thank you," Isabel said in a somewhat defeated whisper as she flipped the cap open with unsteady fingers. She squeezed the sugary pseudo-tomato stuff onto her plate and dipped her pizza in it. Without another word, she ate.

"May I?"

She looked at him with narrowed eyes.

"Can I try a bite, please?"

"You may."

He dipped his piece into her ketchup, took an enthusiastic bite, and nodded his pretend enjoyment. Then he shook his head, wanting to spit it out but chose to smirk and chew through it. "For you. I tried it for you." He swallowed and washed the bite back with a quick swig of mineral water.

She broke out laughing. "I didn't ask you to try it. You didn't have to." Her brows lifted.

"I wanted to, Isabel. And 'I want what I want.'"

And I get what I want.

*

The mood was back to fluid now. Between bites and sips of soda, they chatted away for another hour until the place closed. Then they strolled back toward *La Vaca* on the all-but-vacant boardwalk. The conversation weaved and winded, and now had landed on the topic of their respective homes.

Home. God, what a concept. He hadn't had a solid place to land in as long as he could remember. Just countless and faceless hotel rooms around the world, or his private jet.

But Isabel, she felt like home to him. A warm and welcoming, sensual and decadent home.

"Where'd you go?"

"Sorry, sorry…just thinking."

"*Staring at me* and thinking."

"You'll just have to stop being so captivating. Now, what were you saying?"

She sighed, then smiled. "I was telling you the saga of how I inherited my grandfather's seaside condo and how I just love it there. The bay and the beach and the salt air on my skin. I can hardly keep my clothes on when I'm home because I love the—" She glanced at him.

Yes, he sure as hell caught every spine-tingling word. "Yes? Go on," he teased.

Her cheeks were redder than red. She rolled her eyes, then looked up to the sky in complete silence. A redirect? *Hah.* As if he'd ever let the *no clothes* comment go.

"Don't be rude, wedding planner. Finish your thought."

She groaned. "It's just, I've never lived alone. I've always been in the thick of things in town, or before that, with a fuller than full house. So now, I just love *my* place, love the fresh ocean breeze…and, well…I like to do just about everything in the buff."

He heated from his toes to his head. It wasn't just the illustrious image of her goddess-like form, naked, that shot waves of hot energy through him. No, it was that she was spilling her secrets, bordering on official flirting, even though she seemed to regret it the very next second.

Still, he felt fucking giddy. *Strangers, my ass.*

"Completely naked, huh?" God, he was hard at the mere thought. In flat-front pants, no less. He pulled her to a bench he'd spotted so he'd hide his reaction to her while maintaining the near-perfect mood of the night. "Tell me more," he teased. But was dead serious.

"Mopping? And cooking?" Zack asked, smiling at her with his illuminated green eyes. She now had to explain further, since she'd damn mentioned it at all. What the hell was she doing? Teasing this poor man, this sad, gorgeous man. But his puppy dog look weakened her and made her quiver to her core.

She just felt so good with him, so detrimentally right.

So as not to disappoint her captive audience of one, she went on. She told him of the freedom she felt with the windows always open, the purity of the far-off Pacific, its cleansing salt air against her skin. She told him that she'd pretend the sea told her long kept secrets, ones it had been holding, as if waiting for her to finally be alone there to confide in.

"And I love having no one but myself to answer to, you know?" She smiled at Zack then, not meaning to have sent a message directly to him—*Isabel is better alone, everyone is better and safer with Isabel being alone*—but glad if it had come across.

And actually, no, she *had* meant it. Well, at least her protective and prudent brain had. But her heart diluted the conviction of her words. She hated being alone. And simply loved…this.

Mierda! If her mixed messages weren't driving Zack crazy by now, they sure were doing a number on her.

She continued on, though, unable to stop. Probably rambling by then, boring the crap out of the man. But if Zack was bored, she couldn't tell. His eyes were wide, like he was hanging on every word. He was either an amazing actor, or just unbelievably well mannered.

She told him more about her condo by the sea, the current state of it, and some about her dear *abuelo*. How Isabel had been his favorite granddaughter, and how Isabel's mother, Yesinia, had been abuelo's favorite of his six children.

And that's where she caught herself.

Too much, too close.

Another thought about her mother, let alone a word, and she'd crack open and bleed a river of tears. Isabel's right hand gripped her left wrist below the bracelet.

Change the subject, Isabel.

She could tell from Zack's concerned and questioning expression that it was too late. He was going to ask her. But no, she couldn't go there.

Just say something else. "Anyway, the place is beautiful. But it could be a shack and I'd still love it. If I get to be near the sea, smelling, hearing, seeing it every morning," she said and smiled, "then I'm happy."

But the topic of the ocean was a dangerous one, too. She had heard, and blatantly ignored, his attempt at clinching a future date with her. *"After the wedding."*

No, though. No *after*. No anything.

But God, yes, his whole sweet-as-sugar childhood fear of the ocean bit did hit her. It turned her on to no end, the vulnerability in such a powerful, virile man was just too much for her heart, head, and core.

Doesn't matter. She had to steer him away from his second attempt now. Nothing between them could happen. After the wedding she counted on and prayed for his private jet to take care of that.

So, she'd end this now, this tease of a night. "God, I can't believe how late it is," she said, glancing at her phone for a time check. "And I was home early today too. To catch up on much needed sleep from the lack of it last night." She cleared her throat for his benefit.

"Right, of course," he said, a glint of pride in his eyes and maybe a heated memory in his head, of them together, as shown in the curl of his lips.

Oh God, Isabel, please be done here.

"And I can't be an exhausted mess for the biggest gig of my career."

His captivated gaze made her squirm. She had to turn away from him, reacquiring distance. Necessary distance.

Zack touched her hair. "You alright?"

And damn him and that solid, anchored security she felt with him.

"Yes. I'm...fine." *Just fucking torn to pieces by you.* "Just tired."

*

She pointed to the limo that had just pulled up, and he was again taken over by the empty, plunging feeling in his stomach, then chest, and all the way up to his head. He wanted to kiss her desperately, and then to continue talking, or walking, or sitting, just being with her.

But reality ruled. Isabel collected her purse.

He held out his hand. "To strangers-turned-acquaintances."

She let a smile show through her eyes, and when she gave him her hand to shake, he placed an innocent kiss on it, then he said, "Really, Isabel, thank you."

Her brother, Antonio, went around the vehicle to open the passenger-side door for Isabel, giving Zack a good firm handshake as he passed him. Zack hadn't realized that Antonio was Isabel's brother until she'd said so during their stroll. He saw the resemblance now. He had liked the guy from their first handshake at the airport when Darren had arrived. Antonio seemed strong, confident, upstanding, the kind of guy he'd do business with and have a drink with after. Hard to find a no-bullshit type like this man seemed to be. A common family trait in at least two of the twelve. *Holy hell, twelve!* He could not even fathom it.

"Don't worry, I have my car," he said to Isabel, who was already sitting in the limo.

She put down her window. "Don't worry, I wasn't offering." She winked as the limo pulled away.

CHAPTER 27

ZACK WENT STRAIGHT to his brother's hotel room when he got back. It took three hard pounds on the door to get Darren's ass up, and no time at all to dive into a deep, long-awaited conversation about their father. They went at it 'til dawn, going through the detailed history of their lives, things only two brothers could share and know, along with the things Darren never knew.

And he brought up his talk with the *wedding planner*. He smiled to himself, referring to Isabel that way when, *Jesus*, she was so much more to him. Anyway, he was thankful to be able to use Isabel's advice, her clear point of view, because the topic of his father was hard enough. But now he had an objectivity he'd never thought possible. Granted, his father wasn't there with them in the room, but baby steps.

The brothers decided together that they'd take their father to lunch that day, and as an attempt to keep the drama to a minimum, they'd bring Amy along for a more casual tone.

*

Midday Friday, the day before the wedding, Zack watched Antonio and his passengers pull out of the resort driveway and head to *Playa de los Muertos*, a high-end foodie haven. Zack would drive himself and meet his brother, father, and Amy there, a strategic move in case he needed to make an early escape.

On his way into view of the beachside restaurant, he had a strong need to hear Isabel's voice, to speak to her, just to get a quick refresher from the night before. His blood and thoughts were racing. He pulled out his cell, knowing he shouldn't call her. But he had to.

Looking at his phone, he laughed to himself, realizing he *couldn't* call her. He'd forgotten to get her goddamn number again. *Again, for fuck's sake!* Four hours spent with her last night, damn it. How this woman zapped his brain cells and churned his blood! He shoved his phone in his pocket and entered the open-air restaurant. He had her with him in his pounding, sprinting heart, and that had to be enough.

*

Zack spotted the empty chair awaiting him at the four-top across the brightly decorated dining room. His brother was waving his arm high in the air. Zack took a huge gulp of oxygen. *Be objective, and stay calm. For Darren.*

Zack got to the table. *Breathe.* And cue polite smile.

"Son." Bennet stood from his seat, hand extended to Zack.

Zack's fake smile vanished as he cleared his throat before choking on the sudden ball of disgust he didn't even know he had in him. *Keep it together.*

He inhaled the fresh sea air and shook the man's hand. "You can call me Zack. Or Zachary. But I prefer Zack. Please," he said, gesturing for the old man to sit down while he moved to the chair across the table. He nodded at his brother, gripping Darren's shoulder in greeting, and then leaned over to kiss Amy on the cheek.

Menus opened immediately, a flimsy but welcome barrier to hide behind. But he had a surprising desire to look at the man, a more than surreal sight. Curiosity mixed with loathing filled his head, but he remembered Isabel's words, "apathetic freedom." Not so damn easy with the man in his airspace, though.

In fact, he was miles away from apathy. Raw hate clobbered his brain, but also, tingling gratification. At Bennet's frailty, the lifelessness bordering on despair in the man's dreary eyes. His father was so different from the vibrant, opulent playboy he remembered.

Zack forced himself to focus on the menu, but he kept reading the same item, peanut-encrusted tilapia, over and over again, and he not only hated the bottom feeder, but would go into anaphylaxis from the crust. *For fuck's sake, focus, Zack.*

In the meantime, Amy began the obligatory pleasantries and small talk. He was glad that she got chatty when nervous or excited—or both, in this case.

She began to jabber away about the crazy adventure she and *her* father had had locating Bennet James. She had pieced together the small details Darren had mentioned during their time together: Paris, France; Sabrina Rondot; B.C. Properties, and so on.

And Zack's stomach began to churn.

"I finally found one of Bennet's properties in New York in the public records, but a law firm was listed as the one contact." Zack was certain that was his father's lifelong attorney, Artie Deninger.

She detailed her phone call to the firm, but Zack could imagine for himself the sequence of events. The receptionist probably rolled her eyes at Amy's sappy-sweet voice and put her straight through to the voice mail of Mr. Deninger, P.A. She would have left a longwinded message like, "My name is Amy Rine, daughter of Dan Rine…blah, blah, blah…engaged to Bennet James' youngest son…phone number. Blah."

Zack's mental summary ended much quicker than his soon-to-be sister-in-law's. He politely continued his aimless analysis of the menu while pretending to listen. Eyes on desserts now, his mind wandered to Isabel wiping up the ice-cold mint chocolate chip mess from his lap the night before, until Amy's voice elevated an octave, startling him out of his daydream.

"…and I got a return call from Bennet the very next day!"

She continued on about the conversation she'd held with the bastard sitting across from him. *Breathe. Be polite. Smile.* His new mantra. His hands sweaty, he finally put the menu down. His hands began to fidget, so to maintain composure, he picked up the espresso demitasse in front of him, and, sipping it, wondered where it came from because he sure as hell didn't remember ordering it, or even seeing a waiter, for that matter.

Amy's monologue went on, piercing his ears and boiling his blood, but he considered the alternative to the current chatter and quickly regained his appreciation for Amy's presence and verbal energy level. She filled the potential silence, which was why they'd brought her along after all. And he full-well knew it wasn't her, but rather the topic of her prattle, that was killing him.

Beyond the ultra annoying details echoing in his ears, something else nagged at Zack. Bennet's return phone call to Amy—the next day, huh? The very. Next. Day.

*

His mother had gotten the harsh brush-off by Deninger for inviting Bennet to Darren's graduation. Bennet hadn't wanted to be contacted then, so why now had he been so damn easy to reach? What was this self-motivated shell of a man after?

"So, Bennet, how's Sabrina?" Zack blurted out, not even sure if he had cut Amy off. Thankfully, he hadn't. She was mid-bite into her salad, which had appeared out of thin air also. Had the waiter taken their food orders, too?

"Well, Son, I mean, *Zack*," Bennet corrected. "We, Sabrina and I, haven't been together for many years now. Many, many years," the man said in a hollow, solemn tone. God, the man's voice was so different than Zack remembered it. Thick and raspy, from too many cigarettes maybe? Or liquor?

"Sorry...to hear that?" Darren said, who then looked to Zack.

Darren had explained to Zack during their late night talk that he was willing to forgive their father, but it didn't mean it would be easy. Nor would he ever forget. Darren was hurt too. His brother was of course enraged that their own father had left them to start a new family, a replacement family. Bennet James' first family, Darren assumed, must not have been up to snuff when it came to his father's lifestyle. Keeping in line with the whole travelling circus metaphor from their phone call weeks ago, they were small town while Sabrina had offered the man Paris.

"To tell you the truth, boys," Bennet's voice cracked, "I've lost a lot over the years."

You mean you threw away a lot over the years, you fucker... And here it comes.

Was Bennet dying and needed a fucking organ? Was he accused of a crime and needed quick cover? Or was he a gambler, a substance abuser?

Did it really matter?

No, it did not. Because Zack could still put the puzzle pieces together without knowing the man's vice or vices.

The man was penniless and was back for funding!

Amy Rine of Beverly Hills, daughter of Daniel Rine, the shipbuilding tycoon.

Yeah, once a self-centered prick, always…

*

Zack's thoughts tore through his skull while he fumed and shook, suffocating.

"When the stock market collapsed and my REIT funds were in over-leveraged hotel and apartment holdings… I lost everything."

Bullshit. I bought everything. For way over market value.

How had the man blown through all that gain?

And again, what did that matter? The man was here. At his brother's wedding. For goddamn money!

"Then Sabrina left and took the kids with her. She had been stashing away my hard earned—"

"Stop," Zack demanded. He hated that he was right. "Just stop." Clearing his throat, he shifted his attention to Amy and Darren, then Amy solely. "Amy, I apologize. This is up to you…and Darren of course, but if you want to spare yourself unnecessary stress, given that your wedding day is tomorrow, I would recommend you take the limo back to the hotel now and just relax with your friends."

And Zack returned his narrowed eyes to the old man while waiting for Amy and/or Darren to make a decision. He just watched his father's sullen eyes shift uncomfortably under Zack's severe stare, but not one glance up from the man's salad. Bennet didn't dare.

"It's a good idea, Amy," Darren told her.

She pushed her chair out, smiled graciously at Bennet, then at Zack, and lastly, she leaned over and kissed her fiancé on the cheek before standing to leave. The two men and one sniveling coward all stood as she did.

*

Last night was the first time Zack had told Darren any of the gory details regarding their father, along with Zack's *actual* feelings about the man. And Darren relayed his regrets to his older brother—that although contacting Bennet had been a romantic and well-meaning gesture by his fiancée, he definitely saw how poorly timed this reunion was, especially during what was supposed to be such a joyous occasion. Zack and Darren, at the end of their late night talk, had finally put it all to what Zack called "a comedy of errors." *Thank you, Isabel.*

But right then, the comedy was anything but funny.

The waiter and a runner brought entrees, and three plates were placed. Zack now remembered telling the waiter to skip him earlier when their orders had been taken. So now, with his gut twisting from black espresso gasoline and rage, he signaled to his brother to give him Amy's plate, a pasta dish in some kind of cream sauce, to soak up the acid-hate eating him alive.

"I need the trust back," Bennet blurted out, staring down at his thick prime rib.

"Dad, things take time. Trust has to be built…you know? Earned. Hell, you've been gone for how many—"

"No, Darren," Zack cut his brother off, "that isn't the *trust* he means. He's saying he needs the money…the trust fund. The one he left us, when he…left us."

Darren looked in awe at Zack, then at his father. As the reality dawned, Zack watched the innocence drain from his brother's face, only to be replaced with hot red disdain. Darren's nature was kind, gentle, calm and light, but even his brother had his limits. And now Zack could tell that those limits were just about met. Zack put his hand on Darren's shoulder to steady him.

"Who flew you out here, Bennet?" Zack asked, taking over.

"Amy…well, her father," Bennet answered, still unable to make eye contact, the shame written on his face was Zack's exact intent. They all froze and remained that way for what felt like an eternity.

A birthday serenade from across the restaurant brought Zack back. He glanced at his cell phone. Only a minute had passed.

God, his mouth was dry, his chest still heaving. He took a sip of water, moistened his lips, and took a huge clearing breath through his nose.

Composed now, he found words. "I've already given you enough, having paid way above market for your property portfolio. Now, as for the trust that you so generously left us, Bennet, it is in Darren's name, solely Darren's. I relinquished rights to it the day after you left. He's the one you will have to consult. So"—Zack began to push his chair back to get the hell out of there—"I'm not needed here."

Darren looked at his brother with wide, desperate eyes, begging Zack not to leave him there alone.

Zack leaned back instead of standing and began rubbing his temples. He looked at Darren again, his brother was practically shaking with rage.

Fuck. Zack cleared his throat. "Darren, you just finished your master's program the head of your class. A year and a half early I might add. You're a sought-after architect, and that's all you. One hundred percent you, brother. Yes, your education was, as you know, paid for by me…but the work, the time, the sacrifice—it was all your effort and no one else's. And I've never made a better, more sound investment than the one I've made in you and your education. The least risk, highest reward of any I've ever made. And the only repayment I ask for is your happiness. And for your family to be happy, your wife and your future kids. That's it." He swallowed hard, and did not dare look at his brother, who he knew had tears falling from his furious eyes already.

Zack went on. "Now, the trust fund that Bennet is referring to, in fact, has remained untapped since he vanished. There was never a need. The business, my own real estate investments, the projects I slaved over, all yielded well. Very well. And they have supported you, Mom and me for all these years. I can say with all sincerity that I would have rather died than use a penny of Bennet's guilt money, *but*…if you or Mom had ever needed it to survive and *I* couldn't provide, then I was prepared to use it. I swear I would have swallowed my pride and used it."

Zack paused and glanced at Bennet. His father shifted uneasily in his seat. Zack caught what seemed to be a proud look in the old man's eyes just before Bennet shot his gaze down at his own trembling hands. Did Bennet James dare to feel pride in Zack? If that was the case, Bennett had to know, the man had no fucking right. That Zack wasn't *his* to be proud *of.* Bennet had relinquished his fatherly privileges when he'd traded his own flesh and blood for lust, greed, and the other seven fucking deadly sins.

His focus back on Darren, Zack continued. "I respect you, brother. And I trust you. If you see the trust fund as a necessary evil for you and your soon-to-be wife, for your future family, and your future home, then I tell you to use it. Use it to the fucking glory. No one deserves it more than you do… and I wouldn't judge you at all. In fact, I'd applaud you for thinking of the larger picture, the highest priority of all…your family." Zack paused to drive the last part home to Bennet.

His brother said nothing and just shook his head slowly, as if logic and clarity would come of it. Zack wished to hell it was that simple.

"Darren, hey, at least we know that we're a different sort of men, you and I—nothing like…*him.*"

Then Zack looked down, squinting from a sudden headache that spread throughout his entire skull. That last sentence, the very last words he'd spoken—*a different sort of men…nothing like…him*—they lit a fuse in him and tasted sour on his already parched tongue. He took another sip of water and abruptly pushed his chair back. "But if you choose to return the trust money to this man, then so be it. You are brilliant at your career, and you will always succeed, no matter what." He kissed his brother on the forehead, pulled out a hundred spot for the table, and headed for the exit.

"Son…Zachary! Wait!" Bennet yelled. But Zack wasn't slowing his stride.

*

Bennet made it to him before Zack reached his car.

"You need to understand," the man said, panting, holding Zack's elbow to keep him there and for support, it seemed. The man's fragility was extreme. "We struggled, Son…financially, it was really hard! I mean, before you were born. And when we found out Elaine was pregnant with you, we were hardly making ends meet."

"The point? Get to it, fast."

"Well, when you did come, it was as if the world flipped on its axis, one-eighty! It was immediate! I landed a job, finally, after nothing for two long years! Then a promotion, practically a fluke. We were ambushed with good fortune, and one doesn't know how to, you know, handle it when you're so unaccustomed to such wealth, so much power! And all that comes with it."

"Feeling pretty bad for you right now, Bennet." Was his father putting his disappearance from their lives on some frou-frou astrological fortune cookie bullshit? For the entertainment alone he had to hear Bennet out, but he assertively removed the man's hand from his arm and dusted off his shirt-sleeve from where the man's fingerprints lingered.

"I fell in deep. I was never home, and I was never really there when I was home, except in Vallarta, where there was almost no escape."

"Even then, Bennet…yes, you spent the days with us, but I knew you were out most nights, I mean, come on."

"Yes. It's true. It's true." The man paused in thought, eyes squinting shut as if that would erase history. He kept them shut tight as he continued. "Your mother got pregnant again with your brother to try to regain my attentions. But the man she'd fallen in love with when we both had nothing, he was long gone." His eyes opened then to meet Zack's glare. "I couldn't resist the temptations. And at the time, honestly, I didn't want to. But as soon as I left you boys, and your mother, everything started to fall apart; I lost everything, like there was another flip of the axis! Then, I saw the light—"

"The light, huh? But you still stayed away?"

"I couldn't come back. I was too…too ashamed."

"But here you are now." Zack's throbbing headache jumped to the next level and the world around him spun, with Isabel's words punching him in the center of his forehead once every turn. *Not the kind of man you are. Not the kind of man you helped Darren become.*" Her words burned guilt-riddled truth into his heart.

The kind of man I am? What kind of man is Zachary James? The kind who wanted to attack his father, rip him apart for throwing a seventeen-year-old kid into the desperate position of head of household? But even with such a responsibility dumped in his lap, he'd gone out and made his *own* fortune. That was a kind of a man to be proud of, right?

And who else was Zack James? Well, he *wasn't* the kind of man who'd committed to a wife and children and then left them cold for other women, more power, and lavish extravagance. In fact, Zack had prevented it from happening at all by always avoiding commitment. At all costs.

Until Isabel.

And the head spinning stopped.

*

Zack felt himself caught. Had he let the fear of *becoming* his father mold him into the man he despised? Into Bennet James? If he was to be honest with himself...yes, that was exactly who he'd become.

During Zack's mental monologue, his father just stood there, staring. "Zack. I *am* sorry. You must think I'm just pathetic. And I am. My actions then and now are of a pathetic, sad man. I can't expect you to forgive or ever forget. But whatever happens, if being out of your life for all this time has helped you become the man you are today, then, for that alone, I have no regrets. You are what I prayed you'd be."

Zack stared at and through his father, then he whispered, "Comedy of errors..."

With nothing left to say or hear, Zack felt something dark draining from his heart. It was quickly replaced by a rushing wave of the apathy Isabel had promised. And of calm, like the ocean-sized puddle that had attacked him on the first night he'd met Isabel. A washing, cleansing wave.

He held out his hand to his father. They shook. Then he left Bennet standing there. Done.

CHAPTER 28

H E NEEDED TO talk to Isabel.

Fuck it. Zack lifted his hips off the seat to gain access to his phone, then pressed his favorites button set for Amy.

"Yes, everything is, or will be, fine. Darren is still in there…Of course, *you* know him. No worries, Ame. He shouldn't be long. But hey, listen. I need the wedding planner's cell number… Because, well, I need to thank her. Last night, our talk, it helped a lot, that's all."

*

Meet me, again? Same place. Done with father.

Isabel read the text from the unknown number. She put her second earring on and wrote back: *Twenty Minutes. La Vaca.*

She ignored the conflicted thrill spiking her heart rate and the screaming protest ringing in her head.

*

When she got there, Zack had already gotten bowls of mint chocolate chip at their table, melting in Vallarta's early afternoon heat.

"What if I had wanted something different?" She smiled. But he didn't smile back. He was distracted and serious.

"It went well. And, damn you, Isabel, you drilled into my head so deep that I am seeing so clearly it hurts. I fucked up once, and I'm not going to let it happen again." He zeroed in on her like it was the end of the world and they were slated to be the only survivors.

"Let what happen? Zack, what are you talking about, exactly? You said it went well?"

"Yes. I forgave him, well, in my own way. He was…I mean, he *is* here for himself, for money, but who the fuck cares, right? Darren will make his decision whether or not to help the bastard, but, I…I feel nothing toward the man. Empty. And"—he grabbed her hand—"I discovered something else."

Isabel tried to pull her hand back from his, but he softly yet firmly kept it in his grasp.

"I am my father. Or I was my father." He halted there to sigh, then scooped a fast bite of ice cream into his mouth.

Mmmm, that mouth. But, God, he was acting so intense and emphatic and determined and manic all mixed together in a regrettably irresistible package.

"But I thankfully realize this now. It isn't too late. And I have a chance to change. Because of you, Isabel." He squeezed her hand tighter. "For you."

"Whoa there, Zack. Just…wait a minute here." Her suddenly clammy hand in his grip was beginning to lose circulation. He couldn't be falling for her. What the hell had she done?

"Look, you can't say I haven't gotten into your head like you've gotten into mine, Isabel."

She blinked her eyes deliberately to be sure she could believe where this conversation had just turned. "Zack. I don't deny…having thought about you. Or even, admitting that we…you know…*click*. I mean, even beyond the…mutual attraction." Her cheeks got hot. "But the reality is, we live in two completely different worlds," she said, knowing she'd need a stronger argument than that. So much stronger.

"Let me just spend time with you, as much as I can. I mean, after the wedding. Let's just see where things go with us."

"In the day or two before your flight back to wherever you actually live?" She was completely thrown off guard by his entire proposition. She knew he liked her, she knew this went beyond his potential sweet talk, but his urgency was just too much. She didn't expect him to be so hard to shake.

She'd been counting on the whole '*out of sight, out of mind*' thing, but what if she couldn't get him out of sight to kick him the hell out of her mind?

She could only stare while Zack went on. "That's the thing. I don't damn live anywhere! My jet, a whirlwind of hotels with faceless people and deals and luxuries I don't care about. The life I've led so far has literally been my fucking father's. Now that's comic, isn't it? Just goddamn hilarious, really," he said, almost to himself, ending with another hefty spoonful of melting ice cream.

So he was his father, and now he wanted to prove he could be just the opposite of him by using her? Now *that* was comic and as good of an excuse as any to tell him to screw off, right?

And she needed all the reasonable excuses she could come up with for not giving her and Zack James a chance. Because although she wished she didn't care so much about what he thought or how he saw her, she did. The fear of him taking her as a total nut job or discovering the walking curse that she was and being deathly scared of her was a lose-lose she couldn't even bear to think about. She'd rather he leave Vallarta enamored, and be able to hold onto the memory of his sweet, desirous eyes that melted her icy, numb heart and spun her around dizzy.

"Thanks but I'd rather not be used, Zack. Find another way to prove that you're not your dad."

"No, that's not what I meant. And I told you my feelings toward you as soon as I found you at the bar after searching the whole damn town for you, Isabel! I was almost too vocal. My feelings had, and still have, nothing to do with my father. Falling for you just happened, and I can't hold them back. I can't *not* see this through with you."

He stared at her as if trying to make out what she was feeling, thinking, planning.

But she said nothing, at a complete loss for words.

"I'm not asking for your hand in marriage or anything. I wouldn't be that damn bold. Hell, I expect you'd vanish again if I ever went there." He looked down at his bowl. "Believe me, I'm no expert at this relationship thing either, so we're the blind leading the stunningly beautiful blind here," he said, looking back up at her.

So he thinks I am just scared of relationships…? God, it's so much deeper than that.

"This feels so right, Isabel. And I want to just try…*us*. I can't bear the level of regret if we don't at least try." His steady stare was killing her, convincing her, scaring her.

Silent beats ticked by.

She watched his Adam's apple lift and drop again, maybe preparing more words. How to stop his horribly delicious words? Her hand still trapped in his, there was no apparent way.

"I've been planning on consolidating my property holdings and really making my move to Vallarta. That's why I was here so far ahead of the wedding, to close on my father's condo just outside of town, the one we'd stay in every year when we were growing up. That's been my end game all along. I can move here sooner, and nothing would be on your shoulders, Isabel. No pressure…"

No pressure? More like all the pressure in the world! *Think fast, Isabel.*

"Well, good because I should tell you now that I might be moving to Cabo to open a Golden Rings satellite for Lucinda, my own branch," she half lied. Lucinda had mentioned it in passing. Really a pipe dream, though. But it was all she could think to say to stop this insanity. "That is, if I make it through *this* event!" she ended, narrowing her eyes at him in warning, just short of saying, "*Keep the hell back so I can make it through this wedding!*"

"If things—if *we*—work out, then we…you know…work things out! Life happens, right? We would go with it! I'd move."

"You'd move to Cabo, even with your precious condo here, and your love for Vallarta?"

She saw a flare of frustration in his face. He was obviously getting fed up with her push back and excuses. He leaned in, lips pursed, but trying hard to control himself. "There is always a chance for relocation when dealing with work, Isabel." He took a breath. "Again, we'd work it out." His voice was mellow, but his furrowed brow gave him away. He wasn't backing down easily.

At that point, she just wanted to blurt out the truth, rip the bandage off, let him have the real, psycho reason she couldn't be with him, that she had to protect him…from *her*. And she had to protect her heart from yet another shattering loss.

But no, she couldn't. She had to suffer through to the end of the wedding in his presence, and she wouldn't be able to manage if he looked at her in any other way than the way he did right now. Those savage emerald eyes consuming her soul, her heart, her entire being.

And now he just waited. While she spun and whirled in thought and reason, he let the thick silence speak for itself, a true artist in salesmanship and negotiation, damn him.

But she could think of nothing—no next valid argument came to her bewildered mind. "Shit, I didn't realize the time…the rehearsal dinner!" She collected her purse and pushed her chair back. "You know this kind of discussion, it's really too…too big to rush. Rain check for after the wedding," she said with zero eye contact because she just couldn't handle seeing the expression on his face.

*

Zack cracked a smile and said, "Hold it!"

And that paused Isabel in her seat as if she were a child in trouble. He definitely wasn't letting her off that easy. After all, he still held her hand captive.

He couldn't believe how, with each offer he put out there, she'd put up another roadblock. But he saw through each one. Each one of her walls was made of soft white sand, and once he stepped back, he could see the entire sandcastle. All it needed was a big wave to roll in and wash it away. And he didn't mind being the very tidal wave to do it.

He mulled over the clues; her one-night rule, her proud exterior with the insecure center, the scars. She was afraid, and it didn't even matter why.

Because he wasn't *unafraid* of a stable, committed relationship and its risk of shattering. He was just as fucking terrified. A terrific life, a terrific love. With Isabel, his jumbled, tightening network of nerves was what made it all so heart-pumping, mouth-watering, and just plain worth it. Raw reality with his angel, Isabel. It was what he had been missing in his lofty, sugar-coated, loveless life.

"I really have got to go, Zack." She gave him an exhausted, defeated look with her tired eyes. He'd forgotten just how late they'd been out last night on the boardwalk together. And the night before that.

But he'd torture her just a bit more. He had to. With his free hand, he took another spoonful of ice cream into his mouth. He watched her eyes follow the spoon as it went in and then out and as he licked it clean.

Then he stood up. She tilted her head in confusion as he still held her gaze and her hand.

He moved toward her in a flash...

...and kissed her.

Now holding her captive with his mouth, his left hand released her hand to slide up her soft cheek, then back to cradle her head at the nape of her neck. He felt her body's surrender as he lulled and hypnotized her with his gentle assault. He knew that if it weren't for his consuming kiss, her protest would have been loud and strong. But her body alone gave no fight. His passionate demonstration continued until some of the children in the ice cream shop began to giggle and clap.

He let her go slowly, gently, reluctantly. He stood up and smiled down at the serene beauty, her lips parted as if still in mid-kiss, while her lids lingered over her deep golden eyes, fluttering lightly as if she were locked in a dream. He knew he was. Locked and hoping never to wake from it.

But whispers and little pointed fingers in his peripheral dragged him back to the real world.

He nodded at his audience to appease and shush them, then took his angel's hand in his. "Thank you, Isabel, for meeting me again. I'll see you this evening. I can't wait." Then *he* left *her* there.

Yes, he left *her*.

*

Looking back at her through the shop window, at her flushed cheeks, wide eyes and frozen pose in the ice cream shop's neon orange seat, he smiled. She shook her head to herself, as if attempting to get rid of the shock he'd just sent through her. She kept her head down while she collected her purse, then pushed herself back from the table. Before she stood up, Zack watched her take a deep inward breath, which filled her chest, making her glorious breasts rise. She licked her lips, hopefully tasting Zack's lingering mint chocolate chip ice cream he'd left there during his penetrating kiss.

He left the window then. Getting into his car, his heart melted for her and her vulnerability. He wouldn't relent though, not until she melted fully and forever into him.

CHAPTER 29

UNLESS HIS NAME was Zack James, no man would make her radar. She was in so deep, she could hardly function.

Rehearsal dinner, Isabel. Get your shit together!

She spotted him across the banquet hall on line at the bar, looking amazing, just classy as hell. There was a touch of irritation in his evergreen eyes, the maid of honor chatting his ear off. Isabel thought the scene so funny, she laughed out loud, yes, to the confusion of the guests in her vicinity. She smoothed her flowing yellow dress down her legs with heated cheeks and a pleasant smile and continued with the night's tasks as best she could. Damn hard to do since she was still reeling from that afternoon's kiss.

Focus. Go check on the first course. Grinning politely, she weaved through tables of mingling guests, making her way to the service hallway, which led back to the main banquet kitchen.

*

Footsteps clipped behind Isabel, mimicking the rhythm of her low heels.

Always cautious, always ready, she mentally prepared for action, as taught to her by Antonio.

She didn't look back, she just increased her pace.

But so did the pursuing footsteps.

*

A hand grabbed her shoulder.

Isabel threw a backhand blow to the face...

...but Zack caught her wrist before her fist made contact, and he spun her around.

"Jesus you scared the hell out of me!" But desire leapt in to steal away her anger as he slid his hand down her forearm, caressing it until he reached her elbow, then lowered her arm to her side.

"I didn't mean to scare you. I even said your name."

She didn't remember hearing anyone saying anything, but then again, the pulsing panic reverberating in her head might've trumped all. God, Roberto's recent behavior really had her on high alert.

She reset her nerves with a deep breath. "I didn't hear you but, either way, Zack, you shouldn't be back here." Even though her body screamed otherwise, as the dry, electrifying heat of his touch made her damp under her dress. Damn him. And then, completely ignoring her comment, his hand, still cuffing her arm, glided up slowly to her shoulder, which he circled lightly with his fingertips, sending chills through her. Her back arched suddenly in response, the reaction was out of her control entirely.

"Here." With his other hand, Zack took a white lily from his bulging front pocket and slid it behind her ear. "Wear this. You said it was your favorite flower."

Coño! She really couldn't take this right now, but as that thought entered, his warm, igniting touch left her shoulder. It was replaced by an instant, icy void, as if she had been unplugged from the sun. Then all of a sudden, her brain could function, registering that he had already started back down the long corridor to resume his role as best man.

She was one part angry at the contact he'd made, *too damn risky*, while another part of her was in love with his follow-up attention after he had left her vibrating at the ice cream shop that afternoon.

And he'd remembered the lily.

So cliché, but so damn sweet it pained her heart. She forced her feet toward the main kitchen as originally planned before becoming a puddle of sap there on the cold cement floor.

*

Isabel made her rounds, from the stage for a mic check to the bar for wine levels. She sent a message to the kitchen through the headwaiter that it was time for dinner service and then positioned herself in the grand ballroom so she could make eye contact with the bride.

And all the while, the damn photographer kept following her around like a puppy. She kept having to redirect him toward the bride, the groom, the *other* wedding guests, and away from her, for goodness' sakes.

She prided herself as being exponentially more diligent than most coordinators. Not just for career advancement, but because the better an event was planned and prepared, the less chance there was for her inevitable missteps, trip-ups, and fallouts. She made it a rule to never handle any object directly. She hired a slightly larger crew than most of Lucinda's planners so she could reduce breakage and just do the puppet mastery from behind the scenes, be the brain of the operation.

And usually she'd run everything through her earpiece, communicating to each of the major stations, but Lucinda had taken them all for her celebrity affair in Sayulita without mentioning it. She'd definitely have Raquel get new sets in the morning for the ceremony. For now she was just glad she wore the most functional low heels she had in her closet and hoped to hell not to set the place on fire as she scurried—smoothly, of course—from station to station.

And on top of it all, she had to deal with the distraction of all distractions, sitting smack in the center of the room, following her every move with those magnanimous eyes. Zack.

Add a hurdle for fun, why don't you? Really, thanks! Speaking to Fate used to make her feel insane, but now it was just luck she kept the conversation inside her own head.

And she tried like hell to keep her eyes off Zack, which made them wander his direction all the more. Mesmerized, she'd glance then shift her gaze away as quick as her feet moved her around the room. But each time she'd force her eyes off him, they'd land right on Stephanie Rine, who sat as close as humanly possible to Zack, just short of a lap dance distance, for Christ's sakes.

But right at this moment, Zack was alone, just him and his full glass of something, which he circled with his index finger, around and around, obviously deep in thought. And the thought of that finger on her now throbbing bud shocked and embarrassed her as if the room could read her mind.

She shook her head, eyes closed to remove the image, and turned toward her next stop, the photographer on the far side of the ballroom, who had finally left her alone, but was now flirting with the bar back girl and missing the entire party altogether.

She took a step in the photographer's direction, and quick reflexes just barely prevented a direct collision into Stephanie Rine. Isabel's hand flew to her pounding chest in shock.

"Ah, Jezebel, I wanted to—"

"Isabel, Stephanie. My name's *Isabel*." Fluster turned to immediate annoyance. *Only two more days of this one.*

"Yes, right. Well, I wanted to check in on…on…" Stephanie's nose crinkled, and as if waiting for something, the woman froze there, then scrunched her nose more.

"What did you need to check on, Stephanie?" Isabel really didn't have time to stand around waiting for the woman to complete her dramatic build up to a damn sneeze, especially as she watched the photographer head to the restroom with only two minutes before the pre-wedding speeches. "Is it about the adjustments to your dress? Because they're done, and it was delivered to your room two hours ago." Giving an inaccurate dress size was just not okay, Stephanie having made extra and unnecessary work for both Isabel and the seamstress.

"No!" Stephanie spat defensively. "No. The details for…for—"

A loud exploding sneeze interrupted the inherently bitchy tone.

A silence fell over the surrounding guests as they searched the room for the source of the explosion.

Stephanie covered her nose, then got thrown into an attack of more uncontrollable sneezes. When she looked up at Isabel, her eyes were bloodshot, inflamed, and tearing.

"The ladies' room is that way." Isabel turned to point, and when she twisted, Stephanie shrieked then snatched the white lily from Isabel's hair, throwing it emphatically to the floor.

"I'm allergic to lilies! Why do you have a lily in your hair, Jezebel? Didn't you read the details of the bride and her family in your stupid questionnaires?" The woman scoffed. "You did this on purpose! You are—"

But another sneezing fit interrupted the rant.

Isabel didn't forget details related to her events, but had she missed this one? An allergy? The maid of honor's allergy? She knew of the best man's nut allergy, but there were no others. She was sure.

Or was she?

Shit! She needed to get access to the file on her tablet, which was in her purse. To check. To be absolutely positive, even though, again, she never got this level detail wrong! But still she'd double check. She had been so distracted, after all. More than ever before. Between Roberto and this event—so much riding on it! And of course, Zack.

She swallowed back a knot of anxiety. *Be calm, Isabel.*

Okay. First, Stephanie Rine would be fine, she knew that.

But as for Isabel's pride, she hated to imagine the maid of honor's look, and Annette Rine's for that matter, if Isabel had missed this.

Thankfully though, she had no concerns regarding her position with Lucinda's company. Her boss had heard all about the pseudo-deep drama queen and would no doubt support Isabel, even if she had missed this vital detail. Yeah, Isabel was as sure of that as she was sure that she hadn't missed anything at all…

Come on, a lily allergy? The MOH of her biggest gig ever? And her favorite flower, to boot? She'd even dealt with that crazy bride a month ago who'd tried to get her lily-allergic mother-in-law sick—until Isabel put her foot down. No, she'd have caught this in the Rine/James questionnaires. *For certain.*

Rapid-fire sneezes brought Isabel back to the situation. *Diffuse then discovery.* She took Stephanie's elbow, leading her toward the restroom. "No!" Stephanie screamed in between sneezes, and shooed Isabel away.

Fine. So after she watched Stephanie sneeze herself to the ladies' room, hunched over and whimpering the entire way, Isabel speed-walked through the ballroom to the back corridor to her tablet.

And as she scurried—*smoothly, with composure*—she felt Zack's eyes from across the room. She glanced at him over her shoulder. She was sure he had no idea what was going on, but he mouthed the words, "Are you okay?" She didn't have time to respond, though, and continued through the service door with his concerned-yet-searing gaze at her back.

*

He hadn't been able to stop staring at her. She moved quickly, and he watched her every step and interaction. He watched all the waiters, techs, and bartenders eat right out of her hands.

And she had kept the lily right where he had placed it behind her ear. His insides warmed with that tiny morsel of confirmation, however meaningless. She looked like an exotic princess, the Princess of Puerto Vallarta, he mused. He didn't even care anymore how sentimental and cheesy he'd become. It felt too damn good.

At the same time, he was enjoying the Darren and Amy show. His brother was such the man. Darren smothered and doted on Amy like they wouldn't see each other every day for the rest of their lives. Every day. *The rest of their lives.*

God, the rest of their lives…but yes! For Zack, with Isabel…hell, yes!

Then from his peripheral, a strange exchange between Isabel and Stephanie caught his attention, ending with Isabel's marginally calm dash across the banquet room floor. Her expression as she passed was wide-eyed, edged with worry. He didn't think she ever got flustered. She hardly broke a sweat from what he'd seen of her in wedding planner mode. Something was up. He mouthed a message to her, but when he didn't get a response back, he got up to follow her…again. *Stalk much, Zack?* He didn't care, he wanted to be sure she was alright. He made sure no one saw him slip through the side door. But when he couldn't find her in the long passageway, he decided to get back. He was sure whatever drama involving Stephanie was still unfolding. He knew enough about the maid of honor to expect a long-winded saga made out of nothing.

*

Sneaking back in through the same door, he saw Annette Rine and Amy sitting next to Stephanie. Amy was patting her sister's hand while Annette melodramatically wiped her eldest daughter's red and swollen eyes.

Zack approached.

"What happened? Everything alright?" he asked, damn well knowing the answer.

"That Jezebel…" Stephanie started then sneezed, causing Zack to step back a few feet. "I told Mother we should have fought for Lucinda to manage things!"

"The wedding planner girl had a flower in her hair that my daughter is highly allergic to. I'm sure it was on purpose…envy is a very dangerous thing!" Annette Rine touted for her older daughter.

"Mother, Isabel would never do anything to hurt anyone!" Amy chimed in.

Zack cleared his throat. "Ladies, let's focus on getting Stephanie some—"

"Help is here," came a quick and confident voice over his shoulder. His angel's voice. "Excuse me, please. I have Dr. Ortega here to attend to the maid of honor. If we can step out of the Banquet Hall to the seating area?" And *there* was the controlling goddess Zack had longed for the entire night.

Or his entire life.

"My nephew Andrew is an *American* doctor. Get him instead," Annette Rine demanded.

"Now, Annette—" Zack began, but the stubborn old bag had already started scanning the room for her nephew.

"Dr. Ortega has his clinic in this resort, and his medical bag is right here with him." Isabel pointed to the man's side. "In the interest of time...," she continued, looking at Amy for support.

Amy touched her mother's shoulder and with a firm look, forced Annette to concede.

Hell yes! Zack was glad to see Amy taking matters into her own hands.

Zack helped Stephanie to her feet, and as she walked with Zack and the doctor out of the grand ballroom, Stephanie glared behind her in Isabel's direction.

And Zack looked back at Isabel, too, with a subtle smile and a supportive wink.

*

The silence had to be broken, and Isabel was just the one to break it.

"Amy, are you enjoying the evening so far?"

"Oh, absolutely! And so is Darren. Thank you so much, Isabel."

Annette interrupted with a huff. "*You?* And Darren? Did you just see what happened to your sister? You should be furious right now, Amy Lynn! Furious at this so called wedding planner...not even knowing what allergies the maid of—"

Isabel's hand went up to Amy's shoulder, blocking Annette and her tirade. "Oh yes, I needed to show you this, Amy...it's very important." She took out her digital lifesaver. "I got my tablet so I could double check all the questionnaires with you to prevent any other, well, mishaps. But, as my memory serves me, no allergies were listed for *anyone* in the wedding party except for the best man."

She slid her fingers over the screen. "This is your sister's signed questionnaire. Each item is answered with a handwritten *NA*, even question number seven, '*Allergies.*' But she did write her coffee beverage preference and her dress size... albeit a few sizes too"—Isabel cleared her throat—"...snug, as it turns out."

Annette glared, speechless for one glorious moment. Then the woman retorted, "Well, I'm certain there's a mistake."

"Jesus Christ, Mom! There's no mistake. It's a scanned, signed document. See? In Stephanie's own handwriting." Amy placed her hands on Isabel's shoulders and turned her slightly so their backs were in her mother's awestruck face. "As far as I'm concerned, Isabel, my sister deserves what she gets. I'm going to find Darren and get the hell away from this commotion. Please, just…you know…ignore my mother! And Stephanie. God, I can't wait to no longer be a *Rine*." With that, Amy huffed off to find her groom. And Isabel watched proudly as Amy did so.

*

Despite the almost disastrous, but deeply satisfying, white lily episode, the evening went on smoothly after that, especially once Stephanie was escorted up to her room by Dr. Ortega and Doctor/Nephew Andrew at Annette's insistence. Stephanie was so woozy from the medicine that Dr. Ortega had pumped into her that she probably wouldn't remember a thing anyway.

The vibe of the room became drastically lighter. Some of the guests even began to take turns at the karaoke setup on stage. And the bride seemed to have the most to release, as she made that microphone her bitch, letting loose and singing her heart out to Marco's "Struck by Luck" three times straight. God, Isabel hated that song, but she smiled wide at Amy's new-found freedom. Next the bride would be dancing around the place nearly naked. Isabel laughed to herself, wishing she were home doing just that.

*

At 1:00 AM, most guests headed back to their rooms for the night. Beds were calling, especially with the Big Day having officially arrived, only eleven hours until the ceremony. But Isabel noticed some of the wedding party had paired up during the evening's festivities, so sleep wouldn't come to everyone. The very thought made her hot, her throbbing arousal took her off guard again, and her cheeks flamed up.

What is wrong with you, damn it?

But she knew the answer.

He was sitting alone at his table, watching her with starving eyes, not subtly, either. Had he seen her blush? Did he know why? Her wondering only made her cheeks hotter. But she continued to study him. His gaze was glassy and there were too many empty glasses in front of him to count. She felt his intentions from afar. But before his unrelenting magnetism could catch hold of her, she twisted her head to break the spell and wisely decided to get the hell out of there—fast.

She left through the service door, actually jogging in her two-inch Demi Dorns down to the main kitchen. Thank goodness she hadn't worn her spikes. She quickly consulted the banquet manager for closedown and slid out the back entrance into the staff parking lot to her car.

*

In a drunken haze, Zack followed Isabel. The third time that night, down the service passage he went. *God, this would be a perfect place to have her.* To take her. All with that thrill of being caught.

But he knew that would be bad for her. He had to get her in private, in secret. But he was chasing after her to be sure she was okay—and that was all. Because he still couldn't tell if the white lily incident had caused her any major issue.

Yeah, he was just checking on her, really, nothing else to it.

But *he* couldn't even swallow his lame lie. It was Isabel, after all. Of course she was okay. And he knew she didn't want him checking on her.

And of course, he didn't want to *just* check on her. He wanted to consume her whole.

Her wellbeing first, Zack. For fuck's sake.

Yes, of course. And checking on someone you care about, whether they want it or need it or not, is an authentic gesture. Totally justified. He should see that she's alright, be there for her. *Definitely.*

He'd have to wait 'til after the wedding for anything else. Tonight they'd only talk. And maybe even laugh over the whole Stephanie-lily episode. Yeah, with no one around he'd reach her car, and just like their magical time on the boardwalk, they'd laugh and talk and laugh some more.

Then maybe she'd thank him with a kiss from those sensuous lips. He would reciprocate her thanks and press his body into hers, against her car door, turning on all her switches that were waiting there for him, under her thin, flowing silk dress. He would grind his aching cock in between her screaming thighs until he made her cream just slightly into those hot lace panties he'd seen before, the ones he aimed to rip off of her once they got into her tight little sedan.

After all, she'd kept the lily!

His sloshed logic jumped around all over the place as he staggered on, but it didn't matter. His true focus was realized and acknowledged: He would convince her to let him in. Into her car. Into her house. Into her bed. And back before dawn, before any wedding guests awoke.

Fuck, he wanted her so damn bad.

He shook his head to refocus when he got to the hotel's commercial kitchen. Quickly assuming a role of 'meant-to-be-here,' he walked through the stainless steel maze and outside. The fresh evening air hit him, and he took it in. He walked along the side of the building, following the scattered light poles while trying to keep from falling over in the dumpster-lined alley-way. The headlights of some vehicles from a side parking lot told him to veer right. He found himself by the pool and spa entrance of the resort where a few tables were filled with late night schmoozers and smokers, but no one he knew from the wedding. He squinted and strained his dry eyes to search for the silhouette of Isabel in the distant parking lot.

A few more struggling steps forward and his eyes caught something. Yes, about one hundred feet away were the delectable curves of the goddess he had set out to…check on.

He stumbled slightly, but regained his footing, and continued walking toward her. His ear noted some sudden off-pattern footsteps behind him, but they stopped just as quickly, and he dismissed them. *Keep focused, Zack.*

A high Humvee revved by him, blocking his view and forcing him to wait before crossing the lot. He held himself steady by staring at the dim street lamp above him, a balancing focal point. The beastlike vehicle finally passed, leaving him with the full voluptuous view of Isabel.

Who was now accompanied by a second silhouette.

The two shapes suddenly morphed into one, and a scream for help hit his ears.

Solid awareness vanquished his drunken buzz, and he flew to Isabel.

CHAPTER 30

ISABEL WAS LEAN, muscular, but still, her arms shook as they held the man as far from her face as possible. His core had already trapped her groin and torso against the car, and with his legs pinning hers, she couldn't even knee him, although she didn't quit trying.

"Get the fuck off me! Stop goddamn you!" she screamed.

"It's me, Isa, no reason to fight. It's your true love!" His voice oozed innocent sweetness as his hands fought and slapped to touch her skin, her face. Then he forced his mouth onto hers.

Her teeth crunched down.

He threw his head back howling, his hands at his bleeding mouth while his hips still pinned her to the vehicle.

"Roberto! Get off me! Now, damn you!" Her words lingered in the air, maybe paining him more than the bite to his tongue.

Two hands appeared over each of Roberto's shoulders and yanked, ripping Roberto's body from hers.

Boundless relief had Isabel sliding down her car, ending in a ball on the pavement. Her brain was fully aware and weirdly calm while her body shivered uselessly on the ground. She watched the tussle, but the scene played out in slow motion as her racing pulse pounded through her.

The broad-shouldered savior stood between her and Roberto, who threw himself in her direction, leaping at the other man's impenetrable body. With his wide back to her, he'd become a tall, gritty barbed wire fence between her and a relentless pit bull. Seconds-like-years passed while the wall of a man stayed his ground. And all without one swing at her attacker, as if he strategically waited for Roberto's batteries to run out.

She heard yelling and rushing footsteps, then the man, The Wall, yelled, "Gentlemen, over here! This man"—*that voice*—"attacked this innocent woman as she got to her car. I saw the entire thing."

Zack? His deep baritone was unmistakable. His vast, unyielding frame, too. Her heart lifted—then sank on her next jagged breath.

She just couldn't escape him.

Worse, she didn't want to.

And in this particular case—oh, God, thank you for Zachary James.

*

The hotel security guards each grabbed an arm and yanked Roberto back, but her best friend continued his futile efforts.

Zack, now staring at her with tender eyes, maintained his blockade, not allowing Roberto sight or scent of her. Then he took a step toward her and offered his hand. She paused, though, when a far off voice met her ears.

"Is everything okay? Zack! Are you hurt?" a woman called.

Stephanie. Definitely Stephanie Rine. Isabel's eardrums ached from the shattering pitch.

Zack waved Stephanie off, wherever she was shouting from, while Roberto's rantings increased in volume, a last attempt as he was dragged away.

"Are you crazy, Isa? Making it seem like you don't want me! Isa, we are meant to be together, so stop this now! You can't distract yourself with these other men! The German guy, then that Canadian DJ? And *this* playboy! Come on, Isa! Wake up! I'm the one! I'm your new Sebastian! You felt it that night in my arms! Just wait 'til I *do* make love to you! Then you'll know, Isa! Isaaa!" And finally Roberto's screams faded.

Zack heaved a breath, removed his sports jacket, and kneeled down next to Isabel, draping his coat over her bare shoulders. It was hot out, but with the thick angst in her gut, she shivered uncontrollably. All she could muster was a, "Thank you," while she continued her blank stare into the night.

"I'm staying here with you. They're going to want to process reports. It'll take a couple of hours, at least, and then I can get you home safely." But as he spoke, Isabel's mind whirled back to logical reality. "I'll sleep on your couch, the floor, whatever. Just as long as you're not out of my sight."

She looked into his deep green eyes, so soft, caring. "Zack, I think, I mean, I know that I'm…okay. I'm in love—I mean, in debt…Oh God." She winced then exhaled slowly. "Just, thank you. For coming to my rescue." She paused, wanting to give him her hand, to be sure he knew her sincerity, her relief, and gratitude for his presence.

But Stephanie's distant shouting reminded her of her necessary role.

"Let's just get you inside. We'll get through the red tape togeth—"

"No—no, Zack. I mean, really, I'm fine, on my own," she stated, as if to an unruly wedding guest who had pushed her too far. "Please, Zack. I just can't risk it."

"You can't risk being assaulted again in a parking lot!" He'd raised his voice, but apologized with a nod and a blink. "After what happened here, are you still worried about Stephanie? Your job?"

"My career, Zack…yes." She huffed her frustration, then shut her eyes to clear her head. "Listen, I *wouldn't* have been fine," she soothed, "if it weren't for you. That I know. But I *am* fine now. Please, just let me go do this alone. See, I don't even have a scratch on me. I'm just a little shaken up is all."

With hands up and a downturned glance, he conceded. No more radiant green gaze—she felt him unplugging.

But it had to be this way. Just look at what happened with Roberto. Fate was flaring her fucking talons again! She knew where her best friend would end up—prison's just as good as death in Mexico! For Zack's sake, unplugging was the only option. Damn her heart in the process.

*

She watched Zack, dejected, as he spoke to the guard, instructing him to get Isabel inside right away. That he himself would give his full statement in the morning or, giving it another shot, "Tonight even?"

But the officer stated that the morning would actually be better. Zack handed the guard his business card and shook his hand for longer than customary, maybe still hoping that Isabel or the guard might change their minds. But there was no change. Isabel needed him to go. He sighed, his obvious frustration etched in the lines above his furrowed brow, then set himself to leave the scene, toward the hotel and the still-shouting maid of honor.

"Oh," he said after taking his first reluctant step, "do make sure Ms. Ruiz is escorted safely back to her car after the processing of all necessary and *complete* paperwork." The guard nodded, and Zack made his exit.

She watched him walk toward the hotel, hating every step he took. Her heart ached, screamed, thrashed, while Isabel could only look on helplessly, wanting nothing more in the universe than for him to stay with her.

Look back. Just a glance. To tell her he understood.

But Zack James did not look back at her. He did not break his stride or his focus. He was doing exactly what she'd asked him to do, heading straight back to the hotel, to his room, to bed. And it burned her like fiery hell.

And, of course, to add to the flames were the strangling sounds of Stephanie Rine's swooning shouts as the best man approached the horrid woman, and as he got further and further away from Isabel.

CHAPTER 31

H E WALKED TOWARD the hotel's pool entrance, holding an inner argument with himself. She told him to leave her, she'd insisted. But he should have fucking stayed.

On the other hand, he had to take into account Isabel's nature, the strong, fierce tigress that he knew her to be. Isabel was a rock, and although she'd just been shaken to her core, she didn't need nor did she want a savior...not even in extreme assault scenarios.

And he realized that he didn't want a damsel in distress, either. What he wanted, who he wanted, all he wanted, was Isabel.

*

As he neared the pool, he prepared what he needed to say to Stephanie. He was unsure of how long or from which point Stephanie had seen him or maybe even had been following him, but a vague and matter-of-fact response was all he'd give her.

"Oh, Zack, I was so worried! Was that Jezebel? Was she being attacked? Are you alright! God, those types of women and their provocative auras just attract that kind of element. But she was so lucky you were there! So"— she stopped for effect and maybe a moment's breath—"what *were* you doing there?"

A growl of disgust rumbled in his chest. Forget the 'luck' reference, did the woman just insinuate the attack was Isabel's fucking fault? Fury, raw and real, locked his breath.

But this woman wasn't worth the breath.

Speak quick and go, Zack.

"I guess I just got lost in the right place at the right time," he said, walking straight past her. "Well, I'm still feeling the alcohol from the party so... good night." And he continued into the building, the hotel security door closing with a clank behind him.

*

Then the door buzzed and swung open again. "Zachary? With such a scary incident having just happened, I, um...I'm a little worried about going up to my room alone. Would you mind going with me?" Stephanie implored.

He looked up at the ceiling. Was this woman for real? No, she was more like a big wad of artificially sweetened bubble gum stuck to the bottom of a brand new pair of shoes.

"Since we're on the same floor, Stephanie, fine. Let me get the elevator here." And as he went to press the call button, her finger met his, a giggle escaping her lips and a ravenous hunger glowing in her eyes.

The elevator came quickly. Thankfully. "Ladies first."

That is, if there was *a lady* present.

"Such a gentleman," she flirted hopefully.

They got into the elevator, and to Zack's disappointment, the car was empty.

Hoping for elevator-super-speed and Stephanie's silence, he just hit their floor number, and up the elevator traveled.

Besides Stephanie's frequent sniffling and wheezing, her allergic reaction apparently still affecting her eyes and nose, and now her breathing capacity, the quiet was deafening. Again, better than any more words out of her ignorant mouth. Zack just focused on each small creak in the hydraulic-powered elevator cabling and the sound of the *swoosh-swoosh* increasing and decreasing as they passed each floor.

Ding!

The doors opened, but it was only the eighteenth floor. *For fuck's sake.*

A waiter with a catering cart appeared, framed within the elevator's doorway. *Okay, company is good.* But with a look of disappointment being that there was no room for the man and his doublewide food trolley, the waiter, to *Zack's* disappointment, disappeared the next moment. The elevator doors shut, once again sealing in the thick, radiating, awkwardness put out by his wedding party counterpart.

"Thanks for accompanying me," Stephanie said. "And, you know, you're more than welcome into my suite. For a last drink of the night. Or"—she looked at her watch—"the first drink of the day." She giggled again.

Ugh.

Ding!

Finally! The twenty-fifth floor.

"Like I said, Stephanie, I really need to sleep. Big day tomorrow for my kid brother and your little sister," Zack said, doubting she gave a crap about Amy or Darren, being such the spotlight hound. He escaped from the elevator into the hall as soon as the doors opened and moved quickly to his door three rooms down on the left. He pointed to her room only a few down from there. "Here we are, safe and sound. So sleep well, Stephanie. And feel better, you know, with your eyes and nose, and all."

And his hotel room door opened, closed, and locked behind him all before she could ask him again to join her for anything.

CHAPTER 32

ISABEL FINISHED WITH the police and the hotel management's accident report protocol very quickly, thanks to Charlie, who knew Isabel had a wedding to direct in less than nine hours.

What Charlie didn't know was that she'd had less than three hours sleep between last night and the night before. She was running on fumes. Then add the crazy and sickening drama that was just thrown at her, and her emotional state was all that more fragile, shaky, and irrational.

Case in point: Her deep concern, however unwarranted, over Roberto's status.

"Charlie, where did they take Roberto? I just want be sure he's, you know…okay. I mean, maybe I shouldn't press charges?"

"Isabel. You aren't safe unless he's put away and gets some help. And that won't happen unless you do this. Listen, you just need to get some rest." Charlie walked her out to the back door where a guard waited for her. "He'll be booked tonight locally. Tomorrow morning I'll follow up with my contact at the precinct. And I'll press for a psych evaluation. Maybe getting him to the secure mental facility up north will solve all your concerns. But right now, you need to take care of you."

Isabel was escorted to her car. Before starting the ignition, she dialed Antonio. The guard seemed intent on waiting for her to completely exit the resort before leaving her there, so she held up two fingers and smiled in thanks for his patience. There was just no way that she was going home to an empty house.

Antonio answered her call, groggy from sleep, but quickly raised his voice to screaming, and cursed Roberto to the "depths of hell." She let him spew fireballs for a solid minute, but then brought him back down to practical.

"I just need you to meet me at my house right now. I'm leaving the hotel parking lot. I'm fine, just a little shaken up. Roberto's detained and Charlie will keep me posted. He has a connection on the force who'll let me know that Roberto is okay."

"Okay! Who cares if he is okay, Isa?"

"This is my fault on so many levels, Antonio."

"God, Isa, do you hear yourself? We should've listened to you!"

"No, I mean, it's *my* hex, *my* influence, and my blindness! But all that aside, the fact is he is...was...my best friend. We can keep me safe by keeping him away, but we've gotta make sure he gets help! It's Roberto, for Christ's sake!"

"Just get home, Isabel. I'm already pulling out of my garage."

Her car keys rattled slightly as she tried to start the car. She took a deep, calming breath. And with that breath, she thought of Zack.

Zack had been there for her.

And just the thought of him calmed her, comforted her, steadied her.

*

She left the hotel premises, throwing a final wave of thanks to the guard as she went. Merging onto the main drag, her mind shifted up a gear, back into anxiety mode.

Was Roberto safe? And was she the shovel that'd dug the hole he'd fallen into? She just hadn't realized how serious Roberto was about her. Had she been too flirtatious with him? And not direct enough?

But to force himself on her like that! He'd actually attacked her! And it was unforgiveable. Threatening her, hurting her. *Damn it, Roberto, what the fuck were you thinking?*

And, she knew he'd seen her with Zack at the bar, but how the hell did he know anything about Drew from Germany or DJ Chris? God, just how long had he been following her? Watching her? Her head spun. Her date with Drew was before she'd even made the God-awful mistake of sleeping with Roberto! Just how far back did this go?

A whirlwind of instances flew at her at once. *But wait!* Did she remember correctly, or was it just the trauma of the night, the words Roberto had shouted at her as he was taken away. "Just wait 'til I *do* make love to you..."

When "I *do* make love to you?" But they *had* slept together. She'd gotten stupid blackout drunk and broken her rule. He'd told her so. She'd blacked out that night, and he'd told her they'd had sex when she'd woken up naked in his arms, in his bed, that was what he'd damn told her!

Dios Mío! Had he set it up? Undressed her to make her think...and then lied about it? Wait. Was it even worse than that? He had made her all her drinks that night, at least the ones she could remember! Did he drug her? She really couldn't put it past him at this point. She couldn't rule out anything.

And it was all because she'd selfishly hung on to him, to her one friend on Earth. And, no, even that wasn't permitted. Not even Roberto was allowed in her cursed world. She'd broken her goddamn rules long before the night they'd supposedly slept together. She'd blurred her lines long before that. Safe distance? No. Unsafe, lethal.

Her chest was caught, no air. Screaming, sprinting thoughts. *Justify it, Isabel. Justify 'til your heart's content.*

No, damn it! It wasn't rationalization, her attempts had been real, her intentions had been true. She'd tried to keep Roberto from harm, even asked him to keep away. And now, tonight, was this the lesser evil? Her dearest friend having gone out of his mind? She'd driven him to the brink of insanity. Would death have been better than the torture Roberto would face in a damn mental ward for the criminally insane?

Stop being so melodramatic, Isabel.

Melodramatic? *Seriously, fuck you, fate! Just, goddamn you to hell.*

She felt sick to her stomach, ready to spew her guts out. She knew she should pull over, but was too scared to. And so tired.

So goddamn tired. Too tired to work it out in her head

anymore, the unseen darkness that plagued her was draining her dry. Bones-in-the-desert dry.

"Fuck you!" she screamed. She pounded and pounded her steering wheel with both hands, again and again and again. With the last slam of her quivering hands, she mistakenly hit the horn, which startled her into a slight swerve on the thankfully empty road. Then her eyes welled with blurring tears, and she just unfolded.

Sobs, years and years of salty wet sorrow. She had no choice but to pull off to the side of the road then, as she cursed the never-ending shit storm that was her life. She took long breaths to get control while her nausea still threatened, but didn't send her over the edge. Only her tears dove to their deaths. A billion, trillion tears.

What seemed like hours later when only minutes had passed, the glow of a truck's oncoming headlights broke her daze. *Get home, Isabel. Antonio's there. Just get your ass home.*

She pulled back onto the road and reached for her volume control, thinking her heavy metal music would steady her for the rest of her drive. But another cyclone of thoughts came first. *For Christ's sake, leave me alone! Can't I have ten minutes of peace?*

No. An alternative surfaced. The awareness that if Roberto had not been waiting at her car just hours ago, then it would have been Zack…alone. And as drunk as she knew he'd been, having had her peripheral on him throughout the entire rehearsal dinner, he would have done the very same as Roberto.

But Jesus! Here was the undertow of guilt; she would have welcomed *that* attack.

Finally being honest with herself, she would have accepted Zack's advances in the far off, poorly lit staff parking lot. Why? Because when it came to Zack James, her willpower was just too damn weak. And it would have all potentially gone down with Stephanie, *Zack's* "stalker", on the sidelines, which of course would have been the end to her career.

*

Antonio was on the edge of the pullout bed when she got home. He was heaving pissed, God, like she'd never seen him. She broke his zone with the sound of her car keys clanking on the sideboard. And a second later, he had her wrapped in his arms. "God, Isa. I am so sorry. So, so sorry."

Her brother couldn't blame himself. She wouldn't allow it. "Fate, brother. Just fate," she whispered. Not that she really believed that. She still put it all on herself. But she knew Antonio wouldn't accept that. She pulled away from him slowly. "Sleep. I'm fine. Hitting the bed now." She just wanted to end this hellish night.

He nodded, kissed her forehead, and she went straight to her room.

She lay in her bed and focused on the sound of her own breathing—in and out. In and out. Finally, thank God in heaven, no thoughts. Deeply in. And completely out.

Soft sleep came. Then dreams.

CHAPTER 33

IT ONLY TOOK thirty minutes of pacing, inner debate, and outward muttering before he punched a hole in the wall. *Damn her pride! I should be with her now! For the aftershocks. Fuck!*

He wrapped a towel around his cut-up fist, picked up his room key, and left the suite. He wasn't leaving Isabel down there by herself. He'd just keep her company...or whatever the fuck she wanted to call it. And he had every right to be there, to give his account of the assault. It was a fucking real time attack, damn it! Didn't she get that?

He continued his inner defense, preparing what he would say to her when she tried to push him out and away again, her horrible goddamn habit. But he had nothing to prove, he would tell her. And just like he wouldn't abandon his brother, his brother's soon-to-be wife, a friend, or even his fucking attorney, he wasn't about to leave the woman he was admittedly falling for—more like had already fallen for—to deal with this by herself. On second thought, maybe he'd leave the last bit out for tonight. He'd save it, but the rest she'd hear, whether she liked it or not.

Yeah, now he felt empowered, imagining himself standing by her, sitting with her, comforting her like he should have insisted on in the first place. His steps down the hall were heavy, dense, emphatic, to support the argument he'd prepared.

Just then, a clicking sound caught his ear, then a creak, and before he could glance over his shoulder at Stephanie Rine's door, another click-then-bang. *My very own stalker*, he mused, and continued to the elevator.

*

When he got to the front desk, he asked to speak with security immediately. One of the officers who had come to the scene appeared and shook Zack's hand firmly. The officer's other hand held a half-cup of coffee, like he was on break.

The officer called him an *hombre valiente*—Zack had a decent-enough base in Spanish to know he'd been called a "brave man." He didn't feel brave, though, leaving Isabel like he had, but Zack nodded his thanks.

"Can you tell me where *Señorita* Ruiz is now? And is she alright? Have the reports been completed? Can you take me to her?"

But the officer only stared at him and sipped his cup of joe. The man's lackadaisical attitude boiled his blood. *Keep calm, Zack*. The guy's just a graveyard shift security guard.

He swallowed, took a deep breath, then repeated the request in Spanish as coolly as he could, when all he really wanted was to pour the coffee over the guy's head.

"Sorry, *Señor*, but she left already." Spoken in perfect English.

Zack came down hard with his fists onto the granite reception counter, jolting the officer, his coffee, and the front desk girl who stood frozen, phone lines ringing and flashing like crazy.

Zack blinked and sighed. "*Lo siento*." He shook his head then nodded. "Really, I'm sorry." He knew the security dude hadn't done anything wrong. No, it was Zack who had fucked up, again, by leaving Isabel at the scene in the first place, against his own damn gut. He'd fucked up huge, and he wanted to fix it. He wanted to tell Isabel he was there for her.

Before Zack could get his bearings and unclench his iron locked jaw to even utter his next question to the officer, a silver haired man in a full suit, obviously a manager, came out from the back office. Maybe this guy had a more accurate status report, and maybe the officer didn't know what the hell he was talking about. Maybe Isabel was *going* to be escorted…soon, but hadn't been yet.

The older gentleman approached, arm outstretched. "You must be Zachary James. A pleasure. An honor, in fact. Thank you so much for helping Isabel. She had a real stroke of luck tonight with you being there!" The man seemed to know her well and genuinely care for her wellbeing. At the same time, Zack sensed that this man was almost surprised that she was okay, shocked even. "A real stroke of luck…finally," the man reiterated, almost to himself.

Zack knew it was no stroke of fucking luck that he was there to save her. Not because he believed in luck less than he thought the goddamn Loch Ness Monster was alive and kicking, but more than that, he hadn't even been at the right place at the right time for any noble reason. He felt a sting of hot guilt in his gut. He knew exactly why he'd been there originally. His fucking hard-on for Isabel had gotten him there. More disgust flooded him.

You're a fucking asshole, Zack. You don't even deserve her!

He wanted nothing more than to go back to his room and hit and crush and pound more things with his fists.

"My name is Charlie. I'm the customer service manager here at the Bay View," the man interrupted Zack mid thought. "It looks like you're really shaken up, but not to worry, Mr. James. Isabel was escorted to her car by security twenty minutes ago, and she just gave word by text that she got home safe and sound. Her family is with her there."

Damn it! He really had missed her. But at that point, he could've faced her. Zack stood there like a lost fucking stray.

"And I've already followed up with the police. The assailant is in custody and won't be released any time soon. The police will be back for your statement tomorrow morning, before your family's affair. But for now, why don't you get some sleep, Mr. James?" Charlie said, patting Zack's hand like a father would.

Zack shook the man's hand and attempted a smile in thanks, then headed toward the elevator bank. A surge took over as he zombie-walked, worse than the emptiness he'd felt whenever Isabel was far from him. This was more a cold liquid mercury through the veins, a slow creeping paralysis. And he knew the cause. He swore then, if given the chance, he'd never let Isabel down again.

CHAPTER 34

S HE WOKE UP with a jolt. Her bedsheets were wet, and her body was hot, soaked with sweat. She closed her eyes to try and remember her lingering dream and noticed dried tears on her lashes and cheeks. Her clock showed 2:30 AM. She'd been asleep for only minutes. Her toes tingled and her pulse could be felt through all of her erogenous points, especially between her legs. When she took her sweat-soaked t-shirt off, the cotton sliding over her nipples actually hurt. Why were they so sensitive?

Then, a flash entered her mind—Zack's eyes, the color of translucent ocean outlined by pine forest and speckled with sunlight.

Her wet dream came back to her in its full glory. And, God, it had been so damn real. Zack had taken her home that night, and *did not* sleep on the sofa. In her dream, he had taken her and had made her pour so hard, she'd cried. And when her tears flowed, she remembered ever-expanding happiness. She'd been rolling into another climax as he'd moved in and out of her, while his brilliant eyes infiltrated hers.

But then she remembered his eyes had morphed to sky blue, and then his entire face followed suit...until it was Roberto above her, increasing in speed, pounding her like a murderous dagger into her soul. That was when she'd shot awake. God, that image. That feeling. *Please, leave me.*

Now real tears fell, tears sourced from fear, disgust, and violation.

She sobbed without limit until there was nothing left.

Unknown time passed before she connected again to her surroundings. Alone in her bed, her body still pulsating—having been left mid climax—she shivered then sighed. To gain some separation, she got up and grabbed a glass of water. She called up an image of Zack in her mind as she sipped the cleansing liquid, mostly to prevent the nightmare from creeping back in. She stared at the wall ahead of her. How funny, that for all of her efforts in fighting Zack off, he had really only ever brought her immense pleasure, sweet comfort, anchored security and calm.

But again, she wasn't fighting him off because he was bad for her. She was fighting him off because she was bad for him. Deadly bad.

She lay back in bed, her body still vibrating at a heightened frequency. Oh, how she had wished the first part of the dream could be her reality. If only.

And now, no matter how hard she tried, she couldn't fall back to sleep. Beyond her whirling thoughts, she was tight with a crowning sensation left by her dream. *Damn it!* And that haunting image of Roberto.

Screw it! She'd focus on Zack and the first glorious scene of her REM fantasy. Because, hell, if she couldn't have Zack James in real life, then she'd take him virtually.

She fully surrendered to her vision of Zack, his broadness over her and in her. She pleasured herself, finishing the act he had begun in her ever-sweet dream. Now awake and alone, she let him dominate her heart, her body, and her soul. His essence rippled through her until she was ravaged and spent, and sleep could come to take her far, far away. But would sleep or work or anyone or anything ever take away the pain in her heart?—that deep-seated ache that only Zack soothed.

CHAPTER 35

SUNLIGHT SPILLED INTO the bedroom, easing her awake. She stretched, then rolled out of bed and went to shower off her early morning orgasm. After thirty seconds under the hot spray, she heard her phone, and ran to grab it off her nightstand. Lucinda's image showed on the screen and, dripping wet, Isabel answered the call while standing there shivering.

"Isabel, why didn't you call me immediately?" Lucinda spoke quietly, assumedly having heard the parking lot saga from Charlie.

"Why worry you? You have enough drama to deal with at *your* event, and I'm fine! Lucinda, trust me. I would have called if anything more serious had happened."

"Listen, love. You're more than an employee to me. I need to hear about this type of thing, whether it got serious or not! And the brother of the groom, thank God for him! Thank God!"

Isabel rolled her eyes. "Yes, I definitely would have had to call you if it weren't for him."

"Well, you're almost done with this gig, Isa, but if you need me to juggle things and get you out of it, I can call—"

"No—please, Lucinda…" Being replaced at an event would've been a travesty for the event, for the bride, and for Isabel. "I really am fine. I'm not letting another planner step into *my* wedding. I mean this wedding!"

"If you're sure. But listen, Isabel, I also got a call from the mother of the bride earlier…"

"It's not even 7:00 AM! How is that even possible?"

"Well, with Annette Rine, who knows? Maybe her sleeping pills wore off early today!" Lucinda laughed. "She called with some accumulated bullshit about, well…*you*. Some rude remarks you'd supposedly made, some mishandling of an allergic reaction the maid of honor had? So, I want you to know that I told her not to phone me again. I told her that if the bride isn't happy with something, the bride can go directly to her planner. And if her planner cannot help her, then the bride can phone me. '*The bride. Only the bride*,' I said. Then I hung up." She cackled, having enjoyed herself far too much.

Isabel felt good. Being supported by Lucinda was a real relief, but again, she expected nothing less of her boss and friend.

"I just had to call and prepare you, but no matter, you'll pull everything off today without a hitch. I have no doubt. And don't let those bitches get to you, you hear me?"

"I won't. Anyway, the bride and I really clicked, so I'm really not worried. Okay, so let me go get ready. Have good luck up where you are!"

"Luck…hah! Bye, love!"

*

Just as they hung up, her sister, Celeste, came in carrying two coffees. Isabel's clock showed 6:31 AM.

She kissed Isabel on her forehead. "Oh, God, Isa, Antonio called me this morning. I'm so glad you're okay, *m'ija*. Dear Lord, thank heaven! And thank God for the best man, yes?"

"Zack," Isabel said to the floor. "He literally ripped Roberto off me, Celi."

Celeste studied her face. "Isabel Angelica, do I…do I see a…a sparkle in your eye?"

God, is there a damn "sparkle" now? Isabel hid behind her coffee cup, taking a slow, steady sip. A comment like that from the sister who'd practically raised her was not good. Isabel couldn't just shrug it off.

Celeste walked over to open the bedroom drapes then came back to the bed and took Isabel's hand. Celeste sat there quietly, rare for her sister. And well-played, the woman knew Isabel would talk.

Isabel sighed. "Zack...he...well"—no-no-no, she couldn't tell Celeste— not a good idea—"he didn't hurt Roberto, not a hair on his body. He wouldn't let Roberto near me, but he wouldn't hurt him either. Not a single jab. But I...I was...I am...really scared...and torn. I'm so damn torn, Celeste! Roberto's issue is *my* fault! And Zack...I just wish..."

"What, Isa? Wish what?"

"Nothing. It's nothing..." *Jesus, Isa!* Celeste couldn't know how she felt about Zack. Because they just couldn't *be*. And Celeste would've been impossible to combat with her incessant 'Pin Down a Man for Isabel' campaign. There just was no point.

And since there was no point, Isabel felt a sudden torrent of shame. Knowing her jinxed pattern, how could she have been so selfish, so horrible, so wretched, letting Zack into her life as far and as deep as she had? To even consider leading Zack further, risking his very existence for her own lustful heart? She couldn't even look Celeste in the eyes, couldn't bear the thought of her sister seeing her as the weak and cruel hypocrite that she really was.

Isabel felt Celeste zeroing in on her, as if sensing her inner turmoil.

"Isabel, *m'ija...mi amor*. You are so beautiful. A sweet soul, and so strong, too. Like, you wear this armor...yes, a thick shield of heavy iron armor, which, after all you've been through, I thank God for, Isa. For your survival, I thank the heavens. But please"—Celeste lifted a brow and sighed—"I just don't want you to forget what's under that armor. Please, for heaven's sake, for Mama's sake, don't forget your heart."

Isabel couldn't hold back her emotion, and reached over to hug her sister. Celeste loved her, she knew it and felt it. And Isabel loved her back. But still, there was no way around it, forgetting her heart was precisely what she *had* to do.

She threw back what was left of the lukewarm coffee, then went to get dressed within minutes flat.

She came out of her room in a cream-colored pantsuit that outlined her curves—practical, classy, elegant.

She quickly went over the day's details in her head while her sister fixed her food for the road.

Raquel had confirmed the arrival of the entire *Bella Caroll* wedding wine order, thank God. And the flowers were en route—no white lilies among them. The cake, the priest, the headsets, all set or in progress. The tuxes, too. And lastly, the bride's gorgeous gown, she knew was ready and waiting…yes, the bridal gown.

Vivid detail of her own wedding dress sprang to mind, even after so long. And with the image, a moving memory. Her parents, both singing loudly over the noise of the wind blowing through the four open car windows. Along the winding scenic road running the southern part of the vast *Bahia de Banderas*—to her church.

Isabel's dress filled the entire back seat, the top layer fluttering up ivory satin into her gently made up face. As they approached town, the ornate iron dome peeked over the townscape. The trade winds off the sea gusting through the windows, along with the sun's rays, made her squint, but she wouldn't let her destination out of her sight knowing Sebastian was waiting for her inside.

Also rolling into the bayside town, a glowing yellow blanket of morning fog, its source looked to be a lightning storm farther out over the water. The yellow-tinted mist reached the church, a perfect backdrop for her magical sanctuary.

The building, set on a hill in the town center, peeked in and out of her view as they descended into Vallarta. After minutes of craning her neck, almost a game for her eyes, she had her steady sights on the Church of Saint Guadalupe. She even remembered the warmth that filled her chest.

Until the blinding white crack hit the steeple. One of Vallarta's infamous lighting storms, Fate herself, had hit, leaving only smoke and flames to fill her view.

When she arrived, they wouldn't let her see him. Sebastian had been waiting at the altar in his black suit, a white lily in his lapel, when a large ceiling beam fell, literally crushing his body and simultaneously, her heart.

"Isa!" Celeste shocked her back to the here and now. "Grab your tablet and your bag. Over there, *m'ija*. *Vamos*. Antonio's here to drive you."

She hopped in the front seat with her brother, ready to drive along that same scenic rollercoaster ride that she'd traveled in her trip down memory hell a minute ago. She shook it off with a quick in-and-out breath, and set to wondering how her first large-scale wedding would go off. The list of points stacked against her was a long one. Assaulted the night before; being impossibly in…something that may be love with the best man; getting no more than a few hours of sleep in days; a complaint from the mother of the bride; and now, total cry-eye from her brief talk with her sister.

A longer sigh. *Just how awesome will this day be?*

CHAPTER 36

S HE CALMLY STROLLED through her task list and agenda in the hotel's back office, Charlie's desk was open to her anytime he wasn't sitting at it, which was basically always the case.

"How are you this morning, Isabel? After such a night…" Charlie asked, popping his head in as he passed by. His voice had startled her, but she hid it well as not to make him feel bad.

"I'm okay. Thanks, Charlie. My mind is preoccupied. Probably a good thing, right?"

"Well, no worries. Got confirmation this morning that Roberto got transferred to that inpatient mental facility an hour north. He's secured and he'll get help. I'll get you more details on Monday. You have far too much on your plate right now." Charlie winked, gave her a caring nod, then tapped the wall twice, and was gone.

Isabel sighed with some relief and continued with her preoccupations.

Raquel had already emailed her an update for the morning. All the ladies had their dresses. The men had their tuxes…except for the one hanging on the back of the door staring at her with a note attached. Arnold, as it turned out, had left the tux for Isabel to take up to Zack. *To be sure it is a fit*, the note read. Where was Arnold? He'd had an emergency up in Sayulita—*Lucinda*. A raspy huff. The note also stated he would be back in Vallarta by noon at the latest in case there was any issue. *Damn it, Arnold. And Lucinda!*

She needed to be focusing on the bride! If they only knew what a distraction they had just thrown her way. But thankfully, they didn't know.

Okay. She'd take the tux up to Zack, then go back to check the fit after seeing Amy in between.

And at least Raquel was there, glued to the bride like white frosting on wedding cake. *The cake!* She needed to check on a last-minute change Amy had requested. She walked to the elevator and texted Madeline's at the same time, being careful not to walk into anything or anyone.

*

After a resetting sigh of her eyes, she knocked on Zack's door. Then she knocked again, but louder. A quick glance at her phone—8:43 AM. *Stay focused—no time.*

He opened the door half asleep, golden tan chest and rock-hard abs on display, wearing only boxers, complete with...a total hard on.

"Do you answer the door this way for everyone?" she asked, shoving the plastic-wrapped tux into his tight and toned body to cover him from her conflicted gaze. She couldn't even let her mind go there, especially after her early morning fantasy. *For heaven's sake, please God.*

"Yes, I mean, shit, no. I'm, uh...I just woke up to the knocking. I overslept...from lack of sleep," he stuttered. "But more importantly, how are you doing? Did you sleep at all? I couldn't stop thinking about what happened, about you."

"I see what you *couldn't* stop thinking about," she said, referring to his morning wood, but not missing his sentiments, his sweet and stuttering thoughtfulness. He was genuinely concerned for her, but she definitely couldn't drift to the events of last night, either, not if she was going to pull this wedding off.

He saw right through her. "You have a lot on your mind. Is there anything I can do? To help?" His voice was as smooth as his silk boxers, now completely visible again as he'd folded the garment bag over his right arm, damn him.

In her low heels, she shifted her stance as heat shot straight to her face.

Again, her self-pleasuring session flooded her brain with a mix of desire and guilt, then adding her time crunch, she was in no mood for...*help.* "Just please...try on the tux. I'll be back to check it in exactly five minutes."

And she left him and his raging erection there in the doorway.

*

Not again. He wasn't ignoring his gut again.

Zack touched her wrist gently and begged her with his eyes to stay. "Wait. Give me one minute?" He needed to tell her that he'd gone back for her last night, that he should never have left her, and wouldn't again. And it took him to the brink of madness, the thought of Isabel in pain or hurt and alone.

He could read the worry on her brow, the entire bridal party all residing in that very corridor. He knew Isabel didn't want to be caught entering his room even to do her job.

But..."Just come in. It'll save you time. Then you won't have to come back and check on the tux. We'll leave this door wide open, just like this," Zack told her with a calm, even tone, trying to hold back his intensity. He was splitting at the seams to tell her all that he needed to. He'd hardly slept at all because of the thoughts and feelings swirling inside him, the whirlwind that last night's fist pounding hadn't done a thing to alleviate.

Isabel looked down the hall then pulled out her phone again for the time. "Fine. Only because it'll save me time." She moved past Zack while taking out her tablet from her bag, rushing her fingers over the virtual keyboard. She glanced up for only a moment at the too-large-to-miss fist-hole in the foyer wall, uttered a small, "hmm," and stuck her nose back in her tablet.

Zack followed behind her, keeping the door wide open like he'd said he would. He watched her take a seat on a chair in line with the open door, sitting right at the edge of it, continuing her preoccupation with the device, typing, swiping, tapping. He knew she was legitimately busy with the wedding, being only a matter of hours away, but her complete escape from the present situation, from being present with him, was no doubt convenient.

Then a man's voice in the hall floated in. "Thanks for dessert." It was followed by a shuffling, a click, and two doors shutting, almost simultaneously. Isabel was already standing at attention, nostrils flared and looking more distant, assumedly trying for professional.

"It's cool, just Wret. He was hitting on Jane all night. I'm sure that was his smooth exit from her room," he said, bringing the tux into the large walk-in closet inside the bathroom to try it on quickly.

His whole-body ache from the chronic 'without-Isabel' void, had eased as soon as he saw her face through the peephole, and, no, he'd never open the door in only his boxers to just anyone—Isabel was light years from *just anyone*. Anyway, now the ache was replaced by a jackhammering pulse, and as he slid his legs into the tuxedo pants, he felt lightheaded. And also under extreme pressure. How would he get off his chest what he needed to when his audience was pretending to be less than interested? And in a legitimate rush.

He came out and cleared his throat for her attention. She pulled her eyes away from her tablet to look up at him. And a transformation wiped across her face, her features giving him the confirmation he so craved. Her eyes wide, the rise and fall of her chest halted.

She stood up and seemed to float over to him, out of direct hallway-view, even. When within inches of him, she stopped. Obviously trying to avoid looking into his face, she smoothed his tux jacket at the shoulders, her supercharged energy spiking his pulse to another level. Just short of a heart attack, he kept his arms pasted to his sides, holding back his deep desire to wrap her in them and never let her go.

"You look...amazing," she said, suddenly caught in his eyes. But she flicked her attention away, assessing the fit of the rest of the ensemble. "Arnold did a great job."

"*You* look amazing," he said, his eyes following her gaze, insisting she hear him. "You *are* amazing, Isabel," he told her, his hand moving to her chin, disobeying his internal orders and her past verbal ones.

His light touch lifted her face up, forcing her to look directly at him. "I was wrong to leave you last night at the car. I went to security to check on you afterward, but you were already gone. I should have stayed, should've ignored your stubborn ass."

She couldn't move her face, but she could shift her gaze. Her eyes looked to the ceiling and stayed there. Then her hand went to his and removed it from her chin. She stepped back.

"I don't know how to thank you, Zack, for what you did for me last night." She took three more steps backward, back in line with the open hotel room door. "And you were sweet to check on me." She spun on her heels to grab her tablet and bag from the chair. "I'm honestly fine, though, especially with this wedding keeping my mind busy. And I really do have to go now."

She was in the doorway a moment later. "You make a fine best man, Zack. You really are...I mean *do*." And she was gone.

CHAPTER 37

OFF TO THE side of the flowered altar, Zack stood at the ready. His brother, the groom, stood next to him, tall, proud, eager, and mildly panicked.

Zack felt relaxed and quite entertained. To help calm Darren's nerves, he nudged his brother to join him in people watching as the guests filed in. The brothers quietly mumbled closely held family secrets about each arrival to one another, but all the while, Zack scanned the church sanctuary for the most intriguing person in his world, the remarkable and stunning puppet master of the show, the wedding planner.

As he continued his search for Isabel, Darren elbowed him when their father entered. Bennet gave a far off, straight lined smile and nod and then seated himself in the last pew. Zack's handshake yesterday, and Darren having decided to help his father out financially, seemed to have further humbled the man, an obvious glaze of shame noted even from the last row. But Zack thought it something of an act of courage that Bennet stayed for the wedding. Either way, Zack was relieved the man took to the sidelines. One less provocative ingredient in the day's wedding stew. Because Zack's biggest concern was his mother. She was already being amazing about his presence there, and as long as Bennet kept his spectator-level distance, his mother would be okay, and even maybe still enjoy herself.

But for Zack, a separate side disappointment came with the whole Bennet drama. Zack's plans to tell his mother about Isabel had been interrupted.

Soon enough, though. First things first, to get through this wedding weekend in order to get the chance to get through to his angel, his Isabel.

Minutes later the church was full, and the music began just as quickly. Darren looked with wide eyes at Zack, ready, willing, and suddenly spotlight-phobic. He slammed his little brother on the back, smiling.

"You're ready for this, big man. You're so ready."

With the guests silenced, the organ introduction began filling the hall, and their mother, Elaine, came down the aisle looking very proud and, Zack thought, very elegant. She was arm-in-arm with Annette Rine, who seemed slightly medicated or buzzed, but at least the woman was smiling.

The lavender dressed bridesmaids followed, escorted by the grinning groomsmen.

Stephanie made her way down the aisle next, still swollen and red around the eyes, shaded by a white wide-brimmed hat and perfectly overshadowed by the young ring bearer and the adorable flower girl. *Damn, Isabel was good.*

Zack prepared himself as he was up next to the pulpit, coming in from the side, just preceding the groom.

*

Isabel watched Stephanie promenade down the aisle. She had, of course, come prepared for a maid of honor meltdown. She'd tossed Stephanie the large *almost* elegant white sunhat then gently nudged her through the entrance of the church hall. The flower girl and ring bearer led the way as planned.

Isabel cued her assistant with a low directive through her earpiece. "Best man, go. Groom, go."

She intentionally kept her attention on the bride, and only on the bride.

Isabel nodded at Amy, who she thought looked truly beautiful. She signaled to Daniel Rine, who gave his youngest daughter, Amy Elizabeth Rine, his arm.

While Amy's father beamed warmly at his daughter, Isabel smiled, seeing Amy's sharp focus on Darren at the end of the long aisle

This part, always this part, warmed and chilled Isabel to her depths.

But against her better judgment, masochistic Isabel followed Amy's gaze. And seeing the best man's glowing eyes of emerald at the end of the aisle—it was more bone-chilling and heart-smashing than any and all of her other weddings combined.

*

A successful ceremony. Now, the ecstatic bride and thrilled groom were ready to party. And Isabel was ready to make their celebration everything they'd hoped for, a grand finale for them, which would double as a giant relief to her. She could now see the light at the end of the tunnel, nearly free from the torment of being in such close proximity to the magnanimous Zachary James while never being able to have him.

She moved to the *palapa* bar where the beautifully decorated expanse of patio met the white-as-snow sand. Raquel was doing all of the scurrying for her, so she could afford a moment's peace to just observe.

Everyone was moving. Dancing, laughing, eating, schmoozing, drinking; all with the white sandy beach, the rolling blue tide, and the glorious Vallarta sunset as the incomparable backdrop.

Amy and Darren whirled around the dance floor, as did Zack, her ever-distraction, with his mother, Elaine, in his arms, both dripping with joy. The kindness in Zack's face and the authentic sweetness of his embrace made Isabel's chest clamp down hard, on the brink of an utter and total breakdown, threatening tears, lip quiver and all. She swallowed it back and sighed, deciding immediately to watch any other aspect of the party, even the pathetic drink-fest had by Annette and Stephanie Rine in a far off corner, than to torture herself further with Zack in view.

Check on the chef, Isabel. Check on dinner. And maybe grab a drink for yourself while you're at it.

*

After touching base with Chef Diego, and downing a quick glass of fluid chill-the-hell-out, she returned to the party right when the best man began clinking his glass for everyone's attention.

The toast.

"My kid brother, Darren James, everyone. Isn't he just such *the* man?" Zack began.

Isabel watched him handle the crowd, teasing his brother lovingly while putting his new sister-in-law on the highest of pedestals, then knocking Darren down some more, all with flare, wit, humor, and charm, like the charm he'd used on her the afternoon they'd met, albeit slightly less suave. But like a true showman, he finished to a standing ovation.

After the rest of the toasts, dinner was served.

Then something intriguing. She watched Zack head over to where Bennet James was sitting. He interrupted his father deep in thought. The man's sullen eyes lit up as his oldest son extended his hand to shake then sat down next to him.

And in silence, they ate together.

A lightness filled her chest. She was proud of him. God, Zack James was a much bigger man than she even knew. A really wonderful man. But beyond her happiness for Zack and his victory over his anger-saturated past, Isabel felt a bit hollow inside. And it was distinctly different than the usual protective numbness that pervaded her view. She found herself wanting to go to him, to share in his happiness like they had won a battle together, because really, they had. She was an integral part of this landmark in time for him.

She imagined going over there, sliding her hand across the wide breadth of his back, pulling up a chair tight to his, kissing him on his perfectly rough cheek, and sitting with him, being with him. Together they would make meaningless small talk with his father, the man who had wounded Zack so deeply. But together they had turned Bennet James' reappearance into a source of true catharsis.

But no, she of course couldn't do any of that. It was far beyond the scope of her work, and that was all she could ever be to Zack James—his brother's damn wedding planner.

CHAPTER 38

THE PARTY ENDED and Zack helped get his very buzzed and truly blissed-out brother to his room to change, grab his luggage, and go. The honeymoon cruise was due to leave within the hour. He got Darren to the lobby and into Antonio's safe hands in plenty of time. He man-squeezed his baby brother, whispered a few words of wisdom, and headed back to his room, drunk with liquor, happiness and exhaustion.

He called the elevator. A chime announced its arrival. The doors slid open with a hydraulic hiss. And there was Stephanie Rine, quite seriously posing against the back wall of the car, and maybe also using the back rail for support to keep herself upright? Either way, this was not cool.

Fuck. He couldn't avoid entering at that point, so he offered her a polite grin and stepped inside the déjà vu of a nightmare. He selected their floor and stood facing forward, trying hard to pretend he was alone. Her heavy breathing filled the small space with the scent of alcohol and impotent breath mints. Zack was well oiled, yes, but Stephanie smelled like a damn distillery.

It was when they passed the eighteenth floor that her hands reached around to the front of his pants. And at the nineteenth, he pushed her off him with swift yet gentle firmness. And there she stood on the opposite side of the car still maintaining her scorching pseudo-sexy gaze. She began licking her bright pink lips as if he were a piece of prime rib on a platter.

But then a sick and pained expression appeared on her already swollen face. She was no longer hungry for anything, that was safe to say. She was turning green. Stephanie getting sick in the elevator, or on him as was likely, would surely delay his goal, which was to sleep in his hotel room—alone. Well, alone, but with his angel, if only in his dreams for now.

Anyway, he chose to stand next to Stephanie, giving her a steady frame of reference until they could exit, thinking it might delay the pending explosion. When the elevator came to a halt, she moaned, and then he led her out and down the hall to her room. Sad, that her being sick was the only way to halt her super-aggressive advances, but it was at least doing the job for Zack. He'd get her to her room and let her pass out safe and sound and yes, alone, too.

He took her key, unlocked and pushed open the door, and edged her inside. He couldn't hold her upright and the door open at the same time. He had to let the door shut behind them.

And once it did, Stephanie sparked up and pushed him to the room's foyer wall with the weight of her entire body and a whole lot of enthusiasm.

But he didn't even have to push her off because within a second's time she was sprinting to the bathroom to retch her guts out.

He went to leave then, but as his hand grabbed the door handle, she came back out, her face redder and her eyes more bloodshot. "Heeelp," she moaned, stumbling with one shoe still on. He groaned as he made his way back across the room to guide her to the bed.

Then he went to leave.

"Staaaay?" she whined, patting the spot next to her.

He ignored her and continued for the door.

"I've seen you eying that slut of a wedding planner, Zachary James. I get it, you like 'em dark. So hey, that wetback border-bunny's just perfect for you!" she slurred.

Seething, Zack couldn't see straight, only flashes of fury and a severe need to crush something. But he held it back, kept himself in check, still not wanting to waste a single breath on this wretched woman. He knew all too well that she wasn't above saying the same bigoted fucking remark sober as she was piss drunk. And despite his light pity for the lonely woman, he took a little too much pleasure in the idea of punching her right in her already swollen face for saying fucking anything derogatory about Isabel. He'd given the woman a pass last night. This was number two.

Just leave, Zack. His fists clenched, white knuckles visible in the room's blackness. *Leave.*

Nope. "Look, you miserable, pathetic, heartless excuse for a woman! You can't even know how little you matter, and compared to Isa—"

Snoring. The horrid woman's loud, guttural nose noise swallowed up his angel's name and the rest of his would-be rant. He shook his head. She probably wouldn't have heard a single syllable through that thick, arrogant skull of hers, anyway. But still, he needed to say what he'd said, at least the start of it... That Stephanie Rine was nothing.

And his Isabel was everything.

*

He couldn't have left the room fast enough, and once he did, the enveloping nausea was a welcome relief to what he had felt inside Stephanie's room.

Stephanie's door slammed shut behind him. Still boiling, he turned toward his room. And there, bending over across the hall with her full and magnificent backside staring back at him was Isabel, picking up something she'd dropped in front of Amy's room door. She took his breath and anger and pain away in a single heartbeat.

Replaced with raw, pure want and heat and joy. For fuck's sake, how he wanted her. How badly he wanted every loving inch of her.

And the wedding was finally over.

CHAPTER 39

SHE STOOD AND turned to find Zack staring at her with drunken, ravenous eyes. And then her mind processed which hotel room he had just come out of. It was for certain Stephanie Rine's.

While she was still mentally processing what that may have meant, he grabbed her hand tight and pulled her down the hall toward the far off exit sign. She wouldn't scream, too risky—in that particular hallway especially. But she couldn't pull away either. His hold was too tight.

And, damn it all, her body didn't want him to let go.

They were moving so quickly, one of her heels flew off midway, and for safety, she kicked off the other. His grasp on her hand was tightening, but she didn't feel scared. Angry, yes, but she wasn't scared of him, her savior only twenty-four hours earlier.

She knew inherently that Zack would never hurt her. It wasn't like the confidence she'd had in Roberto, because although she still couldn't believe that Roberto had attacked her—it still being so surreal, a fog really—she'd had that gut feeling telling her over and over that things with her best friend were far from alright. With Zack, though, her gut told her of a completely different type of danger, and it was Zack who was at risk of being hurt. Well, Zack and her heart again.

There was definite anger in her, though—hot flames, yelling, raging upward from her bare feet. He was risking her career right now with this public scene, and after having just come out of another woman's room? How drunk could he possibly be?

But, *por Dios*, if it were in any other context, how she would have been thrilled and elated at being romantically whisked away by this man.

What did it matter, though? He obviously couldn't give a damn about who saw them, and he definitely *had* just exited the maid of honor's room.

And even if those things weren't issues, her damn curse still was. And always would be.

But she was stuck, her hand still in a vice grip hold. The only thing she could do was to keep up with him.

He slammed through the heavy door under the red exit sign, pulling her into the echoing stairwell with him. As the door closed behind them with a hiss then a hard clank, he pushed his body against hers, pressing her firmly into the cold cement wall. Grinding into her with his thick erection, which practically screamed from inside his perfectly fitting tux pants.

Then he kissed her desperately.

Isabel put her two hands on each of his strapping shoulders to stop him. "*What* are you doing, Zack!"

"The wedding is over," he delivered in a hot whisper to her ear.

She pushed him harder to get space enough to look at his face, make him process her words. "We are in the guests' hallway at the hotel *of* the wedding! You are fucking risking my position right now!"

"But no one is coming, Isabel...not yet anyway," he said, sighing with pleasure. The strong smell of scotch hit her nostrils.

"Damn it, Zack!" She was just able to slide out from behind his chest's blockade. "You've just come out of some other woman's hotel room. *That* woman's hotel room and you dare touch me? You're drunk...and disgusting."

"Isabel...please. It was Stephanie, she was about to get sick in the elevator, so I got her to her bed," he said while reaching out for her still.

Her mind was reeling as she stepped back to avoid any and all contact. Which part of this clusterfuck to tackle first in her whirling mind?

She wasn't sure if she should believe his story about Stephanie. A man was a man, and a drunken man was a drunken man, after all. So what if he seemed genuinely annoyed by the woman? She had a willing and attainable cunt, so she couldn't be counted out.

The image of Stephanie bouncing up and down on Zack's muscular thighs, interlinked with him—she just couldn't stomach it. Her ego wouldn't allow her to plummet into the same class, or rather the same category, as that *classless* bitch. If he *had* stuck his all-loving cock into Stephanie Rine, what would that make Isabel? Yes, just another plaything, played by the master player himself.

Mind-fucked again. All his talk, the dedication crap and deep connection bullshit. All so laughable, she wanted to cry.

And, with that, it dawned on her. Despite the sound and feeling of her heart-blood draining out of her, this all might be for the best. Her last card, the one to end the game.

But playing it would be excruciating.

Zack spoke in his most serious tone, hard to find in his state, she imagined. "I only want you, Isabel. I only want *you*."

More words. Why the hell was she still standing there? But before she could make another move toward the exit, he grabbed her hip and pulled her back into him, his other hand sliding behind the nape of her neck, forcing her to look at him.

His gaze…it made her know for that moment, undoubtedly, that what he was saying was true and real. *Goddammit.* And she hated him for it.

While she was hating him, he leaned in and kissed her again, sweeping his tongue into her mouth, forcing hers to dance and giving her body another delectable and regrettable taste of him.

She hated him more.

She was so irate, but so ignited. She could feel his raw need for her, that sensual power, but it was laced with a tenderness that she so longed for in her lonely world. He and that kiss made everything fade away, and she melted.

Damn it! She was about to break her rule again, which she would absolutely never forgive herself for, but she wasn't pulling away. She wasn't pushing him away, either. She just understood him, empathized with his infinite excitement for her, because she felt the same surge of energy for him, no matter how hard she fought it.

So she caved. She totally caved and began to return his kiss.

And his angst and urgency lulled, softened, like she had somehow soothed the savage beast. And at that exact moment, the stairwell's heavy fire door opened.

CHAPTER 40

T HERE STOOD A disheveled Stephanie Rine, ice bucket in one hand, Isabel's shoes in the other, accompanied by the radiating stench of vodka and vomit.

Both the bucket and high heels dropped to the floor. Followed by the woman's jaw.

"I was lost, looking for the…ice machine." And with that, Stephanie Rine spun around, and the door thundered shut behind her.

*

Isabel was in a haze of a new silent kind of fury. Her blood raged through her. She could not look Zack in the eye. All she could do was grab her shoes and speed down the stairs barefoot with heaving, frantic breath. Down twenty-five flights to the first floor service corridor. And he followed her, despite her evil glares back at him.

She wanted to get the hell out of there, away from him.

"She won't remember a thing," Zack said, out of breath.

"She won't remember catching us together in a mouth-to-mouth lock? Or she won't remember you fucking her? Which?" Isabel yelled.

"Back to that, now? Check the fucking hotel cameras, damn it! I was in and out of there in one minute flat. And *you* know I take way longer than a fucking minute!" He exhaled, shaking his head. "You insult me.

Stephanie-fucking-Rine? That bigoted bitch? I mean, God, I have not thought of anyone but you, Isabel. Constantly, you… It's driving me insane!"

"You selfish bastard! If you thought of *me*, cared about *me*, you'd have just kept your distance like I asked. Her seeing us together like that…it's an absolute early death to my career! I'm officially screwed—fucking finished! God, Zack, what the hell were you thinking? Never mind. I know. It was your cock…of course! Just, goddamn you!" She said it, but immediately felt a rush of heat to her face, knowing she was guilty of the same lustful lack of control and that it had stopped her from leaving him in the stairwell in the first place.

And she saw in his face the sharp pain she'd just inflicted.

He stared blankly at her. "Fuck! Isabel, I'm sorry. I just…want you. God, so bad. I want to be with you. I *am* sorry for jeopardizing your job—"

"Career, Zack. My hard-earned career. My livelihood."

"Yes, but…" He paused, as if thinking out his next words carefully. "You know, I can more than take care of the both of us, Isabel. You don't need a job—a career, sorry—if you're with me."

Yes, he did just say that. She shook her head at him, then at the floor. She prayed the alcohol was talking. She couldn't have fallen for such a chauvinistic prick. Impossible, right?

"You chauvinistic prick! You spout *your* feelings for me, but ignore mine at the same time. My career is fucking important to me! So what do you have in mind? You make me the trophy on your arm? Or I continue with my event planning 'job' somewhere else, if that's even possible, and you resent me for it?"

"No. And not what I meant…at all! I was just…"

"Just what? Listen, my career is—*was*—everything to me. But how could you understand? Zack James, who flies around the world, calling on his minions to do all of his work for him. And oh, so depressed, so sad, being eaten up by boredom and emptiness from his luxurious, grandiose life! Cry me a fucking ocean! You don't even see how fucking lucky you are! Opportunities come at you like a tidal wave, but for us regular folk, we have to fight and struggle for a chance, like the chance I *had* with Lucinda!"

"How the fuck can you know jack shit about my opportunities? Everything I have, I damn well earned with hard work, my blood, sweat, sacrifice. I was the one who acknowledged and seized each and every opportunity, took the risks, took the leaps. And now I fucking create opportunities for others. Goddammit! *I* could hire you if you want me to?" His eyes were blazing at her with raw and intentional condescension.

But she shot her death stare up to the ceiling. She had to. Or she'd lose her nerve, her backbone, her will. She held back the threatening tears. She would have rather died than let him see a single one. He didn't damn deserve a molecule of a teardrop of hers.

So her eyes zoomed in on the chipped paint above her head, the end of a long web of cracks from old age. Then she swallowed hard trying to find her voice and said in a lifeless tone, "You and I, it'd never work, Zack. We're just too different. Great sex and hot chemistry don't compensate for, well, *everything* else that's lacking. You're going through this thing with your father, your new perspective on life. I just don't have time to wait for you to figure it all out. And by the way, I don't take charity. I'll find a new *job* on my own. Anyway, I can't do *this* with you."

He scoffed. "Running away *is* easiest, I get it."

"You have no clue about *my* reality. My obstacles and hardships." Now she was ready to explode. If he would just give up already! End this relentless chase or attack or whatever the hell it was!

Zack eased his arms down to his sides, looked up at the ceiling with a sigh, and then back at her. "Isabel, please listen to me. My life issues, the crap with my father, it was you who got me to be honest with myself. I've been running away from life, doing just about anything not to turn into my father. But I actually ran right into becoming him. I ran from love, commitment…but I'm ready to stop running now. Whatever *it* is that has you scared, we can take it on together, just…stop running *from me.*"

Isabel studied the ceiling cracks again, noticing then how far back the web began, following the network of rigid lines and fringes all the way to the white cement wall, then down to the hard gray floor. *Nothingness.*

She set her glazed-over eyes back on Zack. "I'm not running from anything, Zack. Don't assume we're anything alike. We aren't. My priority is just…beyond *you*! It's that simple. Let me ask you, does this *newly enlightened* Zack get that he is not the center of the fucking universe? Can he even consider that I have my own life and I need to make my own way for myself? Without distraction…like tonight's chaos…not at all necessary!" She kept pulling from her mental arsenal of excuses, which was so close to empty. Why the hell she didn't just leave then, she didn't know. Like the night on the beach, her traitorous feet just stayed stuck, immoveable.

Maybe it was her search for closure. But he just wouldn't give it. Jesus, she could see what he had meant by him always seizing his opportunities. She definitely felt him trying to seize *her*. She had never had a man fight so hard for her, and she hated feeling the sensation. But worse, deep down, she relished it.

"I don't even know what we're talking about anymore. You're confusing things just to slap on another copout. But I told you, I *will* find out what you're keeping from the surface," he reminded her. "You wouldn't have spent that time with me, those hours on the boardwalk, *on the clock*. And none of that night was one-sided—you opened up to me, too, Isabel. And not because of my pressing. And now, I'm not even on your radar all of a sudden? It isn't me who has the issues, Isabel."

His words stabbed and stabbed some more. "Look!" she yelled, then pulled back quickly. *Breathe.* What did she have to hide anymore? She had already stated again and again that this…*thing* between them was over before it had even started. But he was relentless! He would just keep calling her out on anything she came up with. She just needed to end it, and if he didn't believe the real reason, well then, his thinking her insane would do the job, no matter how he saw her afterward. And how fucking endlessly horrible that would feel. But he'd pushed her to it at this point.

*

"Zack, it happens to be the case, that…I am, in essence, a cursed soul, and…"

"Oh Jesus…really?" he jeered. "Cursed…?"

"Let. Me. Finish. Please. I have always had this undeniable pattern of tragedy following me, like, ever since I can remember. Anyone close to me has ended up…" She glanced up at his unbelieving eyes, but continued on just the same. "Zack, judge and speculate all you want, but the last three men who loved me died fucking horrible deaths. And my own mother took her life, also because of me. Now, look what's happened with Roberto! I…I just couldn't be responsible for another life. You've just got to let it go…let me go!"

"Wow, aren't *you* the self-absorbed and all-powerful one now? You have the power to kill, huh? And didn't you say you didn't believe in luck and this bullshit? The first time we met?"

"I said that *luck* doesn't believe in me. Because fate…fate has made sure luck stays far, far away."

"I fucking cannot even believe what I'm hearing! No. You're just fucking with me. Or you're fucking crazy! Either way, just say you don't want me. Say that, but don't you dare mock me, Isabel!"

"Don't you dare mock *me*! It's all true!" But what was she yelling for? She had expected his skepticism. In fact, she was banking on it. "Look, let's not waste our time anymore." Then softening from exhaustion, "I just…I care… about your safety! We just can't be together, Zack. We just can't."

"Okay. So, fuck! I thought you were strong, brilliant…but this superstitious bullshit?" He paced a few feet then spun around, "But if it's the case that you're 'cursed,' why get involved with me in the first place? Why let us get this far?"

Fuck. Good point, and yes she was a horrendous, selfish witch.

But it was not something she'd admit to out loud right now. "I tried to not let it get here! You just wouldn't fucking quit!"

"Then why not tell me your crazy-ass theory? That would have stopped me in my tracks way back!" he scoffed. He mumbled something else under his breath. It made her nauseous. She knew this would hurt, but Jesus, the new look in his eyes—his hateful, patronizing glower—it was cutting her chest open in slow motion while she watched.

It was obvious to him that she loved him and that it terrified the fuck out of her.

And cursed? That was the final straw. This bat-crazy reason was just too hard for him to swallow.

If, hypothetically, he were to ever *believe* in her insane theory, believe in such things at all, it would mean that he, that *they*, were all powerless to affect anything in any of their own lives. It would be the improvised comedy of the universe, with no rhyme or reason. *Hell no!*

Then his logic called up the constant *insulting* insinuations he had heard about himself his entire life and now again from Isabel. That *luck* had played a part in so much of what he had achieved in his existence. *No!* As if *luck* had anything to do with his victories, with his success at raising his brother, his financial stature, his survival. And then, in walks his deadbeat dad, implying that he was Daddy's fucking lucky rabbit's foot and was sorry to have "lost" him!

He'd hear none of that bullshit—no more!

And he couldn't fight for, or with, Isabel any harder than he had.

He'd reached his limit.

"What the fuck am I still doing here? I mean, you...you insult *me* with accusations of sleeping with Stephanie, of being an arrogant, ungrounded asshole, and then you round things out with the excuse that you are a fucking walking curse? Jesus, what a waste of time and energy," he spat then fumed. "You're a damn fool, Isabel Ruiz—a goddamn fool."

He couldn't look at her to see her reaction. He just turned and walked off, completely drained, wrung out and hanging. The picture of his future with Isabel, the *one* who'd filled his void, spiraled down and flushed itself out of his reality.

And his stomach, chest, and head all pounded painfully in unison, like a hellish chorus of sad, lonely souls.

CHAPTER 41

FUCKING SUNDAY. ZACK couldn't even depend on the trivialities of the wedding for distraction anymore. With a complete lack of direction for the day, and without the perfect whimsical blueprint he had drafted in his mind with Isabel as the primary pillar, the stark aimlessness was too much for him.

He had been so sure about her. *Fuck!*

Having had entirely too much alcohol last night, or more like, for the entire past month, then add the severe lack of sleep and far too much drama shoving and prodding him over the edge, he couldn't have felt worse. When he went to the mirror, he saw that he couldn't have looked worse either. He peered closer, scrutinizing his face and his hair, finding another gray speck in his thick reddish-brown waves.

And then he looked closer.

A strange feeling overcame him. He felt dizzy, woozy, as if he were drunk still, though he was for sure *not*.

He saw deep into the mirror, past his own image somehow, through himself, like an optical illusion. But it was an animated scene. A hallucination? Or a damn delusion?

What he saw was his entire life on fast forward, farther and farther beyond his reflection. He saw more flights to different places, different people, different women. He saw his brother and new wife getting older, with their growing children. His mother, shrinking through her life, then vanishing—gone. His own hands held out in front of his eyes, turning older, more frail. He was alone.

And he jumped away from the mirror when the movie of his future-life ended. All he could see now was his tired reflection staring back at him.

Holy fuck! Just holy fucking hell…

*

He put clothes on. Got his room key, car key, wallet, phone. He left the room, the hotel, then the parking lot and headed to *La Sexta Noche*. It was 5:30 AM. He drove fast. The roads were empty on that Sunday morning in Vallarta, except for an early morning bicyclist and two horsemen taking up a lane of traffic, not an uncommon sight in Vallarta, weirdly.

He got to the club, took the disabled parking spot, and sprinted inside. No bouncer that early, or late, rather. Now inside, he asked the lone bartender, "Canadian DJ?"

The bartender pointed to the DJ's booth. "Lucky, 'cause you almost missed him. And he's hardly ever here this late…" she blathered, but Zack let her trail off as he headed across the dance floor, jimmying through straggling partiers.

The guy was packing up to leave when Zack arrived at the booth. "Hey man. I don't know if you remember me?"

And no. The guy obviously had no recollection of him whatsoever, per his stoned-out-of-his-head stare.

"I'm Zack, a…colleague of Isabel's. Isabel Ruiz? Gorgeous, long dark wavy hair, Mexican goddess." He waited a second for the guy's bells to ring. No one could forget Isabel. "You replaced her mirror?"

A light came on in the guy's eyes. "Yeah, yeah, Isabel. Shit yeah, man. And you're the dude from the booth the other night, I mean 'colleague,'" he said with air quotes and an all-knowing albeit completely glazed-over look. "I'm Chris." He extended his hand to Zack who shook it firmly but quickly. He needed to get what he came for and go.

"So, listen man…her passport and phone fell out of her purse and I…" Zack trailed off, noticing the guy's head cocked, eyes narrowed. He was high, but he wasn't that far gone. "Look, dude, the truth…I'm in love with her. I need her address, and since you replaced the mirror at her condo… And she wouldn't take my calls even if I tried. I've got to get to her. I've just got to."

The guy nodded, deep in thought for a nanosecond, then without hesitation, DJ Chris jotted something down on a napkin. "Here's the condo complex name, but I heard that complex just got a new security gate with a guard and all, so you can't get in without her buzzing you in, dude. Sorry. But, she's in like the fifth or sixth unit."

Zack checked the scribble. It was at least legible: Paradise South.

Holy fucking hell?

The complex that he'd practically grown up in! His condo, the one he'd just purchased, unit number nine—it was in Paradise South.

Go, man. Move! Zack transferred a fast cash thank you to Chris as they shook hands.

"Good luck, dude! She's fucking unbelievable," the guy said almost wishfully.

"Fuck luck, but thanks, man. Really," he said, then sprinted out to his car.

He was going to Isabel. His future was unbearable without her. Just absolutely unfathomable.

Once again he was speeding through sleepy Vallarta, literally flying over the random unmarked speed bumps littering the town roads. But he was on autopilot, unable to see much else but the movie of his life sans Isabel. It haunted him and lit him on fire at the same time. He drove faster, hitting scenic 202 now, the winding cliffside byway toward his condo. And hers. *How fucking crazy is that!*

Please let her take me back, forgive me, want me. Because if not, he swore, the drive off the edge into the bay seemed more enticing than the mirror's projection, the movie that showed him life without her. *Please, Isabel.*

CHAPTER 42

SUNDAY MORNING AT dawn, Isabel was up early with a cup of tea on her back deck overlooking the bay. And being confident that Roberto was no longer a threat, especially since the fence had been finished during the wedding on Saturday, she sat there practically naked, back to comfortable in her desired state.

But nothing else in her life felt comfortable. Or right. She was ragged from worry over her position at Golden Rings, and fuming, confused, and nauseous over Zack, the entire cluster it had all become. God, that look in his eyes, it suffocated her—still.

She blinked it all away and sipped her tea slowly. *Find something to distract you.*

Okay. She focused on the rolling tide below. Always soothing to her. The roll in and out, like breath, like life.

Just then a flitting monarch butterfly caught her eye. She had been in awe at their great migration as a little girl, but this one was without its group, its kaleidoscope she recalled learning in school. The lone soul fluttered over her and out over the bay. Her heart sank knowing that if the orange and black beauty continued its course west, it would never reach its destination, nor would it ever find rest—the sea would destroy its wings if the thing tried to touch down. Its only hope would be to meet its end with a hovering seabird, a quick, and likely painless, conclusion. What a shame—such a delicate and dazzling creature. She turned her head, unable to watch.

And as she faced her front door now, a sudden knocking, then the door-bell, brought her back to her own cruel reality.

Too early, even for a *Mexican* visitor, well, except maybe in an extreme situation.

This is it. Lucinda must need to do this in person.

She wrapped herself in her soft satin robe, took a breath for courage, and went to her front door.

*

Peering at him through the stained glass window was the vibrant yet blurred image of his Isabel.

"I needed to see you, Isabel." He had heard the light patter of her bare feet from inside. "And you don't have to let me in if you don't want to, but please just listen to what I have to say from out here?"

Nothing.

He stood outside like a door-to-door salesmen, completely at her mercy. Minutes passed.

Looking around, waiting and hoping, Zack couldn't fucking believe that only four units down was the place he'd called a second home for his entire young life. The old gardener trimming the bushes on the grounds waved to him, the man had been working the property for so long.

Zack smiled and returned a wave, then turned his attention back to Isabel's door when he heard four beeps, a deadbolt clank, and a chain lock drop.

She opened the door.

*

Without a word, but in all her stunning glory, she let him enter her home. His entire being quivered. He always wondered how she did that to him. No one else on the planet ever had.

Upon entering, he tripped but caught himself and recovered before she even noticed. *Keep it together, Zack.*

He continued to follow her into the main room, soaking her in with his anguished eyes while breathing her coconut scent deep into his lungs as if his life depended on it. She continued out onto the deck, still without a single word. All he could hear were the waves tumbling in below them, they got louder as he moved farther out onto the deck. He paused then. With Isabel at the deck railing and the wide blue Bay of Banderas set behind her, he couldn't breathe for an instant. The ultimate masterpiece. He squinted his eyes to better capture the exquisite subject of the virtual photograph: Isabel, in her gossamer satin robe highlighted by subtle reflective light from the sunrise to the east. He couldn't be sure that she, or any of it, was real at all. So much like a dream, he feared that breathing would wake him from it.

"Tea?" Her soft-spoken offer startled him back.

She's real…that's a start.

"No. No, thank you."

He sat down at the patio table across from her, and as he adjusted his chair to see her more fully, a strange chorus of screaming whines floated past his ear from somewhere close by, maybe to the north? Zack searched for the origin from his seat because having been haunted by the mirror that morning, such eerie sounds couldn't just be shrugged off.

"Just cats…next door. The place is abandoned now. Actually, the one on the other side of me too. That one's overrun by sea birds now. When I moved in, the neighbors moved out."

He digested what she said and shook his head. She was obviously referring to her "curse."

"That's insane," he mumbled. Was Vallarta, or the entire country, even, so superstitious? It was such foreign thinking to him. And he thought he knew Vallarta so well. So maybe it's a deep cultural indoctrination that Isabel had grown up with that made her actually believe she was cursed. Things started to become clear. He remembered the bouncer at the nightclub who wouldn't let her in. The guy wouldn't even look her in the face! So crazy. Mind-boggling! No wonder she believed this…curse. It completely surrounded her!

And the mention of her mother last night…had the woman ended her life because she'd believed her youngest was a walking hex?

Well, he'd asked for this, wanting to know what she had been hiding, what she was so terrified of.

But it wouldn't terrify him. No, nothing could terrify him more than his future without Isabel in it.

*

They sat there in silence for some time just watching the tide. Then a sigh escaped her lips, showing him a sense of surrender he hadn't seen in her before. As if she stoically awaited an oncoming storm and was completely resigned to it.

He moved an inch closer to her with his chair. "Isabel, I realized something this morning. You care enough about me that you'd choose to deny yourself a chance at happiness *with* me…just to protect me. Whether *I* accept your theory, your *curse*, or not…I'm willing to take the risk. I've been told, fairly warned, but I'm choosing to take my chances. They are *my* chances to take. I just need you, Isabel. Bottom line."

"Zack, you need to understand, my decision isn't all selfless. *I* can't handle the loss—*another* loss. I can't handle any more guilt! Years of guilt, starting with Sebastian." She paused and looked away from Zack's gaze. *Sebastian.* He'd heard Roberto say the name and deduced from there. Hey, she was at least opening up to him. A good sign, even if by mistake.

"My heart was *yanked* from my chest, Zack. From my life. I was left to face the blame, knowing I was the cause of his death and of the others' deaths." She held her chest and took in a deep breath. Her eyes closed, letting glistening tears show from behind her long dark lashes.

God, her pain was raw. And it knifed him.

Please, Isabel, let me in. To ease the hurt, calm the storm, she just had to surrender.

*

"Listen to me, Isabel." He leaned in to her, so wanting to take her face in his hands. But he knew not to. She had a strong invisible wall up around her that he needed to respect. For now.

"I've been taken by you. Fuck it!—I am indisputably and undeniably in love with you! And I would rather die at the end of a single, glorious, unbelievable Isabel-filled day than to continue living a life of pure nothingness without you."

She had no response, not a word. A good sign, no bullshit rebuttal. He couldn't take anymore of that.

"I'm sorry for the drama I've caused. I'm sorry for threatening your career, for the stress, for putting your needs and goals behind my own. Damn it, just all of it. I'm just learning how to get my own head out of my ass." A grin, then a straight stern line. "I beg you, take a solid day to think on what I've said. Think on *us*. I will walk out of your life if that's what you want, even though it would be worse than the most torturous death. But I will do it if you ask me to. But just give it a day?"

She turned her head from him and stared out over the water. Her rare silence meant to him that she'd agreed to think on it.

He stood up, having said all that he'd intended. He walked by her to let himself out, only allowing his fingertips to brush over her hand in passing. His heart fell. Would this be the last time he'd ever feel the warmth of her skin?

CHAPTER 43

SHE CLUTCHED HIS wrist before he could take another step, as if she'd been possessed by her alter ego. Then words fell out of her mouth in the form of a question.

"Do you promise that when I give you an answer…tomorrow, that you will accept whatever my decision is? If it's no, that we cannot be together, you will agree to let me be and we will never see each other again?" She heard her own words as if a separate voice spoke them.

What the hell was she considering? What exactly was her plan? She felt the warring elements within her battling to the death.

"If I have to wander this planet alone, rotting in misery"—he scoffed, but still deadly serious—"yes, Isabel. I will respect your decision." He'd whispered it while staring at her strong hold on his wrist.

She didn't know why, but she needed him so badly, even for one last time, one last injection of his all-loving energy straight into her soul. She had nothing more to lose, and she trusted he would let her go if she told him the following day that was how it had to be. Which of course was the case. That she knew.

But Isabel Ruiz, whose alter ego was in complete and utter control at that point, pulled down hard on Zack's arm, taking him to his knees. Both of his arms landed on her thighs to catch himself.

She sat up and leaned forward. She lifted his chin to hers, and with gazes locked, she slowly touched her lips to his. A delicate last kiss.

Which she could not bear to end.

She combed her fingers through his wind-strewn hair, and then devoured his mouth whole, her tongue meshing with his while tightening and clenching between her thighs, trying to control the need for him down deep inside her.

*

He yanked her to him, pulling her off the chair onto his hard lap. The light mesh chair tipped forward onto her and he tossed it backward with ease.

He enveloped her tight in his arms and relished the rise and fall of her breasts against his own anguished chest. The tide below mimicked her heavy breathing and at that moment, he had to be one with her. The satin robe loosely tied at her waist opened with ease, presenting the lack of any barrier for his thick, pulsating entry.

He kept her on his lap with one arm, and with his other, released himself from his pants, starved to fill her infinite universe. He was hard and ready, dying to dive into the deep pool of warmth and home residing between her forever-sprawling legs.

But first he lifted them both up to allow his hand access to his rear pocket for his wallet.

"Condom, inner fold," he told her as her fingers fumbled and found, tore and rolled it over and down his length.

He exhaled then brought her back down onto him, gliding her ever-so-smoothly onto his throbbing lust. He raised up and then down with her, echoing the coming waves below.

Her body tensed, her long canal squeezing his steel within her as if she would never let him go. She moaned, competing with the sound of the sea. He could tell she was ready to release, but he couldn't bear to have it end yet. He took her soft warm ass in his clutches and lifted her up and off his shimmering erection and devoured her breasts, one then the other. She whimpered. He lined his lips with each nipple, relishing their sharp response.

She begged him, "Please, Zack. Be back in me. Please…" He loved it. He felt her tortured bliss in the raw quality of her plea.

He would give her anything, anything at all. He let his grasp slip from her supple bottom, and slowly slid his hands up her sweat-soaked back, while letting his yearning cock plunge back into her tight, silken lotus.

She let out a loud yell laced with what sounded to him like never-ending sadness.

He gripped her long salt-crisped hair and pulled back slightly, getting her to a deeper place of pleasure, her body buckling on top of him. She gushed relentlessly while he kissed her face sweetly, tasting her salty tears as she went and went and went.

He began his deluge again, knowing he could bring her to yet another wave of elation and join her there. Pumping her smoothly and rhythmically with his engorged and insatiable length, he added his finger moistened with the sex juices from her recent spout of release, and delicately circled her clit.

She moaned longingly while her core constricted his thickness again. Taken off guard, a wave of full sensation drove up *his* back from his very center. He rolled with her down to the deck planks, vibrating from his pre-ejaculatory orgasm, holding on for dear life to not let it end. He needed to keep her for as long as forever, if only he could.

His cock engulfed again by her sweet hot serum, she opened her eyes wide and brought her face to his. With her burgeoning lips at his mouth, and with her body under him, full breasts pressed against his chest, her hard nipples angry and sharp, he plunged into her infinite tunnel and exploded like a geyser, infusing every last inch of his hope that this would not be their last time fitting perfectly together as one.

CHAPTER 44

I SABEL SAT THERE, tired and spent. The scene from minutes before flashed in her mind, him lifting her up with him to her feet, shaky and feeble from him and his torrent. He had steadied her, then stepped back and walked around her as if to mentally record her figure, her birthmark he outlined with his finger, then her arms and her back, then coming back to the front of her, his finger delicately outlining her swollen lips. He'd closed her silk robe over her body, dragging his two thumbs down the lapel of the wrap, down her cleavage, down to her belly. As chills rocketed up her, he'd brought her robe tie around to her front, his fingers dusting her loins which were still reeling. He'd pulled her to him, leaned his face to the side, and pressed his lips to her neck—as if he'd shatter with even one more shared look.

And then he left her standing there.

Now her phone's buzzing brought her back to present. A text message: *Lock the front door behind me.* She smiled, forced herself up, and went to secure the house. She saw him still in her driveway and texted him back. *Thanks, and why are you still here? Stalking won't help my answer ;-)*

She resumed her position on the back deck, vibrating and thinking and waiting while the bay's warm morning breeze swept her face. Like a kiss. Was it Zack riding the wind? Because even as he drove away, he felt so close, so near.

Startling her out of her second round of stillness, her phone went off. She was sure that this time it was her boss. She reached for it with less hesitation than she expected of herself, but still, her breath caught in her chest as she looked at the screen.

She shook her head, another text from Zack: *No stalking, I promise.* Her breath released and her lips curled up for an instant.

And as if on cue, the lone butterfly that had taken its earlier suicide mission out over the bay fluttered back in her direction. It landed on the railing right in front of her and her nearly empty teacup. It slowly opened and closed its wings as if in disbelief that it had finally come to a solid place to rest, and that it was even alive to do so. Or maybe Isabel projected that onto the delicate little thing. Either way, she was glad, relieved. Maybe fate wasn't as evil, as sadistic, and as merciless as she'd thought. Maybe, amidst torturous flights over vast and dangerous waters, fate decided from time to time to give beautiful and helpless creatures a rail to rest on—just every now and again.

She picked up her phone, set to text Zack back with her decision.

CHAPTER 45

H E PULLED OUT of the driveway just after sending her his last text. He was sure they were right together, two lost puzzle pieces that had finally found each other's perfect fit. He came to a red light and checked his phone eagerly for anything back from her, but nothing yet. He continued down the winding byway toward the hotel. He was exhausted and looked forward to his bed. He would just crash and wait.

Then a text buzzed in. He glanced at it hopefully, like an excited puppy. But it was from Wret: *We're going marlin fishing. Meet us, 20 min.*

He literally laughed out loud. Zachary James hadn't been fishing since his father had taken him and Darren last and had boycotted the entire sport after Bennet left. *How ridiculous*, he mused. *Fifteen plus years of avoiding… fishing? Hell, yes I'll go!* He'd go, and in doing so, he would further clinch the newfound apathy he held toward his father and the newfound freedom that came with it. He quickly texted *Yes!* as he drove, rerouting himself toward the marina.

He breathed deep, picturing the day on the open water, the speed, the catch. Why the hell had he ever made his missing father so important, such a symbol in his life? Whatever. Now he would embrace the day, and at the same time, distract himself while he waited for Isabel's answer.

Another text came in, and thinking it was from Wret, but hoping it was from Isabel, he cruised through a turn into a straightaway, then glanced at his phone: *Are you coming fishing with us? Stephanie.*

What the hell? And *who* the hell gave Stephanie Rine his cell number?

He tossed his phone, along with his annoyance and disappointment, onto the passenger's seat in disbelief of the woman's persistence. And then there was another incoming text...

Another one from that prejudiced bitch?

He reached for it but the phone slid to the floor. The tiny sports car made for an easy reach while still keeping half an eye on the road.

At first glance, it was hard to know what it was that flashed into his partial view while he was still halfway below the dash. Going 60 mph with one hand still on the steering wheel, there was no place to veer. No moment to think.

As if in slow motion, the horse flew over the hood on impact, rolling up the windshield, crushing the roof. The all-encompassing implosion slammed Zack into the passenger's side glove compartment.

The living nightmare began and ended in an instant.

CHAPTER 46

ISABEL WOKE UP Monday morning, stiff and disoriented. She'd apparently drunk several pints of Mexican *tuba* wine, because the empty bottle lay on its side at her head. She had a hazy recollection of a number, one hundred and eight? Dolphins? Ah, yes, she'd used dolphin spotting as a distraction during the painful waiting game. Waiting and waiting for any incoming texts, calls, visits—hell, a sky written message would have done her. But nothing. Not from Lucinda, and nothing from Zack.

God, nothing from Zack.

She looked at her phone hopefully, maybe something came in while she was passed out. But all she had were a few outgoing calls from the morning before, which she immediately remembered making. Thank God before drowning in coconut wine, she'd gotten a hold of Raquel to handle the Rine/James Sunday brunch, and had spoken to Antonio for the airport runs. She couldn't bear to show her face at the Bay View, or to see anyone at all for that matter. All she could do after Zack left was wait. And drink.

And now, with no more wine, she'd have to go back to dolphin counting.

*

At dolphin number one hundred and ninety-seven, her phone rang.

She took a breath, moved the empty wine bottle back from the table's edge and slowly picked up her cell. Lucinda's image appeared on the screen.

And here we go.

She let it ring just one more time before answering. Then she hit *Accept.* "Isabel."

"Good morning, Lucinda." Decidedly no guilt or apology in her voice, Isabel reminded herself that she couldn't really know for certain why Lucinda was calling. It could be for a phone number, or an airlift for an elderly guest?

Sure, Isabel, get optimistic now. More like, delusional.

So she knew it was the end of her career. And it was the end of her special relationship with Lucinda. But she also knew in her heart that she'd tried in earnest to combat the Zack situation. With all the best intentions. For the company's reputation, and for her own, she'd implemented pure professionalism.

And it burned her that she honestly hadn't known Zack was a wedding guest when they'd met, and met again, and had the most skyrocketing sexual and emotional connection ever. And come to think of it, Lucinda hadn't known he was the best man either, when the woman left Isabel at the Five Breezes that day, the day she and Zack first met!

But it didn't matter. Not a damn. Because Isabel knew what mattered in the end to Lucinda Carlyle.

"Isabel, can you tell me it isn't true? What the maid of honor saw?"

Isabel remained silent. She couldn't say it wasn't true. So she wouldn't say a word.

"Was it…another assault? Did she misinterpret it all? If so, I'll prosecute that son of a bitch, Zack James! Saving you one night, then preying on you the next!"

Oh God…No!

"No, Lucinda, it was nothing like that!" Isabel did remember Zack coming on hard and strong, but it was from genuine excitement with the wedding coming to an end, a mutual excitement really. And despite her attempt at stopping things, it being the wrong place, wrong time—and the small issue of him leaving Stephanie's hotel room—all in all, it was just another cosmic fucking joke, a big fat joke on her, yet again!

But definitely nothing close to an assault!

"Then *what*? I was grooming you, Isabel! To take over someday, and someday soon! What possessed you?"

Should Isabel tell Lucinda that she and Zack had met before the event? He was the guy Lucinda pushed her direction? And that he had fallen for her...and maybe, likely, *shit,* definitely, she for him. After all of Lucinda's lectures, Lucinda of all people would be ecstatic, right?

But, then, how did Isabel let it get physical *during* the event? On hotel grounds, no less? On the same damn floor, same wing as the wedding guests!

No. She decided she wouldn't stoop to explain herself, especially not over the phone. There was no way around sounding defensive, bordering on pathetic. Isabel had too much pride.

Lucinda accepted the silent reply. "I just hung up with Stephanie Rine with Annette conferenced in. I, of course, would have hung up on both of them, since they are not the bride, but it was when they began threatening that they'd kill my business with horrendous reviews on all the wedding sites! And on and on. My contract protects Golden Rings from slander, but to defend and litigate it would cost more than the company's worth. And legal doesn't stop the irreparable damage of bad press. I have staff, contracts, my pending retirement hinges on all that I've built, Isabel!" Lucinda paused. And Isabel just shook her head at her end of the phone. *Those horrid bitches.*

"The cardinal rule, Isabel! I just expected anything but this from you. Was the best man even worth it? No, don't even answer that. It doesn't matter anyway. They've agreed to sign a Covenant Not to Sue or Slander Agreement if I let you go. I'd have to release you anyway, since the entire office knows now. So"—Lucinda huffed—"for the benefit of my company...Isabel Ruiz, your services are no longer needed. Goodbye."

Isabel sat there on her back deck, phone still at her ear, but the only sound left to hear was that of the tide rushing in. With a blank mind and a frozen stare out at the water, she had no tears. She was just too numb to even cry. Her jaw tightened. She reached across the table for the bottle of coconut wine. *Fuck.* She forgot it was empty. Just bone fucking dry.

CHAPTER 47

HIS EYES BLINKED.

"Oh, thank heaven!" he heard his mother's voice cry. Then he heard medical terms being exchanged between two others in the room. And saw the time on a wall clock through his haze…4:23…*in la tarde o la mañana?* He couldn't tell in the artificially lit and windowless room.

"A severe concussion, twenty stitches in total, from the left temple to the center of his forehead, and several broken ribs," the doctor repeated from the chart, and then Zack faded away again.

*

"He needs more. And I won't leave until he gets it." He woke again to a woman's shrill voice.

He half opened then squinted his eyes. "Lights," he murmured.

"More light? Just open your eyes more, sweetheart."

Stephanie Rine?

"Off. Lights off." His head throbbed. Where was he? He had recalled his mother's voice. Where was she? Was he left floating in a void, left with just Stephanie-fucking-Rine to hover over him?

Isabel! Where is Isabel? Fuck it hurts to breathe. Had she texted? Is she here?

"Hello. I'm Doctor Acharya. Can you tell me your name?"

"*Me llamo* Zachary James." Zack looked confused. His words were out of his control. "*Por qué…?*"

"It's fine, Zack, don't be too worried. With such a trauma, speaking a foreign language, eating with the wrong hand, things like that may happen during your recovery from time to time."

Forcing his brain, Zack stammered, "How...long was I...out? *Qué día es hoy*...I mean, what day...today?"

"It's Wednesday. You were out for three days, Zack. You were in an extremely severe car accident. In fact, you're not only tremendously lucky to be alive, but you are lucky to be able to talk, to move your limbs, to be conscious right now! After seeing the photos of your vehicle, it's all downright... miraculous, son. Just a laceration to the head and several broken ribs."

"It hurts...to breathe. *Hablar*...to talk," Zack rasped.

"Don't strain yourself, sweetie," Stephanie soothed with an unsolicited pat on his arm. Zack flinched slightly, but moaned in pain from the minor bit of movement.

The doctor continued. "Yes, and it will hurt for some time. The button by your right hand is for the morphine drip, to alleviate the pain. And the button below that is for immediate assistance from the nurses' station."

"*Dónde está*, I mean, where's Mom? I heard her. And Isabel? I need Isabel."

He heard Stephanie sneer and then excuse herself from the room, telling the doctor in a huff that she would send Zack's mother in.

"Zack, your healing time will be some weeks for those broken ribs, and I'll take your head sutures out in fourteen days." The doctor nodded, pleased. "For now, just get some rest. You'll be out of here in two or three days so... soak up the service." The man chuckled, then went to leave.

"*Esperas!* The phone? Can I talk from my phone...someone?"

"Best to rest now, but here's your mother. Maybe she can communicate something for you."

*

"It's really hard to hear you, Amy... What about Zack? Because he didn't return my text, I'd been wondering—"

Amy's garbled ranting cut off her words, then her breath.

Her phone slipped from her fingers and dropped to the floor, bouncing several times while she could only stare at it. As if it was possessed. *Pick it up. Talk to Amy. There's nothing new here, Isabel. Inevitable torture, remember?*

Robotically, she grabbed the phone with a quivering hand and brought the now cracked screen up to her ear.

"Amy? Are you there?"

"No, it's Darren, Isabel… Can you hear me? Cell reception…not… best…first stop…now."

"I hear you now! Darren—how? And, when?"

Darren began to explain Sunday's sequence of events to her as she remained surprisingly calm, collected.

Until he told her that the accident had happened after leaving her house.

*

Jolting sobs erupted from her, and she dropped to her knees on the cold tile floor. The hard shock to her kneecaps physically reverberated through her, but the pain didn't register at all.

"Are you there, Isabel?" Darren's voice echoed in her head.

Was she? Was she really there? Or here? Again? Fuck! And fuck fate. She knew and ignored and now would face the fucking consequences, the loss, the heartbreak. All-the-fuck over again.

"God, I'm not sure if she's still on," she heard Darren say.

She somehow brought her desperate gasps to smaller, hardly audible whimpers. And then found her voice. "Sorry, I'm here. Darren I can hear you." The voice of a hollow ghost drifted out of her mouth. Just an unrecognizable, raspy hush.

"Isabel, he's going to be alright. Really."

Darren had no clue. "Right, of course, I just—" She was about to lose it again, so she just quit speaking.

Darren somehow took his cue and went on. "He told me to call you, Isabel. Made me promise to get you down there to see him. He needs to talk to you. He needs you there. St. Maria's, Room 303."

She heard the shakiness in Darren's voice then. Pained emotion being held back by all the courage the newly married man could muster. Zack was

Darren's surrogate father. What the fuck had she done? How could she have been so selfish? All to fulfill her own lust, and to reverse her own loneliness. Zack was almost gone because of her! *Damn you, Isabel!*

"I'm a world away, Isabel, and I can't get to him for at least three days. He's always been there for me, and I'm...look, it doesn't matter. The self-less fucker made me promise not to come back from the honeymoon! And it turns out, Isabel, it isn't me he wants to see anyway—it's you, only you! Please...will you go?"

She said nothing as her emotions got the better of her again. She took a deep breath and found her voice. "I will. Of course I'll go see him."

Darren sighed relief into the fuzzy phone connection. "Isabel, listen, separate from how he treats my mother and me, Zack's been a narcissistic prick for, like, his entire adult life. But he's changed. I noticed it when I got to Vallarta. But now, with this accident, it's extreme. Like, I've called him the luckiest bastard in the world since forever, and it always pissed him off. But when he was on the phone with me only ten minutes ago, he called *himself* 'blessed' and 'the luckiest man in the universe'! And said that you, Isabel, you're his 'lucky charm.' That kind of talk from my brother's mouth, unheard of. Completely, just, unreal!"

She didn't know what the hell to say or what to think. But a skeptic turning believer didn't make the near death of Zack any less real. Or any less her damn fault!

"Darren, I'll go there now. Let me hang up with you and get on the road. You and Amy just try your best to relax and be with each other. I'll tell Zack you send your love," she said quickly. "And I'll talk to you both soon."

She hung up and dried her eyes, then switched into high intensity mode, grabbing her keys, phone, and bag. She looked at her unconscious, hardly legible scribble on the border of the old newspaper on her coffee table to recall the hospital room number and then bolted out of the house.

CHAPTER 48

S HE GOT OUT of the elevator into the waiting room. She walked past the evil glares of Stephanie and Annette Rine, and the subtle and muted greetings of the remaining friends in the wedding party who must have extended their stay in light of the accident.

Isabel looked for the nurse's desk. A wall sign directed her beyond the waiting room through a set of heavy electronic doors. She took a breath, then quickened her pace, because if she didn't, she'd lose her nerve altogether— she was certain that the red illuminated exit sign behind her was summoning. Loudly buzzing her name.

As she approached the nurse's desk, she saw an older woman leaning over the counter talking to the nurse. Isabel came upon them quietly as not to interrupt, but within five feet, the woman turned around.

Zack's mother, Elaine, a relieved smile spreading wide across her tired face. "Oh God, thank you. Isabel dear, you've come. Darren called and told me you were on your way, but, oh goodness, here you are, and…I am just so glad to see you, and meet you," the woman said with welling tears in her weary eyes. And on the next breath, Elaine had Isabel tight in her grasp and wouldn't let go.

A strange, morphing minute went by. Feelings of guilt, then sheer sympathy, on to oozing warmth filled Isabel's chest until, finally, she surrendered to the woman's embrace. Almost against her will, though. This was Zack's mother. She couldn't have him, she couldn't have his mother, she could have none of it.

And what made it worse, Zack had told her so much about Elaine, such tender stories, Isabel felt like she already knew and, God, even loved the woman. Zack's mother was holding Isabel as if she were the woman's own daughter.

Dear God, this is too much, too hard.

Isabel began pulling away, trying to unlatch, to separate from the whole-hearted woman.

But Elaine took control. She slid her hands down Isabel's arms, and held her firmly at the elbows. Then she looked Isabel dead in the face. "Isabel. My precious boy has found his heart in you," she said. "He's alive *because* of you! He almost left us, but fought his way back for you. To be with you! Thank heaven for you, my dear Isabel. Just thank heaven." Elaine James hugged her again, clutching Isabel to her even harder this time. And then Elaine released her grasp, and kissed Isabel on the forehead. "He's waiting, dear. Oh he's been waiting and waiting. Go to him." She turned to the charge nurse behind the desk. "Maria, this is the one. My Zack's Isabel."

"Hello, Isabel," the nurse said with a tender smile to match Elaine's. "Please sign in here and I'll take you right back to him."

Please, no. "Okay, thanks." Her pulse filled her throat as she signed the form. The nurse stood to take her to Zack. There was no turning back now, and she'd promised Darren.

Elaine patted Isabel's hand and nodded. "I will see you shortly, dear."

Oh, how Isabel wished she would see Elaine shortly, or ever again. God, how she wished.

*

Isabel went with the nurse, while Elaine made her way back to the waiting room through the automatic doors.

And through those slow opening and closing doors, she heard a familiar crowing, Stephanie's loud, shrill voice, her hike in volume maybe even for Isabel's benefit.

"Rumor has it that she's killed four husbands. She's like a real-life witch! Bad juju! The Mexi room service girl at the resort confirmed it! And then she almost kills Zack! I could kill her myself!"

Used to such talk, Isabel tuned out the noise, even though, ironically, every word the crazy woman uttered was true. It strengthened her, in fact, to keep moving toward Zack. She had to save him from herself.

"Just this way," the nurse said. Isabel followed the woman to the door of the next wing, and just before entering, she could hear another voice from the waiting room, one even louder than Stephanie's.

"Stephanie Rine, you're just a stupid, insecure…hussy!"

Elaine? The nurse, Maria, looked at Isabel as if she'd read Isabel's mind, and nodded. Yes, it was indeed Zack's mother. The electronic security doors shut, blocking any other delicious reprimand Elaine may have delivered. Isabel smiled, a tiny burst of justice leaked into her heart. She lifted her chin and let the feeling fill her chest.

But as soon as she looked down the long white gleaming hallway ahead of her, the burst fizzled to dust.

"The room is just at the end of this hall," said Maria, waving Isabel on.

Isabel wanted to sprint the other way. She wasn't ready. She needed time. So much more time. If only the long, sterile hallway in front of her could have stretched miles more, taken forever to walk down. But it didn't. In fact, her feet had already carried her to the room door, as if unconsciously and absolutely against her will.

The nurse opened Zack's door, but Isabel stood back against the corridor wall, unable to move or think or breathe. *Breathe, in and out, Isabel.* Then one last tight breath in and a choking, choppy breath out and she was ready, but not really at all, for what would be her official and final goodbye.

CHAPTER 49

HIS HEAD POUNDED, while his nausea was controlled only by his fear of leaning over, because leaning or bending, even breathing, inevitably resulted in shattering pain throughout his fragile rib cage. He pressed the morphine button and immediately relaxed, closing his eyes, thankful for the slightest relief.

"Mr. James," the nurse whispered. "She's here."

He willed his lids open against the heavy morphine daze, and then forced his eyes to come into focus.

A flood of déjà vu. Although he knew this was her first physical visit to his hospital room, he was sure that the vision that stood at his bedside, this bronze angel in white flowing silk scarves, had been right there watching over him during his entire hospital stint. "Isabel," he murmured. "Isabel."

He felt a strained pressure through his entire spinal column just having his head rotated an inch, trying to keep his gaze on her, but he took care of it with another click of the button. His mouth and throat were desert-dry, so instead of trying to form sound just yet, he held out his hand for her to take.

"I am so, so sorry," she sighed, then he heard and saw her swallow, her emotion tripping down the smooth column of her throat.

Oh don't be sad, my angel. But he still couldn't get words out.

She took his hand in her own and squeezed hard. "I knew...and I told you! Here's our glimpse, Zachary James. I just couldn't take it if you had..." Tears streamed down her silken cheeks now. He wanted so badly to reach over and wipe her tears and all her sadness away. But he couldn't even sigh without stabbing pain.

"But...I'm right here," he managed to scratch out from his parched throat.

He had so much to say to her, but first he pointed his finger to the side table where a lone cup of water stood, a straw bent over its edge. She brought it to his mouth, he pulled a few sips. Between the shallow incline of his pillow and a small bubble of air getting into the straw, he coughed on the last gulp, and his roar of pain startled Isabel, and the water spilled down the side of the bed.

The charge nurse flew in. Zack was holding his sides with his crossed arms, as if his skeleton would just collapse, bones falling limp to the mattress if he didn't keep himself together. He could see Isabel out of the corner of his eye—she looked terrified, her back flat against the room wall. He couldn't stand to see her fear, her dread that he'd reduce to ashes from a goddamn cough. But again, he was here. At least he was alive and here.

The nurse increased the incline on the automatic bed, brought in a new cup of water with a lid, and cleaned up the small spill at his bedside.

"All good?" she asked.

Zack blinked yes while Isabel nodded, relaxing her expression and her shoulders just a bit as she returned to Zack's side.

"I hate that you're in so much pain." She took his hand again.

His voice cracked to a start as he wove his fingers into hers. "With this button here, I'm just fine." He smiled, hitting it again.

Then he cleared his throat with a tiny grimace. "My mom, you met her?"

"Yes. Yes I met her. Very sweet woman." She gave him a warm yet distant smile.

"Just wish I could've seen the look...the look in her eyes. She must be in love. Like I am——" Then a small start of a cough interrupted his words and sent pain through his middle. She got him more water, and after a few sips, he pushed the cup away.

He was ready to tell her what he'd been dying to say.

He took a painfully deep breath. "Isabel...the doctor, he actually used the word 'miraculous'! It's a miracle that I'm alive. And I see now, I have *seen!*" He flinched from the slight excitement of his words, but signaled for another drink and was ready to go again, now in a slow whisper. "I'm so lucky," his raspy voice confessed. "I'm the most... the most fortunate man in the universe. And you...you're the one who brought me back. My God, I have so much...to tell you, Isabel. But"—he smiled—"it will probably take our entire lives for me...to explain it all. They say I was in a coma for three days, but where I went, there was no"—he swallowed and winced—"no such thing as time, Isabel!" he told her in his morphine haze, his voice becoming quieter and quieter, even hard for him to hear. "Just...no such thing as... as...time..."

*

And then that haze swallowed him up to sleep, his head falling back onto the pillow, a smile still on his perfect mouth. And his grip of her hand slipped, letting her hand go free.

"Goodbye, Zachary James."

CHAPTER 50

HER LAST WORDS to him tasted like bitter poison as she'd said them. But fate, for once, had let her off easy, relatively speaking. Zack, being such the fighter, and Isabel, having proved to be so weak-willed and unable to combat his charms, she had been sure that their end would be a horrendous, battle-torn one.

So if she had to choose, she couldn't have imagined any better way to slip out of his life.

Ah, the illusion of choice.

Because it was absolutely not her damn choice, she fumed. There was a knot the size of a boulder in her throat, and the pounding of red-hot misery in her head was blinding. At the doorway, she glanced at Zack one more time, her last vision of him, and then flew down the hall, stopping just before the doublewide exit door to the waiting room.

There, with no one around, she threw herself against the wall for balance and then slid down, crumbling to the floor.

*

She realized the loss of an immense something accompanied by a great fear, like she was plummeting into darkness. It was familiar to her, similar to the out of control feeling the day Sebastian had left her alone in this hell called her life.

Fucking fate!

Furious, she frantically took out her cell phone from her bag. She scrolled through her photos, ignoring the cracked screen and her own splintered reflection it showed. She found what she was looking for.

Her home screen image, *Sebastian*.

Delete it, damn it. Forever.

And with just a tap of her finger, it was done. The photo trashed. The end. And with no images of Zack to replace it with, she was free of the pathetic reminder, the idea, the hope that she could find and hold love. Because she goddamn couldn't! Not ever.

All she got to keep a hold of, tight and true, was her endless void, a void she hadn't been prepared to add to, to deepen, in this lifetime. But here again, deeper it went. *Endless* plus *infinity*.

But as her tears began to collect, despite her best efforts, Zack's face came to mind. And those sweet and sensual eyes of his, clear as the sea. She bit down on her bottom lip hard, pain-clearing hard, then surrendered her head back against the wall. With eyes closed softly to the world and tear drops now crashing to the sanitized floor, the only thing willing her next breath was that she at least knew Zack would go on. He'd live. That wonderful man would live the hell out of life. He'd be an amazing lover, partner, friend, and God, a father, to a lucky someone else, somewhere else, very far away from her.

CHAPTER 51

OVER TWO DAYS' time, Isabel had gathered up enough courage to go into the Golden Rings office to collect her things. She went in early so she could avoid Lucinda and all of the staff, except for the receptionist.

When Isabel got to her private office, her desk was all just how she'd left it. She hadn't been in for a while—not with her remote access and the bum rush of events over the last weeks—but still, God, she'd miss her desk. And the energy and bustle of the office, the clinching of clients, and even the unending hours of preparation. She'd miss her position, her purpose, having a hand in solidifying potential soul mates for life.

And Lucinda. She'd miss Lucinda most of all.

She sighed in surrender, then began to box up her belongings.

A photo of her and her favorite nieces, Celeste's girls, was the only thing of significance. The rest, just stuff. And when she was done with clearing the surface and emptying the drawers, she stood back. And peeking out from under the keyboard on the now barren desk was an envelope with just her first name on it. In Lucinda's handwriting.

*

She picked it up. The envelope's contents were firm, rigid, but light. She wanted to get out of there as quickly as possible, but with the office empty and her curiosity piqued, she just had to take a quick look inside. She tore it open and pulled out her last paycheck and a handwritten letter wrapped around some photos.

I hated to let you go, Isabel, love, but I can't risk the bad press. Nor can I start any bad precedents with the staff…but please know that I miss you already! You know, though, my interests aside, you shouldn't be coordinating other people's bonds of love anyhow…you should be coordinating your own, damn it! The photos say it all, and I am and will always be the expert! ~ Lucinda

Isabel pulled out the photos.

That damn photographer! The man had caught Isabel and Zack first in an eye lock at the rehearsal dinner, then Zack staring at her during the ceremony, and one shot at the party…of her only feet away from Zack, her eyes gazing up at his face. His handsome and truly kind face.

"If that's not two people in love, I don't know what is." Lucinda stood in the doorway smiling softly at Isabel.

Awkward, thick vibes filled the room while her ex-boss's comment registered, and was then disregarded. "Lucinda… Good morning."

"What's your plan now, dear?"

Isabel swallowed then sighed, fingering the check under the photos. "With this, I'll invest in vacation rentals. Charlie said he'd throw me overflow during high season. The two condos on either side of me are vacant."

Lucinda released a jagged breath, took one long stride toward Isabel, tapped the photos, then lifted Isabel's chin to gain total attention. "I didn't mean work, love." Lucinda's gaze narrowed. Inescapable. "You'd better make this whole thing worth it, Isabel Ruiz. If you've lost your position here and *then* let that man go, I'll be really fucking pissed."

Isabel sucked in her bottom lip and tried to smile with her eyes. "I know you don't believe in our superstitions, Lucinda…but I've faced so much hell over the years. I can't imagine going through it again. The car accident was my final warning sign. I just can't take the risk. I can't risk…him!"

Lucinda rolled her eyes. "I've run through four husbands, Isabel…does that mean I'm cursed? Wait, bad example." Lucinda shook her head. "The fact is this…" The older woman paused, staring hard at Isabel, who shifted her stance preparing for a longer than usual speech. How funny—she'd be more than relieved and elated to receive a lecture from her mentor, especially now that she had no right to her. While the alternative cold shoulder of shame would have killed her.

"Life is a day-to-day pain in the ass, Isabel—*cursed* or not. It's finding the small pleasures and sharing them with your loved ones, or better yet, your *one* true love, if you can find him. Most don't. And you already know that I'm a hopeless romantic, a true believer in that one true love."

Isabel narrowed her eyes at the woman.

"Okay, well, that may not necessarily apply to *my* life, but that's my case in point! Following?"

"Yes, Lucinda."

"Good, good. Now look, I would go get that delicious hunk of a man myself if I were the young, intelligent beauty you are. Hell, I would try to get him myself being the *old*, intelligent beauty *I* am…but he wouldn't be interested. He's quite obviously not interested in *anyone* but you, love," she said, pointing at the photo from the wedding ceremony.

Isabel stared again at the pictures. Her mind wandered to the recent scenes of Amy and Darren during their first dance. Then her thoughts traveled farther off, to that old black and white of her grandparents, their loving gaze, a forever fixture in her head and heart. And then back to the photos in her hand. She couldn't deny the look of adoration Zack was giving her—or her, him.

Lucinda, as usual, was right. Isabel and Zack were pretty damn magical together…on so many levels.

But could the affection they shared combat her curse? And, more than that, was her heart strong enough to place that bet? Especially when Fate was dealing the hand for the house, and everyone knows that *no one* ever beats the house.

CHAPTER 52

ZACK WOKE TO the news that he was being released. He asked for Isabel, unsure of what exactly had happened the day or so before, but the new nurse didn't know anything about, well, anything.

"Please, have my mother come in."

Minutes later, Elaine entered, dark circles under her eyes, but a wide smile on her aged face. Before he could ask her anything, Dr. Acharya came in and immediately set to examining Zack.

The man took a closer look at how his head gash was healing. The doctor smiled and nodded, then bobbled his head. "Looks good. Phenomenal." The doctor moved to grab his chart. "So, you're leaving us today, but you need to take it really slow the next few weeks, very important. And I'll see you back here for a follow up, which means of course, so sorry to say"—he winked— "you're stuck here in paradise until then."

Zack smiled. He hadn't intended on leaving paradise, near-fatal accident or not.

"Oh, yes...I almost forgot," the doctor went on, "The paramedics found this at the crash site about twenty feet from the vehicle, like it was ejected to safety...anyway, the nurses charged it up for you." The man smiled and handed him a device.

It was Zack's cellphone. He held it in his grasp with great care, as if it was his own pumping heart. He didn't even hear the doctor's next comment.

"Zack?" His mother interrupted his mental wanderings.

"Yeah, sorry." He looked up from the phone.

"Zack, you just remember how lucky you were, and don't take it for granted!" the doctor said.

He knew the man's mini lecture was well meaning, and Zack smiled in appreciation. He *was* lucky, the luckiest son of a bitch on the planet. And he needed to talk to Isabel, to tell her that he understood now, that he accepted all of it, all of her! And that they were meant to be together, more than he'd ever realized. He came back from the brink for her and now needed to start his life with her.

"Yes doctor. Thank you for everything."

The doctor shook Zack's hand, then his mother's and left the room.

Finally. "What happened to Isabel, Ma?" he asked, looking down again at his hand clutching the phone.

"I didn't even see her leave, sweetheart. I don't know. I'm sorry. Let's just get you to the hotel and go from there, dear. I'm sure there is an explanation."

Yeah, there was. And he'd have to prove her explanation wrong. He'd have to show Isabel that he was the cure to her curse, and she was the missing piece to his heart.

*

"I'll go and sign the release papers, dear, and will be right back."

He nodded to her, then refocused his attention on the phone in his hand.

He inhaled, pain taking firm hold of his middle, then he eased out a long breath. He powered the device on. The screen lit up. *Unbelievable!* He couldn't believe the damn thing still worked.

The display now illuminated, a frozen screen of text messages stared up at Zack.

All from Isabel.

Wednesday, June 4th, 4:23 PM—the exact time he woke from his coma: *Zack, where are you?*

And scrolling up from there, one from Sunday, June 1, 7:31 AM—the time of his accident: *Zack. I can't fight it anymore…I want you, I want us. I guess we'll just fight fate together.*

His heart was flooded. Hot, pounding, and alive.

*

He dialed her number from his phone four times. No answer.

And he kept dialing as he was wheeled out of the unit and out into the bright Puerto Vallarta sunshine.

A limo was there to take him back to the hotel.

Antonio came around the vehicle. The man gave Zack a firm handshake. "So glad you're okay, man. Anything at all I can do, bro, you just say the word."

Zack nodded in thanks, looking up at Isabel's brother with hope. "I appreciate it. Really do, man. And…I actually could use your help with something."

"Anything, bro. Anything."

CHAPTER 53

S HE PUT DOWN the wedding professionals magazine—yes she was now an officially confessed masochist—and hunted for her robe.

On the third buzz of the doorbell she gave up her search and threw on some stretch pants and a comfy tee instead. The bell rang a fifth time.

"I'm coming, one second!"

She looked through her front door window, and a small flat digital screen had taken up her entire field of vision. Skewed by the bevels and colors of the stained glass, she could just make out what it was.

A smartphone with text bubbles.

"Isabel, I know from your texts what your decision about us is…or was! Please, let me in. The accident wasn't a bad omen…it was just the opposite. Please just let me in."

In an instant, her back was flat against the door, her breath quickened with indecision. She could get over him with time—if she just *did not* open the door.

But Lucinda's words rang in her head, about how few people find their one true love. Let alone, for her, a second love!

Then she recalled other words, words of warning from her scared shitless mind…*Isabel, you can't have love, period! Not Zack, not anyone!*

"Please, Isabel. We love each other, and I understand now! I get it, the curse…my luck…it's…written, the universe's plan! We're supposed to be, Isabel!"

Damn it! Maybe she was meant to say goodbye the hard way. Fate had teased her to believe it had been with Zack drifting to sleep as she uttered the torturous words. But she guessed she was wrong. It seemed *pure agony* would be the way.

And opening the door wouldn't mean she'd change her mind.

Or would it?

"No. Zack, I can't open the door. You can talk to me from outside." She spoke with sudden courage—or cowardice, depending on her ever-conflicted perspective.

"I understand you're scared. So am I, but isn't that life? We can do this... *thing* together, Isabel. I never feel as alive as I do when I'm with you! Do you understand that?"

Yes, she *so* did. But it didn't matter.

And she just couldn't handle a long-drawn-out thing here.

But maybe if she gave him a little token, some lingering words through the door, then he would go. Yes, let him take her sentiments with him at the very least. "Zack, I can't deny...that I love you. So much, it burns. And I know you love me, but sometimes love just isn't enough. The accident was the final warning. I love you too much to be with you, Zachary James. It's all too much!"

"You're scared to lose me, but here you are, pushing me away?"

"Pushing you away alive and breathing!"

"Look!" Zack held up a photo to the window now. It was too morphed to see the detail, but Isabel could make out a flattened car with the roof peeled back like a sardine can. "The doctor said I should be dead and unrecognizable. But here I am, walking, talking. And I would have been crushed if I hadn't been leaning over to get my phone from the floor to see *your* text! Isn't that a sign? Or the sign that my phone survived for me to know your answer, sent a millisecond before the wreck?"

"None of that matters. The accident was because of me in the first place!" Her hands raking through her hair in frustration.

"I can't do this through a door!" And he vanished.

*

Isabel slid down the door, balled up in a daze, staring out at the bay through the back slider. Was he gone? Was that finally it?

She covered her face to block out the sun and to be ready for a downpour of tears, but it didn't come. The numbness washed over her that quickly.

Crash!

A large rock shattered the slider, large glass shards flew across the floor.

Isabel scrambled to her feet, her pulse ricocheting through her body.

"There you are," he said while clutching his sides, the motion used to break the glass must've been excruciating, especially after—*Jesus!*—having to scale her security fence! God, what the hell was he thinking? *And for Christ's sake, broken glass?* Again?

CHAPTER 54

"AY DIOS MIO! Zack—shattered glass! This is so, so bad!" Enraged, she grabbed shoes and then a broom from a closet around a corner, all the while mumbling just loud enough for Zack to hear. "Can there be any more signs to make my damn point?"

"It's okay, Isabel. I'll pay for it, I have a guy, and…give me that broom!" he said crunching right through the glass to get to her. But the wall she put up with her palms, her glare, her steps backing away from him like he meant her harm, it all made him halt in his tracks right there in the middle of the glass-strewn floor. *Crunching glass*, just like the first time they'd met. Only, she had laughed then, while now she just looked terrified.

"No, Zack, it's not okay at—" But she cut herself off, her eyes suddenly pinned on a fluttering monarch coming in through the glassless doorway. She stood there, jaw hanging, clutching the broom handle as if she needed it for balance.

Isabel's eyes still following the erratic movement of the butterfly, completely captivated, he took a step toward her and took the broom, giving her his arm instead, despite the pain shooting through his torso. He moved her slowly with him a few steps so he could lean against the kitchen island, and then he spoke, despite her lack of attention, his tone purposely quiet as not to startle her. "I needed to talk to you face to face, Isabel. I'll leave, but first I need to get these last words out." He lifted his arm despite the agony, and turned her face toward his with his finger. "A comedy of errors," he whispered.

"Excuse me?" Isabel said, finally focusing on him.

"A comedy of errors," he repeated.

She inhaled through flaring nostrils, agitation radiating from her.

"Look, I woke up from the coma, and I saw things more clearly than I ever had before. I can't wrap my brain around the rules of your curse, Isabel, but I believe you…and I know now that I am a lucky son of a bitch, always have been. And the luckiest thing to ever happen to me is you, Isabel!" He took a step closer to her, but she took a long step back. He processed her less than subtle message and moved a meter away from her, setting the broom against the wall by the open doorway.

Fine. Some space. But she would hear him. "From our first time together, before all of this chaos, I felt…whole with you. I felt like I was home. I have never felt so alive. I'm just, well, a better man with you, Isabel. Before you, my life was filled with ease and luxury, but I was an empty shell. Now, being near you, being in love with you, I have challenges to overcome, obstacles to hurdle, but that is what I want! With you! I want to live for the moment, and I want each of my moments to be shared with you, Isabel Ruiz."

"Feelings are just…feelings, Zack. Emotions are temporary, fleeting."

"Life is fleeting!" he yelled. Then sighed. "You love me, Isabel. And you naturally want to protect me *and* want me to be happy. As I do for you. But if only one of the two were possible, which would you want more for me, safety or happiness? Which one?" He looked her square in the face. "The ecstatically happy Zack who risks dying sooner than later, or the tortured and desolate Zack, a goddamn zombie for all eternity?"

She glared at him. "Which one? Come on, this is stupid."

"Stupid or not, Isabel, would you be alright if I was miserable and lifeless?"

"Like I've been miserable for all these years! No, of course not, Zack!"

"Well, without you, angel, that's what I'd be. And above all else, I want *your* happiness. And whatever your answer is, as long as it makes you happy, that is what I'll do. I will go or I will stay, but I believe in the pit of my soul the car wreck proves that I don't need your protection, but what I do need is your love, Isabel. You, your heart. Now and always."

She shook her head, obviously unsure of what to do, but his logic seemed to be making an impact. She looked at him with narrowed eyes, but then got distracted by the butterfly again, which was finally making its exit out the back door.

She flicked her focus back to Zack then shifted toward the ceiling, toward the sky. "What the fuck do you want me to do here?" she yelled. "Because I sure as hell don't know! Tell me, for God's sake, what am I supposed do! What the hell do you want from me?" And with that, she dissolved to the floor, disregarding the remnant glass splinters, crying from the depths of her being.

Despite his pain, he knelt down slowly, not wanting to crowd her, but needing to comfort her somehow and protect her from the scattered glass debris.

"Marry me. That is what I want you to do. I want you to marry me, Isabel Ruiz. Fuck fate, just be my wife. Marry me, angel."

Wincing, he pulled out from his jeans pocket a diamond ring. He got down next to her, pulled her onto his lap, and held her while she gawked at him, then at the ring.

*

She had lost her first love before *they* ever got to say their vows. Then tragedy had prevented two other arranged marriages. But Zack had already cheated death once, and he was willing to accept the unknown threat of tragedy again, and apparently forever after, in order to be with her.

If he was willing to take the risk, why shouldn't she? Why the hell shouldn't she? And in doing so, make him happy, and attain some happiness for herself.

But what of her penance? Honoring her lost love, and her mom, and the others?

Isabel, wouldn't your mother and Sebastian want you to be happy?

Yes. Of course. And she knew her surviving family wanted that for her, too.

Could she finally toss her haunting guilt out to sea and let a wave of joy crash over her once and for all?

Goddamn it, yes! Yes!

For now, which was all anyone really has, why couldn't she and Zack be alive and thriving together? And happy, blissful even.

She shook her head, not believing any of what was happening. Then, melting into his arms, she looked up at his face and gave him a solid nod. "Yes."

She would finally stop fighting Zachary James. Instead, she'd give into his heart and her own.

She reached up, both hands holding his chiseled face firmly in her grasp, and kissed him with a sweet, all-confirming kiss. And he kissed her back, the first of endless kisses to come.

*

He was in a heightened state of bliss. Fucking floating from the virtual morphine straight to his heart.

While his mouth lingered over hers, savoring each dip and brush of her tongue dancing with his, he took her hand and threaded her finger through the simple diamond and gold ring.

"Wait," she murmured through their kiss, then pulled away. She looked down at her finger. At the ring. "I thought I saw"—she slid the ring off her finger—"something inset here."

She took a moment to read it, then read the inscription aloud. "'*Perfecta Combinación del Destino*'—Fate's Perfect Match."

She nodded her head and pressed her lips tight to his again, as if she'd never let them part. He wouldn't ever mind that. Then her arms reached around his body somewhat gently and clawed his back—not so gently. "That's so you always remember this moment," she whispered.

He laughed, which also hurt. Like he needed a memory aid. He couldn't forget this landmark in time if he were in a true brain-altering accident. This moment was imprinted on his soul.

"We'll have to have a really long engagement so I can make sure you aren't clinically insane. Because…*this is really* insane!" she said, soaking him in with her gaze.

He drew his thumb down her cheek, catching a few drops of her salty emotion and licking them off his thumb. Then he held her tight with one arm and grunted from a shockwave of pain as he shifted to reach into his other back pocket. "I almost forgot the other gifts I have for you."

On the way over, Antonio had helped Zack gather a collection of items for his grand gesture, and so he felt obliged to play the full hand in appreciation of the other man's efforts.

"What are you doing? Can I help you?"

"No angel, I got it." He exhaled as he relaxed back into his sit and displayed the first item. "Good, it didn't break, because that would've sucked."

"A ketchup packet?" Her lips pursed, and her eyes sighed.

"Never know when an emergency pizza situation'll crop up." He waggled his eyebrows at her.

She broke out laughing.

"But wait…there's more." He fanned out in his other hand two tickets and a flattened white lily.

She tilted her head to read the horizontal detail of the tickets. "The Marco concert? Really?"

"Yeah—Lucinda helped." He grinned.

"I actually don't *love* Marco's stuff," she said through her laughter. "I'm all about metal from the 90s."

"I knew it!" He squeezed her arm. "I knew! On the boardwalk." He narrowed his eyes. "Well good, 'cause it looks like we're gonna miss the concert anyway."

"Why's that?"

"Because we'll be busy attending the sold out *Isabel show*. It actually starts in a few minutes here and it goes all night long." He tossed the tickets over his shoulder, pulled her tighter to him, only grimacing for a moment from his achingly sore rib cage, and devoured her mouth, a torrential kiss.

*

She shifted her hips, pressing vigorously into his steel, returning the kiss with equal angst. She reached behind him as she gently rocked her hips, and slid her hands in his back pockets, gripping his ass, as if trying to pull him harder into her.

But an involuntary grunt came from his chest, not accurately expressing the total and utter bliss their kiss delivered, but instead, the sharp pain spreading through his torso.

She pulled back, concern in her eyes.

"I'm good, I'm good. More, give me more." He took her face in his hands, and met her mouth again without mercy.

"Wait, Zack, I'm taking you to bed to—"

"Yes, to bed…is good."

"To rest, Zack. However badly I want to *not* rest with you, you're in pain, babe."

But he chose to ignore her and trail kisses down her neck instead.

She slapped his shoulder lightly. "Come on."

Heady and delirious, he lifted his head. "That hurt," he teased, "but fine, my angel, I will let you take me to bed. Tend to me. I'll have my way with you"—he slid the mangled lily behind her right ear, some of the disheveled petals falling to the floor in a delicate heap—"soon enough, my future wife. Soon and always."

"I'm glad you know enough to listen to me." She winked, then slid off his lap. "A good habit from the got go."

"It's 'get go,'" He smirked.

"Huh?"

"Nothing, angel. Nothing. Um, hey, let me have a second here…" He had to gather his strength to get up. As he caught his breath, pooled his energy, he smiled at her. He moved both hands to her cheeks, stroking her smooth skin with his thumbs. "Isabel?" God, he could say her name a thousand times just to feel it roll from his tongue.

"Zack." She blinked her eyes. Emblazoned on his soul, those eyes.

"Did you visit your grandfather, this house, a lot when you were little?"

"Just about every other weekend. We loved it here. We'd be at the beach from dawn 'til dusk."

"Did you have lots of friends, or did you just play with your brothers and sisters?" He wanted to know everything there was to know about her.

And he wanted to jog her memory.

"Most kids stayed away from me. I wasn't called a jinx then, but I was so accident prone and clumsy, I might as well have been. But the foreigners would play with me."

"Yeah, I remember."

"Remember? Remember what?"

"Did you play with a boy named Bennie on the beach? He was scared to surf with the rest of the kids, so he was always left behind, but he'd build—"

"Sandcastles! Yes, wow, Bennie! How...do you know?"

"Bennet Zachary James, Jr.," he said, holding one of his hands out to her in mock introduction. "I dropped the 'Bennet' and replaced it with my middle name the day he left." He watched her eyes studying his, recognizing, remembering.

Her chest lifted, hitched, then finally released as she exhaled a forever breath. "Oh my God, Zack! I had *such* a crush on you...for years! And you stopped playing with me when I was like ten or eleven. I was devastated! This is just...insane!"

Why she was so shocked at anything anymore, he couldn't say. He knew now that Fate did what she had to in order to get *her* story done right, written just the way she wanted it. The ultimate author.

"I crushed on you hard, too, but you were younger than me...by what, three or four years?

"Six, I think." Eyebrows lifted. "Amy told me you're thirty-two. Older than dirt," she teased.

"God, do you remember how huge that gap was as a teenager, though?

But how I wished and dreamed we'd know each other when we were older."
He smiled, leaning in to kiss her neck. He nuzzled her, inhaling her essence.
"So here we are, engaged and neighbors," he said through his repeated kisses,
now to her collarbone moving down to the swell of her breast.

"Just a few condos down…I remember. I used to stalk you…just a little bit."

"I know. And are you ready after all these years to claim your victim?"

"Yes, but you're not ready to *be* claimed. Still damaged goods. Like I said
before, I'm puttin' you straight to bed. You need rest, Mister."

He kissed her cheek. "Fine, but you'll rest with me. Kiss my hurts?"

"Now there's the corny crap I fell for when we first met—or re-met—at
the Five Breezes. Come on my lucky charm," she said with a wink, "I'll kiss
your hurts."

She helped him up and led him to the bedroom. She held his hand tight,
the sweet pressure making him even more eager to be skin to skin and heart
to heart with his angel. Even though each elated breath sent sharp stiches of
pain shooting through his rib cage, he relished the excitement, the joy.

But his body really had been overexerted throughout the day. "Wait,
angel." He paused at the doorway of the bedroom, dizzying euphoria threatened his balance.

But he knew the fix.

Not oxygen. Not meds.

Just his strong, stunning, sensual Isabel to anchor him, to love him.

He pulled her into his embrace and pressed his mouth to hers, parting
her lips, melting into her mouth like it was the last kiss he'd ever give her.
And he'd committed to doing just that for as long as he lived, because they'd
never know fate's plan for them, but he did know that his *now* was absolute
perfection. *Now*, with Isabel, his divine angel.

THE END

AUTHOR'S NOTE

I *so* hope you enjoyed Zack and Isabel's story—I absolutely loved writing it for you!

Now, do you want more good stuff featuring Zack and Isabel and the other couples in the Paradise South series—*for free*?

Just go to www.RissaBrahm.com/Join and you'll get a deleted scene from each of the Paradise South books as they come out:

5 Deleted Scenes from the Paradise South books
Tempting Isabel — (Isabel & Zack)
Taking Jana — (Jana & Antonio)
Catching Preeya — (Preeya & Ben)
Satisfying Ali — (Ali & Dev)
Freeing Kyla — (Kyla & Liam)

And...

You'll receive 1 Free Novelette called *P.S. in Paradise* — (Full Epilogues for all 5 Books, which will only be sold as part of the Paradise South series Box Set) — for FREE!

So, head to [www.RissaBrahm.com/Join] and get your free stuff on!

Also reserved for my newsletter subscribers: first-to-know news on release dates, fabulous giveaways and other cool bonus material like character sketches and interviews, failed flings, and more! So, go check it out! xo~Rissa

P.S. Your candid and detailed review of *Tempting Isabel* posted on Amazon helps other romance readers know if my stuff is for them. Your opinion really matters and is so appreciated! [www.RissaBrahm.com/Tempting-Isabel]

P.P.S. I always love hearing from you directly! Reach out anytime…

e: me@RissaBrahm.com
p: www.RissaBrahm.com/pinterest
f: www.RissaBrahm.com/facebook
g: www.RissaBrahm.com/goodreads
t: www.RissaBrahm.com/twitter

BOOKS BY RISSA BRAHM

PARADISE SOUTH

Tempting Isabel, Book 1
Taking Jana, Book 2
Catching Preeya, Book 3
Satisfying Ali, Book 4
Freeing Kyla, Book 5
P.S. in Paradise (The series' Epilogue Novelette Collection)

All five delectable, deep, and destined romances of the Paradise South series include captivating heroes and heroines to love and lust for throughout their impassioned journeys toward their *happily ever afters*.
Enjoy them all: [www.RissaBrahm.com/Books]

ACKNOWLEDGEMENTS

Infinite thanks:

To my content editor, Tessa Shapcott; copy editor, Kristie Stramaski, and my proofreaders, Michelle Josette, J.F., and Markham Correct.

To my beta readers: Saleena C., Lady P., Penny L., Kirsty F., Sandra L., Kerrie K., Gretchen H., Tiffany S., Zana K., Argie S. and Margo K.

To my Launch Team for their time, feedback, and energy. Kirsty F., Phyllis P., Saleena C, Mary B. H., Kerrie K., Penny L., June M.

To Phyllis B., for enjoying my stories and encouraging me on.

To June M., for your time, perspective, care and enthusiasm.

To Authors Kimberly Llewellyn, Lynn Carmer, and Joanne Rock for your expert guidance and support.

To the works of Jasinda Wilder for helping me find my voice.

To the works of Laura Kaye for showing me deep point of view.

To the works of Nalini Singh and Megan Hart for helping me go beyond the surface of a character.

To the RWA TARA chapter for all your support.

To my Mom, always there for me.

To my husband, for the *best* twists and turns, reining me in when I went dark and dramatic, and for spending endless hours brainstorming and offering your oh-so-vital male perspective.

To my daughter, for bearing with me and for pushing me on: "Go work, Mom."

To VK and GRP, for time, support, goals, cattle prods and love.

ABOUT THE AUTHOR

Contemporary romance writer Rissa Brahm grew up in New York and has since lived in all four corners of the United States, and beyond. The beautiful paradise of Puerto Vallarta, Mexico—the core setting of her hot & heartfelt debut series, Paradise South—is Rissa's most recent and beloved home.

When not chained-by-choice to her MacBook, she is embarking on outdoor adventures with her husband and little girl, laughing to tears with a good rom com, eating amazing Indian food with something chocolate for dessert; reading good, hot scorchers in bed; biking, long walks, and yoga; zoning out to killer music from across the decades and the globe; and getting lost only to discover a new exciting route home again.

You can connect with Rissa on Facebook, Twitter or by email anytime by heading to www.RissaBrahm.com.

www.ingramcontent.com/pod-product-compliance
Lightning Source LLC
Chambersburg PA
CBHW032142190626
46814CB00005BA/1802